THE TIGER IN THE SMOKE

THE TIGER IN THE SMOKE

Margery Allingham

Carroll & Graf Publishers, Inc.
New York

Carroll & Graf Publishers, Inc.
260 Fifth Avenue
New York, NY 10001

ISBN 0-7394-0313-3

Manufactured in the United States of America

THE TIGER IN THE SMOKE

IN THE SHADY WAYS OF BRITAIN TO-
DAY IT IS CUSTOMARY TO REFER TO
THE METROPOLIS OF LONDON AS THE
SMOKE.

ONE
GHOSTS

"It may be only blackmail," said the man in the taxi hopefully. The fog was like a saffron blanket soaked in ice-water. It had hung over London all day and at last was beginning to descend. The sky was yellow as a duster and the rest was a granular black, overprinted in grey and lightened by occasional slivers of bright fish colour as a policeman turned in his wet cape.

Already the traffic was at an irritable crawl. By dusk it would be stationary. To the west the Park dripped wretchedly and to the north the great railway terminus slammed and banged and exploded hollowly about its affairs. Between lay winding miles of butter-coloured stucco in every conceivable state of repair.

The fog had crept into the taxi where it crouched panting in a traffic jam. It oozed in ungenially, to smear sooty fingers over the two elegant young people who sat inside. They were keeping apart self-consciously, each stealing occasional glances in the same kind of fear at their clasped hands resting between them on the shabby leather seat.

Geoffrey Levett was in his early thirties. He had a strong-featured uncommunicative face and a solid, powerful body. His brown eyes were intelligent and determined but not expressive, and both his light hair and his sober clothes were well and conventionally cut. There was nothing in the look of him to show the courage of the man, or the passion, or the remarkable if untimely gift he had for making money. Now, when he was undergoing the most gruelling emotional experience of his life, he appeared merely gloomy and embarrassed.

Meg Elginbrodde sat beside him. He was much more in love with her than he had ever believed possible and every social column in the country had announced that she was about to marry him.

She was twenty-five years and three weeks old, and for the five years since her twentieth birthday she had believed herself a war widow, but during the last three weeks, ever since her engagement had been announced, she had been receiving through the post a series of photographs taken in the city streets. They were all recent snapshots, as various landmarks proved, and in each of them there had appeared among the crowd a figure who either was her late husband, Major Martin Elginbrodde, or a man so like him that he must be called a double. On the back of the latest picture to arrive there had been a roughly printed message.

"It may be only blackmail," Geoffrey repeated, his deep voice carefully casual. "That's what Campion thinks, isn't it?"

She did not reply at once and he glanced at her sharply, accepting the pain it gave him. She was so lovely. Queen Nefertiti in a Dior ensemble. Her clothes seemed a part of her. Her plum-coloured redingote with its absurd collar arched like a sail emphasised her slenderness. Since it was fashionable to do so, she looked bendable, bone and muscle fluid like a cat's. A swathe of flax-white hair protruded from a twist of felt and underneath was something not quite true. Exquisite bone hid under delicate faintly painted flesh, each tone subtly emphasising and leading up to the wide eyes, lighter than Scandinavian blue and deeper than Saxon grey. She had a short fine nose and a wide softly painted mouth, quite unreal, one might have thought, until she spoke. She had a husky voice, also fashionable, but her intonation was alive and ingenuous. Even before one heard the words one realised, albeit with surprise, that she was both honest and not very old.

"That's what the police think. I don't know about Albert. No one ever knows quite what he thinks. Val certainly doesn't and she's his sister. Amanda may, but then she's married to him."

"Didn't Amanda talk of it at all?" He was trying very hard not to be irritable. One of those solid men whose feet seemed to keep by very nature firmly on the ground, he was finding the inexplicable and unconventional unnerving.

Meg moved her head slowly to look at him and he was aware of her new perfume.

"I'm afraid neither of us did," she said. "It was rather a beastly meal. Daddy kept trying not to say what was in his mind and she and I behaved like nicely brought-up little boys and didn't notice. It's all a bit unbearable, darling."

"I know." He spoke too quickly. "The Canon genuinely thinks it's Martin, does he?" and he added, "Your husband," with a formality which had not existed between them for a year.

She began to speak, hesitated, and laughed uncertainly.

"Oh dear, that was terrible! I nearly said, 'Daddy always thinks the worst,' and that isn't at all what I meant—either about Daddy or about Martin."

He made no comment and there was a long and unhappy pause during which the cab leapt forward a foot or so, only to pause and pant again, frustrated. Geoffrey glanced at his watch.

"There's plenty of time, anyway. Now, you're sure it is three-thirty that you're meeting Campion and this Inspector?"

"Yes. Albert said we'd meet in that yard place at the top of the station, the one that used to smell of horses. The message just said, 'Bath train, three forty-five, November eight,' nothing else."

"And that was on the back of the photograph?"

"Yes."

"It wasn't in Martin's handwriting? Just block capitals?"

"I told you."

"You didn't show it to me."

"No, darling."

"Why?"

She met his glance calmly with her wide stare. "Because I didn't want to very much. I showed it to Val because I work for her and she called up her brother. Albert brought the police into it and they took the photograph, so I couldn't show it to anyone."

Geoffrey's face was not designed to show exasperation or any other of the more helpless emotions. His eyes were hard as he watched her.

"Couldn't you tell if it was like him?"

"Oh, it was *like* him." She sounded helpless herself. "They've all been *like* him, even that first one which we all saw. They've all been like him but they've all been bad photographs. Besides——"

"What?"

"I was going to say I've never seen Martin out of uniform. That's not true, of course, but I did only see him for a short time on his two leaves. We were only married five months before he was killed—I mean, if he was killed."

The man looked away from her out into the fog and the scurrying shadows in it.

"And dear old Canon Avril seriously believes that he's come back to stop you marrying me five years after the War Box cited him 'Missing believed killed'?"

"No," she protested, "Daddy fears it. Daddy always fears that people may turn out unexpectedly to be horrible, or mental, or desperately ill. It's the only negative thing in his whole make-up. It's his bad bit. People only tell Daddy when it really is something frightful, I know how he feels now. He's afraid Martin may be alive and mad."

Geoffrey swung round slowly and spoke with deliberate cruelty aimed mainly at himself.

"And how about you, pretty? What are you hoping?"

She sighed and leaned back, stretching her long slender legs to dig one very high heel into the jute mat. Her eyes were watching his face and they were entirely candid.

"I knew I'd have to tell you all this, Geoff, so I thought it out." The drawl was not unsuited to frankness. Each word had its full value. "I love you. I really do. As I am now, with these last five years behind me, I am a person who is quite terribly in love with you and will always be—or so I think now, today, in this taxi. But I did love Martin when I was nineteen, and when I knew—I mean when I thought—he was dead I thought I'd die myself." She paused. "Somehow I think I did. Your Meg is a new girl."

Geoffrey Levett discovered with horror that he was in tears. At any rate his eyes were smarting and he felt sick. His hand closed more tightly over the slender gloved one and he banged it gently up and down on the cushion.

"I'm a damned fool," he said. "I ought not to have asked you that, my dear, dear girl. Look, we'll get out of this somehow and we'll go through with the whole programme. We'll have everything we planned, the kids and the house and the happiness, even the damned great wedding. It'll be all right, I swear it, Meg, somehow it'll be all right."

"No." She had the gentle obstinacy of her kind of woman. "I want to tell you, Geoffrey, because I've thought it all out, and I want you to know so that whatever I do—well, at least you'll understand. You see, this message may mean just what it looks it means, and in an hour I may find I'm talking to Martin. I've been thinking how horrible that'll be for *him*. You see, I've *forgotten* him. The only thing I keep remembering and dreading is that I must tell him about the dog."

"The dog?" he repeated blankly.

"Yes. Old Ainsworth. He died soon after Martin was—was presumed killed. Martin will hate that. He loved Ainsworth. They used to sit and look at each other for hours and hours. It's horrible, but it really is the clearest thing I remember about either of them. Martin in pyjamas and Ainsworth in his tight brown skin just sitting and looking at each other and being quite happy."

She made a small gesture with her free hand. Its arc took in a lost world of air raids and hurried meals in crowded restaurants, hotels, railway stations, khaki, sunlight, stolen pools of peace in chaos.

"When he was in the Desert he wrote a poem to Ainsworth—never to me, you know—but he did write one to Ainsworth." Her husky voice filled the rain-drenched world. "I've never forgotten it. He sent it home, probably *for* Ainsworth. You'd never imagine Martin writing verse. It went:

"I had a dog, a liver-coloured mongrel
With mild brown eyes and an engaging manner.

He had a studious mind and thought
Deeply about himself
And food and sex.
He was also a liar.
He wasn't proud:
He'd shake hands very gravely
With almost anybody not in uniform . . .
I'd like to talk to him again:
Now I'm a soldier we've a lot in common."

She was silent and Levett did not move. It was as though the fog had brought coldly a third person into the cab. At length, since something had to be said, he made the effort.

"A queer chap," he murmured briefly.

"I don't think so." It was evident that she was trying to remember. "He was being a soldier then, you see. He was doing that all the time I knew him."

"Oh God, yes!" He recognised the haunt at last from his own days in that strange hinterland of war which was receding faster and faster with every day of the fleeting years. "Oh God, yes! Poor little chap. Poor silly little chap."

Meg bowed her head. She never nodded, he noticed suddenly. All her movements were sweeping and gracious, like an Edwardian woman's, only less studied.

"I never saw him out of war," she said in much the same way as she might have said, "I never saw him sober." "I didn't know him, I suppose. I mean I don't really know him at all."

The last word faded and ceased uncertainly. The taxi started again and, seizing an opportunity, swung sharply into the station approach.

"Are you coming with me, Geoff?"

"No." The disclaimer was altogether too violent, and he hastened to soften it. "I don't think so, do you? I'll telephone you about five. You'll be all right with Campion and his bloodhound, won't you? I think you'll be happier without me. Won't you?"

The final question was genuine. The flicker of hope appeared in it unbidden. She heard and recognised it but hesitated too long.

"I just don't know."

"You go along." He kissed her lightly and had the door open just before the taxi stopped. As he helped her out she clung to his sleeve. The crowd on the pavement was large and hurried as usual and they were crushed together by it. Once again he saw her as he had been seeing her at intervals all the afternoon, afresh, as if for the first time. Her voice, reaching him through the bustle, sounded nervous and uncertain. The thing she had to tell him was altogether too difficult.

"I haven't really *told* you, Geoff. I'm so muddled. I'm so *sorry*, darling."

"Shut up," he said softly, and thrust her gently away.

The crush snatched her and bore her away from him into the dark archway of the entrance, which was festooned like a very old theatre proscenium with swatches of fog. She turned to raise a small gloved hand to him, but a porter with a barrow and a woman with a child frustrated her and she was swept on out of his sight as he stood watching, still with the cab door open.

Meanwhile Mr. Albert Campion and Divisional Detective Chief Inspector Charles Luke, who was Father Superior of the second most tough police division in metropolitan London and proud of it, stood in the covered yard of the southern end of the terminus and waited. Apart from bleaching him, the years had treated Mr. Campion kindly. He was still the slight, elegantly unobtrusive figure exactly six feet tall, misleadingly vacant of face and gentle of manner, which he had been in the nineteen-twenties. The easiest of men to overlook or underestimate, he stood quietly at his point of vantage behind the rows of buffers and surveyed the crowd with casual good temper.

His companion was a very different kettle of fish. Charlie Luke in his spiv civilians looked at best like a heavyweight champion in training. His dark face with its narrow diamond-shaped eyes and strong sophisticated nose shone in the murky light with a radiance of its own. His soft black hat was pushed on to the back of his close-cropped curls and his long hands were deep in his trouser pockets, so that the skirts of his overcoat bunched out behind him in a fantail.

Members of that section of the district who had most cause to be interested in him were apt to say that, "give him his due, at least you couldn't miss him." He stuck out like a lighthouse. He was some inches taller than his companion but his thickset build made him seem shorter. As usual he conveyed intense but suppressed excitement and rigidly controlled physical strength, and his bright glance travelled everywhere.

"It may be just some silly game, a woman playing the goat," he remarked, idly sketching in a pair of horns with his toe on the pavement. "But I don't think so. It smells like the old 'blacking' to me. All the same, an open mind, that's what we want. You never know. Weddings and so on are funny times."

"There's a man involved, at any rate," objected Mr. Campion mildly. "How many photographs have you got of him in all—five?"

"Two taken in Oxford Street, one at Marble Arch, one in the Strand—that's the one which shows the movie advertisement which dates it as last week—and then the one with the message on the back. That's right, five." He buttoned his coat and stamped his feet. "It's cold," he said. "I hope she's not late. I hope she's beautiful too. She's got to have something if she can't even recognise her old man for sure."

Campion looked dubious. "Could you guarantee to recognise a man you hadn't seen for five years from one of those snapshots?"

"Perhaps not." Luke put his head under an imaginary backcloth, at least he ducked slightly, and sketched in a piece of drapery with waving hands. "Those old photographers—mugfakers we call 'em—in the street don't use very new cameras or very good film. I'm allowing for that. But I should have thought a woman would know her own husband if she saw the sole of his boot through a grating or the top of his hat from a bus."

Mr. Campion regarded him with interest. It was the first trace of sentimentality he had ever observed in the D.D.C.I. and he might have said so, but Luke was still talking.

"If it's blackmail, and it probably is, it's a very rum lark," he was saying. "I don't see how or when the bloke expects to collect anything out of it, do you?" His eyes were snapping in the smoking mist. "The ordinary procedure is 'give me fifty quid or you'll be up for bigamy.' Well, she's not married again yet, is she? Crooks can be peculiarly wanting on the top storey, but I've never heard of one who'd make a blob like that. If it had been her wedding which had been announced and not her engagement it might have made sense. Even so, what's the point of sending her one picture after another and giving us all this time to get on the job?"

Mr. Campion nodded. "How are you getting on with the street photographers?"

The other man shrugged his shoulders. "I'd rather ask those sparrows," he said seriously, nodding towards a cluster of the little micelike birds twittering over some garbage in the gutter. "Same result and less halitosis. They all take several hundred snaps a day. They all remember photographing someone exactly like him, only it wasn't quite he. They all lost money on the deal. My boys are still working on it, but it's a waste of time and public money. The pics themselves are covered with fingerprints. All five show the same bleary, smeary figure in the street. Nothing to help at all. This last one with the train time on the back is the craziest of all, to my mind," he added earnestly. "Either he *wants* to get the police on the job or else he expects the young woman to be a darned sight more windy than she appears to be. You say she's not lying. I haven't seen her; I wouldn't know. I'm just taking your word for it. That's why I'm here getting so perishing cold."

His pile-driver personality forced home the suggestion, but he spoke without offence. If one of the great West Country locomotives which lay panting and steaming on the rails ahead of them had advanced the same argument, it could hardly have been more powerful or impersonal.

"No, she's not lying," said Campion. "Hasn't it occurred to you that Elginbrodde may be alive?"

"The War Office says 'No, go away.'"

"I know. But they've been wrong before."

"If it's Elginbrodde himself, he's 'psychological,'" The D.D.C.I. let his eyes cross horribly and for an instant his tongue appeared, loose and lolling. "I hate psychiatry." His glance darted off again, scanning the hurrying travellers. Almost at once a soft but unmistakable whistle escaped him. "This is it." His tone ran up in triumph. "This is our young lady, I'll bet a pound. See that where-are-you-I-hope-or-don't-I look? Am I right? What a smasher!"

Campion glanced up and started forward. "Clever of you. That is Mrs. Elginbrodde."

Meg saw them bearing down upon her. In her hypersensitive mood they appeared monstrous.

There was Campion, the amateur, a man who never used his real name and title. In appearance a middle-aged Englishman typical of his background and period. She saw him as kindly, unemotional, intelligent, and resourceful, all inbred virtues ensuring that his reactions would be as hidebound as a good gun dog's. She knew his kind so well that she was prepared to find almost any hidden peculiarity in him. It was typical of his variety that he should perhaps be very brave, or very erudite, or possibly merely able to judge Chinese prints or grow gardenias.

On the other hand, the man behind him was something new to her and at first glance she found him frankly shocking. Hitherto she had thought very little about policemen, classing them vaguely as necessities which were on the whole beneficial, like banks or the parliamentary systems. But here, as she could see, was a very male person of considerable if not particularly pleasant interest.

Luke came bounding forward with the unaffected acquisitiveness of a child espying a beautiful cuddly pet. His eyes were flickering and his live shrewd face expressed boundless tolerance.

The interview was so clearly just about to get off on the wrong foot that they all recognised the fact just in time. Campion performed the introduction with iron under his velvet words, and Charlie Luke shut off his magnetism regretfully, like a man switching off a light. He watched the girl cautiously, noting her beauty but discounting it, and when he replaced his hat he put it on straight. Yet there had been no chill in her greeting; she was simply obviously worried, a woman so torn by her loves and loyalties that her genuineness was unquestionable.

"I was so sorry I couldn't find you any snapshots for comparison," she said earnestly. "My husband didn't live in England before the war, so none of his things were here. We didn't have very long together and somehow we didn't seem to run to snapshots."

Luke nodded. He recognised her mood. That preoccupation with the problem so acute that it excluded even the ordinary social preliminaries was familiar to him. He had seen worried people before.

"I understand that, Miss—I mean Mrs. Elginbrodde. He was in France, wasn't he, brought up by a grandmother? And he wasn't very old when he died, twenty-five, I think?"

"Yes. He'd be thirty now." She looked round as she spoke, nervously and yet not entirely unhopefully. The movement was quite subconscious and it struck both men as pathetic. It was as though the war years had peeped out at them suddenly and the coloured clothes all round them in the fog had been washed over briefly with khaki. To add to the illusion, the dreary thumping of a street band away out in Crumb Street behind them reached them faintly through the station noises. It was only the ghost of a tune, not recognisable yet evocative and faintly alarming, like a half-remembered threat. Luke hunched his wide shoulders.

"The studio portrait and the passport didn't really tell us much, you know," he said, sketching in a very large square followed by a very small one with his restless long-boned hands. "I think I ought to tell you that as far as our experts can tell from measurement of the features, as far as they can *tell*, it's not the same man." He was watching her, trying to appraise her reaction. The face she turned to him was both disappointed and relieved. Hope died in it but also hope appeared. She was saddened and yet made happy. There was shame there and bewilderment. She might have been going to cry. He began to be very sorry for her.

"I did find this last night," she said, turning to Campion. "I'm afraid the whole thing is very dark, but it's a snap a child took of a dog we had, and that's Martin in the background. I don't know if it's any use at all, yet I think anyone who knew him would recognise it."

She brought a little faded square from the depths of her big handbag and handed it to him. The D.D.C.I. looked over his shoulder. It was the yellowing print of an overexposed snap of a plump, negroid-looking dog wallowing on a London lawn, and far in the background, laughing, with hands in pockets and head thrust forward, was a boy wearing a braggadocio moustache. There was nothing definitely characteristic there except perhaps his spirit, and yet the picture shook them both and they stood looking at it for a long time. At length Luke tapped his coat pocket.

"I've got one of the street pictures here, but this isn't the time to get it out," he murmured, and once again his glance roved round the vast station. He was puzzled and making no secret of it. "Yes, I see why you got the wind up."

His shrewdness and friendliness took any offence out of the observation. "There is a look there. I see what you mean. Yes. Tell me, Mrs. Elginbrodde, did your husband have any young brothers or cousins?"

"No, none I ever heard of." The suggestion was a new idea to her and in the circumstances hardly attractive.

"Now look here"—Luke became a conspirator and his overpadded shoulders seemed to spread even wider to screen her—"the only thing you've got to do is to keep your head. It all depends on you. It's a million to one that this will turn out to be the usual blackmail by a customer with a record as long as a train. He's behaving altogether too cautiously so far and that may mean that he's not sure of his ground. He may just want to look at you, or he may risk talking to you. All you've got to do is to let him. Leave the rest to me, see?"

"Time is getting on," put in Mr. Campion behind him. "Fifteen minutes to go."

"I'd better go to the platform." Meg moved as she spoke and Campion drew her back.

"Not yet. That's where he'll look for you. Don't move from here until we spot him."

She was surprised and her narrow brows rose high on the smooth forehead, which was rounded like a little girl's and had been fascinating Luke for some time.

"But I thought the message meant that he was coming *off* the Bath train?"

"That's what he wants you to think." The D.D.C.I. was in danger of becoming fatherly. "He wants you to watch the train so that he can pick you out at leisure. The postmark was London, wasn't it? He doesn't have to go to Bath to take a platform ticket."

"Oh. Oh, of course." She sighed on the word and stepped back beside him, her hands folded. In spite of their escort she looked lonely, peering out anxiously, waiting.

The fog was thickening and the glass-and-iron roof was lost in its greasy drapery. The yellow lights achieved but a shabby brilliance and only the occasional plumes of steam from the locomotives were clean in the gloom. That tremendous air of suppressed excitement which is peculiar to all great railway stations was intensified by the mist and all the noises were muffled by it and made more hollow-sounding even than usual. From where they stood they could see all the main-line gates and over on the left the great entrance with its four twenty-foot doors and the bright bookstall just beside it.

The afternoon rush was beginning and wave after wave of hurrying travellers jostled out of the booking hall and fanned on to the wide ledge of one of the longest platforms in the world. Away to their right was the other carriageway climbing bleakly into Crumb Street, and behind them was the tunnel to the Underground and the double row of telephone boxes.

Luke was watching the main entrance with misleading idle-ness, while Campion kept a discreet eye on the Underground, and neither was prepared for the sudden cry beside them.

"Oh! Look! Over there. There he is. *Martin!*"

Meg had forgotten everything else in the world. She stood transfixed, pointing like a child and calling at the top of her voice.

Fifty yards away on a strip of sooty pavement, which was otherwise deserted, a neat soldierly figure had appeared. He wore a distinctive but well-cut sports jacket and the inevitable green pork-pie hat, and had just turned in smartly out of the drive from Crumb Street. He had a brisk purposeful step and was not looking about him. Even at that distance the shadow of a large moustache was discernible, and from behind him, as though designed to increase the somewhat theatrical mil-itariness of his appearance, the rowdy street band thumping out the violent marching song sounded clearly from the dis-tance.

"Martin!" Meg broke away before they could stop her. There was something in the cry which reached the man above the noises of the station. It was not the sound itself but something emotional which ran through the other loiterers, as if between them they had made a telephone wire. Campion saw a line of turning heads and at the end of it the stranger starting violently, stopping, pausing frozen for a moment. Then he ran.

He fled like a deer down the first avenue of escape. A mass formation of porters' trucks, each piled high with luggage, lay directly ahead of him, and his pursuers were sweeping down on him from his left, so he turned right through the open gateway of the suburban-line platform where the slow down train stood waiting. He ran as though his life depended on it, blindly, knocking strangers headlong, leaping over suitcases, darting round lamp standards only just in time to avoid disaster. Luke shot after him, clutching his coat skirts round him and gaining because of his superior stride. He sped past Meg, who would have followed him had not Campion's hand closed firmly on her wrist.

"This way," he said urgently, and swept her on towards the other platform immediately behind and parallel to the stationary train.

Meanwhile the crowd hampered everybody. Luke charged through it like a bull, shouting the familiar "Mind your backs, please!" of the station staff. Porters paused in the fairway, staring. Ticket collectors hesitated and got in the road. Children appeared from nowhere and scampered up and down, screaming, and the great solid mass of apathetic gazers who spring out of the very stones of a city the moment there is anything to look at shuffled after the fugitive, making any return journey impossible.

On the other platform, however, when at last they reached it, Mr. Campion and the girl found themselves practically alone. The suburban train, still unlit and lying like a black caterpillar on the second row of rails, was separated from them by a gulf of blackness striped with dull silver. Since all the excitement was taking place on the other side of it, there were no faces at the windows and no sign of movement from within. Meg was very white and her hands were shaking.

"He ran away," she began huskily. "Martin——"

The word died abruptly. Campion was not looking at her. He was watching the dark side of the train, his coat buttoned tightly and his hands ready. The overhead lamp shining on the fog made it look as though the scene were taking place under muddy water. Distances were deceptive and colours untrue. For Meg it was a moment of unreality. She did not believe in it, and her eyes, as they followed Campion's gaze, were incredulous.

At last the moment he waited for occurred. A door halfway down the train swung back abruptly and a dark figure dropped out on to the line. He tripped over a sleeper but recovered himself and stumbled across to the platform, only to find the stone rim level with his shoulders. He sprang at it and clung there, his head turned from them, as he peered anxiously down the line. Any incoming engine must crush him, but at the moment there was no sign of one, only the fog and the coloured lights.

He slipped back and made another effort, just as Campion's lean arm shot out and caught him by the collar. At the same moment Luke appeared behind him and the train became alive with spectators. Windows rattled down, heads were thrust out, and the shrill clatter of voices broke over them in a wave. Luke dropped on to the line with unexpected lightness. He was in perfect condition, lithe and powerful. He caught the stranger by the waist, heaved him into Campion's arms, and vaulted up beside him, his hat still in place.

A white face with narrow black frightened eyes looked up at them. All the soldierliness had vanished. The swagger had melted and the body shrunk into the clothes. The moustache looked enormous and ridiculous. He made no sound at all, but stood shaking and twitching, ready to run again the moment the grip on his arm should relax.

"Oh . . . oh, I'm so sorry. How crazy of me. Now I see him close he's not even like him."

They had not noticed Meg come up and her wondering voice took them by surprise. She was staring at the captive in bewilderment, the colour pouring into her face, relief fighting with disappointment in her eyes.

"It was at that distance—I could have sworn, I don't know

why. The build, the clothes, the——" She put out her hand
to touch the tweed coat sleeve and the prisoner leapt away
from her as if she had been a live rail. There was a momentary
struggle and as they overpowered him again Luke jerked the
man towards him so that their faces all but met.

"You're losing something, mate," he remarked with ferocious good humour. "Look at this. It came off in my hand."
The movement was too swift to be resisted. The stranger
swore in a husky whisper and was silent again. The moustache
had been lightly gummed and now the skin on the long upper
lip was pale where it had been. Luke tucked the piece of hair
into his waistcoat pocket. "Nice one," he said shamelessly.
"Must have cost a packet and come from a swell costumier's.
I'll take care of it for you."

Without his moustache, it was difficult to believe that the
stranger had ever resembled any other man closely. He had
a distinctive mouth, marred by the scar of a sewn harelip, a
broken tooth in the centre front, and an indefinable air of
slyness which at this moment was overshadowed by a terror
quite out of proportion to his crime, at least so far as it was
suspected.

Meg put her hand up to her cheeks. She was incoherent
with embarrassment and bewilderment. It was evident that
two more different men than the captive and Martin Elginbrodde were impossible to imagine, and yet she had been so
sure.

Luke grinned at her. "He didn't risk coming too close, did
he?" he said. "But he quite took you in at a distance. Quite
a performance."

She turned away abruptly and Luke lifted his chin to peer
down the platform. Two heavy men in raincoats were running
towards them, followed by a small section of the crowd who
had just discovered what had happened.

"Your men?" Campion sounded relieved.

Luke nodded. "I put them on the entrance doors in case.
They spotted the rumpus and used their heads." He raised
his hand to the newcomers as he spoke and returned to his
prisoner. "Well, Chatty," he said cheerfully, "don't go getting
any funny ideas about this being an arrest." He shook the

arm he held by way of emphasis. "This is just a friendly invitation to a cup of tea, for all I know. Understand?"

The man said nothing. He might not even have heard. His face was wooden. Only his eyes shifted uneasily. He was quiet now, but there was still a tenseness in his body. He was still ready to make a dash for freedom the moment he got a chance.

Luke surveyed him, his head on one side, his bright eyes inquisitive.

"Why are you worrying?" he said softly. "There's not more on your mind than there is on mine, by any chance?"

In spite of the hint, which was broad enough, there was no relaxing, no letup. The weak mouth remained tightly closed, the muscles were still flexed under the tweed sleeve.

Luke handed him over to the newcomers, who arrived breathless and unsmiling.

"No charge. Held for questioning." He might have been delivering a parcel. "He wants taking care of. Don't hurry him, but see he gets there. He seems bent on taking exercise. I'll be right behind you."

Meg and Campion walked down the shadowy stone way together and Luke walked beside them. The solid knot of men in front moved quickly. The crowd stared at them but parted for them, and they turned out of the gate at the top and round the bend, out of sight.

The girl was quite silent for some time, but the emotional conflict in her mind was as apparent as if she had explained it. Campion watched her out of the corner of his eye.

"You'll have to put this clean out of your mind, if you can, you know," he said at last. "If I may I'll put you in a taxi outside the station, and then after Luke has had a chat with this fellow I'll get him to come back with me. I don't see the purpose of this performance at all, but I think you'll have to face the fact that it is only a performance."

She paused in her walk and faced him. "You mean you're quite certain it wasn't Martin in the photographs?"

"Oh no, it was this fellow every time. That's practically sure."

"Practically?" Her wide mouth twisted and her eyes looked darker. "Practically sure Martin is dead again. I've been remembering him. He was a very—very sweet person, you know."

A wave of old-fashioned black anger swept over Luke's dark face. In common with everything about him, it was vivid and more than life-size.

"That's the thing which makes me wild," he announced with a bitterness which startled them both. "A chap gives his life and as soon as the grass has grown a bit and there's the chance of a spot of happiness for the woman who is the only thing left of him, a ruddy great pack of ghouls come scrapping round looking for a hap'orth of gold out of his eyeteeth. Forgive me, Mrs. Elginbrodde, but it makes me spiteful."

"A pack?" she said dully. "Are there more of them?"

"Oh yes. I've seen that quivering little mug before somewhere. He's nothing. He's the tailor's dummy. If he'd been on his own he'd have done a bit of talking. I'm not the one that lad is so frightened of. That's the only thing he did tell us."

"Then Martin might——"

"No." He spoke with a tenderness unexpected in him. "No, lady, no. Put that clean out of your mind. That dear chap and his dog have gone, gone where the dear chaps do go, gone with a few I knew. You've got your own life and you go and live it and make a do of it, as no doubt he'd like you to. Now you go home. Will Mr. Levett be there?"

"No. Do you want him? He brought me here and went on to his office. He's going to ring me at five. He has some sort of business appointment this evening."

She saw his expression and smiled to reassure him. "Oh, I shall be all right. My father is there. In fact, there are quite a lot of people in the house. We'd be very glad to see you if you could manage it."

"Fine." It was obvious that Luke thought of clapping her on the shoulder and quite as obviously changed his mind. "Splendid. Wait for us. Now we'll put you in a cab just over here. . . ."

He was still fierce when they closed the taxi door on her some minutes later and caught a last glimpse of her face as it changed after her parting valiant smile. As they pushed up the drive into Crumb Street, Campion was struck once more both by his power and the unexpected emotional depths he had revealed. Luke was as moved as if Elginbrodde had been his brother and was identifying him in his mind with some soldier he had loved. It made him an alarming enemy for someone.

Meanwhile Crumb Street, never a place of beauty, that afternoon was at its worst. The fog slopped over its low houses like a bucketful of cold soup over a row of dirty stoves. The shops had been mean when they had been built and were designed for small and occasional trade, but since the days of victory, when a million demobilised men had passed through the terminus, each one armed with a parcel of government-presented garments of varying usefulness, half the establishments had been taken over by opportunists specialising in the purchase and sale of secondhand clothes. Every other window was darkened with festoons of semi-respectable rags based by bundles of grey household linen, soiled suitcases, and an occasional collection of surplus war stores, green, khaki, and air force blue. The fine new police station on the corner was the chief ornament to the district, and the D.D.C.I advanced upon it with the tread of a proprietor. The impatient traffic was moving a little and they were held up for a moment or so on a street island. As they waited, Mr. Campion reflected that the evil smell of fog is a smell of ashes grown cold under hoses, and he heard afresh the distinctive noise of the irritable, half-blinded city, the scream of brakes, the abuse of drivers, the fierce hiss of tyres on the wet road.

Just above it, like an appropriate theme song, sounded the thumping of the street band. There was nothing of the dispirited drone there. It triumphed in the thick air, an almighty affront of a noise, importunate and vigorous.

The knot of men who were playing were half in the gutter and half on the pavement. They were moving along steadily, as the law insists, and the rattle of their collecting boxes was as noisy as their tune. They were some little way away and it was not possible to distinguish individuals, but there was a ruthless urgency in their movements and the stream of foot passengers narrowed as it flowed past the bunch. Luke jerked his chin towards them.

"See that? Demanding with menaces. What else is it?

Gimme, gimme!" He thrust a long curved hand under Campion's nose and achieved an expression of rapacity which was startling. "We can't touch 'em. Keep moving, that's all we can say. If a cat made a row like that we'd kill it."

Campion laughed. He liked Luke.

"I remember after the first World War those bands were pretty shocking," he remarked, "but I thought the Welfare State had rather seen to that sort of thing. They are ex-Service, I suppose?"

"Who isn't?" Luke was irritable. "I bet you every man under sixty in this street is ex-Service, and half the women too. That little band of brothers is only ex-Service, among other things. Haven't you seen them about? They tramp all over the town. West End mostly. Nothing's known against any of 'em, as we say, but they're not exactly pretty to look at."

He drew a balloon shape in the air with his hands and screwed his eyes up to beady pin points.

"They all wear tickets round their necks. One says 'No Pension.' Nor have I, of course. Then there's 'Invalid' and 'One Arm.' Poor bloke—but he can get a new one from the old National Health free. Where is it? 'No Head' would make you look quicker. Not one says 'Unemployed,' I notice. That *would* be asking for it. They're only beggars. Every big city produces 'em. They've got a fine old ex-Service song there, anyway. Remember it?"

"I've been trying to. Was it called 'Waiting'?"

Luke stood listening, an odd expression on his face. The band was moving very slowly.

"I'll be WAI-tin' for you!" he bellowed suddenly just under his breath. "AT the old oak tree-ah! I'll be WAI-tin' for you. Just you wait for me-ah! Turn up your lips, waggle your hips, and we'll all be set for chapel. So softly we'll glide, where water-weeds hide, and willows make little waves dapple. Most poetic, I don't think, but those aren't the words those beauties are remembering."

"No." Mr. Campion's neat memory had turned up the reference card at last. "Button your purse, shout for Nurse, I've brought my brace and tackle."

The D.D.C.I. laughed. It was a queer little grunt, not entirely of amusement. "That's a respectable one of its class.

But those boys down there aren't thinking along those lines. You can tell it by the way they're playing." He thrust his vivid face close to Campion's own. "I'll be WAI-tin' for you, AT Oflag Seventy-three-ah! I'll be WAI-tin' for you, don't look out for me-ah! Lift up your froat, you'll bleed like a goat, WHOOPS your adam's apple!"

Mr. Campion's eyebrows rose a fraction and he did not smile. If Luke had hoped to shock he had succeeded. The words had not been inspired, but from behind them there had flashed out for an instant the reality of the thing which had been chasing them all the afternoon. He was aware of it in the street now, stark under the blanket of the gloom. For the first time that day he recognised it and it sent a thin trickle down his spine.

"Violence," he said aloud.

"That's it, chum." Luke had seen their chance and they were edging swiftly through the traffic. "That's it," he repeated as they reached the pavement. "It's always there in London under the good temper. D'you remember in the Blitz, 'I wouldn't be dead for a pound'? That wasn't half a joke then. It tickled us, just touched the spot. Poor old George, blood streaming down his face! Laugh! I thought we'd bust our braces."

He paused to assist a woman to disentangle his long legs from her steel go-cart, flashed a joyous smile at her, and pressed on happily.

"I laughed myself," he said.

Mr. Campion listened to him gravely. He had his own brand of humour, but this was not it. The band and its bellow had become hateful to him and the fog bone-chilling and menacing.

"Oh lord, yes, there's violence about." Luke's wide shoulders were winnowing a path for himself through the crowd. "You can't miss it. I shouldn't be surprised if we don't get quite a whiff of it the moment we get inside. That shady little mouse we just caught was frightened of somebody, wasn't he? Hullo, what's up?"

Campion had paused and was looking over his shoulder. He was holding up the stream and half a dozen people jostled him.

"It was nothing," he said at last as he moved on again, "at least I don't think so. I thought I caught a glimpse of Geoffrey Levett just then. I must have been mistaken."

Luke turned into a narrow archway set deep in the blank side of a new building.

"Everyone looks alike in the fog," he said cheerfully. "You can follow your own Ma home in it, certain that she's the girl next door. If Mr. Levett is about here at all he's probably inside, asking a few important questions while we're still getting over the road. Now, Mr. Campion, we'll have to treat this lad very gently. We'll just turn him quietly inside out. After all, we haven't a thing on him, have we—yet?"

TWO
AT HOME

The fog was thicker than ever over in St. Petersgate Square, but there its brown folds hid no violence. Rather it was cosy, hardly cold, gentle, almost protective. The little close was well hidden even on the brightest of days. Ten years before even the enemy had not found it and so, almost alone in the district, the quiet houses remained much as they had always been. By yet another oversight the railings round the tiny square in the centre had been spared by the scrap merchants and the magnolia, two or three graceful laburnums and a tulip tree had overgrown unmolested. It was one of the smallest squares of its kind in the city. There were seven houses on each of two opposite sides, a wall on the third which shut out the steep drop into Portminster Row and the shops, and, on the fourth, the sharp-spired church of St. Peter of the Gate, its rectory and two minute glebe cottages adjoining. The square was a cul-de-sac. The only road led in by the wall, so that all wheeled traffic had to return by the way it had come. But for foot passengers only there was a flight of steps at the other end. The church stood very high, and between its narrow stone yard and the rectory's Regency block the stone stairs wound up steeply to a wide residential avenue behind. The stairs were worn and highly dangerous despite the bracket street lamp on the churchyard wall, but they were much used in daytime by shoppers, who treated the square as a short cut to civilisation from the stucco wastes of fading grandeur which had once looked down on "trade." Yet tonight when visibility was down to nil, the rectory might have been alone upon a moor.

It was a pleasant cube of a house possessing two main storeys, a half-basement, and a fine range of attics just above the cornice. There were lights in every window and the two which flanked the squat porch showed red and warm-looking in the mist.

Old Canon Avril had lived so long in the square that changing times had altered his domestic arrangements without haste or upheaval. He lived on the ground floor very comfortably while his old verger, William Talisman, made his home in the basement and Mrs. Talisman looked after them both. In the fine rooms above Meg had her self-contained apartment, and the attics had been converted into a pleasant cottagey dwelling for tenants of whom everybody was fond. It had all come about quietly and easily, and he knew very well how lucky he was.

In his early days the living had been a fashionable one and he had been glad of the glebe cottages to house the overflow of his servants, but he had not enjoyed it and the newer arrangements seemed to him infinitely more luxurious. At the moment he was standing where he always had stood, on the rug before the living-room fire. It was the room he had brought his bride to thirty years before, and since then, if only for reasons more financial than sentimental, nothing in it had ever been changed. It had become a little worn in the interim, but the good things in it, the walnut bookcase with the ivory chessmen displayed, the bureau with thirteen panes in each glass door, the Queen Anne chair with the seven-foot back, the Persian rug which had been a wedding present from his younger sister, Mr. Campion's mother, had all mellowed just as he had with care and use and quiet living.

At the moment he was brokenhearted. Meg had returned with her story and he had found it so bewildering that his incredulity had made her cry. She had gone upstairs and he was left sorrowing but still very puzzled. His books were in the other room in comfortable chaos waiting for him to return to their sanity and peace, but he was resisting them valiantly.

Normally he was the happiest of men. He asked so little of life that its frugal bounty amazed and delighted him. The older he grew and the poorer he became, the calmer and more contented appeared his fine gentle face. He was an impossible person in many ways, with an approach to life which was clear-sighted yet slightly off centre, and therefore disconcerting to most of his colleagues. No one feared him, simple people loved and protected him as if he were daft, and he had exasperated more great churchmen than any other parson alive.

The great Dr. Potter, who was for a brief time Bishop of London, had been at Cambridge with him in the nineties and had once heard him deliver a scintillating sermon on an abstruse heresy which but twelve men in England could possibly have appreciated to a congregation of four small shopkeepers and their families, five small boys, and a deaf old lady. When he had remonstrated that no one could possibly have followed him, Avril had clasped his arm and chuckled contentedly. "Of course not, my dear fellow. But how wonderful for him if by chance one of them did!"

He believed in miracles and frequently observed them, and nothing astonished him. His imagination was as wild as a small boy's and his faith ultimate. In ordinary life he was, quite frankly, hardly safe out.

He was a big man with a great frame, untidy white hair, and the ease of manner of one to whom every stranger is probably due to become an old friend. His distress just now was all the more poignant.

"She *saw* him," he repeated, his voice urgent. "She saw and recognised him and ran to him across the station. You heard her say that, Amanda."

The only other person in the room, the Lady Amanda, sister to the Earl of Pontisbright, wife to Albert Campion, director of the key firm of Alandel Aircraft Limited and white hope among Britain's backroom boys, sat in the high chair. She was embroidering the word "Sheriff" in very large letters on a small green shirt. The red hair of the Pontisbrights, which in medieval legend is said to swallow the fire of rubies, was cut neatly round her small head, and under it her brown eyes were thoughtful in her heart-shaped face.

She had explained the business very carefully to him twice already, but the cream of her forehead remained unruffled and her clear voice preserved that quality of adventurous common sense which was her chief characteristic.

"But when they caught up with him he wasn't Martin at all. I've done that, haven't you, Uncle Hubert? Especially on railway stations. It's the noise. You can't hear at all, so you don't see too well either."

The old man shook his head uneasily. "But when she first saw him she was sure," he insisted. "She says so. I'm so frightened of this, Amanda, that I'm clinging to it like a drowning man to handfuls of sea."

Amanda's thin brown fingers turned the wool deftly.

"I don't think the man they caught changed clothes with Martin in a train full of people in a few seconds, do you?" she remarked.

He laughed. It was an abrupt crow directed at himself.

"Check," he said. "No. No, perhaps not. Although, you know, Amanda, people do do the most extraordinary things. But you're right. That's wild. That really is absurd. Unless by chance there were two men."

"No, Uncle." She led him away from that loophole with an experienced hand. "No. There was only one man and he was not Martin, but he looked like Martin from a distance and he wore clothes like Martin and he must have moved and walked exactly like Martin or Meg would not have been deceived. Therefore he is someone who knew Martin, and——"

"Good heavens!" He was looking at her in horror, pain and dismay on his fine face. "You don't mean that poor boy is in the background somewhere, in some institution perhaps? Perhaps unrecognisable himself, but teaching someone else, instructing someone?"

"No, my dear." Amanda's tenacity could match his own. "Martin is dead. He was killed in the war. This man who is impersonating him must have known him before. Do you remember how you showed me how Henry Irving walked? You could do that now, but you can't have seen him for forty or fifty years. When Albert comes in I think we'll find that this man knew Martin long ago, perhaps in France before the war."

The old man sighed. His own imaginings had shaken him and he was only half comforted.

"Perhaps so. Yes, perhaps so. And what about this photograph in here? This is the same man in the same masquerade, is it?"

His eye had caught the new copy of the *Tatler* lying open on the couch before him and he bent down to retrieve it. For the first time Amanda frowned.

"That really is bad luck," she said. "When Mrs. Featherstone telephoned this afternoon and told me, and I looked it up, I was awfully sick about it. It was jolly clever of him, whoever he is, and very, very naughty."

"It's so like the boy as I remember him. All that hairy martial rubbish on his face, dear silly fellow." The Canon was holding the page very close to his eyes, trying to find on its shiny surface lines which had never been there. "There's the name too, you see, the name underneath."

"Yes, well, that's all part of the act." She was genuinely worried and her sewing lay quiet in her lap. "I was going to tell you just when Meg came in. I telephoned the paper and Sean was in conference but I got hold of Pip, who was fascinated, of course. When he had finished explaining that one can't libel a dead man he put me on to the photographer and I talked to him."

"Oh, he was standing there, was he?" The Canon was enormously interested.

"No, he was in his own office. You see, the paper buys these news snapshots from a photograph agency. The photographer simply saw Bertie and May Oldsworth on the course and went over to snap them. There were one or two other people standing near who were also in the picture, and as he did not recognise them he asked them their names, as he always does. He remembered Elginbrodde because he asked to have it spelt."

"The man gave his name as Martin Elginbrodde?" The old man continued to peer at the small figure on the extreme edge of a group of racegoers tucked down in one corner of a very full page. " 'The Hon. Bertie Oldsworth,' " he read aloud, " 'who hunts with the Westmeath, in the paddock with his wife, who is a daughter of Lady Larradine. Also in the picture are Mr. and Mrs. Peter Hill and Major Martin Elginbrodde.' Upon my soul, Amanda, I can't believe this man would have given Martin's name to the press."

"But of course he would if he was impersonating him, Uncle. He must have been following the photographer around, waiting for a chance to slip into a picture."

"Why should he be so cruel? What did he hope to gain?"

Amanda had no solution to offer and did not attempt to invent one. In her experience, no one could beat Uncle Hubert on his own ground when it came to conjecture. Instead she stuck to practical matters. The ability of the soberest folk to believe all they read in print was well known to her, and her worry was a real one.

"People we know have been ringing up ever since, asking if Meg has seen it," she said slowly. "There'll be a lot more this evening. People always read the *Tatler* at tea on Wednesdays. And of course they're going to go on telephoning from now till next year as the late ones spot it in the dentist's waiting room or the hairdresser's. Meg's going to hate that. Just now she's expecting a call from Geoff. I hope I did the right thing. I put Sam on to it."

"Sam?" The Canon's face brightened. "Just the man. He knows all about newspapers." A smile of affection had passed over his face as it always did when he spoke of Samuel Drummock, who was his tenant on the top floor. That elderly and distinguished sporting journalist and his wife had lived there many years, and the relationship between the two men was something of a miracle in itself. It was a cordiality based, apparently, on complete non-comprehension cemented by a deep mutual respect for the utterly unknown. No two men saw less eye to eye and the result was unexpected harmony, as if a dog and a fish had mysteriously become friends and were proud each of the other's remarkable dissimilarity to himself.

Amanda sighed. "So that's all right. He's sitting on the top stairs with the phone and a mug of beer. Meg has left her door open and the moment it really is Geoff he's going to call her. He's furious about all this. I've never seen Sam 'right angry,' as he calls it, before."

"Well, you know, it's an evil thing, this attempt to reverse the process of mourning." The Canon stepped back on to his own territory and became a different being. "Mourning is not forgetting," he said gently, his helplessness vanishing and his voice becoming wise. "It is an undoing. Every minute tie has to be untied and something permanent and valuable recovered and assimilated from the knot. The end is gain, of course. Blessed are they that mourn, for they shall be made strong, in fact. But the process is like all other human births, painful and long and dangerous. This attempt to reverse it when the thing is practically achieved, that is wicked, an attempt to kill the spirit. The poor fellow, whoever he is, has no idea what he's doing, that's obvious. Sam forgets that. Hallo, that's the front door. Is that Albert?"

Amanda listened a moment and then bundled the shirt she was holding behind her under the cushion like any other mother six weeks before Christmas.

"No, Uncle, that's the children."

"Oh dear!" He was alarmed. "I'd forgotten them. They must be kept right away from this, Amanda. They're not ready for anything of this sort. This is most shocking to the young Frightening."

"I know, dear. Lugg's with them. We'll see to that. Hullo, how did you get on?"

The door shuddering open had admitted three excited people. Two of them, both male, were almost beside themselves with the joyous adventure of getting home through London in a real pea-souper. One of these was six and the other was sixty. The third of the party, who was pale and a little breathless from the responsibility of controlling the others, was a girl. She was eight.

Mr. Campion's heir, Rupert, came in blinking in the bright light. He was a slender six-year-old, red-haired like his mother, and wiry. He had the innate gentleness of his father's family, but unlike either of his parents, he was shy. He went over to his mother now and, leaning across her chair, burst out with his private worry in a husky whisper.

"The shoe trees for Aunt Val cost two-and-six."

"Oh well, that's all right," said Amanda reassuringly. "That only makes you ninepence down to date. That's not bad, you know, considering the rise in the cost of living."

"You're sure?"

"Certain. We'll go into the whole situation at the end of the week. Was it fun?"

"Tremenjous," Mr. Magersfontein Lugg, breathing heavily in the doorway, was glowing with a good temper foreign to his somewhat lugubrious personality. He was a large globular person, with a vast white face, small beady black eyes, and a drooping moustache. For so many years he had been Mr. Campion's friend and knave, as well as his personal servant, that certain eccentricities which he possessed had long been accepted and forgiven by all who knew them. He wore the formal black clothes and hard hat of an upper servant of the last century, but there the likeness ceased abruptly.

"I don't mind minding kids," he announced. "The little gel saved me from being run over twice."

The third member of the trio smiled faintly. She was not very tall and not very plump, and her thick straight hair hung down behind her almost to her knees. She was very plainly dressed and as formal as only a child can be, but the blue eyes in her short-nosed solemn face were secretly merry under their heavy lids.

This was Emily, daughter of Mrs. Talisman's second son who had got on in the world and achieved an engineering degree, only to be killed with his wife and a second daughter in Portsmouth in the Blitz. Then Emily, who had been a baby at the time, had come to live with her grandmother in the half basement.

Old Canon Avril often forgot she was not his own granddaughter, and Mrs. Talisman brought her up to be worthy of such a distinction, with the result that she might have been a little repressed had it not been for Sam and Mrs. Drummock who prevented all that.

She looked round cautiously. "There were fires in the street," she said.

"That's right. They've got the old beacons out at Marble Arch." Lugg spoke with tremendous relish. "I ain't seen 'em since I was a nipper meself. Flames shootin' up into the sky like Guy Fawkes night."

Rupert regarded him seriously. "We got you away, though," he observed, "and you still have your parcel. Are you going to show it to Mother, or is it a surprise?"

"Now then, now then, come orf it." Mr. Lugg's sallow skin had achieved a dusky redness and his eyes glowered. "Be a sport. Remember all I've learned you. Don't nark it."

Rupert said nothing, but his eyes laughed and he and Emily exchanged a silent joke.

"It is a surprise," deduced Amanda, "and I'm glad to know because Mr. Lugg's surprises are better if they're not sudden."

"All right, all right, I'll tell yer if yer must know. It's only a bloomin' Father Christmas mask. I was trying it on to amuse these 'ere kids and the blessed girl be'ind the counter made me buy it." Lugg was fighting with a string on his limp package and would have produced his purchase there and then had not a key sounded in the lock behind him in the hall.

"Oh." Amanda got up. "Look, Lugg, that's the boss with Inspector Luke."

The fat man met her eyes. "Inspector Luke, eh?" he said in quick comprehension. "Yes, well, you young'uns better get along, get your wet shoes orf or something. We don't want you dyin' on us, causin' trouble. Come on, come on, get a move on, can't yer? Where shall we go? Up top?"

"No. I don't think so. Mr. Drummock's busy for us on the phone."

"Ho." The black eyebrows rose. "General mobilisation, is it? Very well, we'll go down to yer Grannie's, Emily. See what she's got in her pantry. Perhaps she'll 'ave another go at teachin' me to speak proper, pore soul."

Rupert slid his hand into the vast one. "You can if you like," he said with the conscious wickedness of one betraying a confidence. "You said you could."

"Yus, but I don't like, see? And that was between us. You're goin' to get a thick ear. You're above yourself, that's what you are. You get more like your Pa every day. Come on, Emily, where are yer?"

"I'm here." Her voice sounded from the basement stairs. "I've put the light on for you. You fell last time."

They vanished below, leaving the room blank, like a stage after a harlequinade, and the old man laughed.

"How happy they are," he said, "all of an age. Ah, Albert

my boy, come in, come in. Good evening, Chief Inspector.
I'm afraid we're giving you a lot of trouble."

The greeting stopped Charlie Luke, who had come swinging in behind Campion, filling the room to bursting point by
the mere size of his personality, short in his tracks. Suspicion
leapt in his bright eyes. He always suspected people wanting
to save him trouble. One good stare at the old man appeared
to reassure him, and without being in any way discourteous
he soon managed to convey that he had seen faces like Uncle
Hubert's "befuddled old kisser" before. He smiled, with a
secret quirk of sheer street-boy naughtiness in his twisted lips,
only to receive a considerable shock as he found it not only
remarked and recognised but also forgiven by the old priest.
It was the most complete introduction taking place in a few
seconds which Mr. Campion had ever witnessed.

The two men shook hands and after he had greeted
Amanda as an old colleague Luke glanced about him.

"Where's Mrs. Elginbrodde? Did she get home in good
shape?"

"Yes. She's upstairs in her own room. I'm afraid I upset
her." The Canon wagged his head regretfully. "This has appeared too." He took up the social journal as he spoke and
the D.D.C.I. nodded.

"We saw it at the station. The old charge sergeant sits there
reading it, thinking he's a lord. That's going to cause a bit of
trouble, I'm afraid. Well, it's an upsetting time, sir. I think I
ought to see the young lady, though."

Amanda rose. "We'll go up. Did you get anything?"

"A little. Nothing conclusive," murmured her husband,
who seemed unhappy. "Come on, Charles. This way."

Meg Elginbrodde's sitting room, immediately above the
one they had just left, was as different from it as could well
be imagined. Van Rinn had done the décor for her in the
latest lush or Beaton manner, and between the damasked
grey walls and the deep gold carpet there ranged every per-
missible tint and texture from bronze velvet to scarlet linen,
pin-pointed and enlivened with daring touches of Bristol blue.
After a dubious sidelong glance Luke suddenly decided to
like it very much indeed, and he favoured it with a good stare

round which made him look like a black curly retriever arriving unexpectedly in fairyland.

On an elegant side table between the windows there were evidences of Meg's own art, sketches of dresses, swatches of material, samples of braids and beads, and the blue spidery designs from which jewellers work. Since Campion's famous sister Val had acquired the controlling interest in the fashion house of Papendeik, she had sponsored several young couturiers, and Meg Elginbrodde was one of her most successful discoveries.

The girl herself had been sitting in a small gilt armchair by the fire when they arrived and she rose to greet them. She had changed into a long grey dress which suited her slenderness and flattered the white-gold sleekness of her hair, but she looked an older woman than she had appeared, in the station. The emotional experience which she was undergoing had marked her and her muscles were taut and her eyes sombre with new information about herself.

"Who was he? Did you find out?" She spoke directly to Luke as if to a friend, and was met by something new in his attitude. He had become wary and inquisitive, and Campion, who seemed nervous of him, hastened to answer.

"His name is Walter Morrison."

"Commonly called 'Duds.' " Luke indicated exaggerated outline of his own clothes by way of defining the nickname. "Does that convey anything to you?"

"No," she said slowly, her eyes growing puzzled as they watched him. "No. Ought it to?"

"Not particularly. He's been out of jail, Chelmsford"—he sketched in the blank face of a squat building with the flat of his hand, presumably to save himself time—"just six weeks. He was concerned in a holdup." He hunched his shoulders and embarked on one of those pieces of description which were peculiarly his own. It was an astonishing performance in many ways. The man talked like a pump, in gusts, using little or no syntax and forcing home his meaning by what would appear to be physical strength alone. "It was thug stuff, but they planned it, Duds and another man. One knife between them and half a broken bottle. It was on the corner of Greek Street and Soho Square. Night. V-2 time." His diamond-shaped eyes demanded her co-operation. "Remember V-2's? The whole city waiting. Silent. People on edge. More waiting. Waiting for hours. Nothing. Nothing to show. Then, strike a light! Suddenly, no warning, no whistle, wallop! End of the ruddy world! Just a damned great hole and afterwards half the street coming down very slowly, like a woman fainting. Well. It was in that time. These two lay in wait. Dark streets. Quiet. Foreign troops passing. These lads were waiting for a drunk. Two came by at last alone."

His voice dropped a tone or two. "Quietly. Quietly. Up behind . . . Got yer!" He finished with a soft but blood-curdling little gulp and the scene was as vivid and as unspeakably brutal as if it had happened before them. "It wasn't so easy though," he rattled on, unaware of a tenth part of the impression he was creating on that gentle civilised company. "Bad luck really. Or good. Depends which side you were on. A patrol car ran slap into the fight. Money and valuables had passed, so the law was happy. The two were inside and up before the Beak before they knew what had happened to them. Neither was in uniform and there was no traceable sign that either of them was entitled to wear one. They weren't talking, of course, but their fingerprints were on the files so they didn't miss anything that was coming to them. The other man got the full ten years for robbery with violence. But the charge against Duds was reduced to 'Assault with intent to rob' and he got the limit of five. He can't have been a good boy inside in spite of his pretty voice. There was no remission."

Meg smoothed the silk over her knee and the diamond on her hand winked and trembled. She looked a trifle dazed. It was an effect which Luke's descriptive methods were liable to produce on the uninitiated.

"That just makes it utterly incomprehensible," she said softly. "Is that all you know about him?"

"Oh no." His intelligence was sharp and he prodded her bewilderment like a carpenter prodding a beam for rot. "From 1932 to 1940 he was in and out of prison for various offences, larceny, demanding with menaces, assault. After that he vanished, might have died, for nearly five years, which suggests that he was being taken care of by the Army. He might have done well in it. That did happen."

"Did he serve with Martin Elginbrodde at any point?" demanded Amanda, her cool voice deliberately conversational in the tension.

"We haven't established it." Luke met her eyes and flashed a question at her which she either could not or would not recognise. "He says he never heard of him, naturally. His story is that he's an actor by profession. That probably means he once went on the stage for a spell. He gave the name of a provincial management and we're checking on that now. It won't get us far or"—he peered at Meg again—"will it?"

"He certainly had a most professional moustache," murmured Mr. Campion with uneasy lightness.

Meg raised her head. "How did he explain the moustache?"

"Oh, said he used to wear one but lost it in stir, and didn't like to turn up among his pals without one." The D.D.C.I. spoke in a new light voice, with a careful clipped accent. He also twisted his body slightly, and immediately the absent Duds was recalled to the mind's eye. "He gave his present address, which is a well-known lodginghouse just over the river, and we were able to check on that at once. After we let him go . . ."

"You let him go!" Meg looked at him in amazement and he stiffened.

"We couldn't hold him, ma'am." He sounded scandalised. "We can't hold a man because a lady thinks she recognises him as her husband."

"But he ran away."

Luke opened his mouth but checked the retort just in time. He glanced hopefully at Mr. Campion, who did his best to explain.

"If the police arrest a man they're bound to bring him before a magistrate as soon as possible," he said gently. "That's the law the wars are fought for nowadays. Habeas corpus and all that. This man Morrison hasn't even been proved to have got himself photographed in a false moustache to plague you with copies of it, but even if he had I doubt if the act would constitute nuisance. That was why we hoped he'd speak to you. Once he had asked for money, uttered threats, some point in his performance would have appeared."

She shook her head wonderingly and Luke exploded.

"We were only within our rights in marching him off for questioning because the chump ran away," he announced inelegantly. "If he'd raised his hat and wandered off we could hardly have stopped him. The courts can be very mind-my-wig when they begin on the subject of police persecution of the marked man." He threw in a brief but vivid impression of some legal dignitary who possessed a commanding manner, a throat infection, and a small but obtrusive corporation. "However, we're on to the blighter now. He knows we are and——"

The trill of the telephone bell on the landing outside cut him short. Meg had sprung up at its first hesitant note. Her movement was unconscious, as was also her glance at the French clock on the mantelshelf. The golden hands showed the time as a few minutes before seven and in the silence everyone remembered that Geoffrey Levett had promised to telephone her at five. Meanwhile a firm flat Midland voice was speaking in the passage outside.

"Hullo, hullo. . . . Aye, it is. . . . But no, no, you can't speak to her. I'm sorry." The tone was patient but utterly uncompromising. "Oh yes, I've got your name, I'll remember. . . . Yes, she has seen it. . . . Aye, it was indeed a great shock. Someone playing the go-at. Not in good taste. . . . No, I quite agree. . . . Good-bye."

The phone rang off and the tiny sound was followed by a bellow which would have carried across a playing field.

"Meg lass!"

"Yes, Uncle Sam?"

"The Dowager Lady Totham, Park Street. Seventeen going up."

"Thank you, darling." She sighed and reseated herself. "That's been happening all the time. Sam's keeping a list. I do hope Geoff doesn't keep finding this number engaged. I'm sorry, Chief Inspector, what were you saying?"

Luke stood looking at her. His hands were in his pockets, his jacket hitched back into a flounce behind his narrow hips. His shoulders were flat and wide and his dark face glowed

with the half-ferocious, half-condoning knowingness which
was the essence of the man. He had clearly made up his mind
to come clean.

"Mrs. Elginbrodde," he demanded bluntly, "just how well
did you know that husband of yours when you married him?"

Mr. Campion's face became misleadingly blank and
Amanda looked up, her brown eyes surprised and wary. They
were hostile to Luke and he was aware of it and used to
hostility.

"Well, you see how it is," he went on, taking the room into
his confidence. "Now I've had a talk with Duds I see he's a
smooth piece. Nice voice. Plausible. May have come from a
good home, as they say. May easily have had a very good war
record."

Canon Avril, who had been sitting very quietly in the
darkest corner of the room, leant forward.

"If you're asking if he had ever had any serious illness or
nervous trouble, we don't know," he remarked. "I hadn't
known him from boyhood and when his grandmother wrote
me from France she did not mention anything of the kind.
He was introduced here by a young nephew of mine soon
after the war had started. Then, when he returned from the
Middle East, we saw a lot of him. I thought he and Meg were
young to marry, but then life was shorter in those days. Youth
is relative, after all."

The D.D.C.I. hesitated, but his sophisticated eyes smiled
at the old man.

"As long as you satisfied yourself about the chap, sir," he
said, "as long as you did check up on him——"

"Check up?"

Luke sighed. "Neither Mr. Campion nor I ever met Mr.
Elginbrodde. Today we questioned a man called Duds Morrison. There are five years in Morrison's life which from our
point of view are unaccounted for, and it was during those
same five years that Elginbrodde met and married your
daughter. I'm just making quite sure they're not the same
man."

Meg gaped at him. In her amazement she let the murmur
of the telephone outside pass unnoticed.

"But I saw him too."

Luke regarded her stolidly. "I know you did," he said, and added with an irritable gesture which destroyed his official manner, "You're human, aren't you?"

"But of course." To everyone's astonishment the Canon got up and, coming down the room, took his daughter's hand. "Of course," he repeated. "This young man must make sure of that, Meg. Good gracious me. No good purpose is ever served by discounting the possibility of *sin*." He made the word sound familiar if not downright homely.

Luke's smile grew slowly broad and absent-mindedly he turned his thumbs up. "That's all right then. You must take a squint at him yourself, sir——"

"Is there a Chief Inspector of Po-lice in there, Meg? Name of Luke?" The bellow from the landing cut him short and sent him hurrying to the door. "Divisional Headquarters, urgent."

Everyone listened to the ensuing conversation, but it was not revealing.

"Where?" Luke demanded after a long silence, and then, "I see. Right. I'll come there now. No good sending a car in this fog."

He came striding back into the room, unusual touches of colour on his cheekbones.

"I'm afraid it'll have to be tonight, sir," he said to Avril, "and I'll have to ask you to come out again too, Mr. Campion, if you will. I haven't been very bright. They've just picked up Duds in an alley off Crumb Street. He's what you might call thoroughly dead by all I can hear."

Mr. Campion sat up slowly and then rose to his feet.

"So soon?" he murmured. "That's a black mark against us, Charles. I wondered if he had it coming to him, but I didn't envisage anything quite so—prompt."

"Are you saying he's been murdered?" Meg was very pale.

Luke smiled at her from the midst of his preoccupation. "He didn't die of neglect."

The Canon got up. "We must go at once," he said.

As the front door closed behind the three men and its distinctive slam echoed in the apartment upstairs. Meg walked down the room and back again.

"I love Geoffrey," she said.

"Yes." Amanda did not move. Her eyes looked warm and honey-coloured in the firelight. "That's obvious, if you'll forgive my saying so. Did you quarrel this afternoon?"

"No, I tried to explain, though, which was silly. I thought I knew Geoff but I don't, Amanda. I love him unbearably but I don't know him at all." She looked so young of a sudden that the other woman glanced away.

"I don't expect he's very knowable at the moment," she observed. "Getting married is always rather complicating, don't you think? I know it's useless to say don't worry, but I feel you must wait. Waiting is one of the great arts."

"That awful little man in the station wasn't Martin."

"No, of course he wasn't."

"The Chief Inspector didn't believe me."

"Luke was mystified. When he talked to Morrison he must have decided it wasn't blackmail. Now of course he's furious with himself."

"Because he didn't guess the man was going to get killed?"

"Well," said Amanda, who was giving the matter her deepest consideration, "he hasn't looked after him very well, has he?"

Meg made an effort to think about Morrison and gave it up.

"Suppose Geoff *doesn't* ring?"

"Eeh, he'll telephone, lass." The door had been kicked open a little wider by a soft-soled shoe and Sam Drummock came cautiously into the room. He was carrying two large tulip glasses which he had overfilled, and he walked very steadily, like a three-year-old carrying a pitcher. He was a round man with a round bald head, and possessed the great strength which is inherent in the Midland breed. He had small shrewd eyes and a red face and was at the moment clad in his working garment. This was a sort of high-collared pyjama jacket in heavy shantung, most beautifully laundered and worn over tidy little grey flannel trousers. His small round feet were set in neat and shiny red slippers, and his entire appearance managed to suggest the highly conventional costume of some unknown land.

"Gin sling," he explained, handing each of them a glass. "I

mixed it myself so I know it's all right. It's a pick-me-up. You need it. Wait till I get my can. It's on the stairs."

He moved very quickly and lightly, like the boxers he admired so much, and was soon back again, a shining pewter tankard in his hand.

"Well, I listened," he announced cheerfully. "It's a killing, eh? Well, that's bad. Still, cheer up. Thank God it's not uz." A little chuckling laugh escaped him and he roamed over to a bureau on whose lid a design for a wonderful wedding dress was displayed. "I'm going to see the old Queen in this," he said to Amanda with enormous satisfaction. "I'm going to sit in the front pew and hold my little top hat on my knee. If the old Bishop (and he hasn't been looking too good lately, mind you) only foozles it, and Hubert has to do the marrying, I'm going to give her away."

He peered at the drawing again and made an explosive noise.

"I don't like the bit underneath. That spoils it for me, that does. *'Darling, if I could only wear this myself I'd be in heaven.'* Signed Nicky. I'd Nicky the little so-and-so."

Meg smiled in spite of her preoccupation. "Nicolas de Richeberg is the most brilliant dress designer in the world, Uncle Sam."

"So he ought to be." Sam raised his tankard. "Only the best is good enough for uz. But she'd look lovely in calico, my old Queen would. Meg——"

"Yes?"

"It's on my conscience so I'll have to tell you. That girl in Geoff's office rang again. He's forgotten a personal call that was booked to him by his Paris foreman or broker or whatever they call them. She wants him to phone the moment he comes here." Sam was worried. The anxiety peeped out of his kind little eyes and was gone again. "But it doesn't signify." A hopeful idea occurred to him. "Maybe he's gone and had a drink or two, eh?"

"That wouldn't be like him."

"No." He put his head into his mug and reappeared, refreshed. "Mind you," he said, "if it was Martin that was on the tiles I wouldn't give it another thought. I'd *know.*"

Amanda hesitated. "I never knew Martin, of course. Was he a wild person?"

"Martin?" Sam put his head back and crowed aloud. "Oh, a dasher. A lively, dashing, smashing sort of a lad. But we don't want to talk about him, poor fellow, do we?" There were sudden tears in the twinkling eyes. "Oh lord, no. That's done. That's over. My old Queen's going to be happy with a grand chap. She's going to have a good steady sensible manly sort of a huzband." He fixed the visitor with a solemn stare. "A grand chap," he declared. "One of the best. And when I'm talking I know what I mean. A straight clean fighter."

This last was clearly the highest praise he could bestow. He hesitated, glanced at the door and back again, and his very head shone with exasperation.

"But if he's *not* flat on his back under a bar table, why the hell doesn't he ring oop?" he said.

THREE
THE SPOOR

It is not easy to tell when enmity first begins, when that force which is part fear, part rivalry, and part the frank urge for survival first springs, but it was on that freezing walk that Charlie Luke caught the first wind of the man who of all his many quarries was to become the chief enemy of his life.

As Amanda had guessed, at that time he was chiefly angry with himself. He was the best of policemen, which is to say that he never for one moment assumed that he was judge or jury, warder or hangman. He saw himself as the shepherd dog does; until he had rounded him up the malefactor was his private responsibility, to be protected as well as cornered. His job was first to locate him and then to bring him in alive, so the fact that he had ignored the terror which he had seen so plainly in the pale face above the grotesque moustache, and had sent Duds Morrison out alone to die, made him furious. It had been a professional slip of the worst kind and he hated himself for making it.

Yet behind his self-criticism there was something more. Just then he had a presentiment, a warning from some experience-born sixth sense, that he was about to encounter something rare and dangerous. The whiff of tiger crept to him through the fog.

The walk itself was an experience. Without old Avril, who knew his parish blindfold, they might never have achieved it. The fog was now at its worst, rolling up from the river dense as a feather bed. It hung between street lamp and street lamp in blinding and abominable folds, and since in that area the architecture is all much alike, and the streets are arranged in a series of graceful curves in which it is easy to walk in a circle in sunlight, the mile from the rectory to Crumb Street might well have been a maze. However, the Canon plunged into it with complete confidence, walking very fast.

As he strode behind his uncle, Mr. Campion eyed the somewhat picturesque figure with affection. Canon Avril's coat in particular was remarkable, and even famous in its own small way. It might have been designed by Phil May, for it brushed its wearer's boots and was fastened by a double row of bone buttons, each as large as a small saucer, which ran down in a double line to well below its owner's knees. Moreover, since it appeared to be cut from a shepherd's plaid carpet, it had acquired with the years the complete mould of the old man's form, even to the bulge in his right-hand jacket pocket where he carried his tobacco tin, and he marched along inside it as if it were a shell.

The story about it that Campion knew was that it was often in pawn. Uncle Hubert was notoriously unsafe with money, so Miss Warburton, a pleasant spinster who lived in one of the glebe cottages and devoted herself to the church, had, since his wife's death, taken complete charge of his private expenditure. She allowed him so much loose change every Saturday, placing the money in the brass box on his study mantelshelf, and she was absolutely adamant. If he overspent in the early part of the week, penniless he remained until payday.

Financially embarrassed parishioners from the poor streets behind the shops knew all this as well as he did, and whenever possible confined their importunities to the week end, but when, as must sometimes happen, some vital need arose at a moment's notice, there was still just one other way. On these occasions the Canon's coat was carried through the square in daylight over the arm of the borrower to the little pop-shop on the corner, and old Mr. Hertz paid out forty-three shillings and sixpence on it. It was not worth the money. The Jew never forbore to say so. Thus the whole performance was a penance as well as a relief. Only the old and trusted availed themselves of it, and then only in exceptional circumstances, so that, in certain circles, "it'll be a case of the Canon's coat" had become a phrase denoting the end of the tether in money matters.

To do him justice, Avril knew exactly what he was about. He had no illusions and possessed in his own queer way a quality of blazing common sense. Almost always he had to redeem the pledge himself. He did not set up as a charitable institution and was in no respect sentimental, but he was humble, he had charity, and he had friends.

Moreover, in common with many Christians of this classic type, he felt sincerely safer and more at ease when he had given away all he had, like a man passing a ball in a game. In his case the result appeared to be a strange material freedom. He walked, as it were, on the water. The compulsion which demanded his small possessions gave him in return Miss Warburton. It was a splendid exchange.

He took his nephew and Charlie Luke to Crumb Street by a series of short cuts, while they followed him with their fingers crossed. They came upon their goal unexpectedly. A last spurt through a pitchdark mews brought them into the heart of its murky length, not a stone's throw from the police station. Here he paused and looked round at them.

"Now, where is this poor fellow?"

"Pump Path," said Luke promptly. "Up here on the right, past the Feathers."

Once out of the wilderness of plinth and portico, he knew his own manor as well as any man alive, and he led them swiftly down the dark pavement beside the shuttered shops. It was no night for strolling and there were few people about, but the inevitable group of the under-entertained were lounging round a dark entrance beside the Four Feathers public house. This tavern was of the lesser gin-palace type. It leered at them through the mist, flaunting offhandedly a drab gaiety of tile and trademark, while all along the brass rail which bordered the frosted glass diapering of the saloon window, a row of half heads, grotesquely bisected, were turned to peer at them curiously as they swept by.

As they brushed through the group a gleam of silver appeared in the alley's dark mouth and a constable saluted as he recognised Luke.

"The trouble's at the other end, sir, near the Bourne Avenue entrance. You'll need a torch. It's very thick in there."

Luke had already produced one. It had a yellow silk sock tied over it and gave a fairly penetrating beam, but even so progress was difficult.

The stone way was very worn and sloped sharply from each side to an open gutter in the centre, while the high walls which lined it leaned together, their dark surfaces blank as cliffs.

"What a place to die in!" The Chief spoke with disgust.

"Or to live in, of course." Mr. Campion's light voice sounded affable. He had just reached the end of the wall and had come upon a crooked wooden fence which would have appeared self-consciously rustic in a Sussex village. Some little way behind it the square of a small window shone orange in the mist.

"Back garden of 37 Grove Road," said Luke over his shoulder. "Last of its kind. (Hands off our beauty spots.) There used to be a row of 'em over here, but they've all been built over, except that one which is kept tidy by the caretaker of the solicitor's office. It's quite a sight in the summer. Four marigolds in a fancy flowerpot. The old man has nuisance-by-cats on the brain. Goes down to the station to complain every Friday. I wonder if he heard anything tonight. Look out, there's a bit of a bend here somewhere. . . . Ah."

The torch beam turned and, following it, they came upon the scene of the trouble. It was a dramatic picture. Some resourceful policeman had unearthed one of the old naphtha flares which are the only real answer to fog. Like a livid plume, it spat and hissed above the heads of a knot of men in the chasm, its vigorous smoke trail mingling with the other vapours, making Rembrandtesque clouds above them.

"Chief?" The brisk voice of Sergeant Picot came to them hollowly as his chunky silhouette detached itself from the dark mass.

"Wotcher, George." Luke was ferociously cheerful as usual. "What have you got there?"

"Quite enough, sir. Can you get by? There's not much room. The doctor's here." This last was clearly in the nature of a friendly warning. They advanced cautiously, the little crowd parting for them.

Duds had died in a hole. In a narrow angle where two walls met there was a space perhaps a foot wide and eighteen inches deep, and into this the body was crammed in a sitting position, the legs drawn up, the chin on the breast. It seemed impossible that any human being should take up so little space. He sat, a heap of unwanted rubbish, and the red shadow which spread out over his sports coat like a bib had crept over his hands and on to the stones. He looked very small and negligible, scarcely even horrible, in the circle of dark heads about him.

Luke squatted down on his heels and the constable brought the flare a step nearer. Picot bent towards his Chief.

"One of our own men found him at six-forty, but he may have been here an hour or more," he murmured, his heavy-featured face catching the light from Luke's own torch. "This path isn't used very much, and anyway, I doubt whether one would have seen him if one was hurrying by."

"Or stopped if one had. He's no wayside flower," muttered Luke, getting up to make way for Mr. Campion. "What was the exact time he left us this afternoon?"

"Well after five, sir. I can't say for sure. I was hoping you'd have noticed. I came along as soon as I got the report, of course. We've had the photographer and made the survey. Here's the doctor, sir."

The reminder was scarcely necessary. A steady grumble from the region of the Chief Inspector's elbow had been audible for some time. Now Luke turned his head towards it.

"Funny how we always disturb you at your dinner, Doc," he said mildly into the darkness. "I've got a parson just behind me. No offence. I only thought you'd like to know."

The rumbling ceased abruptly and a clipped schoolmaster-ish voice remarked acidly: "Very good of you to bother about my immortal soul, Chief Inspector. I'm afraid I'd ceased to concern myself about yours. I've been waiting here for over half an hour, and of course any sort of examination in these circumstances is quite useless. If you'll have this sent along I'll do the P.M. at nine tomorrow."

"Righto." Luke did not turn his head. "Just before you go, what is all that? Throat cut?"

"The haemorrhage? Oh no. That's from the nose. That's nothing."

"Get away!" The D.D.C.I. sounded relieved. "It's natural, is it? Had a nosebleed and just sat down and died?"

"Not unless by so doing he cracked himself over the head with sufficient force to fracture the vault." The prim voice was smugly amused. "I think that, as you might so easily say yourself, Charles, someone has been 'putting in the leather.' I have no intention of committing myself, but I should say that was done with a boot. We shall know in the morning."

"Can we wash his face?"

"If it gives you any satisfaction. Good evening." He trotted off and his plump figure was swallowed by the fog.

"Steak and kidney pudding night," murmured Luke, glancing after him. "I hope she's kept it hot for him. Can we get this face fit to look at, George?"

"Here, sir?"

"Yes, please. I've got someone to see it. Get on with it, old man, will you?" He broke off abruptly as Campion touched his shoulder. Old Avril had come into the circle of light and stood now bowed before all that remained of the wretched Duds. He was uncovered, his tufty untidy hair sticking up like rough grass on his fine head. He was wiping the blood very gently from the face with a great white handkerchief, performing the operation inexpertly but with a certain clumsy care which suggested to the minds of everybody present the same sort of operation performed on a child with a cold. He betrayed no trace of distaste or hesitation and Sergeant Picot for one was frankly scandalised. He made a faint noise in his throat like a startled pheasant and was on the point of intervening when Luke's hand bit into his arm. The Chief was very still. He stood poised, every sense alert, his eyes snapping and the great kite-shaped mass of his shoulders cut into the picture, lending it new drama.

The Canon continued his ministrations quietly and inexpertly, making a considerable mess of himself. It was clear that along with sin blood had no terrors for him.

"There," he said at last, apparently to the corpse, and he

looked long at the now no longer horrible but dirty and infinitely pathetic face. Presently he pulled the lids down over the dull eyes.

"Poor boy." All the wastage of Duds' manhood was expressed and commiserated in unself-conscious regret.

As Avril took up the dead man's hands to fold them, the jacket sleeves caught his attention and for the first time he became puzzled. He lifted the right arm and ran his hand up to the elbow.

"Some light, please," he commanded gently, and Luke's torch shone down for him at once. It fell on a neat leather patch on the elbow and on a smaller one nearer the cuff. It was good amateur work, an Army batman's job.

"Seen him before, sir?"

The old man did not answer. He finished his task, folded the hands, and rose. He leant over to Luke.

"I should like to talk to you."

"Very well, sir."

"Where are you taking this poor fellow? Can we go there?"

"No, sir, we'll go along to the station, if you don't mind. It's just round the corner. The body must go down to the mortuary. The van will be here now." Luke was firm but respectful and the old man nodded. The two appeared to be in complete accord, Mr. Campion noticed, as if they had known each other a very long time.

"I want that jacket," said Avril. "I want to take it home."

"Very good, sir." Luke did not bat an eyelid. "We'll have all the clothes, George, as soon as you can, down at the station. Okay?"

Picot stepped back to give an order. The atmosphere of the entire proceedings had undergone an abrupt change. The query had gone out of it and life and bustle had returned.

While Mr. Campion was taking from his uncle the terrible handkerchief, which he appeared to be on the verge of stuffing into his pocket, Luke paused to give the routine instructions. The power of the man became almost frighteningly noticeable at once, as if a truck engine had suddenly started up in the narrow way.

"Detective Slaney there?" he enquired, and hurried on as a compact shadow hurried in out of the dark. "Mrs. Gollie,

Bill. You know her well, don't you? Nip along to the side bar
of the Feathers and see what you can pick up. She'll open
her mouth, of course, but if you don't fall right in you may
be able to sort out something from the shower. Keep it as
quiet as you can until this lot is out of the way. Detective
Coleman."

"Here, sir." The young voice just behind Campion was unsteady in its eagerness and a heavy figure brushed past him.

"Look alive, look alive! Zeal, energy, that's what we want
in the C.I.D.! Don't tread on Exhibit A." Luke's irony was
ferocious as his smile in the dark. "Now, just down here behind us there's a low fence with a wicket in it. If you can't
find the wicket climb over the fence. You'll see a little window
all lit up. When you've fallen over the graveyard of little images which fill the perishing place, tap on a window and a
door will open just beside you. Inside there'll be the damnedest old man you ever saw, called Creasey. Listen to him, and
if you don't lose your temper you'll make a good policeman.
If you can get him to tell you if he heard or saw anything
unusual in this alley between five-thirty and six-forty tonight,
you may grow into a detective. He's sure to have been in.
He's got a bedridden old mother in there who he can't leave.
Got it?"

"Yes, sir."

"Right. Off you go. Step on it. Sergeant Branch about? Oh,
there you are, Henry. The deceased has got some relations,
nice decent little people called Atkins. Mrs. Atkins is a sister.
They live in Tufnell Park. I've got the address here somewhere. I took it down when I looked him up this afternoon.
Yes, here it is: 22 Smith Street. Can you see to that?"

"Right, sir." The crowd of detectives were thinning and the
mortuary attendants had appeared. Luke took Campion by
one arm and the Canon by the other and moved them gently
round. "We must get back," he said. "The Boss will be down
by this time."

Avril looked back. "That poor fellow, will they take him
home?"

"Well"—Luke was amused—"they tell me Chelmsford's a
modern prison and it's amazing what they're up to nowadays,

but even so I doubt if they see their old boys off with plumes and four carriages for the mourners."

"But you said something about relatives."

"Oh yes, next of kin." He sounded gloomy. "It comes hard on people like that. He gave the poor woman's name at his first conviction, I suppose. We never forget. Still, someone's got to stump up for the box and shovel, if we can persuade them to. The public must be protected. This way, sir. I think you want to talk to me. Did you know him?"

The torch in the hand which was through Campion's arm happened to slip up at that moment, and the beam played over the fine old face.

"No. He was a complete stranger." The Canon sounded regretful. "I should have known Martin. I should have known Martin anywhere. He was a strange, distinctive lad. This poor boy was not like him in feature at all."

There was a moment's interruption as they came out of the path and found the wider pavement. They were all three walking very fast, all tall men, their heads close together.

"But the jacket," Luke began, and Avril nodded.

"The jacket was Martin's, and it came from my house."

"Did it, by Jove! When? I mean, when did you last see it?"

"I've been trying to think. I don't know, exactly. I'm not very observant. Some weeks ago, perhaps. Perhaps two months."

Luke pursed his lips for a whistle and changed his mind. They had reached the station and he led them into its austere carbolic-scented interior and through to the C.I.D. room and his own modest office beyond. Even here the fog had penetrated, hanging in the atmosphere like a smoke haze. But the light was quite good enough to show the younger men something they had not noticed before: the Canon was in no fit state to be sent home uncleansed. The only occupant, Detective Constable Galloway, a round-faced young man who was Luke's clerk, sprang up from his desk at the first glance, supposing no doubt that a murderer had been brought in red-handed, and even Mr. Campion looked startled.

"Yes, well," said Luke, eying the old gentleman with incredulity, "we'd better continue this in the washroom. Has the

Super phoned yet, Andy? He hasn't shown up yet, I suppose?"

"No sign of him yet, sir. There are one or two items, though. There have been several enquiries concerning Mr. Geoffrey Levett. His secretary is creating. It appears he was speaking at a dinner tonight, rather a big show, and he hasn't turned up. Both the secretary and Mrs. Elginbrodde suggested he might have contacted you. They seemed very worried."

The two younger men exchanged glances and then Luke shrugged his shoulders and touched Avril's arm.

"You'd really better come along with us, sir," he said, and in the washroom, while they attended to him with considerable efficiency, the interrogation continued.

"Oh no, my dear fellow, it was not years ago." In his shirt sleeves Avril stood talking to the back of Luke's neck as the Chief Inspector scrubbed the front of the famous coat with a wet towel. "That particular jacket—one could hardly mistake it—has been hanging in the cloakroom at the rectory for years, but it was there quite recently. It was certainly there when this winter began."

"How do you know, Uncle?" Campion was running warm water over the old hands, slender, clumsy scholar's hands whose fine almond nails took care of themselves, and he put a piece of soap in them as he spoke.

"Because I saw it there when I took my heavy coat from over it on the first cold day of the autumn. That was St. Matthew's Day, the twenty-first of September, very early for cold weather. We old men notice things like that." Avril took the soap and washed his hands with the obedience of one who was used to tyranny in small matters. He made a long thorough job of it, exactly as he had been taught long ago. It was clear he had no idea what he was doing and his eyes were very grave and thoughtful. "Yes, it was there then. That's less than seven weeks ago. I always hung something over it, you see, and I looked round for something else to cover it with. There was a mackintosh there and I put that round it."

"Why?"

The Canon put out his hands for the towel. "Because I thought Meg might go in there and see it. It always reminded

me so vividly of Martin. I saw no reason why she should have
the same experience." His glance flickered over to Luke, who
was watching him, nodding, his diamond eyes live as coals.
Avril echoed his faint smile. "I might have put it away,
mightn't I, folded it and hidden it in my study? But I didn't,
you know. I just left it there and covered it up every time.
Queer how the mind plays these little tricks. One isn't thinking, I suppose. You understand that, don't you, Inspector? I
thought you would."

Luke's face grew a shade darker and he laughed, only to
become serious again immediately.

"Have another look at it, sir. Best to be sure. You see what
it means."

"Of course I do, my boy, of course I do." Avril struggled
back into his clothes. "Someone very close to us indeed must
be involved, and it's a very curious thing because as I see it
this strangely cruel deception is aimed directly at Meg, and
I should not have said that anyone who knew her would do
it. That's why I must have that jacket and I must take it
home."

From force of habit he took the lead back to Luke's room,
talking freely, his pleasant voice resonant in the bleak corridors.

"You think you can find out who it was, do you, sir?" Luke
got in front just in time to open his own door.

"Oh yes." For a moment the old eyes met his and he saw
there that strange sternness which hitherto he had associated
only with the Bench. Its utter ruthlessness shook him once
again, as it always did. "Oh yes," said Avril again, "I shall find
out."

They had been longer than they thought and Sergeant Picot was waiting for them, his horrible brown paper parcel
open on a table and each item, neatly labelled, set out upon
it. His stolid eyebrows rose as Avril pounced upon the stained
and sodden jacket and spread it before them.

"The contents of the pockets is in here, sir," he murmured
to Luke, indicating a second, unopened parcel.

"We shan't want that." Avril brushed him aside and concentrated on the garment. "It's what we used to call 'loud,' "
he observed. "The tweed is loud. That's what Meg recog-

nised, do you see? She sees a great deal of material in her work. She'd forgotten this, but the pattern stuck in her mind and was associated with the boy. Do you see that?"

He pointed to the place where the tailor's tab had been carefully unpicked on the inside of the breast pocket.

"How extraordinary! Now who in the world would have thought of doing that?"

"Quite a number of our clients, sir. You'd be surprised." Luke was grinning. "It's the patches you recognised, though, wasn't it?"

"Yes." The Canon turned the sleeve over and found them again. "Those two patches. I used to wonder—idly, you know—why there were two. Why not put a large piece of leather over both holes? I know nothing about such things, but it struck me as being most odd."

"Perhaps the holes were made at different times, sir."

Sergeant Picot, whose thick dark hair shot out of the top of his head as if he were in a permanent state of shock, decided that his Chief was determined to humour a harmless idiot and attempted to play too.

Avril was unconvinced. "It may have been that, but I still think it would have been wiser to have a single patch," he said. "However, I can swear to these, that's one thing. I sometimes feel that all these very small things have a purpose, you know. One mustn't be precise, and that line of thought leads one to some very strange conclusions, but I do sometimes wonder. Now, if you'll wrap that up I'll take it home and find out how it came to be where it was."

He handed the jacket to Picot and indicated the brown paper.

The sergeant shot a questioning glance at Luke, who nodded.

"I'm going to send George here down with you, sir," he said. "Do you mind?"

The Canon frowned. "I'd rather do it alone. I shall be dealing with my family. Everyone in the house has lived there so long."

"Exactly." Luke was handling him with affection rather than merely with care. "That's why I want to give you George. He's my senior assistant, a quiet, discreet sort of man," he added firmly, eying the sergeant with open menace. "He's so self-effacing you won't know he's there."

Avril remained dubious. "I should find it much easier," he said sadly, and Luke hesitated.

"No," he said at last, "I daren't. It's evidence, you see. Got to be produced in court. George has signed for it. He can't let it go."

"Very well." The Canon gave way not only with grace but with generosity. "In that case, Sergeant, you and I must make good friends. Come along, I warn you, though, my dear sir, I fear this may be very painful for you, very embarrassing and painful indeed."

Picot regarded him blankly, but he was experienced and did what he always did when in doubt, falling back on silent obedience. Nothing could have been more fortunate.

As the door closed behind the unlikely pair Mr. Campion offered Luke a cigarette and took one himself.

"You would have trusted him," he remarked, "in fact, you are trusting him, quite amazingly. You're right, of course, but I don't see quite why you decided to."

"Don't you?" Luke was uncharacteristically embarrassed. He thrust long fingers through his hair. "I know that kind," he said. "There's not a lot of them and they're seldom much to do with the church—except there was one old girl I remember who ran a convent down in Leyton when I was a child. She was one and she was religious, wore all the doings." He made himself a coif with his plaited fingers and lightly sketched in a swinging crucifix. "But it doesn't follow. The one I got to know best was a dear old bloke who had an eel stall in Paddington Market. They crop up anywhere, you can't miss 'em. All you know is that you can trust 'em where you wouldn't trust your Ma. They've *got* to be on the up-and-up, see?"

"Not entirely." Mr. Campion conveyed that this was a field of police knowledge entirely new to him.

Luke sighed and turned to his desk, where the chits had accumulated.

"Because otherwise they fall flat on their kissers, chum," he said cheerfully. "Look at 'em. By ordinary standards they're not safe out. They ought to be starving in the gutter, imposed on by every crook in creation. But are they? Are they, hell! There they go, picking their way like a drunk on a parapet, apparently obeying instructions which no one else can hear. They go barging into filth and it runs off them as if they were lead-glazed. They see all the dirt and none of it shocks 'em. They hand over all they've got and yet they never want. All you and I can do is to spot them when we see them. I recognised that old boy the moment he spoke to me. He'll come back with the truth about that jacket whatever it costs him. He's got to."

Campion's eyes had grown dark behind his horn-rims.

"But who," he demanded, "who in all that household could have smuggled that jacket out to Duds Morrison?"

Luke was turning papers out on his desk and he spoke without looking up.

"Who could, except the girl?" he said slowly. "Either she, or that new chap of hers, who seems to have disappeared."

"You're wrong."

"I hope so." He glanced up and smiled. "Perhaps it's a miracle."

"Perhaps there's another card in the pack," said Mr. Campion.

FOUR
THE JOKER

Mrs. Gollie came into Luke's office as if she was hastening to the scene of some terrible personal disaster, or perhaps merely going on the stage. There was drama in every curve of her splendid young body, in the swinging sleeves of her camel-hair coat clutched tightly round her shoulders, in the turn of her beautiful neck. She was hatless and her well-dyed black hair sat neatly round her head in stiff waves which might have been fresh from the drier, but her fine eyes were ingenuous and her mouth, for all its bright paint, was kindly and innocent.

"I had to come down myself, Mr. Luke," she began without preamble. "I saw him, you see, and I mean to say you want to know, don't you?" She had a gentle voice and that kind of London accent which is like the waters of the Thames at the Pool, by no means unpleasant but the least bit thick. "I told Bill Slaney here I must come myself. 'I'd better go down there at once,' I said. I mean, Bert and I want to help all we can, naturally. 'It's not very nice for us,' I said, 'right on our doorstep and in all this fog.' I mean, it gives you the willies, doesn't it? I mean, you don't feel safe. No one would. I shan't sleep, you know. I couldn't if you paid me. I shan't sleep a wink tonight and if I'd known what was going to happen I shouldn't have slept last night. And——"

"You wouldn't look half so lovely now." Luke's leer would have stopped a train and she paused in full spate.

"I *beg* your pardon?"

"That's right. You didn't come here to listen to that sort of thing, did you? You came to answer questions, didn't you? We can skip all that. So you shall. Sit down."

He grinned at her, waved her into the chair before the desk, and winked briefly at Campion.

"Now," he began, bending over the blotter without seating himself, so that he looked like some great horsefly spread-eagled there, "name, age, occupation: wife of licencee. Slaney, you've got all that engraved on your heart, no doubt, same as we all have." He glanced over her head at the solid plain-clothes man and returned to the girl. "Okay, then, you saw the deceased, did you, duck? When?"

"Well, I mean, I was telling you. You'll have to listen, won't you? I must get a word in, mustn't I? Fair's fair, I mean to say. It was just when we were opening." Her voice was gentle, placatory, and never-ending. "I was just getting my keys for the spirits when I looked round and there he was——"

"How do you know?"

"Well, I've got eyes, haven't I?" She had lost her sense of theatre and was on the defensive, but her wits were gathering about her. "Oh, I see what you mean. Well, it was like this, see. Bill—I mean Mr. Slaney—told me what he looked like. I mean, he came in and asked me had I seen anyone like him in any of the bars today, and I had, so naturally I said so. I'm only trying to help, aren't I? Don't listen if you don't want to. Bert and I don't want to go into any witness box. That sort of thing is not as good for business as you may think. But I did see both men. They came in——"

"Both?" The circumflex accents which served Luke for eyebrows shot up on his forehead. Behind Mrs. Gollie, Slaney signalled confirmation, and they let her flow quietly on.

"I was in a hurry, see, so I didn't notice them particularly. I thought they'd come off a train. The lights were shocking. I told Bert so. He was further along the bar in the saloon, and I called to him that I'd have to have bigger bulbs if I was to see what I was doing. All the time these two were talking. The other man—not the one who was killed—gave the order. Two small gins, they had."

"Were they alone in your little bar?"

"I've just told you so. We were hardly open."

"Did they meet there or did they come in together?"

"They came in together. I've said so. Oh, *do* listen, Mr. Luke. They came in talking very quietly, confidentially, as if they had business. Well, I know enough to stand back when I see that going on. I haven't been in what you might call my own business for five years without learning when customers want me and when they don't, so I just served them and went along to Bert for the bulbs. When I came back I was just in time to see the smaller man—that's the one Bill asked me about, the one with the well-cut sports jacket, green porkpie, and pale delicate sort of face—shoot out through the door, pulling his arm away from the other chap."

"Pulling?"

"Yes, you know, shaking him off." Her white elbow, round and milky, shot out from the folds of camel hair with a jingle of gold bracelets. "The other chap started after him, remembered me, and shoved ten bob down on the counter. Then he went after him. All night I expected him to come back for his change, but he didn't come in."

"Did you hear anything they said at all?"

"I didn't, Mr. Luke. It's no good me saying I did. I didn't listen, you see. Besides, there was such a row going on. Bert had the wireless in the saloon, listening to a play. There was a band in the street, bawling. I was talking myself about the electric-light bulbs——"

"In fact, the place was the same old parrot house it always is." Luke spoke without heat. "What did the second man look like?"

She clicked her tongue against her teeth. "I wish I'd looked, but I never thought of a murder, see? He was tall and he was clean, sort of scrubbed-looking. A thoroughgoing gentleman, if you can imagine what I mean. Might have been in the Navy. He smiled when he gave the order, but not *at* me. I might have been any sort of girl."

"Was he fair or dark?"

"I couldn't say. He had his hat on. He'd got brown eyes, and although he was young he looked important. Respectable, that's the word I've been looking for. Respectable. I know I was surprised to see him run. It was like seeing him turn into an ordinary man."

"Not a usual Crumb Street type, perhaps?" murmured Mr. Campion.

"You've got it." She shot him a surprised smile. "He wasn't. I mean, there he was in a good dark overcoat, black hat, and white collar. He wasn't this district at all."

"Formal clothes." Luke scribbled on the blotter. "Why couldn't you say so before?"

"Because I didn't think of them before." Her voice was soothing and patient. "When this gentleman here mentioned Crumb Street I remembered why I thought he'd come off a train. He had a navy tie with two little stripes on it, very wide apart. Silver-grey and sort of puce and a little sort of flower with a bird's head coming out of it, very small, between."

"Had he though?" Campion sighed. "I wondered about that." He leant over Luke's shoulder and wrote on the blotter, *Phoenix rugger club tie. Geoffrey Levett?*

Luke stared at the scribbled words for a moment before he straightened his back and stared at his friend.

"Get a-way!" he said softly. "You thought you saw him outside here this afternoon, remember?"

Mr. Campion looked very unhappy. "It hardly proves——" he began.

"Lord no. It doesn't prove it wasn't King Farouk, but there's a healthy supposition there. Hallo, Andy, what's that?" The final remark was directed to the clerk, who was hovering at his elbow, his round face shining with excitement.

"Going through the deceased's effects as directed, sir, this was in the wallet. Note the postmark, sir."

Luke took the used envelope from him and turned it over. It was addressed to G. Levett, Esquire, at the Parthenon Club, but on the back an office address with a telephone number had been added in pencil. The postmark was unusually clear and the date was the current one. The letter had gone through the mail that morning.

Luke pointed to the pencil. "Is that his handwriting?"

"I'm afraid it is. That's his own office address, of course."

They stood looking at one another and Luke put the thought into words.

"Why did he give him his address, and then run after him

and——? That won't wash, will it? I could do with a chat with that young man."

"Well, have I helped?" It was Mrs. Gollie, glowing with excitement. "I mean, I——"

Luke turned to her and stiffened. The door behind her was opening and a tall sad figure came quietly into the room.

Assistant Commissioner Stanislaus Oates, chief of Scotland Yard, wore his honours as he wore everything else, gloomily. He had not changed since Campion had first met him over twenty years before. He was still the shabby dyspeptic figure, thickening unexpectedly in the middle, who peered out at a wicked world from under a drooping hatbrim, but he brightened a little at the sight of his old friend and, after nodding to Luke, who was standing like a ramrod, came forward with outstretched hand.

"Hullo, Campion. I thought I might find you here. Just the weather for trouble, isn't it?"

A great reputation has many magical qualities; for instance, Detective Slaney got Mrs. Gollie out into the C.I.D. room without her uttering a single word, Galloway faded into the recess which contained his desk, and the three in charge of the case were to all intents and purposes alone in a matter of seconds.

Oates took off his ancient raincoat and folded it carefully over the back of a chair.

"Superintendent Yeo is tied to his telephone, all his telephones," he said, his cold eyes resting on Luke for a moment, "so I thought I'd slip down and see you myself, Charles." He had a sad voice. The words came slowly, like an old schoolmaster's. "You may have a little more on your plate than you realise. How far have you got?"

Luke told him, reeling out the essential details with a minimum of gesture and the precision his training had taught him. The Assistant Commissioner listened, nodding gently from time to time as if he were hearing a well-learned lesson. When it was done he picked up the envelope and turned it over.

"Humph," he said.

"He must have been waiting for Duds outside here. Probably kept an eye on the doors from the foyer of the hotel opposite." Mr. Campion spoke thoughtfully. "When we let Duds go he must have followed him, taken him into the first pub, tried to get the tale out of him, failed, given him his office address, and then—what?"

"Duds was windy because he wasn't on his own—wasn't working on his own, that is," Luke supplemented, "so as soon as he got a chance he hooked it. Levett went after him, pausing to pay his score, which argues he wasn't fighting mad, and missed him because Duds doubled back up Pump Path. We know where Duds finished, but what happened to Levett? Where is he now?"

"Your Superintendent would like to know that, because that apparently is what three quarters of the people who are still influential in this bedevilled old town keep telephoning and asking him." Oates made the announcement with a sour little smile. "Mr. Levett seems to have planned quite an old-style evening: telephone calls half over the world, an after-dinner speech at a banquet, and a business interview with a gentleman from the French government in his flat after that. None of his friends can find him and they want to know why we can't." He glanced at the clock over the desk. "He's staying out late, isn't he, for such a busy chap?"

Mr. Campion slid off the table where he had been sitting, his hands in his pockets, his foot swinging.

"Medical opinion, for what it's worth, is that Duds was kicked," he said. "I don't see Levett doing that, you know, I really don't."

Old Oates looked up. "Do you see him killing at all, Mr. Campion?"

"Frankly, no."

"But on the other hand, do you see him cutting all his appointments like this? They're important appointments, every one of them."

"It's odd." Campion was frowning. "Geoffrey is a punctilious, solid sort of chap, I should have said. On the sober, stolid side. Unadventurous, even."

"That's what most people think." Oates' grey face was puckered into the faint smile which showed he was enjoying himself. "But he's not, you know. I've been hearing about him. He's Levett's Ball Bearings and one or two other very sound old-fashioned little companies, and he's a very rich man. But we don't like riches in this country these days, and what we don't like we get rid of. I've been making some enquiries tonight and I hear that when Levett came back from the war he found that after he had provided for all the people whom he felt had a genuine claim on his family and estate—his pensioners and so on—he found he had thirty-seven pounds, five shillings, and threepence per annum to live on himself after taxation had been paid. There were two courses open to him. He could spiv around with an army of accountants, looking for loopholes in the law, or he could gamble on the Exchange. For two years and six months he was one of the biggest gamblers on this side of the Atlantic. He quadrupled his fortune. Then he stopped."

Mr. Campion's pale face showed no astonishment. "I'd heard that, but I'd also heard that his name was excellent."

"It is." Oates was vehement. "I'm saying nothing against him. He's done nothing illegal and nothing reprehensible. Gambling is the only thing they don't call you to account for these days. It's not like working; you can be penalised for that. Gambling is respectable. I have two bob on the pools myself every week, I've got to think of my old age. My pension won't keep me. I only say that boy Levett is not unadventurous. He's not a man who doesn't take risks. For over two years he took risks all the time, and once you're used to taking risks, you're used to 'em. The drawbridge is down. You're not impregnable any more."

Charlie Luke had begun to fidget. The muscles of his back showed through his jacket as he strode restlessly down the little room.

"Duds wasn't alone," he said. "He was terrified in the station and he was terrified in here. And he wasn't frightened of me and he wasn't frightened of Levett. He couldn't have been working for Levett, as I had thought at one time, because in that case he wouldn't have had to have the office address written down for him. Levett must have given him that in the pub. The envelope was new. It only went through the post last night."

"That is why I slipped along." Oates felt in his pocket. "Seen any Express Messages tonight, Charles?"

Luke pulled up sharply, his forehead wrinkling. "No, sir, can't say I have. I've been on this business since I came back tonight."

Oates waved his hand. "Don't excite yourself, my boy. Quite probably it hasn't come in yet. Very occasionally they tell me an item first. By some oversight, of course." He was dourly amused. "We're wonderfully highly mechanised at Central Office these days, Campion. Teleprinters, radar, coloured lights everywhere. It's only when we get a power cut that the whole blessed police system is liable to go out of action. Well, I put on my hat and came down here myself because a convict called Havoc had made a getaway from the Scrubs."

Luke drew a deep sigh and his smile became contented.

"Havoc. That was the man who was cased with Duds. They did the holdup together. So that's it. I wondered when we were going to see a little daylight."

Oates did not respond. He had taken two blue slips of paper from his pocket and was busy comparing them. He looked indescribably mournful, his spectacles crooked on his sharp nose.

"It's very unsatisfactory," he said at last. "Your people picked up Duds Morrison's body at six forty-two, I see, but at six forty-five Jack Havoc was only just making his break half across London. He was killing another friend of his, as a matter of fact—at least I assume he's dead. The report which I saw just before I came out said 'sinking.' "

Charlie Luke became uncharacteristically annoyed. He stood jingling the coins in his pockets, his dark face lowering.

"These perishing crooks, who do they think they are all of a sudden?"

"Gods," said Oates calmly. "Splendid and superior beings, with winged heels and thunderbolts in each hand. Yet you'd think that any old bit of looking glass, let alone a long period of prison food, would cure any man of a delusion of that sort. But it never does. You know that as well as I do, Charles. But what you don't know is why I've come traipsing down here, splashing the beautiful motorcar with which a thoughtful Police Council provides me, so that the shabbiness of my clothes doesn't undermine my authority."

He paused, and Campion, who had been watching his old friend curiously, became aware that the new thing about him was that he was embarrassed. This was so very unlike him that the younger man was astounded. Clearly the old man had something on his mind of which he was more than half ashamed.

Meanwhile Oates leant back in his hard chair, his legs stretching out across the room.

"I received the two reports side by side, and then I had a word with Yeo and he told me what had come through from here on your interview with Duds this afternoon. I thought it over and presently I thought I'd come down myself. Havoc, I remember Havoc. Everyone is looking for him, and the chances are that he'll be pulled in in two or three hours, but if he's not, then I think you'll be finding traces of him here in your manor, and I thought I'd like to talk to you about him. Both you and Campion were overseas when we jailed him last and so you missed him. You missed quite a phenomenon." He repeated the words softly: "Quite a phenomenon."

Mr. Campion found himself fascinated. Oates was stepping right out of character. No one in the world had spoken with more force or at greater length on the stupidity of creating a legend round any wrongdoer. It was a creed with the old man and he preached it freely. His theory was that every crook was necessarily a half-wit, and therefore any policeman who showed more than a kindly contempt for any one of them was *ipso, facto*, very little better. This was a new departure with a vengeance.

Oates caught his expression and met it steadily, if not with ease.

"Havoc is a truly wicked man," he said at last. "In all my experience I've only met three. There was Harris, the poisoner, a fellow called Timms whom I don't suppose you've ever heard of, and this fellow Havoc. I thought at one time that Haigh was going to qualify, but when I met him and talked with him I decided he didn't, quite. He was mentally deformed. There was a sense missing there. The thing I'm talking about is rather different. I can't describe it, but you'll recognise it when you see it, if you have time. It's like seeing

Death for the first time. Even if it's quite new to you, you know at once what it is."

He laughed to and also at himself. "I know what I'm talking about," he added, and Campion, who had never known a time when he did not, was prepared to believe him.

Charlie Luke had not known his chief so long. He was far too intelligent to appear sceptical, but he hastened to bring the conversation on to a more specific basis.

"Are you saying he's a born killer, sir?"

"Oh yes." The heavy lids flickered up and the old policeman's chilly glance rested on his subordinate for a moment. "He kills if he wants to. But he's not casual about it like your gangsters. He knows exactly what he's doing. For a crook he's unusually clear-sighted. Take this latest performance of his. If Sir Conrad Belfry is dead——"

Campion sat up. "C. H. I. Belfry?"

"That's the man. Distinguished doctor. About half-past six tonight Havoc throttled him and slid off down the fire escape without the warder, who was sitting outside the door of the consulting room—strictly against regulations, by the way—hearing a sound."

"Good lord! Where was this, sir? Not *at* the Scrubs, surely?" Luke was describing the narrow proportions of a cell window in the air.

"No. In a second-floor consulting room in Wimpole Street. After badgering the authorities for months, Belfry had got Havoc out for an experiment." Oates leant forward as he spoke. "This will give you some idea of Havoc. It's taken that man three years of careful self-discipline to get his nose outside prison walls, and I'll lay a fiver he's done it just exactly as he intended to do it from the moment the idea entered his head. Sir Conrad's murder was planned before Havoc even knew the man existed. When Havoc was sentenced he was sent first to Chelmsford, where his conduct was bad, and he got moved to Parkhurst. No one but a mug tries to break from there because of the water, and for a time he seems to have attempted to work his ticket to one of these new-style open prisons. But his record didn't fit that bill."

"So he went sick and got pushed up to the Scrubs hospital,

I suppose, sir?" Luke could not help making a leap in the story, but his eyes were bright with interest.

Oates remained unruffled. He was studying his own notes on the back of the police slips.

"You're underestimating him, Charles, my boy," he said. "I thought you might. He went sick, but in a most ingenious way. Three years ago he developed a—where is it? Oh, I see, a compulsive neurosis concerning the number thirteen." He lifted his eyes, caught sight of Luke's expression, and laughed outright. "I know. It was so hopeless, so damned silly and forlorn as a lead-swing that in the end he got clean away with it. His performance appears to have been amazing. Apart from his 'little trouble' he became a model prisoner, and for the first year—*year*, mind you—it got him exactly nowhere. He did the thing not only thoroughly but progressively. He went sick on the thirteenth of every month, and later on the twenty-seventh. Thirteen letters in twenty-seventh. When he found his cell number added up to thirteen he starved himself until they moved him. He was always polite and apologetic, and also, as far as anyone could see, puzzled. He explained he knew he was being silly, but said he couldn't help it. Of course the idea spread—you know how it does in a prison— and there were signs of mass hysteria developing. Then the M.O.'s got interested. It's a well-known buzz bug, I understand." He looked at Campion enquiringly.

"I have heard of it."

Luke's mobile lips moved soundlessly. He would appear to have remarked, "Cawdblimeah!"

Meanwhile Oates went on placidly. "It took him another eighteen months to get himself moved up to the Scrubs, where they've got a psychiatry unit. There he came up against the experts, but by that time, of course, the thing was pretty well genuine. Anyhow, they kept him, and he was so docile and intelligent that they seem to have made a sort of pet of him. Sir Conrad was nothing to do with the unit, of course, but he'd got a favourite pupil who was the Consultant attached to it, and one day last month he went down there to see him and was taken round the exhibits. Havoc took his fancy and nothing would satisfy him until he'd got the man up to Wimpole Street to try out a new American machine

he'd got over, a thing called an 'Association Motor Appara-
tus.' "

Luke's glance turned to the man in the horn-rimmed spectacles and his brows rose enquiringly. Mr. Campion, embarrassed to find himself considered an expert on a subject so
highly suspect among his friends, nodded once more.

"I see the Chief Inspector thinks that either we're barmy
or he is," Oates observed without malice. "I'm just giving you
the facts. Sir Conrad got his own way in the end—they have
a lot of pull, these fellows. Havoc was sent up to him in a
cab just after six this afternoon. Two warders went with him,
as decreed in the regulations, but one stayed in the hall downstairs and Havoc was not handcuffed to the other. For a time
the second warder stayed in the consulting room, but Havoc
appeared so eager to help and yet so oppressed by his presence that old Belfry at last persuaded the chap to sit outside
the door. The rest of the story is just what you'd think. The
doors in those houses are mahogany and very nearly sound-
proof. By the time the wretched warder got nervous and
made up his mind to take a look, it was all over. Belfry was
lying on the floor, the window was open, Havoc had vanished."

Campion frowned. "Are you absolutely serious when you
suggested that the thing had been planned so long?"

"I take my oath on it," said Oates, "and it wouldn't surprise
me if he had timed the attempt for November just on the off
chance of a fog like this."

Charlie Luke threw away his incredulity with a generous
gesture; indeed he appeared to wash his hands of it literally.

"I suppose he has a sort of a way with him, sir?" he suggested at last, favouring the two of them with the most win-
ning of smiles. Unconsciously he had arched his lean stomach
and might have been about to burst into musical-comedy
song. He had donned frank, open-hearted charm like a garment.

Oates regarded him with gloomy interest. "No," he said,
"nothing like that."

Luke gave it up. "I'd like to see him."

Oates hesitated. He looked a kindly man of vast experience.

"I should like to see him dead," he said at last, and in his mouth the words were simple and convincing.

Mr. Campion was aware of a faint uneasiness between his shoulder blades, and Luke, his sophistication pierced, was briefly blank-eyed and uncomfortable.

In the pause, an apologetic sergeant came in quietly to whisper an enquiry. Luke glanced past him through the open doorway of the C.I.D. room, where a grim-faced young man, dressed with all the careful casualness of the modern clerk, stood clutching his raincoat and folded evening paper. He was waiting before a desk, looking over his shoulder at the sergeant's back, and his savage resentment, together with the dull courage with which he was controlling it, was as vivid as if he had displayed them on a banner.

"Who?" When lowered, Luke's voice was inclined to set the walls vibrating. "Duds Morrison's brother-in-law? No. No need for me to see him. What? Oh, the newspaper? Well, we'll do anything we can. Publicity can't be helped. One of those things." He waved his subordinate away and the door closed, but Duds Morrison and the problems he had left behind him had returned to them.

"Respectable relatives?" said old Oates with interest. "Funny how many of 'em have 'em. His sister's going to have a baby, I suppose? They always are." He felt for his pipe. "Well, Luke, I think we've got on a bit, you know. Havoc is somewhere in this puzzle of yours, I think you can be sure of that. Havoc was the man Duds feared, but I don't see how he killed him. In fact, he couldn't have done in the time, even if he'd known where to find him, which is unlikely."

Luke said nothing and Campion, who was beginning to know him, recognised the shoot of his underlip. Despite his veneration for Oates, at that moment Charlie Luke did not altogether believe in Jack Havoc.

The immediate development, therefore, gained considerably in drama. Police stations are as human as any other places of business, and when it came the wave of outrage spread through the new Crumb Street building in the same electric way in which it was later to spread through every newspaper office in the country. It began with a flurry of words in the outer hall, where the heavy sergeant who read the society journals in his spare time listened to a hatless, collarless elderly gentleman who had come bursting in on him, half inarticulate with shock and horror. From there it spread over the house phones and down the concrete corridors, gathering in speed and intensity until it culminated in Luke's little office a few seconds after Oates had finished speaking. The actual message arrived over the telephone on the clerk's desk in the corner, but afterwards not one of those three men, who knew more about giving evidence than anyone in London, could have sworn on oath that it had not been shouted in their ears.

"A nasty job just down the street at Holloway and Butler's, sir, 37 Grove Road. Someone broke in the front and rifled the office on the ground floor. Old Creasey, the caretaker, who was in the basement at the back talking to one of our own men, young Coleman, must have heard something, so they went up, leaving the bedridden old woman behind. They're all dead, sir, the woman as well. Knifed. Blood everywhere, the witness says. He's Mr. Hammond, an elderly employee of the firm's who lives alone in the attics. He took his time getting downstairs, which was wise of him. Whoever did it got clean away through the little bit of a garden at the back which leads to Pump Path."

In the split second before the Chief Inspector went smoothly into action, ordering calls to the fingerprint department, the divisional surgeon, the photographers, the forensic laboratory, and all the other units which make up the machinery of detection, Campion caught a picture of him which he never forgot. Detective Coleman had been one of Luke's white hopes. He had liked the boy for his eagerness and had taken a great deal of trouble with him. The present assignment had been in the nature of a personal pat on the head from him.

He did not speak as he heard of his death, but a grunt escaped him, a sound of rage, and he stood momentarily arrested, one long hand outstretched, warding off realisation. No great actor ever expressed the instant of tragedy more vividly or with greater economy. To see him was like glimpsing a flame, an epitome of grief's impact. Yet he was sublimely unaware of any self-betrayal and as he snapped out the orders his voice was clear and impersonal.

Meanwhile, Mr. Campion's own response to the news was of interest. "Holloway and Butler were Elginbrodde's solicitors," he said. "Meg mentioned it the other day. In fact, I went down there for her and had a word with the senior partner, a Mr. Frederick Smith. We were trying to get a better photograph of Martin, but they couldn't help." His eyes met Luke's own. "Elginbrodde's jacket, Elginbrodde's solicitor——?"

"And Elginbrodde's successor, by God!" said Luke, startled into impiety. "There's still no sign of Levett."

Oates had moved out into the C.I.D. room, where the first reports from the detectives who had raced to the scene of the new crime were just coming in. Now he stepped back for a moment. There was colour in his sallow cheeks and his eyes were bleak.

"All three victims have clean, expert wounds," he said briefly. "Over the collarbone, into the jugular. Schooled professional stuff. Victim taken utterly by surprise in each case. Notify the Flying Squad for me, Luke. Tell Bob Wallis he's wasting his time hunting for contacts. This is where Havoc has been."

FIVE
BROTHER DOLL

Meanwhile, earlier that afternoon, by the time Geoffrey Levett had accosted Duds Morrison some thirty yards up the dark street from the police station and had persuaded him into the Feathers by the simple process of gripping his elbow and thrusting him through the door, one great anxiety was safely off his mind. This man, whoever he was, had never been married to Meg.

From Geoffrey's point of view the whole afternoon had been a nightmare and the last two hours of it very nearly unbearable. He was not an experienced shadower and was by nature rather a participator in than an observer of events. Nor had he realised before that he was capable of such jealousy. This discovery embarrassed him, putting a foreign restriction on his actions and introducing him to the misery of indecision. Acting on impulse, he had paid off the cab and had followed Meg at a distance because he wanted to see for himself the man who was threatening his happiness, but for a reason which he refused to pursue, he would rather have died than let her know it.

The result was that he found himself hanging about outside the dreary Crumb Street police station, like a boy outside a rival's window, terrified of being seen. He had no idea what was happening inside and was tortured not only by curiosity but by anxiety lest the business was not being handled intelligently. But above all he wanted to make sure for himself that Elginbrodde had not returned from the dead.

Therefore, by the time Duds stepped swiftly out of the police station and set off up the pavement, Geoffrey was in the mood for reckless action.

He hurried after the man, hampered by passers-by, slipping upon the greasy stones, and caught up with him at last just as Duds himself was cornered by a woman with a load of parcels and driven up against the windows of a shop. Geoffrey took him by the elbow.

"Listen——"

The man made a futile effort to escape, found it hopeless, and began to whine.

"You can't do this, you can't do this to me. I've been on the carpet all the afternoon and they've let me go. The rozzers have let me go."

The sound of the voice, the slang, the whole attitude of the man, poured soothingly over his captor. Relief produced its own reaction and his grip tightened.

"Splendid. Now perhaps I can help you. I want to talk to you, anyway. Come on."

The bray of a street band starting up not far behind them seemed to devitalise Duds. He shuddered, struggled half-heartedly, and gave in.

Geoffrey pushed him on down the street and into the doorway of the first hostelry they reached. The little bar parlour was deserted and dim with fog, and the noise in it was considerable. A radio was relaying a noisy adventure play on the other side of the glass screen which divided the room from the saloon next door, the woman behind the bar was talking relentlessly to someone who was presumably listening to her, and from the street the cacophony of the band came ever nearer.

Geoffrey fixed the stranger's dull black eyes with his own.

"Listen to me," he said distinctly. "Get it well into your head from the outset. This may be worth your while."

It was an approach which he had used with varying degrees of subtlety to a great many people in his time, and had seldom known it to fail. He noted the flicker of interest, faint but unmistakable, with rising satisfaction. The tenseness in the arm he held slackened and the stranger stood more firmly on his heels.

As the talking woman moved along the bar towards them Geoffrey gave her an order hurriedly. She served them without wavering for a moment in her harangue to the unseen radio listener. Levett drew out his wallet and pencil, still keeping an eye on his captive, who watched him with the apprehension of the cornered. He was licking his lower lip, however, and had come a step nearer.

By now the street band was immediately outside the door and the noise was so great they could not hear themselves speak. Levett scribbled on the back of an envelope and handed it to Duds, who took it dubiously and read it. When he raised his eyes, Levett had taken a treasury note from his case and appeared to be studying it. After a while he looked up.

Duds remained interested and after a further pause Geoffrey handed him the money. The band passed by.

"The rest when you come to see me."

Duds regarded him sulkily. "What do you want?"

"Only the story."

"Newspaper?" All his terror returned and he made a movement towards the door, but there something seemed to check him, although there was nothing to see. He glanced back uncertainly. Geoffrey was shaking his head violently. The abominable band had returned and until it repassed the door he was forced to be silent.

"No," he said when speech was at last possible. "Nothing like that. It's purely for my own personal information. Surely you can understand that?"

To his astonishment, it was clear that Duds could not. There was greed in the pale face fighting a losing battle with fear, but no comprehension whatever.

Geoffrey was bewildered. As far as he could see, his name, which he had written clearly on the envelope, had not registered on the stranger at all. The explanation occurred to him, bringing with it a return of all his former alarm. He took hold of the coat sleeve once more.

"Who employs you?" His anxiety made him overeager and he saw the white face grow wooden.

"No one. I'm unemployed. I told the rozzers so. I'm an actor. I'm not working."

"I don't mean that. I only want to know one thing, and make no mistake. I'll pay for it. Who instructed you to get your photograph taken in the street?"

The man's leap for freedom took him by surprise. Duds jerked his sleeve out of his grip and flung himself at the frosted glass panel of the swing-door as if he were pitching himself into water. A draught of freezing air broke over the parlour like a shower of spray. Geoffrey slammed down a ten-shilling note and shot after him, leaving the woman behind the bar gaping, too astonished, for once, to speak.

He was on Duds' heels, but the street had darkened considerably since the shops had put up their shutters, and for a second he thought he had lost him in the fog. But almost at once he reappeared, running back, this time almost into his arms. Geoffrey stepped forward, but Duds saw him in time and swerved, darting into an unsuspected opening between the houses.

It did not dawn upon Geoffrey that some other enemy must have turned his quarry. He merely saw his man and went blindly after him into the alley, led by the sound of his flying footsteps, hollow and panic-stricken in the narrow way.

The noise behind him did not register on his mind for several seconds. He was closing on Duds, who had slowed as the path turned, and his hands were within inches of his coat before he became aware that they were both being overtaken. A rush of lightly shod feet, accompanied by the heavy chink of something which sounded like harness, bore down upon them both, and an instant later a violent blow on his shoulder sent him reeling past Duds and against the wall.

Then a tide of men swept over the two of them, pinning them close in the dark. At first there were no voices, no words, only heavy breathing, the slither of soft feet on the stones, and once more the chink of metal.

Very close to his shoulder Duds whimpered. It was a shred of a sound, high with fear.

"Where's the Gaffer, Duds?"

The faces were so close that the question came warm out of the icy mist. It seemed to Geoffrey, spread-eagled against the wall, that the enquiry came from many lips. Urgency was there, and menace, but they were muted, controlled, kept just under the surface. "Where's the Gaffer? Where's the Gaffer?"

"Inside." The word arrived explosively. "Parkhurst. Been there years."

"Liar. You always was a liar, Duds." The blow which followed the statement passed so close to Geoffrey's own face that he felt its wind, and the sound it made as it touched flesh made his own wince.

He felt Duds sliding down slowly at his side. He struggled to get an arm up to shield his head, but at that moment the crowd yielded to pressure from behind as Army boots thudded down the passage. Geoffrey was carried forward some yards away from the figure on the ground. Panic swept over him and he struck out, swearing savagely and loudly in the darkness. Instantly he was seized and lifted bodily off his feet. A hand found his mouth, almost dragging his chin from his face, and something hard and round hit him above the ear so that blackness denser than the fog descended upon him and he fell.

His first conscious thought was that even for a nightmare it was extraordinarily cold and uncomfortable, and the noise was incredible. The sensation of being unable to speak was more familiar to him in dreams, and he moved his throbbing head restlessly, fighting, as he thought, with sleep. Soon he realised that he was awake, but in such an astonishing position that he doubted his sanity.

He was wedged tightly into a little wheeled chair, midway between an invalid carriage and a child's go-cart, his arms pinioned to his sides under an old khaki mackintosh fastened behind him, and his cramped legs drawn up and strapped to the undercarriage of the chair. His mouth was sealed with a strip of adhesive plaster, which irritated abominably and paralysed the lower part of his face. He was wearing a knitted Balaclava helmet which covered his entire head save his eyes, and he was being wheeled swiftly along a foggy gutter in the midst of a rabble of marching men who kept time to the thin music of a mouth organ.

At this point he remembered what had happened to him up to the instant at which he had been knocked out, and he had the presence of mind not to attempt any violent movement which would have betrayed his return to consciousness. Having made certain that he really was helpless, trussed neatly by experienced hands, just able to breathe but no more, he concentrated cautiously on his kidnappers.

There were ten or a dozen of them, drab, shadowy figures who kept very close to him, shielding him with their bodies from passers-by who could scarcely see their own hands in front of their faces in the brown mist.

From where Geoffrey sat, very close to the ground, they towered above him, and lighted buses crawling by looked big as showboats and as remote. His head was spinning and he was still fighting with incredulity, but by this time the shuffling ghosts nearest to him had resolved into men and he noticed with a shock that there was something odd about each one of them, although for people with such emphasised disabilities they seemed to move with surprising freedom and lightness. The only heavy feet were those which stamped immediately behind his chair. The rest padded softly round him in the lamplit gloom, their clothes whispering and rustling in his ear.

The man directly in front of him was leading the way. He was tall and made monstrously so by the fact that on his shoulders he carried a dwarf, a small man whose normal conveyance was no doubt the wheeled chair now occupied by the prisoner. It was the dwarf who played the mouth organ. Geoffrey could see his small elbows moving in an ecstasy of excitement and pleasure. Geoffrey's own dark hat, punched up into a billycock, sat on the back of the little man's bulbous head, and from time to time he paused in his playing to jam it more securely in position.

It was the tune which gave Geoffrey Levett the essential clue. He remembered it as a sentimental dirge of the second World War called "Waiting." He had been hearing it at intervals all the afternoon, played by an "Ex-Servicemen's" band up and down Crumb Street. This was the same band.

He made the discovery with a certain amount of relief, since it took him at least out of the region of pure fantasy and into the merely thoroughly outrageous, with which as a modern he was by now more or less familiar. The group had haunted him all through his nervous vigil outside the police station, pestering him with offhand importunities. But he saw now that it must have been his own quarry, the man in the sports jacket, for whom they had been waiting. They had certainly found him, but what they had done with him he had no idea. He did not appear to be with them.

He decided that the business was doubtless some kind of minor gang warfare, and his own part in it must be entirely accidental. By some mistake he had been knocked down and collected instead of the man they had called "Duds." Doubtless they were taking him somewhere now with the idea of questioning him.

The Gaffer. The words returned to him suddenly. That was it, of course. He was on the track of Duds' employer at last. In spite of his discomfort he felt a deep satisfaction. He had made up his mind to solve the mystery which had been up-setting his life, and he seemed well on the way at last. The method was bizarre enough, goodness knew, but at least he appeared to have landed in the heart of the matter. The thought that he might be in actual danger did not occur to him. London is still a comparatively law-respecting, if no longer conspicuously law-abiding, city, and in his time he had escaped from an Italian prison camp into a desert very much more alarming than this familiar bricky wilderness. He had every confidence that he should be able to deal with the situation, unless of course Elginbrodde proved to be alive.

He flexed his muscles against his bonds and settled down stolidly, as he had settled down in that crowded Italian lorry long ago. Meg was necessary to him. He loved her very much. He was going to have her.

Once he had felt the same way about liberty. In the end he had achieved liberty.

In the meantime he had other worries. He remembered the call he had laid on to Paris with irritation. He hoped Miss Noble would use her head and not call out the fire brigade. His absence from the Pioneer Club dinner would take a little explaining, unless he could still make it. He had no idea of the time, nor even where he was, for that matter. They had left the traffic and were swinging along a dark street which was almost deserted. He was aware of high buildings, but there was no way of telling if they were warehouses or offices closed and darkened for the night.

The little procession halted abruptly. It took him by surprise and jerked him forward in the chair. The mouth organ squealed and was silent, and he was aware of nervousness all round him. One man on his left giggled stupidly.

A silver-crested helmet loomed out of the fog and the voice of the law, casual and consciously superior, drawled down at them.

"Packing up for the night, Doll?"

"That's right, Orficer. It's a nasty night. Warmer at 'ome."

Geoffrey recognised the courage in the new voice, which came from behind him. It belonged to Heavy Boots, he decided, for he felt his carriage quiver as the hands on its rail trembled. Yet the tone was perfectly easy and ingratiating.

"You're right there." The law spoke with feeling. "What have you got there?"

Geoffrey achieved a snort through his muffler and at once an iron hand closed on his shoulder. He became aware of the stink of fear reeking all round him, but Heavy Boots seemed quite equal to the occasion.

"It's only poor Blinky, Orficer." And then with dreadful confiding, "Fits. 'E 'as 'em."

"I see. Very well." The law granted his permission to the ills of man with condescension, not to say haste. "Good night, all."

He moved on with steady dignity.

"Good night, Orficer." Heavy Boots showed no signs of relief, but his voice rose warningly to cover any signs of eagerness in the others. "Get along, Tom, can't you? Strike up ' 'Ercules.' Blinky ought to be in bed, Blinky did."

The procession was moving at speed, and the dwarf, after much prompting, achieved a few scattered notes on his mouth organ. Heavy Boots swore softly for a little while. He had an ugly vocabulary and a line in suppressed savagery which was startling. Geoffrey heard "the Flattie" consigned to several sorts of perdition, some of them new to him. As an introduction the incident was revealing. Geoffrey understood he had but one man to deal with.

With the danger past, the temper of the band rose noticeably, and the man on the left who giggled showed signs of hysteria until he was silenced by a kick in the shins from Heavy Boots, who scarcely paused in his stride to administer it. The dwarf was playing merrily again by the time they turned out of the dark street into a lane, which despite the fog was ablaze from end to end with light and bustle.

It was a market, Geoffrey saw, one of those small Alsatias which are still dotted about the poorer parts of the city, protected by ancient custom and the independence of their patrons. Ramshackle stalls roofed with flapping tarpaulin and lit with naked bulbs jostled each other down each side of the littered road; their merchandise, which ranged from whelks to underwear, was open to the sooty air, while behind them tottering shops, open-fronted and ill-lit, cowered odorously.

The band kept to the middle of the road and closed very tightly round the chair. For the first time Geoffrey was aware of their faces and he recognised some of them from seeing them in Crumb Street that afternoon. The giggling man turned out to be a hunchback, taller than most of his kind but typical, with a jaw like a trowel and lank black hair which flapped as he moved. A one-armed man, his sleeve swinging mightily, strode close beside him, while a flying figure, festooned with picturesque rags and moving with amazing speed and dexterity, swung himself between a pair of crutches just in front. No one spoke to them. There were no greetings from the traders, no pleasantries. They passed by without a head being turned.

The end of the journey came suddenly. At a gap between two stalls the group swung sharply and they plunged into darkness again. This time it was through a doorway beside a greengrocer's shop, partly shuttered now but still sprouting wilted leaves and damp straw all over the pavement.

The hallway was narrow and chill and it smelt of dirt and damp and that particular stink of city poverty which is uncompromisingly cat. It was also pitch-dark. But there was no delay. The procession dived like rats into a hole and Geoffrey and his little chair were swept on and down until an inner door swung suddenly open and he found himself at the head of a dimly lit flight of cellar stairs. There he was stopped, held precariously on the top step while the rest swept past him, bobbing and weaving down the dangerous way with the ease of long practice.

He found he was looking into a vast shadowy cavern, warm and smelling unexpectedly wholesome and countrified, like a toolshed or a barn. He was struck first by its neatness. There was order, even homeliness, in its arrangement. Its size was enormous. It took up the whole cellar of the building, which was very high, and although black and cobwebby as to rafters, the walls were clean and whitewashed up to a height of ten feet also. A mighty iron stove, gleaming with lead and very nearly red-hot, stood out in the room, and round it was a circle of seats, junk-shop chairs and settees covered with festoons of clean sacks. Three plank tables placed end-to-end, covered with clean newspaper and flanked by packing-case benches, stood waiting behind them, and far away against the further wall a row of couches stacked with army blankets presented neat ends to the view.

Geoffrey recognised it at once. He had seen places like it before when a company on active service under a good sergeant had dug itself in in some long-held position. Everywhere there were signs of discipline and a particular kind of personality. No rubbish or odds and ends were in sight, but all round the walls little packages of possessions, tied up in sacking, were hung neatly on nails, very much as one finds them in old-fashioned cottages or blacksmiths' shops. It was a definite variety of bachelor establishment, in fact; primitive and wholly masculine, yet not without a trace of civilisation.

His scrutiny was cut short in a most terrifying manner. The men below him scattered. There was a shrill scream, wild and ecstatic, from the dwarf, and at the same instant the hands holding his chair were suddenly withdrawn, so that the little carriage began a dreadful descent down the steep stairs, while he was powerless to leave or guide it.

The utter brutality of the gesture, its careless savagery and recklessness, terrified him much more than the physical danger. There was nothing he could do to save himself. His weight speeded the little wheels and he hurled himself backward, his spine arched, in an attempt to prevent himself from pitching headfirst on to the brick floor. By something which he dimly realised was not quite a miracle, but some peculiar adroitness in the method of launching, the chair did not over-balance, but it rocked wildly as it touched ground and sped through the whooping crowd to crash into a pile of paper-filled sacks stacked against the wall. Their position was far too lucky to be accidental. Without them, the chair itself, not to mention half the bones in his body, must have been broken, and he realised even before the dwarf had ceased his delighted yelping that this must be a cruelty which had been practised on the little man himself many times, perhaps every day.

He felt deathly sick. The adhesive plaster was suffocating him, and in the warm air the knitted helmet irritated unbearably. Once, to his horror, he thought he was going to faint, but the heavy feet were clattering across the bricks towards him and he made a great effort at control. The newcomer approached and bent down.

Geoffrey looked up and for the first time set eyes on his persecutor. He saw a big shambling figure, stooped and loose-jointed, middle-aged but still very powerful. The startling thing about him was his colour. He was so white that he was shocking, his close-cropped hair so much the colour of his skin that the line of demarcation was scarcely visible. Black glasses which hid his eyes explained him. He was an albino, one of those unlucky few in whom the natural pigmentation of the body is entirely absent. He was seeing his prisoner for the first time. The dim light suited his weak eyes and he swung the chair round slowly to get a better view.

SIX
THE SECRET

The albino pulled the woollen helmet from the prisoner's head and the others came closer. They were a strange company of whom perhaps six at most could possibly ever have seen service with the armed forces. Geoffrey particularly noticed the tall man who had carried the dwarf home. He was a thick-featured, mild-looking youngster with a strangely dazed expression. The older, shorter man who was clearly his brother, since the resemblance was remarkable, and the ragged acrobat who had now laid aside his crutches and was moving with perfect ease without them, these could well be ex-Service. The rest were oddities, collected no doubt for their freak value. They clustered round the prisoner, inquisitive but unnervingly silent. Heavy Boots was the declared leader and main personality. There was no doubt of that. He conducted the proceedings with complete assurance and the same tidy methodicalness which was so evident in his surroundings.

Geoffrey was liberated from all his bonds save the cord which bound his hands behind him and the plaster over his mouth. It was a long and deliberate proceeding. The albino rolled each strap and folded the helmet and mackintosh as he removed them, handing each item to the dwarf, who scampered off with it to some safe place before returning for the next.

Geoffrey made an attempt to rise as his feet were freed, but he was too numbed and cramped to move, and was forced to sit where he was while the blood crept back again into his legs.

As his good dark overcoat, his haircut and formal linen

came into view, Heavy Boots hesitated, and for the first time
the solid smirk of satisfaction which had been his only expression gave place to a certain thoughtfulness. He turned to
the smaller of the brothers.

"Now, Roly, who's that? Who is it?"

The man stepped forward and looked earnestly at the
square pugnacious face of the captive.

"I ain't never seen 'im before."

"Ain't that he? Ain't that the Gaffer?"

"No-no." The pronouncement, packed with contempt,
came from the tall brother and caused something of a sensation. Geoffrey understood that it was unusual for him to
speak at all.

Heavy Boots frowned. "Bill, come you here, boy." His accent had broadened. Both he and the brothers were not
speaking cockney but a softer, more natural tongue from
higher up the coast. "Now, look steady, who is it?"

The ragged man, whose weak face was actually painted with
shadows, Geoffrey saw, and who had a strange febrile gaiety of
his own, minced forward, peered down, and laughed.

"Search me. No one I know. Friend of Duds, I suppose.
The Gaffer isn't that type. If that was the Gaffer I shouldn't
be here, I can tell you. You wouldn't see me for dust."

Geoffrey made another effort and this time succeeded in
rising to his feet. Heavy Boots thrust him back with a hand
which had the strength of a horse behind it.

"Set still, won't ye?" he commanded. "I reckon we'll have
to see who you be."

He ripped open the seated man's overcoat and thrust his
hand into the breast pocket. The hunchback brought an upturned tea chest over and, using it as a table, the albino set out
the contents of the pocket neatly and expertly. Geoffrey was far
too wise to attempt resistance. He sat quiet, waiting stolidly.
He was not a man who carried a great deal about with him, and
the search yielded little remarkable. He had a few pounds in
his wallet, a chequebook, his driving licence, and a small engagement book. There was also a handkerchief marked with
his name, a pencil, a cigarette case, a lighter, and the letter he
had taken out of the envelope which he had given to Duds.

The only unusual item was a set of miniature medals. He had

been due to wear them to the banquet and had remembered to collect them from the jeweller's that morning. Heavy Boots studied these with great interest. It was clear that he understood the history they told and he touched the purple and white ribbon of the M.C. with respect as his frown grew deeper.

He laid them aside with regret, and when the dwarf put out a hand for them he cuffed the small man's large head with a force which made him yelp.

Roly fingered his own collection, which were full-sized and included one for a campaign fought well before he was born, but he said nothing, and the rest, although they gathered round, kept well away from the box top.

There was no talking whatever. The albino continued his unhurried examination with the dignity which springs from complete authority. The chequebook and driving licence interested him, but the trophy which turned the day was an unexpected one. The letter which had arrived in the envelope which Geoffrey had given to Duds happened to be a circular begging letter from the Royal Institute for the Relief of the Orphans of East Anglia. It was a dignified appeal, drawn on fine paper beneath a heading which incorporated a list of patrons, led by royalty. "My dear Mr. Levett" was neatly matched in at the beginning, and the facsimile signature of Lord Beckenham, the President, who had described himself as both grateful and sincere, was printed in convincing blue ink at the foot. While not actually designed to deceive anybody, the document yet managed to present an impressive front to the uninitiated. The effect which it produced upon Heavy Boots was startling. He removed his dark glasses and held the sheet very close to his red eyes. His lips moved soundlessly as he read the words over and his pallid hand shook a little.

" 'Ere," he burst out suddenly, swinging round on the company, " 'ere, what ruddy fool's made this mistake, eh?"

His alarm brought out the full force of the bully in him, and he made a considerable figure, heavier and more vital than the rest, who displayed a wispish, raggedy weakness when considered in the mass.

His eyes, terrible without their glasses, were narrowed with fear and anger.

"I've kept you all out of trouble, haven't I, up till now? I've

wet nursed you, by God I 'ave. Who's got us into it proper
this time?"

He was too startled to swear with any conviction and his
alarm was infectious. The company swayed away from him.
Only Roly showed any truculence.

"You can talk," he began, "you can talk, Tiddy Doll, you
always could. Proper Tiddington man you are. What's the
matter, eh? Who is he? A busy?"

"Busy! P'lice!" Tiddy Doll spat. "He's only my dear Mr.
Levett, friend of Gawd knows 'oo. That's what this 'ere paper
shows. This 'ere is from Lord Beckenham. I seed the old
gentleman once down at our camp, near Ipswich. This is what
some ruddy fool's done while I was blinded by me poor eyes.
Come on, step on it. Get the cords orf, can't yer? 'Oo was so
silly as to make the mistake, that's what I want to know?"

"But he was *with* Duds, Tiddy. We all seed him. They both
ran when they saw us, first into the boozer and then down
the alley."

"Shut up, big-mouth. I'll see you get your time to talk."
Doll was having trouble with the rope on Geoffrey's wrist.
His breath, warm and odorous, flowed over him as he embarked on a sort of mendicant singsong of apology. It was
urgent and powerful and quite horrible. " 'Alf a moment, sir,
I shan't be long. There's been a mistake in the fog. One of
my lot 'ere—you can see they're most of them wanting, pore
chaps (the war come very 'ard on some of us, sir)—one of
'em, I don't know who but I will, one of 'em 'as took you for
a friend of ours."

He got the knot loose and ripped off the cord with searing
speed.

"I couldn't see meself. My eyes are very bad, 'ave been
from child'ood. They ain't quite like other people's eyes. You
can see that if you look."

He gave Geoffrey an opportunity.

"I wasn't allowed to do all I wanted to in the dear old Army,"
he said. "I 'ad to stay in camp doing woman's work when I
might have been much more useful if only they'd given me the
chance. But I saw service. I saw service same as you, sir. So
you'll have to excuse of me being half blinded and led astray."

The time had come for the sticking plaster to be removed.

The prisoner was putting up a numbed hand towards it, and for the life of him, despite all his anxiety and precarious position, Tiddy Doll could not resist the opportunity to hurt. He tore it off so suddenly that the excruciating agony took Geoffrey by surprise and brought a sound from him as tears of pain rushed into his eyes.

"That's better, ain't it?" Doll smiled. He could not control it. The little grimace tugged at his narrow lips even while his alarm froze them. "We was only 'aving a game on a friend, sir," he went on hurriedly. "I don't rightly know as how I can ask you to believe that, but as God's my judge, sir, I never had such a shock in all me life as when I see you down here in the light. I knoo at once you wasn't no friend of ours, sir. I can tell. I'm not an ignorant person like some 'ere."

"That will do." The words came softly from Geoffrey's dry mouth. He began to cough, retching and gasping.

"Give 'im a drink, can't yer? Lord alive, you're all carney, the whole lot of you." Doll was dancing in his excitement. "Poor gentleman, 'e's been treated very rough owing to some loony's stoopidity."

Geoffrey waved away the enamel cup which the hunchback brought him, and struggled painfully to his feet. He had himself very well in hand.

"Where's the other man?" he demanded. "Where's the man I was with?"

"There you are, Tiddy." The elder of the two brothers was eager to justify himself. "That's what I said. They was together. Him and Duds was together. Now he's admitted it. They was friends."

"I met him for the first time this afternoon." Geoffrey turned a chilly eye on the speaker and enunciated with the careful clarity he had learned in his adjutant days. "I wanted some information from him and I took him into a public house to get it. Your abominable noise seemed to frighten him and he ran off. Because I still wanted to talk to him I went after him. You mobbed us, and one of you had the infernal impudence to knock me out."

It was stilted talk, but as he guessed it was the language of authority which they all understood perfectly.

A man he had not noticed before, a wall-eyed, thin-necked figure who still clutched a pair of cymbals, responded at once.

"It was Tiddy's cosh wot hit you. He don't carry no moosical instrument, Tiddy doesn't."

"There's gratitude!" A stream of invective drove the point home. "There's gratitude! I got this chap out of the blessed gutter, sir, starvin', he was. A lay-about, nothing but a lay-about. Now he's got a bellyful, that's how he repays me."

Geoffrey ignored the outburst. He was feeling much better.

"Where is the man I was with?" he repeated. "You knew him. You called him by name." He took a chance and picked on the elder brother, whose voice he fancied he recognised. "You there, what's your name? Roly? You called him a liar."

"No, that wasn't me, sir. That was my brother Tom. Young Tom's funny, sir. He got blowed up and 'as never been the same since. That's why we're both on this lark with Tiddy. We come from the same part of the country, sir. We're all Suffolkers, me and Tom and Tiddy. Tom knew Duds. Duds was the corporal, see?"

Geoffrey thought he did. He had a moment of inspiration.

"And the man you call the Gaffer was the sergeant, I suppose?"

"That's right, sir." Doll, the Tiddington man, could not bear to be left out of the centre of the stage for long.

"Were you under him?"

"No, sir." Roly intervened again eagerly. He had the awful innocence of the true countryman. "No, Tiddy wasn't with us. Tiddy never saw the Gaffer. There was only me and Tom and Bill who really, as you might say, see the Gaffer in the flesh. We are the only three left who was with him at the time. Tiddy is helping of us, see?"

"I'm a-leading of you to get your rights, that's what," said the albino. "I'm holding of you up. I'm keeping your minds clear, that's what I'm doing heart and soul, and I hope no man here has been stoopid enough to muck it all."

Geoffrey ignored him and spoke to Roly.

"Well, where is this sergeant?"

"That's what we want to know, sir." Roly was delighted to get the ball again. "We've been looking for him for close on three years now. It's Tiddy's idea. Tiddy says everyone comes to London who's got the money to enjoy theirselves. Stay in the streets of London long enough, he says, and you'll see everyone you know. Besides, it's a living for us, isn't it? Tom gets his share, and he wouldn't in no other work."

"I was right," cut in Tiddy Doll. "I was proved right. We seed Duds, didn't we?"

"That's right," said Roly. "We see Duds all dressed up in Oxford Street and we lorst 'im. That was three weeks ago. Then today we see 'im again and we followed 'im. I called to 'im, but 'e did a bunk and ran down to the railway. Then 'e came out with the busies and went to the police station with them. We knew 'e couldn't say nothing about us, though, if only we kept on movin'. That's the law, that is. They slung 'im out after a bit, as we knew they would. Then you came up to 'im and we followed you both and waited outside the pub. When 'e come out 'e ran right into us and Tom, 'oo 'asn't noticed nothing for years, caught sight of 'im and started after 'im as if 'e'd come to 'imself all of a sudden. When they both went down the path we started after 'im, naturally. We 'ardly noticed you, sir, to tell you the truth."

"Of course we noticed the gentleman," protested Tiddy with exasperation. "We see 'im and we thought that 'e was the Gaffer, that's the long and short of it."

"What happened to the corporal?"

"Tom 'it 'im by mistake." Roly looked at his brother. The tall youngster was standing at the back of the group and his heavy eyes had no light in them. He seemed both morose and vacant and there was no way of telling if he followed the proceedings. "Tom 'it 'im," Roly repeated, "by mistake. Tom's very strong still, but 'e don't never use it now. Then Tiddy come up and we set on you, sir, and then Tiddy went back to Duds."

There was a moment's silence, owing mainly to puzzlement at their own foolishness at concentrating on the wrong man.

"You come back laughing, Tiddy, saying you give 'im something to go with," put in the man with the cymbals unexpectedly. "That's what you said, Tiddy. That was when you got the idea of putting this bloke in the chair."

Tiddy Doll resumed his glasses. Their black patches gave him a secret look. Much of his impressiveness lay in that concealing half-mask.

"He was setting snivelling with 'is nose bleeding," he said in disgust. "I only give 'im a little one to 'elp 'im on 'is way, and then I come back to get on with the job. I thought we'd got the Gaffer."

"You didn't, Tiddy, you didn't, because I told you 'e weren't the Gaffer." Roly was speaking with passion, his mouth ugly.

"Tiddy thought we'd got the orficer." It was the high flat voice of the hunchback and he giggled.

The remark was so obviously true that it took the whole company by surprise. For a fleeting second Geoffrey saw them in a sombre static group, like faces caught in paint. It was Tom, the young brother who had never been the same, who spoke first. He lifted his head and looked steadily at the stranger with eyes which betrayed a fleeting reawakening.

"Major Elginbrodde," he said in the slow Suffolk speech, "that who you are."

" 'E ain't!" Roly was startled and protesting. "Why, Tom, you're all at sea, boy. Major Elginbrodde were a little dark fellow. Besides, 'e's gone, poor chap. No one knows that better than you."

The young man shook his head. " 'E don't look like 'im and 'e don't speak like 'im, but I reckon 'e's the same."

" 'Ere, Tom, you set down." Roly led his brother to a snap-box. " 'E's strange. 'E's wonderfully strange at times," he explained over his shoulder. "Major Elginbrodde and Tom was together when they trod on the mine. That was on the beach in Normandy, four months after our own little job. We'd had our leave since then and the Gaffer and Duds were A.W.O.L., so they weren't with us that time. The Major were wiped right out, but Tom wasn't touched, or so we thought until we found out he'd gone strange. Never told anybody anything, Tom didn't, except me, and that was one night two years after we were back in civvy street."

Geoffrey brushed through the group. His chin stuck out. He had forgotten the present and was back in a world of sweat, petroleum, and khaki.

"Tom," he said, his voice sharp with authority, "pull yourself together, man. Is Major Elginbrodde dead?"

The boy lumbered to his feet. It was as though a chunk of Suffolk soil, long-suffering and eternal, had stirred itself.

"I thought so, sir." The gentle singsong of the coast rolled out the terrible pronouncement like pebbles under a wave. "I see 'im go. I see 'is 'and and 'alf is 'ead come by me. But now I'm a-listenin' to you I'm a-wonderin' if 'e ain't got 'imself some new body, like. Ain't you he?"

"No. My name is Levett. I'm another major."

"So you say, sir." He sounded humble but unconvinced and presently sat down again. His brother was embarrassed and inclined to be angry.

"Don't take no notice of 'im," he begged. "He's a proper fool, Tom is, now. He weren't at one time. When 'e were a young'un he was proper smart, Tom was. We 'ad our own boat in my Dad's time. That's why we was chosen, you see, sir. That's why the Gaffer picked us. The Gaffer found the men for the raid."

"Nark it, chum, nark it!" Tiddy Doll's warning was frantic. "The gentleman doesn't want to hear your life's history nor your brother's. Your big mouth always was your trouble, Roly. The gentleman's got 'is own position to think of."

The threat was an open one and Geoffrey wheeled to stare coldly at the dark glasses.

"You've considered your own, I suppose, Doll?"

The albino regarded him steadily. They had the enormous advantage of understanding each other perfectly. The position was relatively simple. In a city like London, on an island like Britain, which for all its vagaries still possesses a police force superior to most, the prisoner has the upper hand so long as he is aware of it. Geoffrey knew that unless they actually murdered him, and disposed of his body successfully, never a simple business, they must at some point permit him to go free. Since he was not a man whom a good beating would intimidate, but appeared to be a person of backing, the position must eventually resolve into a question of whether or not he lodged a complaint. Once he did complain, the future of the band was not even problematic.

However, Tiddington men are notoriously not without cunning.

"There are some gentlemen 'oo wouldn't like it to be known they was mistook for friends of persons they wasn't friendly with, and so got theirselves into muddles," Doll essayed none too hopefully.

"There are also gentlemen who could not care less," said Geoffrey, "but," he added carefully, "they are usually reasonable people who do not want to do others any harm if they are sensibly treated and their questions answered."

Doll smiled. He was delighted by the oblique form of the intimation. He could not resist sending a glance of triumph towards the others, who remained worried and a little foxed.

Geoffrey turned back to Roly. "Which raid are you talking about?"

"It didn't have no name, sir. It was secret."

"Four months before D-Day?"

"Yes, sir."

"To the Normandy coast?"

"I don't rightly know, sir. We were took over by submarine and put off in a little boat. Me and Tom managed the boat. It was wonderfully rocky. We didn't go up to the house, even Bill didn't go up to the house. Bill sat on the beach with the torch to give the signal should we need it. We was all starkers and painted black, and Bill 'ere was covered with weeds."

Geoffrey glanced at the ragged man who had used crutches in the street and needed none indoors, and was startled to see that he was smiling and that there was a glint in his dirt-ringed eyes. He made no attempt to join in the story but was remembering it with pure pleasure. It had been an hour of utter and appalling danger which he had enjoyed to the point of ecstasy. It went through Geoffrey's mind that the Gaffer, whoever he was, had chosen his men intelligently if not orthodoxly.

"Who were the others?"

"There was only Duds and the Gaffer and the Major. Duds didn't go into the house. He stayed below. They knew the fellow we were after would drive himself, so there wasn't likely to be no chauffeur. The only chap who might come, they thought, would be on a motor bike carrying messages. None of us carried a gun. Guns wasn't allowed because of the noise."

"Who were you after?"

Roly shook his head. "We never heard. Duds said it was a general, but the Gaffer told me and Tom it was a spy."

"I see. And he was expected to go to the house alone?"

"Well, they reckoned there was a woman there. It were only a little house, all by itself. Sea and rocks on one side, private road on the other. They reckoned he'd put her there."

Geoffrey nodded. The picture was extraordinarily clear. He believed the story. Some very strange things had been done along the French coast in those months of waiting before the great invasion. Five men and one officer: at such a time a small force was well worth risking on good information to remove a single dangerous man.

He came to himself abruptly. Roly's voice, which had grown softer and broader as the story continued, was still droning on.

"The Gaffer done the job all right, both of 'em we reckoned, though 'e never said nothing about the woman. He liked the knife, Jack did. I doubt not he liked the knife."

It was his first sign of relish. It flared up jarringly in the country tongue.

Geoffrey looked up sharply. It occurred to him that his first guess had been the right one: it had been Roly and not his brother who had hit out at Duds in the fog. The next moment the man confirmed it.

"Duds told me the Gaffer was in stir—that's prison to you, sir—but he was lying, same as he always did. Jack was too smart for that. Even if they catched 'im they'd never hold 'im. We know better than that. Jack has collected the treasure and he's a-living on it in glory, in glory while 'is mates are tramping the gutter. That's why we're a-looking for 'im."

Tiddy Doll, who had been making signs for some minutes, gave up in despair.

"Now you've said it," he burst out, adding a stream of bad language from which an expert could have deduced his entire history, civil and military. "Now you've opened your mouth so wide you've swallowed yourself. Now you've given everything away."

Geoffrey ignored him. The story was taking shape. Elginbrodde, who he was now nearer liking than at any time in his life, certainly appeared to be out of it, poor chap, but in that case Duds' impersonation of him became even more inexplicable. He tackled Roly again.

"Major Elginbrodde went to the house on the coast, I suppose?"

"Of course 'e did. The Gaffer 'ad to 'ave the Major with 'im to get about so silent. It was the Major's house."

"Do you mean his home?"

"Why, yes, sir. He'd lived there as a kid. It was an old place, a kind of little stone castle. They would never have got up the rocks so quiet in the dark save that he knew the way. That's why 'e was chosen. That's how we come to go at all."

"What happened to the Major's family?"

The ex-fisherman looked blank. "I don't think there was but one old woman, 'is Grannie. She went away and the Jerry left the place as it was. Then the spy we was after put 'is lady there, but they never found the treasure. That was still there when we went, because the Major went to look."

The inflection upon the operative word was not lost upon Geoffrey, but he had had some experience of the fighting man and his notions on "treasure-trove, its probable value." As he glanced round the ill-assorted group in the cellar he thought he saw the whole story. Each face was solemn, engrossed, and avid. Treasure. The ancient word had worked its spell once again. It was holding them together as nothing else could ever have done, and was supporting them even while it sucked them dry.

Of them all, Doll was the most completely enthralled. His narrow lips were working. The fact that yet another pair of ears should have heard the tremendous news was agonising to him. He was the basic material of which great fools are made; a country dolt tormented because of his deficiency, he had dreamed wildly of becoming a tyrant in a city paved with gold. He had achieved the tyranny and had certainly found the pavements. Nothing would convince him that the gold was not there also, if only he could get his hands on it. He saw plain evidence of it wherever he looked; in the great shops, on the painted women, in the hissing automobiles. Golden Treasure, Treasure meaning "after one has dreamed one's fill, yet *more*."

Geoffrey caught a glimpse of this, yet he had no idea of the depth of the illusion.

"The sergeant described it all to you, I suppose?" he enquired good-humouredly.

His amusement was recognised and resented immediately. Nothing he could have said would have inflamed them more. The Treasure was sacred. It was the one thing they believed in in all the world. A murmur, ugly and irritable, escaped the whole group. It rumbled from these rags of humanity like a growl.

"The Gaffer didn't say too much. He was far too fly." Roly spoke bitterly. "But he knew all about it. He knew it was there, and you can bet he went back for it as soon as he knew the Major had got his packet. That's the one certain thing."

"And 'e's a-living on it now, with wine and motorcars and pickles," burst out Tiddy Doll, unaware of any incongruity. "You can tell that from the way is friend Duds was dressed up. That was proof, that was."

"I thought you couldn't see 'im, Tiddy."

"Well, of course I see 'im. I see 'im when we was following 'im." The albino covered the slip and changed the subject adroitly. "There's the Souvenirs. Don't forget the Souvenirs. We know there was treasure there once. You all 'ad a taster, didn't you?"

There was a moment of hesitation and then Roly went over to his brother and, after a muttered conversation, came back with a package wrapped in a rag.

"Major Elginbrodde give us each a Souvenir," he explained to Geoffrey. "He brought them out with 'im in 'is pockets. The rest of us 'ave 'ad to part with ours at different times, but Tom's kep' 'is. 'E 'ad to. It was too valuable to sell. No one wouldn't touch it."

In complete silence he unfolded the parcel. He might have been about to display a holy relic. Under the rag there was a piece of coloured handkerchief, and beneath that a much creased square of oiled silk. The final covering was a piece of lead paper off a tobacco package. Roly pressed it back, smoothing it with hands as black as his clothes. He held out the contents for Geoffrey to see.

It was an early miniature, beautifully painted on wood, a man's head surrounded by a full wig of chestnut curls. Geoffrey was no expert, but he could see that it was fine work and obviously genuine. The treatment it was receiving was doing it very little good. The plaque was cracking and the paint flaking.

"It used to have a frame. Solid gold, that was, set with little bits of coloured glass. A fellow in the Walworth Road gave Tom seven pounds ten for it."

"That was before I found yer," put in Doll furiously. "You was chiselled over that. Even a sovereign's worth thirty-five bob today."

"Bill got twelve quid for his music box." Roly added the information hastily. "A little gold bird in a cage. Wind it up and it sung."

"You only got a fiver for your box," cut in Doll accusingly. "You told me so yourself scores of times. But that was painted, wasn't it, just like this?"

This pathetic history was cut short by a curious interruption. At the far end of the room a folded newspaper suddenly appeared through the ceiling and floated down the wall. The cellar was built out some few feet under the roadway and there was a grating there let into the pavement which was used as a letter box by some obliging news vendor.

"Late Night Final," exclaimed the man with the cymbals cheerfully as he hurried off across the bricks to retrieve it.

"Dog racing," said Tiddy with contempt. "A tanner each way on the dogs, that's 'is idea of romance, that is. Waste o' money. Well, sir, I don't know how you're feeling about this 'ere little mistake of ours?"

Geoffrey looked away from the miniature and Roly wrapped it up again very carefully, rubbing the fine work with his dirty but reverent hands.

"What did you say the sergeant's name was?" Geoffrey had ignored Tiddy Doll's question, but he was gathering up his possessions from the box top.

"Jack Hackett," said Roly. "At least that was 'is Army name. I don't know what 'e was borned with. 'E was a man with many names, I reckon."

"You can lay he won't be Hackett now," put in Doll contemptuously. " 'E's a lord by this time. Perhaps you know 'im, sir? Perhaps you know 'im well and don't know 'is history. You'll hear it all right when we come up with him. What was you a-thinking of doing, sir?"

"Doing?"

"About our little mistake."

"I shall forget it." The educated authoritative voice carried conviction. Doll accepted the statement as he would have accepted no signature, however illustrious. But the performance was not complete. Geoffrey realised they expected a warning from him and he prepared to give them one.

"But if I hear of any similar incident, if you make a silly mistake again, Doll, then of course I shall consider myself free to speak. Do you understand?"

"Yes, sir." It was a smart military answer and the man drew his heels together.

The absurdity of the situation was not really clear to either of them. No one was watching the man with the cymbals. He was sitting on a box, the late edition held close to his eyes, spelling out the Stop Press stencilled in the blank column on the back page. His startled burst of profanity shook everybody.

"Bloke found murdered in Pump Path, W.2. That's Duds. 'E's a deader."

"That's a lie." Tiddy Doll swung across the floor to him to peer at the crooked line of print at the foot of the column.

"You done it, Tiddy." Roly's face had become green and he and the others huddled together, shrinking from Doll. "You done it when you went back. You said you give 'im something to go on with."

The albino crushed the paper in his great hands. His brain worked much more quickly than theirs and he had courage.

"Hold your mouths!" he shouted. "If one of us done it we all done it, that's the law." He turned savagely and pointed at Geoffrey. *" 'Im as well."*

Geoffrey was just too late. There were eight men between him and the stairs.

"Don't be idiots!" he cried out to them. "Don't be fools. Pull yourselves together. If this is true you've only got one hope. A statement to the police now, at once, it's your only chance."

"That be damned!" Tiddy's roar filled the building and he bent his head for the charge.

SEVEN
THE USURER

Across the city in St. Petersgate Square it had been one of
the most alarming interrogations of Sergeant Picot's experience, but by eleven o'clock that evening he was prepared to
admit that the Chief had known what he was doing when he
let "the old parson" have his head. He sat silent in the leather
chair in the corner of the study in the rectory, his notebook
decorously hidden in the folds of his raincoat, and reflected
that if only the police were permitted the licence calmly assumed by the public life would be infinitely more simple.

Canon Avril had either never heard of the Judges' Rules,
or considered that in his own family they did not count. Im-
practical he might be, but as an extractor of the truth he was,
as Picot was forced to admit, remarkably efficient.

They were getting on like a house on fire. He had begun
with his nearest and dearest, and Meg Elginbrodde had been
subjected to a catechism which had not only satisfied but
scandalised the sergeant. Sam Drummock and his dear worried wife had received the same treatment. Miss Warburton,
fetched in from her cottage next door, had been shaken up,
shocked, and subjected. And now, after William Talisman, the
verger, had exhibited a somewhat spineless innocence, his
wife Mary stood before the Canon's desk and at last they were
getting somewhere.

Uncle Hubert had cleared the desk by sweeping its entire
contents into a large dog basket which he kept beneath it,
doubtless for just such an emergency. The sports coat in

which Duds had died, folded lightly to hide the worst of the bloodstains, lay upon its shabby leather top. The Canon's spectacles were pushed up high on his broad forehead, and his eyes, naked and inexorable, looked out sternly from his kindly face.

"This is what your husband has already told me," he was explaining, most improperly if the laws of evidence had carried any weight. "Will says that he's fairly sure that he saw you wrapping up this jacket in a piece of brown paper on the kitchen table about a month ago. Don't cry. How can I hear what you're saying? And don't lie any more. Lying wastes more time than anything else in the modern world. Think what bores the Nazis were."

Mrs. Talisman was plump, carefully girt and coiffured, and she possessed a little foolish pride which showed in her face. Her life was spent in waiting on the Canon, her husband, and her granddaughter, and because she had that privilege she thought herself a little better than other people. She had nursed the old man before her like a sick baby a score of times, and an ill-ironed wrinkle in his shirt stung her like the evidence of personal sin. A dirty back step or a wilting curtain in the basement window could worry her for a week, and she had once boxed the ears of a van man from the Stores who had observed in all innocence that times were changing and the clergy becoming of less and less account.

"Oh, I did!" she exclaimed at last, giving up in a flood of wretchedness. "I did. I took the old coat and I gave it away."

"Well, then." He sighed with exasperation. "Why couldn't you say so before, you silly girl, instead of insisting you knew nothing about it? Did you ask me or Meg before you gave it away? I don't remember being asked."

It was perfectly clear to Sergeant Picot that no one would dream of asking the Canon before giving away any garment in the house. He felt quite sympathetic towards the respectable old girl. She made no answer save to gulp, and Avril continued.

"It's so silly to give away something that is not your own," he said. "There seems to be a mania for it nowadays. But I should have thought it was obvious that the good you do on the one hand must be offset by the irritation you cause on the other. It's woolly-minded, Mary, woolly-minded and shortsighted, and gets none of us anywhere. Work for it first. Then give it away. To whom did you give it? Some poor fellow at the door?"

She hesitated and a flicker of temptation appeared in her red eyes. The Canon was on to it like a flash. Picot had to hand it to him, the old fellow seemed to spot deceit as if it reeked like a goat.

"Ah, I see. It was someone you knew. Now who was that?"

Mrs. Talisman made a helpless gesture with the palms of her hands.

"I gave it to Mrs. Cash."

"Mrs. *Cash?*" The listening Picot understood that this was a revelation. Avril was leaning back in his chair, his lips parted, his eyes comprehending, and also, unless the sergeant was very much mistaken, dismayed.

Presently the old man rose and put his head out of the door.

"Dot!" he shouted.

"Yes, Canon." Miss Warburton's high cheerful voice floated down the stairs from Meg's room. "Coming."

Picot awaited her arrival with embarrassment. They had already had one session with her and she was not his kind of woman. It appeared that the Canon did not need her either, however, for he continued to shout instructions.

"Please fetch Mrs. Cash."

"She'll be in bed, Hubert."

A fresh outburst of weeping from poor Mrs. Talisman distracted Uncle Hubert's attention and he waved at her to be silent.

"What was that, Dot?"

"She'll be in bed, dear." She was coming nearer and they could hear her shoes on the stairs.

"Then fetch her out of it." He seemed astonished that she should not have thought of that way out herself. "Tell her to wrap up and not to stop to do her hair. She can put a cap on. Thank you very much, Dot."

Having settled the matter with kindness and politeness, he shut the door firmly just as the lady reached the hall.

"Now, Mary," he said as he reseated himself, "think this

out very carefully and don't upset yourself more than necessary. Do be quiet, my poor girl. Moderation. Moderation in all things. Did you offer this coat to Mrs. Cash or did she ask for it?"

"I—oh, I don't know, sir."

To the sergeant's astonishment, the old man seemed prepared to accept this statement literally.

"Ah," he said, "yes, I see that. Did she say why she wanted it? No. No, she wouldn't. Forget that. That was foolish of me. But listen, did Mrs. Elginbrodde show you any of the photographs which she had been getting through the post?"

"Of the Major? Yes, she did, sir. I told her I didn't see how anybody could be quite sure."

"Didn't you recognise this sports coat on the man in the photograph?"

"I never thought. Oh, is that how it was done? Oh dear, it never came into my mind."

"Why didn't it, Mary? It didn't come into mine."

"I don't know, unless it was the colour not being there, sir. It's the colour that makes this jacket outstanding, and of course it wasn't in the photo."

"I see. Now you go and make yourself a cup of tea and sit in the kitchen and drink it, and don't move until I call you. Understand?"

"Yes, sir. Yes, I do. But oh, Canon Avril, if Mrs. Cash——"

"Be off," commanded Uncle Hubert sternly, and he took a piece of sermon paper from the dog basket and began to write upon it in his fine neat hand.

Clearly this was the one signal of dismissal from which there was no appeal. Mrs. Talisman made a gesture of resignation and, taking out her handkerchief once more, wept herself out of the room.

"I don't suppose you'd ever get another housekeeper like that these days, sir." The remark was wrung out of Picot. This selfless omnipotence was getting on his nerves. He felt someone ought to tell the old boy. It wasn't fair, somehow. It wasn't fair on the police.

"Of course I shouldn't. I've often thought that. How odd that it should strike you, my dear fellow. I should die in six months without that woman. She saves my life every January when I have bronchitis." Uncle Hubert was frank and even cheerful about it. "The girl is a snob," he went on, "quite a dreadful snob. What an astonishing number of pitfalls there are, aren't there? Have you noticed? We seem to be like those contortionists at fairs—boneless wonders, they call them— able to fall down in absolutely every way conceivable. It's very wonderful."

Picot did not reply. His fresh-complexioned face was perfectly blank. He could not believe the old man was genuine, because people, especially of "that class," never were. Every copper on the beat knew that. All the same, the old boy was unusual. Psychological, perhaps. A kink somewhere, that was about it. This Mrs. Cash, now, he hadn't wanted to discuss her with his housekeeper, and he had been taken aback when her name was mentioned. He wondered what there was between the two. He'd like to see the lady.

The desire was granted almost immediately. The front door opened with a squeak and a burst of Miss Warburton's cheerful noise.

"*Come* along, Mrs. Cash, *come* along. In you go. There's a nice fat policeman in there—oh dear, I hope he can't hear me—so the Canon can't eat you. How lucky you were up. I should have had to have fetched you, you know, whatever you were wearing, or weren't. *Come* along."

The study door shattered open and she came in. Miss Warburton was a middle-aged English gentlewoman who had had the misfortune to mould her social personality at a period when gay and feckless madcaps of the Paddy-the-next-best-thing variety were much in vogue. Her moulding had been slapdash and her basic type pronounced, so that the effect thirty years later was mildly embarrassing, as if a maiden aunt from the Edwardian stage had elected for a day to be untidy, offhand, and bright. However, the woman herself remained what she was bred to be, very feminine, very honest, very obstinate, innocent to the point of being uninstructable, and nearly always right.

"Here she is, Canon," she said, "dr-r-ragged from her couch. Beauty sleep ruined. Do you want me to stay?"

Her nice eyes in her plain face were merry, and her form,

on which every garment always looked as if it were still on its hanger, was arch.

The other woman was still invisible behind her.

"No, Dot, no." Avril nodded and smiled at her. "That was very kind of you. Thank you very much. Now go back upstairs."

"I shall expect to hear all about it, I warn you." She was actually swinging on the door handle, Picot noticed with disgust. Fifty if she was a day, and how the old fellow ever brought himself to call her by such an unlikely diminutive he could not imagine.

The explanation might have puzzled him even more. Canon Avril had bestowed the name on her not because her name was Dorothy. It was not. He called her Dot because he pretended she was a mathematician, and as he said, he could hardly call her Decimal Point. Avril saw her for what she was, a gift of God in his life, and if he often found her trying he was far too humble, and indeed too experienced, to expect that the Almighty's more quixotic benefits should ever prove to be unadulterated jam.

"I daresay you will, Dot," he said mildly on this occasion. "I daresay you will. Come in, Mrs. Cash."

Miss Warburton gave way with the carefree crow of her chosen role and withdrew, dropping a hairpin and a handkerchief behind her.

Mrs. Cash came in. At the first sight of her every experience-sharpened wit which Picot possessed came smartly into play, yet at first sight there was nothing outstandingly peculiar about her. She was a sturdy little person, nearer sixty than fifty, very solid on her feet, very tidy. Her very good black coat was buttoned up to her throat and finished with a tippet of very good brown fur. Her massive face and the thick coils of wonderfully arranged iron-grey hair, together with the sleek flat hat which sat upon it, seemed so much all of one piece that the notion of them ever coming apart was slightly shocking. She carried a large black bag, holding it squarely on her stomach with both neatly gloved hands, and her eyes were round and bright and knowing.

She studied Picot, made a note of him as openly and casually as if he were a door marked "Exit," and walked steadily over to Avril.

"Good evening, Canon. You wanted to see me about the jacket?" Her voice was like the rest of her, bright and bold and not very nice. It contained a jar in it, as if a comb and paper somewhere entered into its production, and her teeth, which looked as if they were made of china, shone in false bonhomie. "I'll sit down here, shall I?"

She moved the small armchair before the desk so that it was directly in Picot's light, and sank into it. Her feet only just touched the ground, but she kept her shoulder straight and the sergeant could see her hat, steady as a rock above the low back.

The Canon was on his feet, looking at her gravely across the desk.

"Yes," he said. He made no apology for summoning her so late and the watching Picot realised with a shock that these were not so much old friends as old enemies. There was the familiarity there which belongs only to the years and is almost a cosiness, but they were not on the same side.

"Mary tells me she gave it to you some weeks ago. Is that true?"

"Well, no, Canon. I don't want to get anybody into trouble, as you know, but Mary's not telling the truth. I bought it. Three pound ten of good money. You can see I didn't make much on it, although it was for charity." She was brisk, straightforward, apparently as open as the day and neither man believed a word she said.

"So you bought it from Mary."

"That's what I've told you. I've told you straight, haven't I? Of course, I felt sure she'd had it given to her. You know me well enough for that after six and twenty years. I've been in the second glebe cottage twenty-six years last month."

The old man did not move. Picot could see his fine face, grave and regretful and also withdrawn, as if in some strange manner he were keeping right away from her. He did not query her statement at all but pressed on with the main enquiry.

"And when you had bought it from Mary, what did you do with it?"

"That's my business, Canon." She was reproving but still affable. Picot guessed that her round eyes were laughing.

"Of course it is," Avril agreed. "Your business entirely. You will recognise it, though, and that will be a great help. Won't you come over here and look at it?"

Picot was surprised. He had not expected the parson to get so tough. He moved so that he could see her face when she first caught sight of the terrible stains. She was unprepared, he noticed, for she bent forward casually and drew the bundle towards her. As she shook it open the appalling lapels curled stickily before her and her busy hands in their tight gloves hesitated, but so momentarily that the check was scarcely perceptible. Her face did not change at all. It remained bland and bright and good-tempered, no way, in Picot's opinion, for any disinterested female face to remain when confronted by such a sight.

"I don't suppose that will clean," she remarked, and refolding the garment, put it back on the desk. Her cracked voice was perfectly easy. There was not even a tremor in it. "Yes, that's the jacket I bought from Mary. Well, it's no good me saying it isn't, is it? You can all recognise it for yourselves. It's been lying about the house for I don't know how long, hasn't it?" Her little laugh sounded practical and full of resignation.

"The police will want to know what you did with it," said Avril.

"Then I must tell them, mustn't I?" She seemed very sure of herself. "I must look it up in my little book. I think I noticed a bit of moth in it and put it in the lot I sent down to Mr. Rosenthal in Crumb Street." She swung round in her chair so that she came face to face with the hovering Picot. "I'm not a rich woman but I like to do my bit for the Church," she announced, smiling at him broadly with all her china teeth. "I sometimes have to take a little percentage for my trouble, that's only reasonable, because if I can't live I can't give, can I?"

"You deal in secondhand clothes, do you, Mrs. Cash?" The sergeant was not to be intimidated by this sort of thing. He thought he knew the sort of handling she needed.

Eyes quite as sophisticated as his own met him squarely.

"I do a bit of good wherever I can," she said, "and I can show you books to prove how much I've been able to donate to the Mission to the Underpriviledged, the Charles Wade Society, the Churchman's Aid, and I don't know how many more. It's all down, all kept properly. Anyone can see it any time they like. Can't they, Canon?"

In response to the direct appeal Avril bowed his head and looked very unhappy about it. The sergeant, on the other hand, felt more at ease than he had been at any time in the evening.

"That's not an answer to my question, is it?" he remarked reasonably.

Mrs. Cash smoothed the lap of her good black coat.

"Well, I'm not an old-clothes woman if that's what you mean, young man," she said complacently. "You've been in this district some time. I think I've seen you about the Barrow Road and Apron Street, haven't I? You knew the sort of district this is. A lot of very good houses going down, and a very good lot of people going down too. Old ladies needing money more than jewellery and not knowing how to go about selling it. Bits of nice lace and a piece of old furniture on their hands, perhaps. Well, I'm not proud. Living near the Canon all these years has taught me how to be humble, I hope, and, like him, I like to do a bit of good where I can. So I trot round helping. There's many an old woman under a good eiderdown at this moment much more comfortable than if she only had her mother's cameo in a chest of drawers instead. I go everywhere and I know everyone. Sometimes I buy and sometimes I sell. And sometimes I have things given me for charity, and I turn them into money and send the little cheque to one of the societies."

"And you put it all down in the book," said Picot. He was nodding, a wide smile on his face.

She echoed the smile exactly. "I put it all down in my book."

"It's the jacket I'm interested in at the moment."

"Yes, I can see you are. Someone's had a nasty accident in it, haven't they? Well, I must help you too if I can. I'll look in the book."

"I'll come with you."

"There's no reason why you shouldn't." She hoisted her big bag on to her knees. "I feel certain it went down to Mr. Rosenthal. His shop is quite near your new police station. He keeps it very nice and clean. He's a good businessman."

"Yes, I know Rosenthal." The sergeant's expression was rueful. "He keeps books too."

"Of course he does. You have to in business. Are you coming?"

"Wait." Old Avril, who had been listening to this exchange with growing depression, intervened at last. "Mrs. Cash, you know your way about this house. I wonder if you'd mind going down to the kitchen and asking Mary to come here. Stay there if you will for ten minutes, and then Sergeant Picot will come down to you. Will you do that?"

"Of course I will, Canon. Don't think I mind the kitchen, I've done enough work in it in your dear wife's time. Very well, young man. You come and fetch me and then we'll go to my little house together. Good night, Canon. I shall be sending something to the Church Restoration Fund in a week or so, just a little something. I've spoken to the churchwardens. They say you can't stop me if I want to do my little bit."

She rose very lightly for one of her build and trotted out, looking like a pottery figure designed to hold mustard. Picot could just see her with a spoon sticking out of her hat.

Avril bent over his scrap of sermon paper, and the sergeant, who was near enough to read the fine hand, saw him write the words: *"Wardens meeting, Mrs. Cash, subscription, No."*

"They say all money stinks, sir," he observed, grinning. "You think you can afford to draw the line somewhere, though, do you?"

Avril's reply punctured his tolerant sophistication.

"How obvious she is, poor woman," he said. "A green bay tree in St. Petersgate Square. Ah, Mary, there you are. Don't knock, come in."

Mrs. Talisman crept in looking deplorable. She was drowned in tears and had been in their salt water some time.

"Oh, sir!"

Avril pushed his hand through his wild hair and sat down. "Did the three pound ten cover it?" he demanded. "Come along, my girl, speak up. Was three pound ten all you owed her?"

"Oh, sir!"

"Was it? Was it all?"

"Yes, sir. On my soul, sir. It was only a pound at first, you see. They had some lovely white shirts at the Stores. Only thirty-five shillings, and Talisman is so particular and I do like him to be a credit to us. And they were so cheap. I'd got the fifteen shillings put by, but of course I knew they wouldn't stay in the shop at that price, and so when Mrs. Cash came in collecting I—well, I did. She offered it and I took it. It was only a pound."

"The rest was interest?"

"Yes, sir. Five shillings a week. It mounted up so fast. She didn't bother me, you see—in fact, I didn't set eyes on her until it was two-fifteen. But then she started coming round, and I know you don't like her in the kitchen. I offered her several things of my own. I didn't want to tell Talisman, sir, he'd never forgive me. I offered her the blanket off my bed that was a wedding present to Emily's mother, and all kinds of things. I did really. But she wouldn't take anything except men's clothes, she said, and not Talisman's black ones either. Then she asked me if Miss Meg hadn't given me any of Mr. Martin's things, and——Oh, sir!"

Avril sighed. "Run along, Mary. Don't do it again. I told you that last time. When was it?"

"Seven years ago, sir, nearly eight. Oh, sir . . . !"

"No," said Avril. "No, no, no, no more. Enough. Go away."

"Forgive me. Oh, please forgive me!"

The Canon glanced helplessly at Picot. "I warned you this would be embarrassing," he said. "I can't forgive you, Mary. I can't forgive sins, my dear girl. Whatever next? But if you want my professional opinion on it, I think you've had the hell you're due to get for this."

"Oh, thank you, sir."

"Good heavens, don't take it as a promise," said Avril, waving her out of the door. "If you want to make sure on that count, confess all to William and do penance by nagging cheerfully borne. But, Mary, don't do it again. Silly old women like you encourage wicked old women like Lucy Cash."

"Twenty-five per cent, per week," said Picot as the door closed. "That's coming it a bit, even in her business. It *is* her business, I suppose, sir?"

Avril did not reply immediately. His hands were folded behind his back and he raised his sensitive chin in the air. His eyes were half closed.

"For nearly thirty years I've seen Lucy Cash trotting about these streets," he began at last. "As the houses have grown shabbier she has grown sleeker. Yet she has always been the same, like a little jug. Didn't you think she was like a little jug? When you see her she is never loitering, never hurrying. She is always going somewhere purposefully, always smiling, always bright and level-eyed. That great bag of hers is like a badge of office. She holds it with both hands. As she passes down these great airy streets, where so many of the houses are let out now in single rooms, window curtains tremble, blinds creep down, keys turn softly in locks. She passes by like a shudder. The air is always a little cooler where she is. When you go to her house look round you. You'll find it full of knickknacks, every single one of which has been treasured by someone." He blinked and, lowering his head, looked at Picot with wide serious eyes. "Whenever I see them they look to me like petrified morsels hacked out of living pain," he said gravely.

Picot shrugged his shoulders uneasily. This was not his kind of talk. Besides, there were many women of a similar sort in the world he knew best. Mrs. Cash seemed a pretty fair specimen, however, and he was looking forward to a private word or two with the old haybag.

"I suppose she does make these donations to charities from time to time, sir?"

"I'm sure she does." Avril conveyed that he feared it. "Sometimes people give her things to sell for good causes. I believe that some of them afterwards like to see her books. She never makes any trouble about showing them."

"What a wonderful 'blind' for her," said Picot earnestly. "She could run anything with a cover like that. We shan't get much out of her or out of Rosenthal either. Of course, it could have happened like that. A coat picked up, secondhand. It's not likely—in fact, it's not credible—but I can see it's going to be very hard to prove anything different. All the same, if you've finished, sir, I'll collect the old dear and see what I can get."

He broke off and looked round. The door had opened and Miss Warburton, tiptoeing exaggeratedly, came creeping in.

"A most extraordinary thing, Hubert," she said, dropping her affectation as she closed the door. "I thought I'd better report at once. Sit down, my dear policeman. I'm so sorry I didn't get your name, but you must forgive me. This may take me a moment or two, but you've got to hear it."

She seated herself on the arm of the chair vacated by Mrs. Cash and, crossing her long thin legs, dropped into a conspiratorial undertone.

"Well, Geoffrey still hasn't phoned. Meg and Amanda have slipped out, down to the new house. Meg pretended she wanted to fetch something, but I think she just wanted to show the place. The paint is finished. *I* was left in charge. Well, a Mrs. Smith phoned in a tremendous state. Poor Sam couldn't cope at all, so of course little Dot rushed in."

She made a meaningless gesture with a bony hand, unless it was a wave of farewell to all the details she might have included had time been free.

"Listen. After a lot of cross-purposes it emerged that she was Mrs. Frederick Smith, the wife of Martin's solicitor, that nice man in Grove Road. They live in Hampstead, and her husband had been called out from a canasta party she was giving, by the police. Apparently something terrible, something quite dreadful, so awful she couldn't tell me much, but there are three dead, has happened at his office."

She took breath and her candid eyes rested on the sergeant with innocent pleasure.

"It seems amazing that I should be able to tell you, doesn't it, but I was fairly sure you didn't know."

"Why did the lady tell you, ma'am?" Picot was as mystified as ever in his life.

"Me?" said Miss Warburton. "Oh well, I insisted. You see, she wanted Meg because she thought Albert Campion would probably be here. She can't get hold of her husband at the police station. The police won't tell her anything at all, and of course the poor dear is consumed with worry and curiosity. Naturally. I should be myself. She'd heard of Albert and thought *he* might help her, but of course he's with the police, as I told her. I learnt all I could and promised I'd ring her back if I heard anything, and then I came down to tell you two."

Old Avril was looking at her in mixed dismay and amusement.

"Yes," he said, as though the discovery astonished him. "Yes, of course you would."

"But you were busy," she went on, indicating that the story was by no means finished. "I could hear Mary boo-hooing in here through the door, so I went down into the kitchen to wait until she came out. There I found Mrs. Cash drinking tea. I don't know if she'd made it herself and I didn't ask."

"What did you tell her?" Picot asked the question more out of censure than curiosity, but his tone was lost on Miss Warburton, who was enjoying herself tremendously in her way.

"She told me she was waiting for you—I suppose I was looking at the teacup; one does—and I said I very much doubted if you'd be able to bother with her tonight, because I expected you'd have to go straight back if you hadn't been sent for already to the solicitor's office. Three murders in one house! They'll need every man they've got, I said."

"Murders!" They spoke together and she surveyed them calmly.

"I certainly understood Mrs. Smith to say murders. I thought you were both taking it very coolly. Mrs. Cash didn't. In fact, that's why I hurried to tell you. Do you know, Hubert, that woman was really upset? It's the first time I've ever seen her show any feeling whatever, and I've lived next door for over twenty years. She actually jumped." She gave a little spring herself to illustrate the movement. "I didn't imagine it because she spilt the tea, all of it, a whole cupful, all over her. She's gone running off to change, she had to. It must have gone right through everything. And she said if you wanted to see her you must go round and knock. Well, I thought you'd be interested. Are you?"

"I am, ma'am, very." Picot was thoughtful. The news was too startling to be entirely credible, but she seemed remarkably certain about it. "I think if you'll excuse me, sir," he said, "I'll go after the old woman at once. I'll take the jacket, if you please—I mustn't move without that."

He stepped over to the desk and began to repack the sports coat in the brown paper in which he had brought it. Miss Warburton was openly disappointed.

"Won't you ring up your headquarters? There are three telephones in the house, you know."

Picot forbore to remark that he never used more than one at a time.

"No, miss," he said. "If I was wanted I'd be sent for. But of course if a call should come through for me, perhaps you'd explain where I've gone. It's the second cottage, isn't it? Two doors from here on the left?"

"You're quite right, but I shall come and show you," she said. "Our little houses are built right under the church wall. Mine is the shabby one, but you won't notice that in the fog."

She hurried him out so that he could only nod to Avril and grasp his parcel, and she was still talking cheerfully in the hall.

"We shall expect you to come and tell us all about it—even if you don't. If curiosity is vulgar, then I'm very vulgar. I make no bones about it. *Come* along."

Yet when she returned a few minutes later there was little that was stupid or even affected about her.

"Mrs. Cash has the light on in the attic, Hubert," she said. "I could see it quite clearly in spite of the fog. She doesn't want any other visitors while the policeman is there."

Avril was standing by his own uncurtained window, staring out into the brown mysterious world which was the square.

"You say these things, Dot," he exclaimed. "How *can* you know?"

"Because I make it my business to," she said softly. "I've got eyes and common sense and I use them. No one ever visits Lucy Cash when that light is on in the attic. It's a signal to certain people to keep away."

"Certain people." He mimicked her. "What people?"

"Business people, I suppose," said Miss Warburton.

The Canon did not speak for a moment and his face was still hidden. Presently a shudder ran through his broad flat shoulders.

"I hope you're right, Dot," he said unexpectedly. "On this occasion, do you know, I hope you're right."

EIGHT
THE SPOOR AGAIN

It was one of the most pleasant things about Amanda that she had never lost that rustic outlook which regards the wildest illogicalities of human emotional behaviour as perfectly normal and nothing to make a fuss about. Therefore, when poor Meg in her wretchedness proposed to drag her out at past eleven o'clock at night to inspect the partly furnished bridal house in which even the power was not yet connected, it struck her as the most natural and sensible move in the world.

She was relieved that it was no further away than the last of the "good streets" on the other side of the square, but she would have gone out to the suburbs quite cheerfully had she been asked.

On inspection, the house proved to be a delightful place. Even when seen in the beam of torches held in very cold hands, it displayed enormous charm. Geoffrey had been determined to satisfy both his own somewhat pathetic dream of solidarity and permanence in his unstable world and his bride's natural good taste, so that the house had been restored to its original smug Regency comfort but given a practicalness and a gaiety which it had never before possessed.

They had peeped at the "Edwardian" bedroom with the flower-snow paper and Honiton bedspread, and the bathroom off it which was like a comfortable lily pool, and had come at last to the object of the exercise, Meg's own studio at the top of the house where the attics once had been.

It appeared to Amanda's candid eye as if Geoffrey had planned its essential layout so that its conversion to a nursery suite could be accomplished with very little difficulty at the earliest suitable opportunity, but at the moment it was a studio, severely utilitarian and not yet furnished. A quantity of Meg's personal belongings, still to be unpacked, was stacked round the pale walls where the moving men had left them.

Meg gave up pretending suddenly and dropped to her knees before one small sacking-wrapped bundle. She looked very young indeed, crouching there, her soft fur coat trailing in the dust behind her and her sleek fair head bent intently as she unfolded the hessian.

"I wanted to find these and burn them," she said without looking up. "I wanted to do it at once, right away, tonight. They're only Martin's letters. That's why I've dragged you out, though. Do you mind?"

"Not at all." Amanda sounded infinitely reasonable. "Jolly sensible of you. There always is a moment when one makes up one's mind about these things, and then it's much tidier to act at once."

"That's what I thought." Meg had uncovered a small nest of drawers in a battered Italian leather case and was emptying them hastily on to a sheet of packing paper.

"I've been feeling vaguely guilty about these for months," she went on, betraying a charming streak of naïveté which suited her voice much better than her sophisticated make-up and hair-do. "I haven't looked at them for years, but I knew they were here and when my things came over I let them come too. Then tonight, when I was thinking about Geoff, and—well, needing him, I suppose—it suddenly seemed terribly important that they shouldn't stay in his—I mean our—house, even for a night. Do you think I'm being hysterical? I am rather, I suppose."

"If you are, I don't see it matters, do you?" Amanda had seated herself on a box of books and seemed perfectly content to stay there all night, should nothing more than ordinary politeness demand it. "Why bother about being anything? This is just the end of Martin come rather suddenly, don't you think? I mean it's the end of the painful bit. It was going to happen anyway, but circumstances have hurried it. There was a little storm and the last leaf fell."

"Yes. Yes, that is it." Meg was eager. Her words came quickly in a rush of relief. "I had forgotten him, or at least I thought I had, and then the photographs brought not so much Martin as my husband back and I didn't know what I did feel. Sometimes I seemed to be being unfaithful to them both, and then tonight the whole thing crystallised and no one but Geoff existed any more for me. I can think of Martin objectively now as an ordinary person. I never could before."

Amanda said nothing, but she nodded complete agreement in the dusk.

Meanwhile, as the neat packages of letters, most of them photostats from the Desert, were piled on the brown paper, something hard and bright fell out from amongst them. Meg held it to the light.

"Oh," she said slowly, "yes, I suppose I ought to keep that. It must go down among the other pretties in the show table in the drawing room. There was something awfully queer about it, a secret, something to do with the war."

She handed the discovery to the other woman. It was a miniature, a girl's smiling face in a jewelled frame, a frame worth rather more than the few pounds which the dealer in the Walworth Road had given a soldier for its fellow.

"How beautiful!" Amanda shone her torch on the painting. "Carolean. I think this must be the original setting, don't you?"

"Perhaps it is." Meg spoke wonderingly. "D'you know, I don't think I've ever considered it before. It just scared me when I first had it and I pushed it away and forgot it. Martin gave it to me a few weeks before he went overseas for the last time. He'd been away for a little while on some trip he couldn't tell me about. Do you remember those years, Amanda? They seem quite mad at this distance. Dull, and uncomfortable, and full of awful secrets and half-guesses."

Her voice sounded youthful in the half-dark.

"Martin came in one night, tired and sort of excited, and just pulled it out of his pocket wrapped up in a dirty handkerchief. He said it had had a companion but that he'd had to give it away because 'there weren't enough to go round.'

I said something about loot and he laughed and I was rather shocked, and then in the next breath he told me he remembered looking at this through the glass of a cabinet when he was a child, and how he always thought it must be Nell Gwyn because she was laughing." She paused and added thoughtfully, "I often wondered if he could have gone back to Ste. Odile somehow when the place was occupied. That sort of incredible thing did happen. It was right on the coast, almost in the sea."

"Ste. Odile? His grandmother's house?"

"Yes, she had to clear out very quickly at the beginning of the war. She died down in Nice just before he was lost. We didn't know that, though, until long afterwards."

Amanda returned the miniature. "What happened to the house?"

"Oh, it's still there, deserted but almost intact. I had to go over and see it some time ago. Daddy couldn't come, so Dot and I went. She's the business brain of the family." She laughed and sighed. "And it was quite dreadful; Martin being only 'presumed killed' made no end of complications, and you know what French legal proceedings are. There was some sort of forty-second cousin, too, somewhere in East Africa. Martin had made things even more involved by leaving a will with a firm of solicitors here in Grove Road, which was full of the most specific instructions. For some reason he was terribly anxious that the *contents* of the house should come to me eventually. He didn't seem to mind about the building itself, but everything inside bothered him enormously. Smithy, that's the solicitor, told me he thought there must once have been something of great value there, or something Martin set great store by, although he wouldn't define it. It was left so that I could claim everything movable, garden tools, flowerpots, everything. But of course the place had been pretty well ransacked by the time we got there. I had what was left. There was a dreary little sale, and the house is just going to pieces waiting for the old gentleman from East Africa."

"How sad," said Amanda. "Was it a pleasant place?"

"It may have been once." The young voice had a shiver in it. "But it was beastly when I saw it. Something horrible had happened there in the war. The locals were very discreet and maddeningly vague, but some enemy bigwig—a back-room boy, I fancy—had installed a mistress there, and one night either they killed themselves or were murdered, and there was hell to pay afterwards, trials and tortures and heaven knows what. The place was stripped even of anything interesting, let along valuable, and there had been a fire in one room. I didn't like it and I was awfully glad Martin never saw it like that. He loved it when he was a child."

"How queer he should worry about the furniture and not the building," murmured Amanda. "When one's a child it's the place, not the thing, one loves. We lived in a mill, and its clumps of willows I remember best, and the pool under them. Of course our furniture wasn't very impressive. It had tears in it." She laughed. "I loved my mill. It's still in the family, still running at a loss. Perhaps there was something rather important at Ste. Odile which the Germans took away."

"Anyway, there's nothing there now." Meg's sigh had relief in it. "I'm so glad I came and got these letters, Amanda. I'll take them home and bury them in Mary's boiler. Martin would approve. I know it now, I know it for sure."

She was scrambling to her feet with the parcel in her arms when a thin brown hand cut into her shoulder and held her still.

"Wait," whispered Amanda, "listen. Someone has just come into the house."

For a moment they held their breath. Beneath them the dark building lay quiet, shrouded tightly in the damp swaddlings of the fog. There were no faraway sounds from the city. The street outside was deserted, and the mists made an insulating blanket, cutting them off from the world.

It was the draught Amanda had noticed first. It crept up from below, chill from the outside air. The sounds came later, a swift patter of feet, a door opening cautiously, the nervous ring of metal, the squeak of a chair on the parquet.

"Geoff." Meg was still whispering, but the word was happy and excited. "No one else has a key. He's got back at last and come to look for us."

"Listen." Amanda was insistent and her hand was still firm. "This person doesn't know his way."

They waited. The sounds grew and came closer. Someone was stumbling through the house with a restless, fumbling eagerness, looking for something. They became aware of anxiety, exasperation, and haste. The sense of urgency was violent. It reached up to them through the dark, unmistakable and frightening.

"Ought we to go down?" Meg's whisper sounded breathless in the cold airless room.

"Where's the fire escape?"

"Just behind us. On this window."

"Could you get down to the next house and call the police? You mustn't make a sound or he'll hear you. Meg, could you?"

"I think so. What about you?"

"Hush. Try. See if you can."

Downstairs a door slammed with startling noise. It was followed by utter silence. As they listened they were aware of other ears straining below them. The pause seemed interminable, and then at last there were footsteps again in the hall, receding now, ceasing and going on again.

"Now." Amanda gave the shoulder a little push. "Shut the window after you and—not a sound."

Meg did not hesitate. She was rather alarmed but quite capable. She rose silently and tiptoed to the casement. The house was well built and her lightly shod feet made no sound on the boards. The window was a new steel one and opened easily. Amanda saw her dark figure silhouetted against its pallid square of light for an instant. Then she was gone.

The other girl remained where she was, listening. She heard the faint whine of the drawing-room-door hinge, and a single step on the wood. Then there was a long silence, followed by a movement in the bedroom immediately below her. The intruder must have come up the stairs without her hearing a sound. She stifled her breath and was aware of the noise of her own heart, and this irritated her. The British burglar is not as a rule the bravest of men, and she knew that should he discover her as his torch beam wheeled across the unfurnished room, the chances were that he would be far more startled than she. But despite all reason she was trembling. There was something peculiar about this particular intruder. His movements were so hurried and, when they were heard at all, so oddly violent.

Suddenly she heard him again, very close this time. He ran up the first few steps of the attic stairs outside and paused. A thin pencil of light ran under the closed door of the room in which she sat. It touched her foot and vanished, and there was silence again. Very slowly she rose and stood waiting.

He went back. She heard him distinctly. He had decided that the top floor was unused. After a long interval she heard him down in the hall again.

Amanda considered the fire escape but changed her mind. The police would respond to Meg's call immediately, but the fog was very thick and might delay them. It seemed a pity that the burglar should get away without being seen. She decided to go down.

Once having made up her mind, she crept over to the door. The first flight of stairs seemed to promise the only difficulty, since the boards were bare and newly stained, but she let the balusters take her weight and moved gently, feeling her way.

On the first landing it was very dark. The bedroom doors were closed and the small circular window little more than a blur, but she remembered the design of the house and by following the wall came softly to the top of the graceful winding stairs. Her overconfidence was almost her undoing. She put out her hand for the newel post, missed it, and regained her balance only just in time. Hovering, one foot down, her hand feeling for the rail, she heard him once more.

He was in the little study, whose door was immediately to the right at the foot of the stairs. She heard the unmistakable scratch of a match in the inner room, and a flicker of grey appeared in the black of the wall.

A trickle of fear touched her, but she ignored it resolutely. Her hand found the rail and she took another step or two down and came under the level of the upper floor. The study door was wide open and through it a light, very faint and unsteady, crept out across the hall to touch the bright casing of a Kandy chest and the pool of a looking glass hanging above it.

Amanda edged forward. The burglar was very busy. He was still taking care to make no unnecessary noise, but he was hurrying and at last she recognized the element which had been puzzling her from the beginning. It was an impression of pursuit. Now that she saw it she could feel it distinctly. It was as though the whole house were running away from forces descending upon it rapidly from outside. Yet from beyond the walls there was no sound at all. The fog pressed round the elegant stucco box, drowning it utterly.

One more step brought her flat against the rounded wall just above the open door, and, glancing across the hall, she saw that a patch of the room was reflected in the looking glass. The first thing she made out was the candle. It was a long green taper which had been set with three others in a gilt sconce on the further wall. The newcomer had taken it down and it now lolled drunkenly in a vase, dripping hot wax recklessly on the polished surface of a Sheraton desk which occupied the centre of the little room.

It took her some seconds to realise that the shadow between her and the rest of the picture was the man himself. He had his back to her and was wrestling with something on the desk. She could not see it, but she guessed it was the spice cabinet which Meg had shown her with such pride, bewailing the fact that the key had been mislaid so that she could not display its fittings. It was a charming affair made of mahogany and inlaid with ivory, and was to stand on the desk to hold note paper. The burglar appeared to be wrenching it apart. She heard the scrape and splinter of the wood.

Sudden rage at the wanton destruction of the pretty thing swept over her and she opened her mouth to protest. The words were almost out when a question shot into her mind and stayed there. What was he opening the thing with? She was never certain if she saw the knife, if it caught the light and flashed in the mirror, or if she merely heard the blade biting into the fragile wood, but the words died on her lips and she was suddenly very cold.

With a final squeal of protest the tiny doors of the cabinet split open. In the looking glass she saw the man's shadow contracted and then grow large, and she heard his intake of angry breath. Then the empty ruined toy shot through the door into the hall at her feet, and immediately, as though at a signal, the whole world became alive with noise.

The hammering on the front door was like rolls of thunder. There was an echo of it below in the basement and the shriek of a window flying up somewhere at the back. From all sides came the sounds of feet, heavy and hurried on stone, and the unmistakable voices of police demanding admittance.

Close to Amanda in the heart of the sudden storm, there was brief but utter silence. Then the candle went out, swept vase and all from the desk, and the stranger came out.

She did not see him, but he passed so close that he brushed against her in the whirlwind dark. She caught something of him in that moment, fear and recklessness and a violence which was new in her experience. He fled past her up the stairs, bolting like some huge animal, fleet and silent, into the house above.

After that it was pandemonium.

Mr. Campion found his wife huddled against the wall on the bottom stair, clutching a broken box like a child on a kerbstone, while the thunder of police boots and the flash of police torches made traffic above and around her. He jerked her to her feet and drew her roughly into the comparative safety of the study doorway.

"How damned silly!" he exclaimed irritably. "Really, ducky, how damned silly!"

Amanda was too experienced a wife to take the outburst as anything but a compliment, but she was very startled to see him at all. For the first time it occurred to her that this avalanche of official aid could hardly be merely the outcome of Meg's telephone call.

"Oh," she said with sudden enlightenment, "he was being chased!"

"He was, my dear, and they've now got him, I should think, unless you've mucked it completely." Mr. Campion was still angry and his arm was so tightly round her shoulders that he hurt her. "Upstairs," he said furiously to a uniformed figure who barged in on them. "This room's all right. I'm here."

Dozens of men appeared to be stampeding through the house. The noise was outrageous and, to a relieved onlooker, slightly funny. Amanda laughed.

"What has the poor man got? The Crown Jewels?"

Campion looked down at her. In her torch beam she saw his eyes round and dark behind his spectacles.

"No, my addlepated girl," he said. "He's got a knife." His arm tightened again. "Oh, my God, you are an idiot! Why didn't you come out with Meg? It was because you were in here that we had to rush him. Left alone, he would have walked into the arms of the regulars, who would simply have sat outside until he moved."

"You got Meg's call then?"

"Good heavens no!" He was contemptuous. "We came up just as she reached the ground. Don't you understand, my dear? It's so simple. The moment Luke talked to the solicitor we all began to see daylight. A man was sent down to watch the rectory and another to keep an eye on this place. Their two reports came in almost simultaneously. Naturally we were half out of our minds. We thought you must walk in on the fellow. As it happened, it was the other way round. While you were pottering through the house like a couple of lunatics, he was forcing a basement window. He must have arrived just after you came in. Our man out here missed you completely."

His voice ended on the triumphant note of one who has put the thing in a nutshell, and Amanda, who had only understood that he was more badly rattled than she had ever seen him, was too polite to comment.

"Let's have some light," she suggested. "Have you got some matches? There are some candles on that wall. Be careful how you move. I think he's been terribly untidy."

Campion produced his lighter but he did not let go of her arm, and when the three tapers were casting an elegant radiance over the wreckage of the pretty room he still stood with his arm across her back.

Amanda considered the damage, her brown eyes pitying. "What a shame! And also silly. There were no small valuables here yet, no silver or anything."

"He wasn't looking for silver," said Mr. Campion grimly. "He was looking for papers. He didn't find them at the solicitor's office, so he came here. Hullo?"

The last word was directed to the doorway, where a drooping figure in a disgraceful old mackintosh stood hesitating.

"Stanis!" Amanda sounded delighted.

"My dear girl." The old man came forward and surprised them all, including himself, by shaking her hand warmly. "Dear, oh dear," he said, "I'm getting old. D'you know, I didn't like to come in, afraid of what I was going to find. Well well, young woman, you've frightened us all very badly, you know. Put the fear of hell in us. Good lord, yes. Well, thank God that's over."

He pulled a chair out and sat down on it and, pushing his hat on the back of his head, wiped his grey forehead.

Amanda was gratified but surprised. It was nice to know they were all so fond of her, but the relief seemed a little excessive.

"Have they got him?" she demanded.

"Eh? I don't know." He smiled his wintry smile at her. "I'm such a big policeman now, you know, that I hardly know anything that goes on at all. I leave the footwork to the young-sters. But even if he slips through their fingers now, it won't be long. At this stage it can hardly be more than a matter of hours. It was you I was worrying about. Why did you want to go and look at a house in the middle of the night? Why don't you shin up Nelson's column one evening?"

"Oh, forget her," said Campion testily. "Where's Luke?"

"Skipping about the roofs or halfway down the drain." Oates was returning to his normal gloom. "Yapping like a skeltie, trying to do everybody else's work. That fellow's an-gry, Campion. He's been touched on the raw. He's what the village I was born in used to call 'wholly riled.' I like to see it. I like to know a man has it in him. Yet it always makes me nervous. I don't want him doing anything with his bare hands, so to speak. We have to be very dignified, we senior dicks."

A remark neither dignified nor even particularly senior, al-though it possessed a certain colourful sophistication, floated in to them from the hall, and a few moments later the D.D.C.I. appeared. He came stalking in, coat skirts flying, his fingers rattling the change in his pockets, and his diamond eyes glowering. At once the little room became grossly over-furnished.

"Lost him," he announced, throwing up great hands in a fine impressionist sketch of flight. "We shall get him in the next hour or two. We can't help doing that. If we continue to be lame, blind, half-witted, and cloth-eared for the rest of our naturals, we shall pick him up. Alive, too, if we don't crush him to death getting out of each other's way. Twenty-five men! Twenty-five men of various branches, counting five drivers and six senior officials, and what happens? The bloke slides out of the bathroom window, the only one in the house which hadn't got a dick sitting under the sill, and leaps into the fog. He has to jump blind, the night is thick as canteen coffee, and does he kill himself dropping on to the spiked railings round the area? Does he hell!"

He had been talking to Oates all the time, but not openly. Ostensibly his remarks had been addressed to Amanda, whom he did not know very well.

At this point he condescended to recognise her for the first time.

"I'm glad you're all right," he said with a brief smile, "but Campion here has gone down in my estimation socially. He's not the nob I thought he was. He just took on like any other common chap. 'Get her out! Get her out!' No old-school-tie stiff-upper-lip stuff there. I couldn't have behaved worse myself." He laughed abruptly at her amazed expression, which he mistook for embarrassment. "Don't worry. It wasn't your fault. We should have lost him anyway. We should have lost him if there had been enough of us to play ring-a-ring-of-roses all round the building, or if we'd been allowed to shoot on sight. We'd have missed him because we underestimated him. We just weren't thinking in his class."

Oates cocked an eye at him. "He observed your man, knew you'd be on your way, took the risk of carrying his project through before you got here, and marked that one window as the one you didn't guard because you'd estimate the drop as unnegotiable."

"Yes," said Luke. "That's right."

"Did anyone see him at all?"

"Two uniformed men saw a shadow and went after it like good 'uns. But he melted. The whole area is alive with us now. It's like looking for a flea in a bust feather bed."

Oates nodded. "He's got nerve and he's got quality, I grant him that."

"Likewise spring heels and rubber bones," Luke spoke grudgingly.

"I shouldn't like to attempt that drop myself, in daylight. I don't suppose the lady happened to see him?"

"I?" Amanda shook her head regretfully. "No, only as a shadow in the looking glass. He was in here, you see, and I was out there at the foot of the stairs."

She noticed that she was causing a sensation and was deeply puzzled by it.

"I can't describe him either, I'm afraid, because it was so dark. I only saw his back in some sort of rough coat—light buff, I think."

"Buff?" They were on to her at once, eager with enquiry.

"I think so. I couldn't swear to it."

"It wasn't a Navy raincoat anyway?"

"No. It was lightish."

"Any hat?"

She hesitated. "I can't remember any brim," she said, "and yet I don't remember any hair either. My impression is that he had a round, tight sort of head. The thing I do remember and the thing I'd know again is the extraordinary atmosphere of the man, if that's the right word. He was urgent, somehow, rather like you, Chief Inspector."

"That's Havoc," exclaimed Oates, highly delighted. "You can't go saying that in evidence, Amanda, but it satisfies me. Don't misunderstand us, Luke my boy, but I know what she means. He's an extraordinary vital animal. He's got force."

Luke hunched his shoulders. "I don't know about force," he said bitterly. "Just give me his direction. I'm not saying I've not got plenty to go on. His prints were all over the solicitor's office, and I don't doubt they are here. He's leaving a trail like a drag hunt. We're bound to get him before dawn. But meanwhile there's four people dead who ought to be alive. One of them a famous man, and another of 'em one of the best kids who ever lived. When this is over I've got to go and see Coleman's old mum. He was her only one and she hoped he'd turn out like me, God help her. Four murders in my manor since six tonight and the chap jumps quietly out of a ring of us."

He stuck his long right forefinger through a circle made of

his left hand, and took a swinging grab at it with his right fist. It was an expressive illustration, but its point was lost in an uncharacteristic explosion from Amanda, whose brown eyes had become wide and horrified.

"That man murdered four people tonight? You didn't tell us. Meg and I might have been killed."

Her reaction was so angry, and so exactly an echo of their own earlier performances, that it punctured the emotional tension like a bubble. Mr. Campion began to laugh and Oates joined him. Amanda remained furious, her flaming hair no redder than her cheeks.

"I think we might have been told," she said. The unreason of the statement occurred to her the moment it had escaped her, and her expression grew blank. "I say, how horrible," she said in an altered voice. "Who is he? A maniac?"

"Not if I know it." Luke was softly ferocious. "No psychiatrist is going to get him off through that door. He'll see the inside of the topping shed when I get hold of him."

"And you think you'll get him soon?" Amanda spoke absently. She was shivering and she glanced behind her into the shadows.

"Luke will get him soon." Oates stirred in his chair. He looked very mild and elderly sitting there, the candlelight falling on his close-cropped head, but his voice was chill with certainty. "The animal is trapped," he said. "Nothing can save him. He has a start on us, but now that the machine has gone into action the odds against him are lengthening every hour. By this time his record has been studied. That means that every living soul who has ever been known to have anything to do with him is going to be contacted, questioned, and kept under observation. For instance, we know he had a visitor in prison. So far that woman (she's a lodginghouse keeper in Bethnal Green) has not heard from him since he escaped. She won't hear. She won't have a chance. All *her* associates will be examined. He'll have no help there."

"He picked up a knife somewhere," grumbled Luke, "and a buff hairy coat. He was in issue clothes when he escaped."

"That was at the beginning." Oates still spoke mildly. "You'll find that phase is over. From now on he must become more and more alone. I've seen it happen again and again.

Quietly and steadily the holes are stopped, the net grows smaller and smaller. Now he has reached the stage when he can never take another step knowing it to be a safe one. He can never enter another room, never turn another corner, without taking his life in his hands." He paused and regarded them with cold grave eyes. "Tomorrow, if he has not been taken, we shall probably offer a reward. An enterprising newspaper will double it at once. After that he'll never be able to trust another living soul."

Luke breathed heavily through his long nose. "Fair enough, but we ought to have taken him tonight. This was our best bet. He'll keep away from Mrs. Elginbrodde and her friends now, whatever he's looking for."

Amanda was astonished. "Why Meg? What is he looking for?"

"Some documents," said Campion. "Something to do with Martin. He went for Martin's file at the solicitor's."

He made the explanation briefly and his hand on her arm tightened, warning her to be discreet. She nodded, but her next question was unfortunate.

"What happened to Geoffrey?"

"You may well ask." Luke's bright eyes were very keen. "Not a murmur from that young man since he went down an alley with a crook who was picked up dead soon after. There's another person who can vanish like smoke."

Campion's restraining hand became ever heavier. "My dear," he murmured with an old-fashioned primness which was becoming increasingly noticeable in him as he grew older, "you and I are going home. If Luke needs either of us he knows where to find us—as he would say himself, at the old address. Meg has been taken home to the rectory, where there are quite a dozen good people anxious to comfort her. We have got to get across the town to Bottle Street somehow in this fog and I feel the time has come when we should try."

"Good idea," said Amanda quickly, and she slid her arm through his.

They left the sad little house to Luke and his minions, who had a great deal of work to do, but had some difficulty in escaping from Oates, who had made up his mind to give them a lift in the official limousine of which he was so vain. Sal-

vation came unexpectedly when they got outside to find Mr.
Lugg was waiting in Mr. Campion's sister's remarkable lan-
dau. The fat man had been thoroughly frightened and was
reacting in the popular way. He was in truculent mood.

" 'Op in the back of this 'ere 'atbox," he said briefly, his
moonface scowling at them through the choking gloom. "It
only took me two hours to get 'ere, but at any rate no one
could see what I was in and laugh. 'Ow did you expect me
to find you—second sight?"

Amanda climbed into the warm cabin with relief. Val's
town car, if highly individual, was extremely comfortable. She
had supervised the renovation of the fine old Daimler herself
and had achieved a modern gaiety of décor which was part
her practical self and part Dali. The glass partition between
the driver and the passengers had been removed, and the
upholstery, carried out in olive-green and an intelligent ma-
roon, was openly reminiscent of Georgian backstairs livery,
so that the vehicle had been rechristened by the family the
Running Footman. It was very gay and gallant and pleasant
to escape to.

Amanda pulled the saffron rug round her and sighed.

"Bless you, Magers," she said. "How did you do it? Telephoned the police station, I suppose?"

"Not me. I don't stick me 'ead into every narks' nest I 'ear
of, like some people." He leant over the back and pushed the
door wide for Campion. "If it 'adn't been for that Mrs. Elginbrodde—wot a smashereeno, eh!—'oo come up outside
the rectory in a police car looking like a jool in a sink tidy,
I'd be sitting in the square still. She told me quite enough to
go on with. Why don't you stick to aeroplanes? They're safer
and they're class. Murders is mud and always 'as been. Don't
forget it."

He cast a baleful glance at his employer, who was at last
inside.

"You're quite content, I suppose?" he enquired. "Up to the
oxters in blood and 'appy as a lark."

Mr. Campion regarded him coldly. "Where's Rupert?"

"Mindin' the telephone. That's where Sexton Blake is."
Lugg settled himself behind the wheel. " 'E and the dorg give

me the only 'elp I get. I give them the night watchman as a
runner."

He let in the clutch with a sigh and pulled out silently into
the fog.

"Now," said Amanda to Albert as their tight little world
moved cautiously through the gloom, "now, what about Geoffrey?"

"Exactly." Mr. Campion borrowed some of her rug. "What
indeed? I don't see eye to eye with Luke exactly, but I wish
that young man would have the grace to turn up."

As usual Amanda was forthright.

"Just how funny does it look?"

"Hardly a belly-laugh." Her husband warmed his hands on
hers. "He was certainly with Duds Morrison the last time the
man was seen alive, and they were then only a few feet from
where the crook was subsequently found dead. From that
moment Levett appears to have wandered off and lost interest. It's not good."

"Where was this?"

He told her briefly, sketching in the story of Havoc's escape
and the triple crime at the solicitor's office.

She shivered, and Lugg, who was both listening and driving, no inconsiderable feat in the circumstances, gave an opinion which, if vulgar, was not unfair.

Campion took no notice of him. "Luke is bitter, naturally,"
he said, "and he's liable to be rude to Levett. He's lost a good
boy whom he liked and he's savage about that. Missing the
man tonight shook him more than he showed."

"But he doesn't really suspect Geoffrey of kicking Duds
Morrison to death, or does he?"

"No. I don't think he does. But he feels, as I do for that
matter, that this is no time for Geoffrey to play the injured
lover. He and Meg have quarrelled, I suppose?"

"No. They haven't. I'm sure they haven't. She's too worried
for that. She thinks something may have happened to him.
Could it?"

"What? You suggest that both these chaps may have run
into a third man, and that Geoffrey is lying about somewhere
unnoticed?"

"Oh, don't. Don't. Don't say it. Meg would never get over that."

"Nor would Master Geoff, on form," remarked their driver with relish. "It's my belief you could lose anything in this drop of brown windsor. But it's not reely likely, is it? I mean, when we've 'ad our laugh we've got to face facts. No corp is goin' to lie about in the street without someone fallin' over it. It wouldn't be natural, would it?"

"It would not. It's not likely, or even possible." Mr. Campion was frankly worried. "I simply can't understand the chap fading away on his own affairs when he ought to have gone to the police himself. He ought to have made a statement at once. Why didn't he report his meeting with Morrison? We shall have to tread very softly in this business, Amanda."

"Yes, I do see that." She echoed his seriousness. "Whatever has happened, he must be made to go to the police himself, that's vital. Isn't there a chance that he may not know what has happened yet? Do you *know* that he went down the path after the man?"

"The inference is that he did. The evidence on that point is rather interesting. The young detective who was stabbed at the solicitor's office had been interviewing the caretaker there when Havoc disturbed them. The detective seems to have been an earnest youth and he had taken down a long statement in his notebook, which he got the old fellow to sign. I can't give it you verbatim, but the old man had stated that he had heard footsteps running down the path which skirts his garden just about the time when Duds and Geoffrey are known to have left the Feathers. He referred to 'the rush of many feet' and 'I heard a number of men.' The detective seems to have queried him but couldn't shake him. It probably means very little, but it hardly suggests that only Morrison ran that way, does it? The caretaker appears to have been in the back room all the evening and said he heard no one else in the passageway until there was all the excitement when the police arrived."

He ended on an upward note, and hesitated.

"Yes?" encouraged Amanda.

"Well, the other thing is rather ridiculous. Probably hysteria, poor devil, but it looked very strange written down."

"Oh, for gord's sake!" exploded Mr. Lugg, a misty mountain in the muffled light from the dashboard. "Drivin' this and listenin' to you, it's like being up to me eyes in the creek. What *'ad* the perisher wrote down?"

"The caretaker said he heard chains," said Mr. Campion, stung into baldness. "The precise words were: 'I heard the rattle of heavy chains as the men ran past, which made me wonder.' "

Mr. Lugg grunted. "Was this bloke 'Avoc manacled to go to the psycho geezer?"

"Of course not."

"Well, you never know these days——Is this a road island we're coming to or the side of Barclay's Bank? Manacles was passy when I was at college, but these reforms always 'ave a catch in 'em. I thought perhaps they'd gorn back to leg irons in the up-to-date 'e's-not-a-felon-'e's-only-a-nut institutions. 'Oo was wearin' chains, anyway?"

"No one, presumably. I imagine the caretake dreamed them."

"Someone else for the bin." Lugg manoeuvred into Park Lane and sat on the tail of a late bus for Victoria. "I could do with a spot of p and q in a padded cell myself. That was Marble Arch I was 'ootin' at. I thought she was takin' 'er time."

"Chains," said Amanda thoughtfully. "What else sounds like chains, apart from Lugg's gearbox?"

Mr. Campion stiffened at her side. "Money," he said suddenly. "Coins. Coins in one of those heavy wooden collecting boxes."

Through all the excitement of the day a recollection had returned to him. He saw again the perambulating group in the gutter and heard the echo of a song, urgent and ferocious.

"I say," he said softly, "I say, it's an outside chance, old lady, but I wonder if I've got something there."

NINE
IN THE FORESTS OF THE NIGHT

Geoffrey lay on the cot furthest from the stove in acute physical misery. He had not surrendered and his overpowering
had been a grim business. He was lying in a far corner of the
room on a string netting mattressed with the inevitable sacks
and covered with a dirty Army blanket.

His mouth was no longer sealed. They had given that up
when they thought he was suffocating, but they had taught
him not to talk. His hands and feet were tied, each with the
same cord, which was drawn up with agonising tightness behind him, and most of his clothes had been removed so that
he was cold as well as cramped. The others were keeping well
away from him.

By now the cellar was almost quiet. Even the dwarf had
ceased his twittering at last, but there was whispering going
on all along the wall. It was Doll's achievement. He had got
them out of a quarreling knot and into their beds, but even
he could not make them sleep. It was in the small hours long
before daylight. The market would not stir for some time yet
and lay sodden and filthy just above them, while on all sides
the city sprawled, breathing heavily, and twitching beneath
its grimy counterpane of fog.

In the cellar the man from Tiddington alone was on his
feet. He was standing before the stove, peering into its red
depths, and he was burning his boots. He went about the task
methodically, hacking the solid leather into strips with a snob-
ber's knife and dropping them one by one into the mouth of

the iron cylinder. So far it was the only sign of fear he had shown, the only concession to human weakness.

Chemists employed by the police can do remarkable things with blood. They can find it in shreds of cloth, in the interstices of floor, boards, on the iron of a heel, and can measure it and can swear to it and weave it into a rope to hang a man.

Tiddy Doll read his newspaper. It was an accomplishment of which he was proud, and he knew a great deal about chemists. He knew something about the treachery of ashes, too, so he was making very sure, taking his time. Geoffrey could see him in the glow, picking out the nails with a small pair of pliers and dropping each one carefully into his pocket like the cautious countryman he was.

But if Doll was afraid, his terror was prudence compared with the abject quaking which was going on all along the whitewashed wall. The cellar had become a pit of fear; it was mindless, irresponsible alarm in men who would have been pitiable had they not possessed that streak of cruelty which is unforgivable in the weakest. Not one was trustworthy. Not one could be relied upon not to give both his friends and himself away at the slightest outside pressure.

In the earlier part of the night Geoffrey had had an opportunity to learn something of the company which the albino had collected about him, and although at first sight it had seemed some physical peculiarity or defect which they all possessed in common, he had soon realised that the true bond between them was the shiftless dependence which had made them beggars. Roly, Tom, and possibly Doll were the only exceptions, and they had no illusions about the rest. Doll had let Roly out, taking the risk because he figured the man had more to lose in flight than to gain. The ex-fisherman had gone down the dark alleys into Fleet Street to pick up a morning paper as soon as the damp piles of newsprint should shoot out to the waiting vans. He had also agreed to bring back some food. There had been wrangling over that already and there would be more tomorrow when the full weight of the situation was recognised by all.

Doll and Roly were now in a position in which they could not afford to let any of the others out of their sight. The cellar with its single staircase and its sunken recess under a grating at the back, which contained no more than a tap and a drain, had become a cage. In it they were safe, at any rate from themselves, but there was no means of sustaining life there, and meanwhile they had a prisoner.

Men who have been manhandled sometimes die, and no one who is hiding from one corpse is anxious to find himself shut up with another. It was a situation horrific to anyone who faced it with imagination, and Doll was by no means deficient in that respect. All the same, he continued his task steadily, giving the nervous eyes which watched him from the wall comfort by his quietude.

Yet behind his deliberate manner he was hurrying. He needed to get the job done before his only ally came back and saw what he was about. The others did not worry. None of them seemed to realise that he was destroying the only valid proof that he was the particular one amongst them who was actually guilty of murder. He knew they were whispering about it, but he understood their limitations. The fearful logic of the law had no place in their emotional thinking. He knew what they believed. They thought they held Tiddy Doll in their hands at last and that any one of them, if he could brace himself to do it, could save his own skin with words and swear his leader's life away. He did not suppose that anyone was contemplating such action yet because he knew that there was not a man amongst them who would not feel more afraid in the world without him than with him. He realised they just thought they could hang him if it came to it, and were taking comfort from the prospect.

He let them get on with it and went on with his destruction, only raising his eyes every now and again to glance at the tin clock propped up on the shelf behind the stove. Yet even Tiddy was not so very clever. Not clever enough. For there had been no mention of the nature of the wound in the paragraph about Duds in the Stop Press column.

He kept his back towards the lonely cot in the corner. The prisoner was very different from all the other witnesses and presented a fearsome problem of his own. As yet the Tiddington man had not made up his mind about him at all. It is one thing to kill casually in the expression of one's natural brutality, but quite another to murder coldly for practical reasons. A thousand country-bred forebears in his blood advised Tiddy Doll most earnestly against that.

He had set himself to finish his boot burning by four at the latest and he achieved it almost to the minute. He threw the last piece of leather into the stove and closed the iron door. The iron horseshoes from the boot heels went to join the studs and nails in his pocket, to be scattered in the street at the earliest convenient opportunity. He glanced down at his feet with satisfaction. They were lightly shod now in a pair of cracked leather pumps which he kept for his leisure hours. He reckoned he was safe, Tiddy did.

At ten minutes after four he began to worry. He did not betray it save by a single longing glance towards the barren ladderway and the savagery of the way he swore at the man who played the cymbals when he began to whine that he was hungry. But half an hour later Tiddy Doll was beginning to sweat, and as though his alarm had had sound, the men by the wall heard it and grew restive, and the complaints became bolder.

Only Tom, brother of Roly, the young soldier who had seen Martin Elginbrodde disintegrate before his eyes and had never been the same again, slept soundly. He lay like a child spread-eagled, with open mouth, and breathed peacefully midway along the restive line.

By a few minutes before five the emotional atmosphere in the cellar had become electric.

"He's gorn. You won't see him no more. He's scarpered and left you, Tiddy." Bill, the effeminate to whom fear was an excitant, spoke with glee from the shadows where he was invisible, but his bed creaked as he bounded up and down on it. "He'll try King's Evidence, you'll see."

Doll turned on him, the muscles of his neck swelling, but he had himself in hand.

"There's many a ruddy fool thought of that and made the last mistake of their lives," he said with comparative mildness. "Them as trusts in the police gets all that's coming to 'em and no error. If you ain't learnt that, you ain't safe to be out of your box."

The man who had carried the cymbals began to cough most horribly.

"I'm empty, gord I'm empty," he complained, choking and retching. "When's the grub coming?"

The demand was echoed with nerve-racking abruptness by the dwarf. His shrill voice was uncontrolled and it jarred and echoed between the high walls.

"Shut up!" The albino's roar was still authoritative. "Do you want me to come across to you, little 'un? Hold yer row. Listen, can't yer?"

He stood waiting, his weak eyes strained to catch the first movement at the top of the stairs, but there was nothing there, no one, only the dark doorway and silence.

"The pull-up on the corner opens at five," whined the man with the cymbals. "I want something out of the kitty to get a bit o' breakfast. I didn't have no supper, Tiddy. You can't starve me."

"Can't I!" The Tiddington man was savage. "Listen, Gutsy, I can stop you ever being 'ungry again. Wait for it, can't yer?"

A step sounded in the passage above and he paused in full flight, the wrath seeping out of him.

"There," he said, his voice hearty with relief, "there, what did I tell yer? Here he is. Here's Roly. What 'appened to you, mate? Got lost?"

The newcomer did not reply immediately. He was descending the stairs very steadily. He had a large grease-soaked newspaper parcel in his arms, but it was not this which occasioned the unwonted caution. Doll met him as he reached the ground and a burst of startled obscenity escaped him.

"Spirits!" he exploded amid the profanity. "You've been down to the all-night boozer in the meat market and bin drinking spirits. You're off your rocker, chum, that's what you are. Off your bloomin' rocker. 'Oo've you been gassing to, eh? 'Oo've you been squealing to?"

He had taken the man by the shirt collar and was shaking him as if he were a branch. In the ordinary way Roly was the only member of the band who was spared this kind of attention from Doll, and in the early days of their association there had been fights between them, but this morning the fisherman was inclined to crumple.

"Stop it," he said briefly. "Nark it, Tiddy. I've not spoke to a soul, I tell you, but I 'ad to go down to the fish-and-fry, didn't I, and I just 'ad one to steady me nerves at the 'ouse next door. I got something to show you, Tiddy. I got something 'ere."

The final announcement was made in an undertone and his sharp-featured face was eager with tremendous news. Doll hesitated. The temptation was great, but once he relaxed, he knew he lost his hold.

"Save it," he commanded, and maintained his superiority. "Give us the grub first. I've got a pair of moaners 'ere." He took the parcel and set it on the table beside a pile of clean greaseproof paper. This was his great refinement and compared with, say, a lace tablecloth in other households. "Now then"—he nodded towards the wall—"you two wot's rumbling, come and get your supper. It's a few hours late and so what? You've got it now."

However, he had underestimated the story. While he was superintending the division of the warm fish, armour-plated in dry fried batter, Roly slid over to Bill. An incautious word flared aloud between them and immediately a flame of interest caught the whole flimsy structure of the company. The half-clad men scrambled over one another to hear. The knot formed again, the whispers gave place to shouts, the hideous quaver of hysteria trembled through the noise, and the mischief was done.

Tiddy Doll reached the centre of the group a second too late. The headlines in the morning paper were too large for even the slowest to miss. They streamed out across the meagre page in that particular assortment of type which in England seems to be reserved for world calamities or ordinary crimes of violence.

KILLER ROAMING LONDON FOG

FAMOUS DOCTOR STRANGLED
THREE DEAD IN OFFICE

Police Cordon Thwarted as Convict Patient Escapes

As the Tiddington man stared at the announcement his face grew swollen and fiery under its translucent skin. Having identified himself with the first statement, the remainder appeared to him to be a fantastic lie, backed, most alarmingly, with the authority of the printed word. He snatched the paper and strode out under the light with it, using his elbows freely as the others dragged about him.

" 'From our special correspondent, London.' " He read each word with equal emphasis, moving his head with the type. " 'At a late hour last night the picked men of London's crack Criminal Investigation Department had to confess that an escaped convict, who is possibly one of the most dangerous criminals this country has ever known, was still ranging the fog-bound streets of their city, possibly with a still crimson knife in his hand. Meanwhile, in a solicitor's office in the western area, three innocent people, one of them a Detective Officer, lay murdered, each, so say experts, butchered with professional skill with an identical weapon. Earlier in the evening, on the other side of the metropolis, in famous Guy's Hospital, the well-loved savant whom men called the Kind Healer, fought gallantly for life. . . .' "

The news story, battling magnificently with too much jam, the laws of libel, and contempt of court, was a work of art of its kind, but to the Suffolk man in the cellar it failed in the first degree and was incomprehensible.

"Knifed?" he bellowed suddenly. " 'Oo said Duds was knifed?"

"No, Tiddy. Look down 'ere. See the pictures?"

It was Bill who flipped the sheet from him with fingers delicate as a woman's and dirty as a monkey's, and turned it down to show the reproduction of two photographs from the police files. Hard lighting and coarse printing had done their worst with them and the result was wooden and meaningless to any but the initiated.

"If you see this man, dial 999 and—take cover," ran the legend above the panel, and underneath in smaller type, "This is the man the police are seeking, Jack Havoc, age 33."

Tiddy Doll remained rigid and Roly began to chatter in his excitement.

"Tiddy don't know 'im. 'E ain't never seen 'im. That's 'im, Tiddy! 'E's changed 'is name like we said 'e would, but that's 'im, that's the Gaffer."

The albino stirred with an effort. "What? That is? That there?"

"Yus. The Gaffer. 'E's changed 'is name."

Tiddy Doll raised a face which wore no expression.

"The Gaffer!" he said, aghast.

"That's right." Roly shook the paper as if he could scatter the words out of it into the other man's mind. " 'E's bin inside, in prison, like Duds told us, but 'e's got out and 'e's done in the M.O. All the dicks in London are after 'im, but they ain't got 'im. That's 'im all right. I knew 'is face as soon as I see it, though the photo's not much like 'im."

The news sank in very slowly, but it got home at last and the revelation had the paradoxical effect of raising the morale of the whole party while it also dispirited it a little. From his shrouded corner Geoffrey could see the change in the very silhouettes which pressed round the three who were doing most of the talking. Roly reached the heart of the matter with his next remark.

"There's only a couple o' lines about Duds, and them's on the back. They don't care about Duds no more. They've got the Gaffer to think about. The streets are full of flatties, but they ain't looking for us. There was a cop outside the door here when I came by the ginger B with the big beezer. He gave me good night same as usual. We're almost in the clear. No one's thinking of us."

"Three others have been slit up," said Bill, who read more easily than the rest when he could keep sufficiently still to do so. "They're on the front page here. Perhaps the dicks think the Gaffer done Duds as well."

Tiddy Doll raised his chin sharply. "And perhaps they're right," he said loudly. He had collected himself, and his forceful personality came into action once more. "So, the Gaffer's bin in jail all the time." There was real bitterness in the observation, regret for a lost illusion. "He didn't get no Treasure."

"How d'you know? How do you know, Tiddy?" Roly was on the defensive. "That's a thing I'd never be too sure of."

"No, he didn't get it." Bill was thoughtful. "It says here he done six years of a maximum sentence for robbery with violence. That means he must have got shopped when we thought he deserted, and that was before the Major got his packet and Tom went queer."

They were digesting this information when the albino took a decision.

"I say that ain't the Gaffer at all," he declared, laying a thick finger on the photographs. "There's no one but a fool would say they was pictures of a man 'e knew. They might be photos of you, Roly. It ain't 'is name underneath. I reckon it's not he."

Bill laughed aloud. "I'd know it was the Gaffer by what he's done, without the pictures." The admiration in the words struck a jarring note in the ears of his new leader, and Doll grew scarlet again.

"I say that's not he," he repeated fiercely. "I say that Gaffer has picked up the Treasure and he's living on it like a lord, and one day we'll come across 'im. As it is, there's this other chap in the paper 'oo must have done poor old Duds in after we left 'im, so the best we can do is to go on like we always 'ave done, taking our money and keeping our eyes open."

As he finished, the snag in this happy programme occurred to him and he glanced over his shoulder towards the bundle on the bed in the corner. The next idea came to him grudgingly. He did not like it. It frightened him. But it came into his mind and he hinted at it under his breath.

"There's no telling what a bloke like this 'ere bloke in the papers might do still," he said.

No one picked him up. At that moment there was a diversion. The prisoner was the first to notice the phenomenon.

From where Geoffrey lay he could see the whole dark arch of the roof, grimy and festooned with cobwebs above the point where the whitewash ended. Now something was happening to the grating through which the news vendor had thrust the evening paper. The irons, lying snugly in a greasy bed of mud in their stone sockets, had been lifted quietly, and through the dark square a pair of legs had appeared. They were elegant legs in well-pressed wide trousers of a pattern very fashionable in certain circles before the war. Suède shoes and bright socks accompanied them, and above there was the suggestion of tweed, thick, buff, expensive coat skirts.

Directly under the grating, which projected into the alley

above, there was a ledge or alcove in the cellar wall. It was thick with the droppings of years, but it provided just enough space for a man to crouch, with the cellar below and in front of him.

Suddenly it was full of colour and smooth movement, and a shower of dust and rubbish floated silently down the white wall.

Everyone in the group round the paper became aware of the intrusion at the same instant. There was a moment of silence, a stunned and timeless pause during which the circle of upturned faces froze into grotesque masks, ludicrous in their astonishment. Then the iron dropped back into place with a thud and the legs kicked out once, as with the grace which belongs to strength alone a man unfolded himself before them. He hung by an arm from the beam in front of the ledge, his feet in their excellent shoes swinging limply two or three yards from the ground. The light fell on him squarely. It found his gay scarf, and the gap of good shirt between his waistcoat and trousers top where his stomach was arched to take his weight, and every man in the cellar saw the tragic face, the forehead on which the coarse hair grew low, and the steady eyes regarding them so boldly as he looked round for men he knew.

Then he dropped lightly to the ground and a smile split a wide thin-lipped cat's mouth in which the teeth were regular and beautiful.

"Dad's back," he said, and his voice was smooth and careful. Only the shadow flitting like a frown across his forehead, and his pallor, which was paperlike, betrayed his weariness. His spirit danced behind his shallow eyes, mocking everything.

TEN
THE LONG SPOON

The silence in the cellar was absolute. No one breathed. Helpless in his far corner, Geoffrey was aware of the tension but by no means clear on the true cause of it. He had not seen the paper and had not been able to catch much of Roly's story. He lifted his head painfully in an effort to see between the men surrounding the newcomer, but he was careful to make no sound.

Inside the circle the stranger was dusting himself down. It was a performance in which he was very much aware of his audience, and yet it was singularly without flourish. All his movements were smooth and economic, but graceful and exciting to see.

He took his time and let them look at him, well aware that he was worth seeing. He was just under six feet, with long bones and sloping shoulders, most of his phenomenal strength in his neck and in the thigh muscles which moved visibly under his sleek pre-war clothes. His beauty, and he possessed a great deal, lay in his hands and face and in the narrow neatness of his feet.

His hands were like a conjurer's, large, masculine, and shapely, the fingers longer than the palms, and the bones very apparent under the thin skin.

His face was remarkable. In feature it was excellent, conventionally handsome and full of drawing, the nose straight and short, the upper lip short also and deeply grooved, the chin round and cleft. His eyes were too full and too flat, but they were a deep bright blue, with very long thick lashes. As much as could be seen of the brown hair under his black beret betrayed an obstinate curl despite the prison cut, and jail pallor, which of all complexions is the most hideous, could not destroy the fineness of his skin.

He was a man who must have been a pretty boy, yet his face could never have been pleasant to look at. Its ruin lay in something quite peculiar, not in an expression only but something integral to the very structure. The man looked like a design for tragedy. Grief and torture and the furies were all there naked, and the eye was repelled even while it was violently attracted. He looked exactly what he was, unsafe. Just now he was very tired and prison had left its mark on him. His clothes had been made for him by a tailor of flamboyant temperament some time in the early thirties; but they were now too loose and there were little scurfy patches on his forehead where the hairline ended.

But he had not lost his grip. Personal magnetism remained glowing in him, as it did in Luke.

He waited for the precise moment when their first shock came to an end and, just as it arrived, nodded casually to the three he recognized.

"Hallo Roly, hallo Bill, hallo Tom. Mind if I take a pew?"

He dropped on to the box at the head of the table where Doll usually sat and, with a grin at the dwarf, took a chipped potato from the little man's sheet of paper and ate it.

"Duds been in yet?" The enquiry was casual. At any rate, he did not wait for an answer but stretched out his long fingers for another potato, laughing when the dwarf, his tongue lolling, shovelled a whole handful towards him nervously.

But to his hearers the words had a superstitious horror. Duds had never seemed so dead. With a warning glance at Roly, Tiddy Doll began to edge backwards towards Geoffrey, while the ex-fisherman burst into nervous disclaimers.

"No, 'e ain't. Duds don't come 'ere, Gaffer. Duds 'as never been 'ere in his life."

"Hasn't he?" Havoc was eating more quickly now, not with any show of eagerness but steadily, shooting out his hand for one grease-sodden strip after another. "I didn't know that. He let me have all the gen on you, of course. That's how I knew where to look you up, actually. Quite a reasonable joint you've got here."

He had an artificial accent, rather more successful than most of the refinements of cockney, the words very carefully if not always correctly enunciated, and spoken as if he were listening to them with pleasure.

"I've not seen him yet." He paused and his mouth split into a smile of sudden and frightening frankness. "I've been on the bash."

The step behind him was light, but he turned so quickly that they all scattered, and Bill, who had been sidling towards him, squealed as he sprang back.

Havoc laughed in his face. "Bill, you damned old iron, don't do that," he said. "I've been under a doctor for my nerves for so long I've begun to believe in them myself. You don't know."

"But we do know, Gaffer. That's what I'm trying to tell you. We do know. We were all reading this when you came in."

Bill laid the limp wreck of the morning paper on the table, his ragged cuff shaking like a fringe round his dirty slender wrist. The sight of it already in their hands was a shock to the newcomer. They realized it at once, but not because he betrayed it. His magnetism faltered for a moment, like a current switched off and on. That was all.

A moment later he had bent forward to take a handful of potatoes from the main parcel and had dropped them on the headlines contemptuously.

"That?" He looked round him. "I've been reading that myself. In fact, I had a copy in my pocket, a cleaner one, more sanitary. Do you remember old Sanitary? Captain Miller? Anyone run into him? He's back inspecting drains for the Council, I suppose."

Bill still hovered. He looked as if he were incapable of getting away and yet fidgeting to do so. He made little thrusting gestures just behind the other man's ear.

"Did you read it all, Gaffer?"

"All that interested me. Go away, Bill."

"Did you read the back page?"

"No. I used the whole paper for a bit of tidying up. I had

something on me that needed cleaning, and when I'd finished
I screwed it up and chucked it into the doorway of a police
station."

It was not true. No one believed it, and yet it impressed
them, as he knew it would.

"You ought to have read it, Gaffer, because there's a bit
about old Duds on it. He's dead. He's been done in. It says
so. Gives 'is real name and everything. 'Is brother-in-law identified 'im."

The ragged man brought out the words in a jumble which
was only just lucid, and stood swaying on his toes playing with
danger.

"Duds?" Again there was the same strange sensation of
shock and faltering power. It was more marked this time and
the man's thick lashes quivered. He pushed the food aside
and turned the paper over. When he looked up he startled
them. "God," he said, "what luck! He did something soft and
it caught him, I suppose." He threw back his head. "Now
what?"

It was a cry which frightened them. All they understood
was that it was a disaster, and if for him, then also for themselves. It was all the more terrifying because until then they
had not realized that they were no longer regarding him objectively. Already he had taken hold of them, swooped them
up and collected them as if they had been a crowd of im-
pressionable girls.

In the far corner, where he had been bending over Geoffrey, Tiddy Doll noticed the reaction and for once he did not
bluster.

Until then he had been quietly busy with his piece of adhesive plaster. He always carried this instrument of torture
about with him because the dwarf was given to noisy tantrums
on occasions and it had been found to be much the easiest
way of dealing with him. Doll had become an adept at its
swift administration, and even now could always take the little
man by surprise. Geoffrey had been neither surprised nor
protesting, but a strong self-preservative sense was keeping
him quiet while he husbanded all the strength he possessed.
He had been in tight corners before, and now had at least
the advantage of recognizing one when he met it.

As Tiddy Doll heard the words and the note in them he bent a little lower over the bed. Geoffrey heard him catch his breath and the little sigh he gave when there was no response.

"When did you lot see Duds last?"

The dangerous question floated across the room and the albino spun round.

"We seen 'im this afternoon," he said promptly. "He come out of the station in Crumb Street and we follered 'im and meant to speak to 'im, but 'e give us the slip."

The lie came out glibly from the corner.

"That's right, ain't it, mates?"

It was the old leader reasserting himself, and they responded at once, relieved at the proffered escape.

"That's right."

" 'E give us the slip."

"Fog was thick just there."

"But we ain't *never* spoken to 'im, Gaffer." Roly could not help adding the information. "We see 'im once in the West End, all togged up, but we ain't *never* spoken to 'im."

"He saw you more often than that." Havoc's weariness was beginning to show in him like a boxer halfway through a prize fight. His eyes were beginning to burn and his face was growing dark with exhaustion. But he had great reserves. "Duds was busy, working for me as a matter of fact. I told you I got all the news from him, indirectly, of course, but I heard all about Tiddy Doll here and Tom's bit of trouble."

The small regular teeth appeared in a smile.

"You've all been looking for me, I hear. 'Living like a lord.' "

Their amazed consternation delighted him. He sat laughing at it, the amusement breaking through the agony in his face.

"You always talked too much, Roly. Sometimes people listen."

" 'Oo give us away?" Tiddy Doll's bewilderment was destroying his caution, and there was a trace of his old bluster in his demand.

The man who sat in his place at the head of the table considered him thoughtfully.

"Your name is Doll and you come from a two-house country town called Tiddington," he remarked pleasantly. "After being rejected on medical grounds from every regimental depot in the East Country, you attached yourself in the middle of the war to the two-stroke-four-oh-oh-nine transit camp at Hintlesham as temporary unpaid hanger-on. After some time your willingness, cleanliness, and talent for organisation got you—God alone knows how—on to the strength, and you even got a stripe. When the war ended you were slung out pronto before anyone noticed you, and you pestered the life out of the officers of your old company until you were reported to the civilian police and were forbidden the district. Do you want to hear any more?"

Doll could not speak. He stood gaping. In Tiddington witchcraft is still spoken of as a commonplace, and the last public burning for the offence took place there something less than one hundred and forty years ago, not a very long time by local standards.

Havoc turned his head away and returned to the others.

"You poor silly blokes," he said, "stamping up and down the streets making a God-awful row. Do you think no one sees you? Every wide boy in the town knows everything there is to know about you. You're no mystery."

The company was startled but on the whole pleased. It may be disconcerting to find that the pool in which one is lurking is under a microscope, but at least it lends one a certain importance. The Tiddington man was shaken, but his pride found some solace. There was one rather important and recent thing about him that this omniscient being did not know. His dark glasses saved him, or Havoc would have seen him wink at Roly.

His momentary superiority gave him dangerous courage.

"There's a slop up 'ere outside the door," he remarked recklessly.

The bright blue eyes rested on him once more. "So what?"

Doll quailed. " 'E 'as a drag up there when 'e ought to be on duty, that's all," he said.

"I know. I gave him a light. I wasn't sure what your arrangements with him were, so I came round the alley and through the letter box."

Doll said nothing but he licked his lips. Roly was more

impressed. His thin face was flushed and he looked younger, more the soldier he once had been.

"You ain't reelly forgot us then, Gaffer?" he said proudly. "We thought you 'ad, me and Bill and Tom. Tom's very funny," he added as a confidential afterthought. "Tom's a little bit don't-understand. I don't reckon 'e knows you."

The tall boy who was still lying on his bed raised his head. "I ain't forgot 'im," he said. "I know you, Gaffer. I know the state you're in. You're like you were that night when you came back to the boat—you know, after you'd done them that time."

The directness of the statement and its simple inference brought the whole terrifying situation into key, as if a casement had swung wide on them. Havoc himself caught the full glare of it. He glanced down at the paper where the headlines were still visible through the grease, and blinked and looked up again.

"Poor old Tom," he said hastily, but the mischief had been done. They were looking at him with daylit eyes. The enormity of his crime was rising slowly through the glamour and reaching fearful proportions as its bright rags fell away. A moment more and he must lose them.

Doll grasped his chance. He sat down at the table and put his elbows on it.

"Listen, Gaffer," he said, "I reckon you didn't come 'ere to find Duds at all. I reckon you come 'ere because you figured we wouldn't see the paper until the morning, and you wanted a quiet lie-down. You've seen your wide boys and you've found that they knew about you, since seemingly they know everything, and you've found out they wouldn't touch you. You've come 'ere because you ain't got nowhere else to go. We ain't much but we've got cover. You've found you made a big mistake when you come out. You didn't know the fighting was over, did you, not reelly, shut up in there? Things 'ave changed since the war. It's bin a shock to you to see that. You're on the run."

The ruthless broadside was annihilating and the ring of truth in it so clear that the most stupid among them could not help but recognise it.

Slowly and gracefully Havoc leant back in his chair. No one

saw any other movement, but as their glances travelled down
from his face to the table they saw that a knife had appeared
in his hand. It had come there as if by magic, or as if it had
grown there, springing from his bony fingertips. It was a com-
bat weapon, sword-bladed and serviceable, with nothing remarkable about it save that it did not look new.

"And again," he said softly, "so what?"

This time there was no power cut, no faltering. He was on
top of himself and them, almost joyous. His excellent phy-
sique, so different from their own, became flaunting and mag-
nificent, and all trace of weariness banished and gone.

"Who moves first? You, Whitey?"

No one stirred an eyelid. There is an odour about genuine
violence, real menace, which tingles in the nostrils with a
pepper which histrionics can never match. There was no
question that the man meant what he said; he was so happy.

"Perhaps you'd like me to give you a demonstration?"

"No, Gaffer, no, no!" Roly was frantic. "No, we've seen
your demonstration. Put it up. Tiddy don't understand, 'e
don't know. 'E don't mean nothing, Tiddy don't. We're with
you, Gaffer, of course we are. Besides, we've got reasons of
our own to think of."

The fatal admission was out before he could stop it.
Havoc's full flat eyes stayed their roving glance and came to
rest on him while the hands grew quiet.

"Oh. Which reasons are those?"

Roly appealed helplessly to Tiddy Doll, expressionless behind his shrouded glasses.

The man from Tiddington made his best effort. He sat solid
and still.

"We've got private affairs, like other people," he said at
last. "We don't want the police round here just now, not on
any account, and that's straight, mister."

There was enough conviction to carry. The man at the end
of the table was impressed. He regarded the albino curiously,
holding his head a little on one side as Luke himself might
have done, his mouth faintly amused.

"Not one of you has got a real record, they tell me," he
remarked at last, "and you don't want to spoil it, eh?"

"It's not a question of records, no, nor of prisons," said

Tiddy presently. "I picked my men and I picked chaps 'oo weren't going to be a nuisance to me. But just lately, only a day or two ago, we 'ad a little accident, so we ain't doing nothing out of the ordinary, not for a week or two." He hesitated and no one knew if his red eyes behind the dark glasses were peering at the little weapon on the table. "We're keeping quiet and keeping ourselves to ourselves like we always do."

Havoc glanced round him with casual arrogance.

"They told me that you were clean in your habits and I hand it you, Corporal. I don't know how you do it."

The inconsequential piece of flattery was an inspiration and the countryman was sidetracked.

"The Queen could eat orf the floor," he said with more enthusiasm than would perhaps have impressed royalty. "We got our rules, and we obey 'em. We got comfort too, and good grub."

The tired hagridden tiger in the good clothes allowed his glance to stray towards an empty cot next to Tom, but he remained a tiger. Doll was feeling his way.

"I ain't chatty, but I'm not funky," he began cautiously. "But I'm not saying we're all quite so strong upstairs." He tapped his forehead significantly. "No names, no pack drill. But you can see for yourself, Gaffer, there's plenty of us to make mistakes."

There was so much truth in what he said that his motive was not obvious. Never had the band looked less reliable or even less human. They were both cowed and excited, and sat round watching the two men as if they were at a show.

There were noises from the market now and, if no actual daylight, for the fog had persisted, the archway leading to the drain was several degrees less black, and there was a faint fluorescent glow on the wall round the "letter box." The city was awake and stretching itself. Very soon now, round warm breakfast tables, families would read the newspapers and from every surrounding police district more and more men, patient and knowledgeable, would come on duty.

Doll sat looking at the table. The knife had gone again. The Gaffer's hands were resting there, his fingers drumming very lightly on the board. Doll did not dare to glance behind him at the bed in the far corner, but he raised his head when Roly's eyes flickered towards it and back again. The idea playing round the cunning country brain was tantalising and the situation, of course, was no less desperate than ever it had been.

Presently he wagged his head towards the stairs.

"That's the only way out."

Jack Havoc watched him with interest. "I know. They told me that. Two ways in, one way out."

Tiddy Doll leant his chin on his hands, probably to prevent himself from clenching them. Far back in the years, in the sunlit church school at Tiddington, where the great twelve-hole privy in the garden and banks of mignonette had fought together to provide the dominant atmosphere, there had been a gaunt old pedagogue who had been as full of sayings as any man Tiddy could remember. One of them in particular had never escaped him:

Who sups with the devil must use a long spoon.

He could see that spoon now in his mind's eye, or one very like it. Iron, it was, hanging up by the brick oven in his great-uncle's cottage. He took a long breath.

"I was thinking, Gaffer, there's enough of us for a bloke to hide among, even in the street, supposing he wanted to get from place to place."

"Your mind works." Havoc was condescending but friendly. "I like that."

"But it would be wonderfully risky, supposing we didn't know what we was doing." The Suffolk accent, soft and broad, was like an apology. There was no more bargaining. Both men were feeling the strain and each understood the other remarkably well.

Havoc stretched himself and when he spoke it was in conscious imitation of the British junior officer in the field.

"I rather think we should have a conference, Corporal, don't you?"

Tiddy Doll sighed and played his master stroke.

"Pick your orficers, Captain," he said.

ELEVEN
THE TIDDINGTON PLAN

At first Geoffrey was the only person to notice Tiddy Doll's peculiar manoeuvre with the conference table. The albino made the arrangement of orange crates with a great deal of ostentatious care, designed, apparently, to ensure that the conspirators would be well away from the rank and file whilst retaining command of the staircase. Yet in fact he seemed to be arranging for the talk to take place so close to the prisoner's bed that the gagged and helpless man must be able to overhear perfectly. It was such an extraordinary mistake for one usually so cautious that Geoffrey was astounded until the diabolical explanation occurred to him. Doll might entertain qualms at the prospect of removing an unwanted witness in cold blood, but Havoc would have none.

The newcomer still sat at the head of the main table, colourful and lonely in the pool of light from the single swinging bulb. From the way they were all treating him he might have been a genuine wild animal sitting up there, fascinating and uncertain. Whenever he forgot them and withdrew into his own agonising thoughts they breathed more comfortably, but for the most part he was irritably aware of every movement, and the strain of having him there was unbearable.

He watched the fussy preparations with growing annoyance and, as usual, it was Roly who precipitated matters. Having noticed what he thought was a serious mistake, he made frantic signals. Havoc caught him and at once the whole interest of the gathering was centered on the bed in the far corner.

"What have you got over there, Corporal?" The languor in the careful voice deceived no one. Doll was ready for it. He had known it must come but had hoped for matters to go a little further first. He made a subservient gesture, bent over the bed to pull the blanket higher, and then bustled the full length of the room. He came round the table so that he stood with his back to the main company, and, setting both palms firmly on the board, leant down to speak confidentially. His dark glasses hid any sign of nervousness and his white head moved close to the dark and stricken face. Only Roly and Billy cared to come up behind him.

"That's our bit of private trouble, Gaffer," he said, lowering his voice to a murmur. "Our little accident I was telling you about. He's spark out, only just breathin'. Bin like that two days and a night now."

The lie brought tremendous comfort to the two men lurking in the background because of the slight mixture of truth which it contained. It seemed to put them in the clear with the Gaffer whilst effectively skating over the delicate matter of Duds. Their admiration for Tiddy became almost affectionate.

"That's right," said Roly.

"Is it?" Doll's angry shrug warned him to keep out. "I figure 'e's goner any time now, and that won't suit nobody. Anyway, 'e's 'armless, Gaffer."

"Who is he? One *of* you?" Havoc sounded as if he were being forced to listen to the troubles of children.

The countryman hesitated. As they would have explained in Tiddington, he felt he was on "the shaky lands."

"No," he said finally. " 'E ain't, more's the pity. 'E's a fellow 'oo was brought down 'ere when 'e was blind drunk. 'E 'ad a bit o' money on 'im and he lorst it, and then 'e turned nasty. We shook 'im up and there 'e is, and that's the gospel truth."

The tale was such an ordinary one that it convinced even the two who knew it to be a lie. To them it appeared to be, as it were, a better truth. Havoc did not question it but he disliked inefficiency.

"Why keep him?" he demanded. "Take him out and stick him in a doorway. In the fog you can't go wrong."

"We know." The albino was humble. "We were going to.

It's my fault we ain't done it yet. I figured 'e'd come round a bit, so we shouldn't 'ave to carry 'im. Now 'e don't look as if he's going to. Besides, we were a bit windy. We didn't know if 'e'd bin missed."

"So that's why one of you went down early to get a paper?"

"That's it, that's it, Gaffer. That's 'ow we come to see your picture." Bill was hopping with delight at the fortuity of the story. "It gives you the creeps, don't it, how it all fits in?"

The flat blue eyes rested on him darkly. "Something has slipped." There was superstition as well as resentment in his voice. "Someone has gone soft. I'm beginning to wonder if it isn't the whole darned town. It's a pity about Duds. I could use him."

"You've got us." Bill was jealous and moved closer. Havoc fanned him away.

"You're right. My God I have! You want us over there, do you, Corporal?" He got up and swaggered across the room, a sound and even splendid animal in every rippling muscle.

In the darkness under the blanket Geoffrey lay still. He had not been able to hear a word of Doll's explanation and had no idea what was going to happen to him as the men trooped over. One thing he did know was that he was helpless. His feet and hands had been numb for some time, and although this meant that his cords no longer burnt him, his legs and arms ached dully and frighteningly, as though they could never regain their use. The gag was nauseating, but he could breathe, for the blanket, although covering his head, was carefully loose about him.

His heart sank when they ignored him and sat down. He had not underestimated Doll.

Havoc sat with his back to the bed, with the albino on his right and the other two on his left. The wide sweep of the cellar lay before him.

"They're quiet because they're windy." Tiddy Doll's voice sounded in the prisoner's ear, it was so close. "They're all right, Gaffer. They don't look much, but I don't want 'em to. I picked 'em for their looks. It's their looks that bring the business. They're all right if handled right."

Havoc made an impatient gesture and Roly intervened nervously.

"You can't tell the Gaffer nothing about men, Tiddy. He could always size a bloke up. That's what we noticed in the Army. There'll be no trouble with our lot, Gaffer, so long as they get their grub."

"That's what I was coming to." Tiddy took over firmly. "It ain't long now before we'll be thinking of a bit of breakfast. Breakfast is important for morale, like they used to say. Usually we all go down to a little place just at the back of the market 'ere. There's an old couple keeps it and they expect us. My idea is we'd better go same as we always do. No one will look at us then, but if we don't turn up people might start thinking. Why don't you come with us? You'd be lorst amongst us if you changed your clothes, and if you wanted to 'ide your face with a bit of bandage, well, there'd be nothing out of the ordinary in that, would there, not amongst us? It could be reccy, a sort of tryout."

"What kind of place?" The smooth voice was interested.

"Small," Doll said quickly, "but there's three doors."

"There's so much steam in the room you can't see across it." Bill giggled self-consciously. He was growing a dreadful new refinement in imitation of the newcomer. "No one there would recognise you. But are you going to trust *us*? That's what it comes to."

"That's what I was coming to," Doll cut in. "The Gaffer's a judge of men, you say. Well, then, 'e'll know I'm right. We all know too much about this 'ere Treasure no one 'as spoke out about yet. We've been thinking of it, for years. The Gaffer 'as shown 'e knows we know. 'Living like a lord,' 'e said. Well, that's what we all want to live like." He made a sudden movement. "We've got to be in on it, Gaffer, ain't we? We've got to be in on it."

"But I always meant that you should." Havoc was graceful even when giving ground. "You can take the place of Duds, Corporal. I always felt that the men who were there ought to share. The rest—"

"I ain't thinking about the rest," said Doll, keeping his voice down. "They'll do what I say, and I'll look after 'em, same as I always do. They'll live like lords' pals," he added sardonically.

"So I imagine." The faint drawl was amused. "I let Roly

into this thing long ago. He and Bill and Tom were with me, serving under me. I chose them."

"That's right, Gaffer. You was never one to let your mates down." Roly spoke with hearty sententiousness and was unprepared for the reaction, which was instant.

"Cut that." There was an alarmed note in the outburst. "Of course I was, and so in any man who isn't mental. I never got taken in by that sort of cant. I chose you because I darned well needed you. I need you again, so I choose you again."

The words slid over one another and the lisping accent of the smarter East End appeared with all its ingratiating warmth. He had become the Big Boy, the Clever Brother.

"You don't often hear me praise myself," he announced, sweeping them into his confidence, "but that's how I've got on, see? I face things. I know that if it didn't suit you to be trusted, I couldn't trust you. You'll hear grown men tell you straight that they trust someone because that person loves them, or thinks they're little tin gods or something. They're mad, aren't they? They're round the bend. Keep your feet on the ground. See straight. That's what I say every time."

All trace of exhaustion seemed to have left him. He was getting energy back, sucking it out of his listeners, apparently, in great vitalising draughts.

"Take the doc who got me out without knowing what he was doing," he went on. "He didn't face the fact that was under his nose and yet he knew. He *knew*, mind you. He said something one day which made me stare. He said, 'Oh, I see, Havoc. You believe with one of our great Prime Ministers that interest never lies.' You could have knocked me down! He knew it and then he couldn't see it. Naturally he had to pay, didn't he? He was asking for it. It wasn't me. I was only giving him what was coming to him."

Only the man from Tiddington understood what he was saying and he did not like it.

"That's sense," he said cautiously. "As long as it's worth my while to go along with you I'll go along. That's me, Gaffer. That's fair."

"It's the living truth," said Havoc. "You can forget the fairness."

"Did you see the stuff, Gaffer?" Despite himself, Roly

could not keep quiet. "You never said. Did you see the stuff all lying there?"

The immemorial romance of treasure-trove, gold in bars and jewels in bucketfuls spilling out over a cave, shone out of his ridiculous mind in glorious technicolour.

Havoc clicked his tongue against his teeth.

"You sound like a kid dreaming of ice cream," he said. "No, of course I didn't see it. It was well hidden. That's why it's still there waiting for us, if we can pick it up quickly. Listen, this is what happened on the raid. After we'd done the job we were alone, Elginbrodde and me, in the house. The orders were that I was to do the necessary and he was to verify they were dead. He didn't like it, he wasn't that sort. He'd had his mind filled up with all sorts of fancy stuff the world has never had time for. He wasn't yellow, but he hadn't got what I have and wasn't expected to have. He got me into the house and made the reccy, and I went into the bedroom and did the job while he waited. When I came out he went in. He came back white as a paper bag, but quiet, as he always was, and gave me the okay. We had one or two other things to do, and when they were done instructions were that we were to come out at once and get back to you on the beach before anyone came up the road. It was dead quiet. You could have heard a petrol engine coming five miles away. When we reached the little garden behind the house he stopped me."

As he listened, Geoffrey caught some of the stillness of the spring night, the scent of the herbs in the little French close, the noise of the sea, soothing and forever, and behind the two in the bedroom, still warm, the dreadful necessary thing.

The re-created atmosphere was all the more startling because Havoc had not found it terrible. It was his absence of emotion, his impersonal picture of the appalled young officer carrying out orders with a perfect but unfeeling weapon, as it were a living knife, which produced the horrific effect.

Havoc was still talking. "Elginbrodde said to me, 'Keep a lookout a minute, will you, Sergeant? I just want to have a squint at something to see it's still all right.' He left me standing there, but presently I saw where he was from a glim from his pencil-torch. He had gone into a sort of stone hut there was by the wall. I went after him, naturally, because I didn't want to miss anything. The way he'd spoken had interested me, see? There he was, letting the little light spot over the stone. The place was empty as a poor box. He told me afterwards it was an icehouse, a thing they had before fridges to keep the food in. It was just a bare hole with a decorated drain running through it, and a garden image at one end of that. There was nothing else, so I said, 'They've got it, sir, have they?' He laughed. I just saw his teeth before the light went out. And he said, 'No, it's safe, thank God. They'll never find it now unless there's a direct hit, and then it'll hardly matter.' "

"But he brought some of the stuff." Roly's anxiety was pathetic. "He give us all a Souvenir. Don't you remember, Gaffer? 'E give us each—"

"That was from the house." The voice was smoothing. "We'd got to make the Jerry think it was a burglary. That was the big idea. No one was to know it was enemy action. It was to look like a civvy job. The place was full of lovely stuff, so I knew that if there was something hidden it must be damned well worth hiding. We just made a mess and cleared the gilt cabinets in the front room. Some of the bits Elginbrodde kept for you chaps, and we chucked the rest in the hedge. I kept one or two, but we were practically naked and we'd got to get back down that ruddy rock face."

"You was a long time getting back." Roly's resentment sounded across the years.

"Of course we were. But that's how I came to know what I do. If you've forgotten the moon, I haven't. One minute the sky was like a feather bed and the next the blasted lamp shone out like a searchlight, and there was me and Elginbrodde on the brow of the cliff looking like a couple of lighthouses ourselves. We dropped and lay there. There was nothing for it but to wait. Elginbrodde kept thinking he heard a car coming up the lane. It was his windiness which made him talk. I saw I could handle him and I started asking him about the icehouse.

" 'What have you got down the well, sir?' I said. 'The family plate?' He shook me. He wasn't thinking of me as another man at all, see? I was just his chap, an object he'd got to get back safely. It made him talk to me as if I was his rifle or something. 'No, Sergeant,' he said, 'that's the Santa Deal treasure there, and it's still all right. I didn't know about it until I was twenty-one or I'd have got it out of the country. By then it was just too late, and I had to hide it. I'm the last of us. No one knows now but I.' I did my best to make him repeat the name, but he wouldn't. It sounded like a ship's treasure to me."

The secret of a ship's treasure handed down in a wealthy family to an orphan boy at twenty-one, technicolour was inadequate for that fantasy. It lit up the cellar with a radiance which was more enchanting than moonlight itself. Roly was past speech and Doll's mouth dry.

From the street above, the sounds from the market were beginning to float down to them. The men on the other side of the room fidgeted a little but they did not move. Havoc's murmur, forceful with the weight of six years' dreaming, held his listeners spellbound.

"Then I asked him what was going to happen if he got hit. 'In that case it stays there forever, I suppose?' I said."

"What did he say?" Roly was trembling.

"He said the damnedest thing I ever heard a man say. He said, 'Then it'll be up to the man my wife marries. I've left full instructions in a sealed envelope, and he'll get it on his wedding day. She couldn't manage it alone, but she'll choose someone like me, always.' "

Lying on the sacks, his head not three feet from the speaker, Geoffrey felt his heart turn over slowly and painfully in his side.

This was the key. He heard the incredulous rumble from the others, like mutterings from another world, but he had recognised the unmistakable ring of truth in the reported words. Of course that was what Elginbrodde had done. When one knew Meg and old Avril, one realised that it was the only thing he could do. Moreover, it was exactly the bold, simple, but unobvious step which in similar circumstances he must have taken himself.

He found this so amazing that his own predicament with all its danger was temporarily eclipsed. Elginbrodde had been so right. The more he heard about him, the more evident that became. They were alike, both the same old mixture, practical but imaginative, conventional but ready to take a chance. All the jealousy Geoffrey had ever felt for Martin flared up to its highest peak in a searing sweep, and died outright like an exhausted flame. He felt freed of it suddenly, as Meg became, mysteriously, entirely his own.

Meanwhile, his immediate danger was becoming more acute. Havoc was growing practical.

"Now," he was saying, "keep steady. I've been working on this and so far I've done absolutely nothing I didn't mean to if it came to it. I arranged with myself that I'd go about it just as we went about the raid, good planning, good organisation, and unhesitating execution. Those are the things which don't fail. No softness, no funking, and no witnesses. The first thing to do is to get the envelope Elginbrodde left. That's vital. The raid was a top-secret job. None of us knew where we went, except Elginbrodde, and you could have crucified him before he'd have told you. We thought it was France, but it might have been anywhere along the whole west coast of Europe. We've got to have the exact location of the house, and the position of the stuff in the house. There'll be legal documents, too, papers giving the bearer permission to take the stuff away. Elginbrodde will have thought of that. He wanted his wife's new bloke to get it without any trouble. That was his whole idea. Once I hold those documents, the foreign police'll be on our side. They'll help us shift it, if necessary. We want the lot, don't we, not a handful each?"

Tiddy Doll sat motionless, his chin raised, the dark glasses hiding any expression in his eyes.

" 'Oo'd Major Elginbrodde give the letter to?" he said at last. " 'Is wife?"

"No. She'd open it. Any woman would. I didn't worry about that. I made certain he'd leave it with his lawyers."

It was the first time the word had been mentioned and at once the atmosphere became tense. Doll wet his lips.

"You went to their office tonight to see, didn't yer?"

"Yes." The drawl had returned to the overcareful voice. "I always meant to do that. As soon as I'd seen a contact of mine and changed my clothes, I went down there." Havoc paused and in the respite Tiddy Doll did a terrifying thing. He slid out a foot and kicked the bed on which Geoffrey lay. He did it very stealthily, but it was a definite movement guaranteed to call the occupant's attention to anything about to be said.

"That's where you went on the bash, ain't it, Gaffer?" he prompted gently.

"Yes. No interference allowed, that was the rule I made."

There was silence at the conference table and after a long time Doll spoke uneasily. Now that the dream which had kept him going for so long was becoming a reality, it was losing its comfort, and his resolution wavered.

"What makes you so certain the stuff's going to be there after all this time, Gaffer?" he asked.

"Because it's waiting for me." The conviction in the tone was absolute and it impressed them. "I'm meant to find it. I knew that as soon as I heard of it, that night on the cliffs." He laughed softly. "You won't understand this, but I'll tell you. Elginbrodde had to confide in me, and probably the blasted moon had to come out just at that moment to make him do it. We *had* to go on the trip together in the first place, and you can tell that's true by the queer way it happened. I was special, see? There were half a million other sergeants in the Army who might have been chosen, but they had to find me for the job, and do you know how they did it?"

He drew them closer to him, pouring out the essence of his belief into their uneasy ears.

"You've never heard of a Hollerith, have you? It was a thing they had in the Army, based on an American business invention. I can't explain it to you, but it was a great room-sized machine, like a glorified cash register, I've heard. They decided on the things they wanted in a chap—athletic, combat-trained, been in a few scrapes, reckless, able to climb and if necessary carry someone who couldn't, age twenty-six, not particular, not known to have a family or a woman, good with men, or anything else they thought of right down to the colour of his eyes. Then they pressed all the buttons and up came his card with his name and number on it. If there were two or three chaps there were two or three cards. Sound like magic to you, Corporal?"

It sounded like something else to the man from Tiddington. He licked his dry lips.

"Go on, Gaffer."

"I was found by that machine," said Havoc earnestly. "Mine was the only card that turned up, and do you know where I was? I was under guard waiting for court-martial. It was looking as though I'd come really unstuck at last. But suddenly I was fetched out, all forgiven, rank restored, allowed to volunteer, trained and paired with Elginbrodde. They wanted *me*. I was the one. It was a tricky time and they were in a jam and I appeared."

He leant back on his box and Geoffrey's bed shook a little as he touched it.

"You'll say there's nothing in that," he went on. "What's a straight invention by a scientist? But the rest isn't. While I was training with Elginbrodde I took the trouble to enquire about him, and do you know what I found? I found I knew the people he knew, and that he was a man I could always keep my eye on. He was the one and only officer in the whole Army who I was in a position to watch all the time. I knew someone who was close to him, see? And they were as close to me as anyone has ever been. That's why, as soon as he spoke to me on the cliff, I knew that what he said was important to me and part of my life."

He waited for their reaction and when they merely shuffled uncomfortably he laughed again.

"I told you you'd never understand it. It's when you're alone hour after hour in a cell like a monk that you see these things. To you it sounds like a coincidence, but there aren't any coincidences, only opportunities. Keep your feet on the ground and you'll see that."

"Sounds like a religion to me," said Bill, and he giggled because he was thrilled and drawn by the emotion ruffling the smooth voice.

Havoc regarded him sombrely. "Religion nuts! This is the thing religion goes soft on. Call it the Science of Luck, that's my name for it. There's only two rules in it: watch all the time and never do the soft thing. I've stuck to that and it's given me power."

"That's right, Gaffer, you've got power all right." Doll spoke hurriedly. He knew men were often a little queer when they came out after a long prison term, but he was frightened all the same. "You've been able to watch Elginbrodde's wife while you was inside?"

"Of course I have. I've watched you all. You can hear more in stir than you can out if you give your mind to it. I got all the information I wanted in, and all the orders I had to give out. I knew she was going to marry again two days before the engagement was announced."

"Married again?" This was news to them all, and Roly sat back, ludicrous horror on his sharp-featured face. "You're not tellin' us she's done it? The new feller ain't got the envelope?"

"No. He doesn't know about it yet, but he will, and that's the hurry. When I got the news I couldn't make my break immediately. The doc I was working on was showing interest, but he wasn't ripe, so I got the word out to Duds and he's been doing the stunt which we arranged if ever this should happen when I was inside. It was a beautiful idea and it was working like a dream. My contact expected the wedding would be called off, but now Duds has come unstuck. He did something soft or it wouldn't have happened. Duds *was* soft. He got us shopped last time because he wouldn't stick a man he'd been drinking with. We had to wait for another, and by that time the luck had changed. I don't know what he did this time. Perhaps the girl's new bloke got him."

So it had come. Geoffrey waited for the next words with the stabbing pain of fear taking his breath away. One of the three *must* put two and two together now.

But when Doll spoke his mind was still on the envelope, that magic Open Sesame which would unlock the cave.

"And it weren't at the lawyers'?" he said thoughtfully.

"No. I'd made so sure of that." Havoc sounded introspective, as if he were searching for some flaw which could account for his lack of success. Bright eyes like rats' eyes were watching him from the further wall. The men had their coats on and sat hugging their wretched instruments, waiting for breakfast and the new day.

"I shall get it, though," he said. "I tried one other place tonight. It was an address I had given me when I got out. My contact had it ready for me. I went to the new bloke's house, the one he's getting ready to take the girl to when he marries her. It was no good, though. They hadn't moved in properly.

There weren't any papers in the place at all." He laughed abruptly. "I nearly walked into trouble there. I saw a busy outside, but I took the risk and went on in. I thought I had plenty of time with the fog so thick, but they must have been waiting for his call, for they came along in strength, and I had to jump for it. There was someone in the house, too. A woman. I smelled her face powder."

Geoffrey's scalp was crawling and his lips moved helplessly against the gag.

"She couldn't have seen me," Havoc was saying. "She was out on the stairs when I was in one of the rooms. I didn't waste any time on her. It wasn't because I went soft. The police cars had turned up by the time I noticed her, and I had to slip off."

"It must have been 'er." Roly spoke in a whisper, as if he were himself hiding in a surrounded house. "It must 'ave been the Major's widow 'erself. There ain't no servant girls now, Gaffer. All that's been done away with while you was inside."

"What?" The question sounded appalled. The unexpectedness of its passion startled them all.

"It was 'er," Roly repeated. "Must 'ave been. Now if you 'ad only woodened 'er, we'd have 'ad all the time in the world," he added weakly.

"I didn't know." Havoc's voice grew high. "I tell you I didn't know. I did like the smell of the powder, but I didn't know."

"That ain't sense, Gaffer, and you know it." Tiddy Doll's intervention was instinctive. He alone recognised Havoc's superstition for what it was and he dragged the man back to solid ground. "What I want to ask is, why was the busy outside the new bloke's 'ouse at all? Did this private contact you keep talking about tip the p'lice orf? Or did one of their dicks spot you was after something of Elginbrodde's when you was at the lawyers'? If so, p'raps they've stopped all the gaps in the hedge."

The direct questions brought an answer which startled everybody.

"Do you know you're not the first person to say that to me tonight, Corporal?"

Tiddy Doll nodded and the light played on his black glasses, emphasising their secretiveness.

"That's the reason your wide-boy friends won't give you no help, Gaffer," he said earnestly. "That's why you 'ad to come to us, who ain't much bottle. You went wild at the lawyers'. You didn't even wear gloves."

"Of course I wore gloves."

"You didn't, you know." Tiddy was wagging his great head. "That was a habit you got out of in the war. It was such an ordinary habit that it went clean out of your mind. You knifed three people at the lawyers' tonight just because they'd seen and might recognise you, and yet you went and left your signature all over the shop. You ain't gone soft tonight, Gaffer, you've gone wild."

There was silence as he finished speaking. Havoc's cold thrill of realisation was so acute that they all felt it. His shock of self-discovery touched them like a draught. Tiddy Doll was merciless.

"It was all in the paper. You couldn't 'ave read it, Gaffer, not like we did." His tone was smug and mocking. He was trying to make the man angry, prodding him, cutting the ground round him like a fighter tormenting a bull.

They were all aware of it, but only the prisoner, helpless behind him, realised its purpose.

"You'll 'ave to stick to your rule now, won't you, Gaffer?" Doll was breathing hard, his blank eyes turned towards the dark unhappy face. "No interference, that's what you said. As you've started, so you'll 'ave to go on."

"Tiddy!" Roly could bear the strain no longer. "You've gorn out of your mind, mate. Shut up, can't yer?"

"But he's dead right." The voice, which was no longer smooth, broke into the quarrel. "He's right. I ought to have worn gloves, and I ought to have seen to the woman in Levett's new house, whoever she was. I—"

" 'Oose 'ouse?" Tiddy Doll forgot every other consideration as the name hit him in the face. " 'Oose, did you say?"

"Geoffrey Levett's." Havoc's suspicion flared and he swung round, ready to see some deep and terrible significance in the slightest of coincidences. "Levett. He's the new bloke. He's the one the envelope is to go to. Why? Speak up, Corporal. Why? Have you ever heard that name before?"

TWELVE
OFFICIAL ACTION

Meanwhile, just above in the street market, the early fish queue, damp as its quarry, struggled out of the gutter and on to the pavement. It was a long ragged line and it idled in the path of the carters carrying sacks into the greengrocer's, apologised good-temperedly, and obstructed again.

This morning the fog was thicker than ever. Twenty-four hours of city vapours had given it body and bouquet, and its chill was spiteful.

The "few words" which were to develop so quickly into a full-sized street row began inside a shop. The owner was a stout woman who had draped herself in quite a dozen knitted garments, each one visible at least in part, but she was still cold and irritable. She spoke her mind to two men who had just confronted her with a polite request.

"But we've *been* measured," she protested. "We was done last week. I don't care if you're the Government or the whole bally Lord Mayor's Show, we've *been* measured for the rates. If they go up again I can't pay them. You'd think Hitler had *won*, the way you carry on."

Her strong voice echoed clearly through the unglazed window and a small man in the queue spat casually into the gutter.

"Say Russia," he remarked succinctly.

"This 'ere Jack 'Avoc ain't no Russian," remarked the fishmonger, half overhearing as he slapped a piece of plaice into the open newspaper which an old woman held out for him.

"He's home produce, like what this is. Run along, Ma, and read all about it by the fire. 'Ave a warm for me."

In the shop the woman was still grumbling. "I'm sick and tired of officials. All over the house they went, only last week."

The taller of her two visitors, a thin mild-looking person who had changed his horn-rims for Health Service issue spectacles for the occasion, regarded her anxiously. Mr. Campion's position was delicate. He had been forced into making the enquiry without police aid, since he was still half convinced that Levett was engaged on some misguided business of his own. This had involved getting the band's address from some very unofficial quarters, and now that at last he had it, it proved to be unspecific. He had understood that the entrance to the cellar was through the back of the shop. He was regretting that he had chosen to introduce himself as a surveyor from the rating authority, but his chief worry was a sudden premonition that urgency was vitally important.

He glanced at his companion, and Mr. Lugg, impressively immense in mackintosh and derby, took it for an invitation to assist. He thrust a sheaf of old income-tax forms at the lady.

"You can't be awkward, not with a dear old lovely face like you've got," he began with somewhat heavy gallantry. "You're goin' to be 'elpful, my dear, that's what you are."

"Reelly?" She sounded unconvinced. "You leave me face alone. I've 'ad it all me life and I don't want to 'ear about it. Go on, push off. Go and measure next door."

Mr. Campion coughed. "It's the cellar, ma'am," he began in a confidential tone. "Our people made a slip and forgot to enter the measurements of the cellar, so we've had to send down again."

"Wasting my taxes! Two of you to measure a cellar. No. I won't give you the key. It's not my place to. My tenants leave their key with me when they go out to work. There it is, hanging on the wall. You touch it and I'll call the cops." She paused blankly and they all stood looking at a large and naked nail sticking out of the green match-boarding of the wall. "It's gorn . . ." she exclaimed. "Who's took it?" and turned on Lugg, bristling with suspicion.

The fat man, taken by surprise, was very hurt.

"Search me, missus."

"I might if I had the time." Her bright eyes, small and dark as his own, took in his great bulk with wicked amusement. "What are you carrying about with you? The dome of St. Paul's?"

"Ho! Who's talking, eh?" As the insult went home he forgot all caution. "Margot Fonteyn of the Covent Garden Ballet, I suppose."

It was absurd. The purely cockney quarrel, personal and infantile, flared in an instant. Her woollen bosom swelled, her face grew plum-coloured, and she raised an earth-stained hand to cuff him. Then, restraining herself as something better occurred to her, she leant out over a pile of gleaming oranges and shouted "Police!" at the top of her voice.

To her intense embarrassment a constable heard her. He was immediately outside the shop, his smooth blue back not a yard away. Moreover, he was delighted to attend to her, for while the argument in the shop had been taking place, a second and much more noisy clash had occurred in the queue. It had begun with an unlikely argument on the probability of Jack Havoc turning out to have originated in eastern Europe, and had blazed into flame when a fuzzy-haired woman with an educated accent and humourless eyes had taken exception to the word "Russian" being used as a term of disparagement. She spoke fluently and loudly but not very pertinently, whereupon the fishmonger, affronted at hearing himself described as a "futile little bourgeois," an epithet of which he only perfectly comprehended the tone and the initial letters, turned savagely upon her and called her "a bloodstained Bolshevik conscientious objector" to her face.

Instantly, as at a signal, everyone within earshot began to air his own strongest views upon the subject nearest to his heart, and the policeman strode over from his corner.

This officer was not a young man. His gingery hair was thinning and he was tired after a long cold night. His mere presence did not quieten the row as it ought to have done, and his warning " 'Ere 'ere 'ere" stood in danger of being ignored.

He was relieved, therefore, when the cry behind him from

enclosed premises made his duty both plain and comparatively peaceful. He turned at once and stepped into the shop.

"Now then, now then, what's going on here?" His powerful voice reached the queue easily, and the words, promising an interesting diversion, worked the charm which had misfired before. The shouting group round the barrow behaved like a howling child who suddenly perceives a sweet. It ceased its noise abruptly and pressed hopefully after him.

The shopkeeper was overwhelmed by the sudden limelight. Her anger vanished and she became reasonable, if over-anxious to justify herself. Her explanations were voluble but perfectly clear. When she had done, the constable glanced from the officials to the nail.

"What gives you the idea the key's lost at all?" he enquired placidly. "Are they out yet? I've not seen them go by."

This was altogether too much of an anticlimax. The woman's hand flew to her heart with the easy histrionics of her kind.

"And it's past nine! Oh my gord, Officer, that stove! I've warned them time and again. I saw a bit in the paper once. A whole family dead in the morning, suffocated from a coke stove just like that."

She had the actor's gift; the clear visual image was projected with a minimum of words. Her audience was startled and pleased. Everybody knew the band at least by sight, and the prospect of the whole ramshackle troupe asphyxiated by fumes in a tomb immediately beneath their feet was sufficient to thrill even the most blasé. Even the constable was impressed.

"Don't say that, mother, don't," he protested. "Much more likely having a lay-in. I don't blame them on a morning like this."

Mr. Campion saw his chance. "All the same," he said firmly, "I think you'd be justified in looking, Officer," and added in the confidential whisper of one servant of the state to another, "I ought just to run a tape over the place if I could."

The constable hesitated. It was not a district in which visitors were appreciated and he still had some time to serve in it. On the other hand, his ears had already caught the whisper hissing through the fog behind them.

"Twenty of them, laid out like sheep. Just like an air raid. Dial 999."

"I can't admit you, you know that," he muttered to Campion, "but if you was to follow me I don't suppose I should stop you."

He turned on his heel and they went after him, the crowd making room for them at first and then streaming behind.

Down in the cellar Tiddy Doll had just thrust back his box and clattered to his feet. Havoc was leaning towards him, his strange eyes dark with eagerness as he waited to hear of some new coincidence which would lend proof to his terrifying philosophy.

"Have you? Have you heard the name before?"

Doll was speechless, but his mind was working. The staggering success of his plan was overwhelming. The awkward witness behind him was as good as dead already. But there was one little difficulty to be overcome first. If the Gaffer should decide to talk to Geoffrey Levett before he settled him—and he very well might in the circumstances—the dangerous subject of Duds was certain to arise. He glanced nervously at the other two and saw to his relief that the name had not registered on them; although they had heard it recently, it had not made any impression.

He was still standing there, hesitating, feeling round for the safest lie, when the street door gave easily under the constable's pressure and the passage became a sounding board for thundering feet as the crowd streamed into it. At the same time, the second door at the top of the stairs swung slowly open before the inrush of air, and every man in the cellar save one sprang to his feet and stared upward.

A policeman in uniform, two officials in regulation raincoats, and a crowd of chattering, jostling members of the general public stood swaying at the top of the steps. They made no attempt to descend, but simply stood there looking down.

In the first frozen second Tiddy Doll felt his arms gripped from behind by hands whose strength was a revelation to him. He was moved bodily, as if he had no weight, and was set squarely between Havoc and the newcomers. He was being used as a shield and would be treated as ruthlessly as if he were nothing more. The discovery steadied him as nothing else would have done, and he kept his head and rose to the occasion.

" 'Ullo?" His voice rang out, clear and belligerent. "What d'you want? We're all at 'ome."

He might have succeeded, got clean away with it. The constable was already muttering apology, but the band was not made of their leader's metal. As the first moment of stupefaction passed, the line across the further wall began to heave and waver. The dwarf emitted one of his hysterical tirades and the whole feckless rabble surged forward into the body of the room like a crumbling barricade.

The constable, who was bewildered by the commotion, turned back again. Havoc loosed his hold. He was looking towards the grating high up in the far ceiling. As a jump it was impossible, even for a tiger, and the panic of the man reached Doll like a wave of icy air behind him. The albino began to roar at his people, forcing his authority upon them as he had done a thousand times before. His voice was like a sergeant major's and the brutal strength of his personality tremendous.

"Form up! Line up, can't yer? Because you've overslept there's no need to panic. The grub will still be there. Got your moosic? I can't wait all day. Look alive."

The dwarf scuttered past him, shouting shrilly in his excitement. Doll thrust out an arm and, catching the little man by the back of his clothes, lifted him bodily from the ground and thrust him behind him to Havoc.

" 'Ere, you carry 'em acrost your shoulders, mate," he said at the top of his voice. "We'll lose 'im in the smoke if 'e runs behind."

The long hands seized him and with a final yelp the little man subsided as he was swung up into his favorite position high above the heads of his persecutors. Doll could have offered his leader no better disguise, for naturally all eyes turned on the mannikin rather than on his steed.

Meanwhile, the man with the cymbals was already on the stairs and Doll strode forward and looked up, his dark glasses peering blankly at the intruders.

"We're just goin' out to have a bit o' breakfast," he announced. "Any objections?"

The constable, who had only remained so long because the pressure of the crowd behind him had made retreat impossible, waved him up without attempting an explanation, and concentrated on clearing a gangway. His helmeted figure retreated slowly and his voice came back to them hollowly.

"Outside, please! You are on enclosed premises. Outside! Hurry along there, hurry along."

Only the men in the raincoats did not retreat and presently the thinner of the two put a foot on the first step down. Doll did not like the look of him at all and addressed him from the ground, mistrusting his silence profoundly.

"We're coming up if you *don't* mind," he shouted warningly. He hoped to get rid of him and to retain possession of the cellar, but once again his own people frustrated him. At his words, the stream pressed round and past him up the stairs. "What d'you want?" he shouted again, and Campion was forced to look at him. As his glance left the line the dwarf, his head towering above the rest and his little hands clutching the lower part of the face of the man who carried him, swept by among the others and out into the passage. Doll came hurrying up last of all. This was disaster, and he alone seemed aware of it. He had no time to listen to the intruders. At the first word, when he discovered that they were not plainclothes men, his interest in them vanished abruptly. The Gaffer was too far ahead as it was. He could just see the dwarf silhouetted against a murky square of light which was the open doorway to the street. If he lost him now he lost him forever, and everything else besides.

He thrust past Lugg savagely. "I can't 'elp you," he said over his shoulder. "Can't 'elp you at all," and he sped out into the fog after the band.

Mr. Lugg recovered his balance with difficulty and turned to his companion, his small black eyes as wide open as nature would permit.

"Blimey!" he said. "What d'you know about that?"

"Not enough." Campion was already descending the stairs. "I don't care for it at all, do you?"

Lugg caught up with him as he reached the ground. Then

they stood gazing round the tousled room where the dying stove stood open and the yellow light still burned. Its habitual neatness was still noticeable under the present disorder, and a cabolic-flavoured cleanliness struck them both. Lugg pushed his hard hat on to the back of his head.

"Mr. Levett wasn't with 'em, cock," he said, keeping his voice down for no specific reason. "I took a good decko at each one as they passed. What a circus, eh? Musical menagerie and no error."

"Did you see the man who carried the dwarf?"

"Bloke in a beret? No, not reelly, but it wasn't 'im. Too tall. What's the big idea?"

"I missed him. The albino meant me to. I wonder why." Campion moved down the line of beds, stripping any suspicious-looking humps among the blankets. He worked with the peculiar thoroughness of one who is afraid of what he may find, but in spite of his care he might have missed the couch in the far corner. The "conference table" and its nest of crates pale in the shadows had been left in a disorder ' which hid the bundle swaddled in its dark blanket, and one box had been thrown on top of it by the resourceful Roly.

Having glanced into the alcove and peered into the recess under the stairs, Campion lifted his head.

"Geoff!" he called aloud on impulse. "Geoff, where are you?"

His voice, characteristic as his horn-rims and pale face, echoed round the vast dim room still warm with the breath of the company which had fled from it.

The two stood listening, and from the open doorway above the clatter of the traffic and the patter of feet on the pavement came floating down to them profitlessly. Then they heard it. It was not very loud, a stifled snort from the corner. And then, slowly, as the man on the bed heaved himself with an effort which tore his cramped muscles, the box on top of him tipped up, wobbled, and toppled on to the bricks.

THIRTEEN
THE CUSTODIAN

When Mr. Campion telephoned Meg from the Crumb Street police station where Geoffrey had been taken to make his statement, she went down there at once. And just before four, on an afternoon of midnight gloom when rain had begun to drizzle through the fog and even Londoners were beginning to wonder why their ancestors had built a city in a marsh, she rang the rectory back and Sam Drummock took the call.

By that time the old journalist had got things organised. With the slightly theatrical efficiency of his great profession, he had rearranged his living room, disconnected all the other telephones in the house, and set up as a newsroom, general information bureau, and hub of family affairs.

He was also writing his piece, an article for a sporting weekly for which the copy had become mysteriously overdue, and his portable typewriter, which had historic associations and had been to the Peace Conference at Versailles, shared pride of place with the phone and his tankard on the kitchen table which Mrs. Sam had loaned him so reluctantly. He was working like a slave, handling police, press, and anxious acquaintances each with the same terse politeness, forgetting nothing, revealing nothing, and enjoying himself as much as ever in his life.

Emily Talisman was his runner, potboy, and audience. Without her, the performance might have possessed an element of sadness, but so long as she sat there, silent on a piano stool, her long hair scraped back under a snood and her bare legs wound round the knobbly column of her pedestal, and watched him with the absorbed attention of worship, the exasperating task never lost its glamour.

Meg was talking for a long time. Emily could hear her voice, squeaky and artificial, the sort of voice a toy might talk in, from where she sat on the other side of the room, but she could not hear the words. She did not mind. She was watching Sam. He said very little. Magnificently collarless, his powerful forearms exposed, and the light glistening on his bald head, he sprawled across the table, notebook at his side. Emily knew it was exciting news because one of his small fat feet waggled in its soft red slipper, but outwardly he was superbly, calm and laconic.

"Aye," he said at intervals, scribbling busily with a pencil as thick as a thumb, "aye, I've got that. . . . Get away! You don't mean it . . . I see, go on."

It was tantalising, but the child did not stir, indeed she hardly breathed. Her wide-eyed stare never left his face.

"Right," he said at last. "Leave it to uz. . . . Steady, my old Queen, steady. Don't you worry. It's as good as done. . . . I'll tell 'em. Leave it to Sam. . . . The lad's all right though, is he? That's all that matters. . . . Thank God for that. . . . Right. In half an hour. Good-bye, love."

He hung up and, wriggling back on to his chair, pushed his glasses up on his forehead and looked at the child. He was thinking out something very difficult. Emily recognised the lively intelligence in the back of his round brown eyes. Something was worrying him. He was making a great decision, as he had to from time to time. She was most careful not to disturb him. He was always so right, was Uncle Sam, if only you gave him time. She loved him very much.

Presently she saw him thrust the worry aside and come out of his thought to meet her.

"Now, pardner," he said. They were both great readers of Westerns and in times of stress the phraseology of the prairie was liable to creep into their conversation. "Cut down to your Grannie and tell her—— No. We'd better make the thing official. We don't want any accidents."

He began to write in a large schoolboy hand, amplifying the note aloud as he did so.

"Mrs. Elginbrodde and her young man and a couple of police big-wigs, and maybe more, will be coming round in half an hour. Albert will be there. Got that?"

She nodded, her thin hand held out for the paper, her lank gold hair falling on his shoulder, her breath sweet on his cheek.

"And Geoff will want a bath, a good hot one. Meg's insisted on that. Oh, she's a grand girl, my old Queen. They couldn't shut her oop, I'll lay a pound. She's looking after her man as she ought, so she's going to be happy. Tell your Grannie that they'll all be hungry, and as you go by ask my old darling if there's no money in the kitchen box, I've got some. Don't bother Miss Warburton, whatever you do. We've got enough trouble as it is. See?"

He ripped the sheet from his book. It bore the uncompromising legend: "Meg, Geoff, police, Albert. BATH. Food. BEER. Half an hour." "Just give that to the old lady with my compliments and tell her it's important. Oh, and love, take my razor—not the best one, the *second* best—and leave it in the bathroom. He'll need it. Off you go! Shorten your leathers. What do you say?"

She paused in the doorway, dancing on her thin legs, her demure face breaking into mischief and her heavy-lidded eyes embarrassed but shining.

"Yippee," she said, but softly, so that no one but he should hear.

"Atta girl!" Sam bellowed. "And then back to action stations, mind. We've got work to do. The copy must go in."

As the door closed behind her he shook his head. His little Queen (as distinguished from his old Queen, who was turning out so well) was too quiet altogether. Sam feared repression like the plague. "It led to trooble," in his opinion. He had a lot to do, he saw that.

As soon as he was alone he got up and went over to the fireplace. Above the tiled grate there was a glass and mahogany overmantel whose natural sombreness was enlivened by a festoon of invitation cards, press cuttings, letters, and spills, which stuck out all round it like a halo of curl papers on a dowager. He surveyed these doubtfully for some time and then, fetching a chair, mounted upon it and peered over the top of the collection. As he knew perfectly well, there was a considerable space between the wood and the wall. He rubbed the heads of the screws which kept the whole contraption in place, shrugged his plump shoulders, and after a while went back to his typewriter.

In common with most writers, he had evolved his own technique for making bearable the drudgery of his abominable trade, and after long experiment had settled on a method whereby he dictated his work aloud to himself, taking it down in a highly personalized variety of typewritten shorthand, unreadable to all save half a dozen psychic compositors who had been dealing with it for years. For real comfort he required, in addition, an unlimited supply of malt liquor and a fascinated audience, so that he was very glad when Emily slipped back into the room and climbed quietly on to her perch.

"Thirteenth of January, nineteen twenty-one full stop. The Albert Hall was packed to capacity," he began, one blunt forefinger twinkling among the little keys. "How well I remember that fateful night. But for the presence of His Royal Highness—a slender boy we all loved—Wilde would never have fought. Some, and there are those who should know, will tell you that Herman's weight——But enough of that. So much water has flowed under the bridges of Old Father Thames since then that it behooves us all to remember old controversies. But who amongst us on that night, when we sat, our hearts swelling under our white shirt fronts, would have believed that after seventeen gruelling rounds in the gamest exhibition the Ring has ever known, we should see our great little champion gathered up in the strong arms of my old friend 'Peggy' Bettinson——"

"Jack Smith, Uncle Sam. Don't you remember?"

"Eh?" Sam blinked at his page, x-ed out one name testily, and put in the other. "Eeh, I'm daft," he said, shocked. "My God, if that had gone through they'd say old Sam was finished, they would and all. And my God, Emily, they'd be right. You remember me telling you about that, do you? There was Jack Smith of Manchester, one of the finest referees—"

"Oh yes." She breathed the words earnestly. "Oh yes, I always remember that bit."

They sat silent for a moment, lost in the remote romantic world, half science, all courage, which was so largely the creation of old Sam and his confreres, whose hero worship, schoolboyish and pure, had enveloped the prize ring in a glory far brighter than any arc lights of Yankee Stadium or Haringay. To Emily, who got it from the fountainhead, it was a realm of chivalry.

Finally Sam slapped his knee. "It's no use, love," he said, "my mind's not on it. There's something I've got to do first. I thought I shouldn't have to attend to this for a day or two, because I believe in sticking to the letter of my word, and that word was 'wedding day.' But, as Mother always said, circumstances alter cases. Never forget that, Emily. There are times, pardner, when a man has to use his joogement. Fetch me a screwdriver."

FOURTEEN
THE DISCERNING HEART

The "Murderer in the Fog" story, which had excited Londoners at breakfast, had shocked and startled them by noon when they had digested it. As there was no arrest, the public mood changed swiftly, and by the time the evening papers were on the streets people were frankly uneasy. For obvious reasons, the police had not released Geoffrey's story, and to the ordinary Londoner the affair remained a man hunt for an escaped convict berserk in a city, a wanton knife striking casually and recklessly in the midst. It was very unnerving.

If the fog had only cleared, tempers might have cooled, but now, at the end of the second day, it had become the father of fogs, thicker and dirtier and more exasperating than any in living memory. The only people who were not astounded by it were visiting Americans, who innocently supposed the capital to know no other weather and took its inconvenience in their good-natured stride.

Everybody else was affronted and nervous. In the streets passers-by walked quickly, hugging the lights. Children were hurried home from school. Doors which were never locked in daytime were fastened by lunch, and men were glad to seek company in club and pub. Business at the theatre box offices fell abruptly, and the outgoing suburban trains were crowded from four o'clock on. No one talked of anything else. The police came in for much undeserved criticism, and the Under Secretary spoke to Oates several times in the day.

Scotland Yard reacted in its own way. Its odd, elastic organisation stretched out to embrace the emergency with smooth purposefulness. Chief Superintendent Yeo, who was in charge of the Number One Division of the Metropolitan force, stepped out of his snug little office overlooking the river to become Investigating Officer, and Luke, his normal duties delegated, became his second-in-command. Behind them, keyed up to serve and dying for the opportunity, was the whole beautiful mechanism of detection. Each department, working tirelessly and with experience, examined every false report, sifted every piece of incoherent evidence, and gave polite and careful attention to every frightened telephone call.

Of these last there were a great many, and as the night wore on there would be more. Already messages were coming in from as far away as Whitby in the north and Bath in the west. Havoc, or someone remarkably like him, had been seen everywhere, all over the island, and the Scots police were on the alert.

For convenience, the Crumb Street station remained the headquarters of the enquiry, but the police were keeping the St. Petersgate Square angle dark and so far no one from the newspapers had discovered the inner story behind the prison escape. The quiet close remained deserted, therefore. No morbid sight-seer risked his neck groping round the dark sidewalks, and there was no sound save of dripping water falling from the branches of the tulip tree.

Inside the rectory the atmosphere was curious. Old Avril's home had a personality as definite and comfortable as his own. It was a place so loved and lived in that violence in any form was apt to seem so out of place there as to become downright incredible when viewed from its quiet precincts. Now, however, it had come too close to be discounted, and the whole house had developed a startled and piteous appearance. Amanda summed it up when she said it was as if one suddenly saw water seeping through a painted ceiling, Irreparable damage was being done to a lovely thing and there was no telling when it would stop.

She and Meg were on the rug before the fire in Meg's sitting room, leaning as close as they dared to the comforting blaze, and Mr. Campion stood beside them, one lean elbow on the mantelshelf. They were not talking as freely as they might have done, because of young Rupert swinging idly on an armchair in the background. He was very much in the way and had been so for over ten minutes, but no one had the heart to send him down to the basement. It was not very far, two flights only, but in the last few hours they had become very long and lonely stairs.

"But even if Geoff could have warned you, you couldn't have caught the man, could you?"

Meg had asked Mr. Campion the question before and had forgotten his answer. She looked very lovely, crouching on the rug, her long legs doubled gracefully under her. "Surely Inspector Luke can see that?"

Mr. Campion smiled at her from behind his spectacles.

"The gallant Chief Inspector is not unnaturally hopping mad," he said lightly. "Geoff managed to call attention to himself, and that was a stout effort in the circumstances, make no mistake about it. He was all in when we got to him, and getting the gag off must have been agonising, with a night's growth of beard embedded in it. But his only thought was to tell us about Havoc. He didn't quite realize who he was, of course, and by that time they'd faded out into the fog irretrievably." He grinned at her. "I was most relieved. The days when little Albert charged into battle singlehanded have gone for good. Havoc is police work, good hefty police work, with medals and promotions at the end of it. Geoff was game, if I wasn't. He was most annoyed to lose them. He *has* something, your young man. I mind you going out of the family much less than I did."

She gave him her quick sweet smile but drew back at once into the terrors surrounding her.

"Bless you, my dear. I was only wondering. I suppose nothing really serious in the way of injury could have happened to him without our realising it? They're a very long time working on him."

"Lugg is always thorough," put in Amanda promptly. "His corpse-reviving treatment takes time, and with Sam helping it may well take more. I think they're pretending to be prize fighters' seconds. Sam had got the bathroom ready. You never saw anything so professional. They'll do him no end of good if only he doesn't lose his temper and knock them both out. But they can't be very long now, because Luke's coming."

Her thin brown hand touched the younger girl's shoulder. "He's all right, pretty. He's all right now."

Meg shot a furtive sidelong glance at her. Her eyes were swimming helplessly.

"I'm an idiot," she said apologetically. "It's the relief, of course, reaction and all that, but I thought I'd lost him and until then I didn't realise quite how much I need him." She shook her long yellow silk hair away from her face and appealed to them openly. "The whole thing seems so utterly insane to me. A man in prison scheming to get another to impersonate poor Martin, to prevent me marrying Geoff. And then because it didn't work, breaking out and doing all these frightful things. He's a maniac, I realise that, but that doesn't make it any better. Madness when you see it is the most terrible thing in the world."

"I don't think he's mad," said Amanda, and her husband, catching sight of her serious heart-shaped face, thought that she looked as he had first seen her long ago in the shabby drawing room of the Mill at Fontisbright. She had the same air of frank childlike wisdom. "He just wants the treasure. That may be wrong, but it's not insane."

"But, my dear, there can't *be* any treasure." Meg sounded helpless. "Poor little Martin never had any treasure. The family had been wealthy, but they lost it all in the first World War. He told me that before he asked me to marry him. We'd be church mice, he said, until we'd got the war over and he got busy."

"A giant killer," murmured Mr. Campion. "Sounds like Geoff."

"It does, doesn't it?" She was briefly amused. "But don't you see, this murderer is making a fearful mistake? Martin must have said something to him which he completely misunderstood. He's been brooding on it all these years and now he's raging about the place like a man-eating tiger, killing recklessly and all for nothing. I can't get it out of my mind. I can see Geoff lying there utterly helpless, while if that man had only guessed who he was——" Her pretty voice quavered out of control and Amanda glanced behind her. Rupert was not listening. He was engrossed by private worries, one of which was his inability to put his head firmly on the seat of the big chair whilst retaining control of his weight. Either his legs were too short or the chair was too high. His other problem was more serious. That afternoon Mrs. Talisman had let slip a most alarming piece of adult information. She had said that it was stated in black and white in the Bible that all the hairs of one's head were numbered, and ever since Rupert had been consumed with anxiety, wondering if the bald-headed Mr. Lugg *knew*. If he did not, the discrepancy on his handing-in papers was going to come as a fearful embarrassment to him, if not worse. Poor old Magers! He'd just have to write "None" and explain as best he could. Yet perhaps something could be done. Even now, although time must be so short. If they could only have a long time together alone, Rupert could break the news gently and they could plan.

He caught his mother looking at him anxiously and smiled at her reassuringly. She would be more worried than he was, even, so he had decided not to tell her. She could come into it if things got desperate.

Meg noticed the exchange and rose impulsively. "Darling, I'm being untidy. I am so sorry. Forgive me. I think I'll go and bang on the door. If Geoff is still retching he'll have to put up with me. After all, that's marriage, isn't it?"

"But not romance," said Mr. Campion as the door closed behind her. "It's an extraordinary thing how the sins of omission catch up on one, Amanda. In youth my generation feared romance like the devil, and now it sneaks up on me, dangerous with all the charm of the untried. I should like to wrap you two in cotton wool and send you down to the country tonight. Do you mind?"

Her calm brown eyes flickered up at him.

"Frightened?"

"A little. Luke isn't happy. Geoff says Havoc has an outside contact on whom he relies, but he doesn't admit that he overheard anything which could connect him with this house."

Amanda frowned. "Who?" Her lips formed the question.

Campion shook his head. "God knows. I can't see it myself. There's no odour of anything but sanctity about this family, and that sort of thing has an unmistakable stink. All the same, 'by the pricking of my thumbs, something wicked this way comes.' Let me send you both home, old lady."

"Are you staying?"

"Yes, I think I'll stick around. I like Geoff and his pretty gal. What a staggering beauty she is."

"I think so." Amanda spoke with a purr of true appreciation. "She's so exquisitely graceful, and in love too, all shiny. She ought to be marked 'with care,' though. Will he give it to her?"

"Yes, I think so, don't you? He's the type, strong and reliable. Ruthless too, I should say, if it ever came to her or the rest. He may be keeping something dark. I wouldn't swear he wasn't. He's out to protect his own, and good luck to him! Oh, I don't like it! Will you go? Once you get out of London you'll be clear of the fog."

Amanda turned to her son.

"How about driving down to the country tonight with Magers?"

"Can we go alone?" His eagerness surprised and hurt them a little. "When can we start?"

His mother returned to her husband. "That settles that. I'll stay with you."

Rupert put an arm round her neck and his hair mingled with hers until there was but one flaming plume.

"You can come if you like, dear," he said, "but we've got to talk, that's all."

She whispered in his ear, "I'd rather stay with the boss."

"Good." He was tremendously relieved. "You take her," he said to his father. "Could Magers and I go now?"

Mr. Campion looked down at him. He was shocked at the intensity of his own emotion, and more afraid of it than of anything he had ever known. One half his life, more than half, four foot tall and as gaily confident as if the world were made of apple pie.

"I don't see why not," he said, "as soon as he comes down from Mr. Levett. Go and get your things. The good-dog-Tray is asleep in the car, I suppose? Say good-bye to Uncle Hubert if he's come in yet. If not, don't bother; he's gone visiting. Be as intelligent as you can on the way home. No trying to frighten Lugg while he's driving."

"No, I won't." The boy was unexpectedly serious. "I must certainly remember that. Good-bye, Daddy." He shook hands gravely and returned to Amanda. "Mrs. Talisman has hung my coat on a peg twenty-two yards high," he ventured apologetically, and tried to help lift her as she moved.

"We'll go and get it," she said. "You'd better have something to eat, too. Come on."

He went off, dancing beside her without a backward glance. His mind was fully occupied. Perhaps there was some stuff Lugg could rub in. Or if the worst came to worst, there were always wigs. Not indetectable to an archangel, perhaps, but surely fair evidence of honest endeavour.

Left alone, Mr. Campion felt that the room had grown darker. He sat down by the fire and felt for a cigarette. As he had said, he did not like the situation. Havoc, and Doll, and the three men who had been on the original raid had vanished too completely. The rest were being brought in one after the other. They were pathetic figures, most of them, unable to help and frightened to try. The police were merely hindered by their numbers. But the ringleaders were gone, as though the earth had swallowed them, and they were tricky quarry, five experienced men driven by a dream and led by something mercifully unusual in the humdrum history of crime.

He thought he could comprehend Havoc and he was in no mood to underestimate him. Oates had been right, as he usually was, the old sinner. The fellow was that rarity, a genuinely wicked man. Amanda had spotted it. He was no lunatic, no unfortunate, betrayed by disease or circumstance, but a much more scarce and dangerous beast, the rogue which every herd throws up from time to time.

Campion was uneasy. The ancient smell of evil, acrid and potent as the stench of fever, came creeping through the gentle house to him, defiling as it passed.

That last message which Luke had thrust over to him just before they left Crumb Street stuck in his mind, sickening him. A waterman had fished the dwarf out of the shrouded Thames just before dusk. He was too late to save his life, but the little man's jaw had been broken before he was put in the water, so he could have told them nothing had he lived, for there was no evidence that he could write.

Campion shrugged his thin shoulders unhappily. The brute was a bad one. It was not often that he wished for police with rifles, but he could have welcomed them now.

He drew his mind away and reflected on Amanda. She had made up her mind to stay, whatever the boy had said. He had seen that in her face. Now that Rupert had grown out of babyhood her prime allegiance had returned to himself and they were partners again. She would look after him and he must look after the three of them. It was not the only sort of marriage, but it was their sort.

He found himself speculating on Meg and Geoffrey, and was interrupted by the sudden arrival of Geoff himself.

The massage had restored him remarkably, although he still bore traces of his experience. But all the same his general appearance verged on the bizarre, for he was naked save for a sporting dressing gown loaned by Sam. This garment was a trifle short for him but made up for any deficiency with as fine an array of coloured horses' heads, racing plates, and fox masks as Campion had ever seen. However, he seemed completely unaware of his clothes or lack of them. His strong, heavy body was taut under the silk and his jaw stuck out belligerently. A less shrewd observer might have thought him angry, but Campion, cocking a weather eye up at him, diagnosed an unusual emotional experience and his first words proved him right.

"So there you are," he said with relief. "Look, this is the damnedest thing. What do you know about this? I don't see why anyone should see it but you, so you'll have to back me if the Inspector gets querulous." His eyes were hard and dark and his hand shook a little as he drew two folded sheets from the pocket of his robe and held them out. "Look, a letter from Martin Elginbrodde."

Campion sat up. "Really? That *is* extraordinary! Where did you get it?"

"Sam. Can you believe it?" Geoffrey was looking at him with open appeal. "He's had it all the time. He says he intended to slip it to me after the ceremony, as he promised Elginbrodde he would, but Meg said something to him on the phone this afternoon which gave him a clue, so he got busy and unearthed it. He's had it hidden behind the overmantel in his sitting room. It slid down there and he knew it was safe and so he left it."

He laughed abruptly and sat down on the opposite side of the hearth.

"I might have guessed," he said. "He was the obvious person, or at least I think so. He's the chap I should have given it to. Read it, Campion. This is the thing Havoc is looking for. He was quite right. There are a couple of notes enclosed for me to take to the local authorities, just as he said there would be."

As Mr. Campion unfolded the sheets the deep pleasant voice went on, by this time a trifle huskily.

"I've not shown it to him. He didn't ask to see it and I didn't think I would, in case it breaks his heart. You'll see. It must have been written just before the kid went out on the raid, and evidently he was still full of it when he spoke to Havoc on the cliff. It was addressed to Blank Blank Esquire, and marked 'Personal.' "

Campion began to read. The writing was small and masculine, the hand of a doer rather than a writer, and the style hit him squarely, its naive and vigorous sincerity leaping out at him like a personality.

Visitors' Club, Pall Mall, S.W.1.

February 4th, '44

DEAR SIR,

I fear I cannot call you anything else but I hope you will realise that I do not mean to be as formal as this address would indicate. I feel very kindly disposed to you. If you get this at all, I shall be out of the picture, where, if you understand me, *I hope to God I stay*. Meg is such a thoroughly splendid person that she deserves a real life with a man who is batty about her. I know you will be [erased] are, otherwise, she would never have married you. Please understand that I realise that my intrusion into your life at this point is rather ''much,'' to put it mildly, but there is something you have got to do.

In the old icehouse of the garden of the house at Ste.

Odile-sur-Mer (Meg will know the place, I cannot leave it to her because it is not mine, but the contents will be, and that I have left her) there is the Ste. Odile Treasure. It is for Meg to do as she likes with so long as she sees it is kept safe. America would not be a bad place for it as things seem to be turning out. If you are poor, make her sell it, of course. Anyone who paid a lot for it would naturally keep it safe. Safety is all that matters. If I go, and I shall have gone, of course, if you get this, our Ste. Odile lot will have ended and someone else must take over.

I am not trusting Meg with the job of getting hold of it herself, nor yet her dear Old Boy, who, as you will know by this time, is not exactly worldly. This is because I can see that, should the place still be in enemy hands, or should France be in a state of upheaval, the job would be much too dangerous for them to risk. Also it would worry them, and I do not want that. The same applies to Sam. He is a grand old scout and the kindest, straightest old duck in the world, but this may be a delicate business. I cannot tell what may have happened, you see. That is what is so worrying. To be frank, I just can't see him managing the thing, but I shall trust him with this letter. You will realise why. He is the boy scout grown up. I *know* that you alone will get it.

I am landing you with the job because I am conceited enough to believe that you will be the same sort of chap that I am, and will make no bones about it but will just go and get it the instant the thing seems at all possible. (It is not possible at this present juncture, as you will appreciate. I am banking on things having changed, if not become actually better.) The old women in the country round Ste. Odile used to say, "One truly loves only the same man." (I have not used the French because you may not read French; if you do, please forgive me, but it is vital you should understand exactly what I am saying.) They meant, as I take it, that a woman only *really* loves the same sort of man all her life, so I am betting that Meg will only marry when she really loves again, and so my guess is that you and I are rather alike in important things.

I hope you will not be offended by this. As I am now
(just off on a sticky assignment), it is a great comfort to
me.

Now do not worry. The Treasure is portable, but it will
take great care. I will put where it actually is in the icehouse on a separate piece of paper. I do not know why I
do this except that it seems safer. I hid it myself, which
is why the whole thing may look a bit odd. Be very careful
how you break in.

Of course I appreciate that all this may be a waste of
time. It may be looted already or it may get a direct hit.
If so, forget it; it can't be helped.

But in that case please do not tell Meg at all. I have
never told her anything about it, for this reason. After all,
if she cannot help she will only worry, and I feel she has
worried enough.

Should the war have ended satisfactorily, it may be all
fairly simple. Just in case this is so, I will enclose some
letters for a few people who may be useful to you if they
are still there.

That is all. Please go and get it the instant you feel it
is at all practicable for you to do so, and give it to Meg.

Give Meg my love but do not tell her it is mine. As
you will understand perfectly well (if you are as I expect),
when dead I would *prefer* to lie down. Over to you, chum.

Good luck, you lucky old blighter, and I mean that.

> Yours very truly,
> MARTIN ELGINBRODDE,
> Major.

Mr. Campion sat staring at the signature for some seconds
before he turned back to read the message once more. The
room was quite quiet. Geoffrey was looking into the fire.

When he had completed the second reading, Campion
handed the letter back. His pale face was blank and his eyes
shadowed behind his spectacles. Geoffrey took it and exchanged it for a third sheet.

"This was the enclosure. You'd better see it."

As Campion read the single line written neatly across it,
his brows rose.

"Odd," he murmured, "but quite clear. Yes, I see. What are you going to do now?"

Levett crushed the flimsy sheets into three tight balls and threw them one after the other on the red coals. Little blue flames leapt out of nothingness to devour them. As they turned from black to white he spoke.

"After all, it was a personal letter," he said, his shy eyes meeting Campion's for an instant. "I don't see a pack of officials breathing over it, do you?"

Mr. Campion did not speak at once. He was thinking how surprising the man was. Just when one thought one knew him, one stumbled on new depths. He had grown to like him enormously during the day, but he had not suspected this sensitivity. He realised with a little shock how right Martin had been, how discerning Meg's heart.

"Oh, I agree," he said aloud. "And now?"

"Now we nip over and get it right away, just as he asks." Geoff had become his familiar self again, brisk, purposeful, and capable as they come. "There's no point in hanging about. That's asking for trouble. We'll settle it with the police and we'll all four go, you and Amanda, me and Meg. We'll drive to Southampton tonight, fog or no fog, and catch the first boat to St. Malo, taking the car with us for the trip down the coast. I feel that if Meg is right away from here it will be safer for everybody, and the job ought to be done, so let's go and do it."

The more Mr. Campion considered the proposal, the more he liked it. He had told Amanda the truth when he had said that he felt that Havoc was "police work." There was no mystery surrounding his guilt. He was something to be trapped and killed, and Campion was no great man for blood sports.

As for the girls, Geoffrey was right. The further they were from the scene of action, the better. He glanced at his watch.

"Luke is due now," he remarked. "Get your clothes on and we'll tackle him. If I know him, he'll be fascinated. What exactly are you expecting to find, by the way?"

"I haven't the faintest idea." Geoffrey stood up, looking solid and splendid, like the man who supports the human pyramid at the circus. "Anything. It's fragile and bulky, that's all anyone knows. A crystal candelabra, perhaps, or a tea ser-

vice even. Something they thought a lot of when Elginbrodde
was a kid. Families do have the most extraordinary treasure.
My grandmother half starved a child rather than sell a clock
which might have been chipped off the Albert Memorial. But
that doesn't matter. It's not a question of intrinsic value at
all. The point is that it was *his* treasure and he wanted Meg
to have it and keep it safe. Values are so relative. I thought
that when I was trussed up, listening to that bunch of crazy
thugs. Hitler wanted the modern world. Well, I mean to say,
Campion, *look* at the modern world! No, I shall be quite
prepared for a bust of Minerva or a set of fire irons, and in
the circumstances I'd risk my life to get them for Meg. I've
got to. It's over to me. Why, you weren't thinking of pieces
of eight, were you?"

Campion laughed. "No," he said, "not exactly. That notion
may occur to Luke, though, and I shouldn't disillusion him.
He's no starry-eyed optimist, but he's got to hunt these chaps
and get them hanged, and it would be merciful to let him
share their dream as long as possible. At the moment Havoc
is at least producing tragedy. As soon as it becomes tragic
farce——" He shrugged his shoulders and did not finish the
sentence.

Geoffrey was eying him curiously. He too was finding more
in his new friend than he had expected.

"Exactly," he said. "He'll let us go, will he?"

"I think so. It's good orthodox procedure. Phase one, re-
cover loot. His only anxiety as far as you are concerned is
that you may be shielding someone here, Havoc's contact."

He made the suggestion lightly, but his eyes were inquisitive. Geoffrey met them steadily.

"I don't think I am. I told him so. Havoc spoke of a contact,
but there was no suggestion that it was anyone in the house.
Who could it be? Are you worrying about the safety of my
future pa-in-law?"

"No. Quite frankly, I feel to do that would be presump-
tuous. Someone else looks after Uncle Hubert. Very well,
then, I'll see you downstairs as soon as may be. I must ask
my wife, of course."

"I've *told* mine." Geoffrey sounded as gay and confident as
Rupert himself. "I met her on the stairs and told her to pack

a bag. She'll go like a shot if Amanda will, but if she won't, of course I shan't let her. We're all set to be old-fashioned that way. See you in five minutes."

His gaudy coattails vanished through the doorway and Campion was left smiling. Geoffrey "would do," he decided. He had liked the remark about the fire irons and had no doubt that the young man had meant what he had said. If the treasure turned out to be the most ordinary of curios, it would still receive honour from him. Campion could see a set of fire irons, arranged in a glass casket five times their worth, let into the wall of a living room and remaining there, an eyesore and a thinking point, for the rest of Geoffrey's life. He was that sort of masculine person, a familiar type of successful man.

All the same, a moment or so later he was frowning in a fruitless effort to remember. Ever since he had first heard the story that afternoon he had been delving in the vast rag bag of miscellaneous information for which he was so justly renowned, trying to find something he had forgotten. Somewhere, at some time, in an old guidebook perhaps, or among the reminiscences of the fabulous *grandes-dames* who had infested his childhood, he had heard tell of the Ste. Odile Treasure before.

FIFTEEN
POOR PEOPLE

An unnatural peace had settled over the house when late that night Luke sat in the study with Canon Avril. The two private cars had left some time before. Rupert and Lugg, with the dog snoring between them, were making their way towards the sanctuary of Suffolk lanes, while the four treasure-seekers groped through the fog in the other direction in an attempt to catch the first St. Malo boat out from Southampton.

The rectory was quiet without them, although it was by no means empty. Sergeant Picot lolled on a hard chair in the front hall, while in the basement two of his men made half-hourly rounds. Under the roof, Sam was still working on the article which must be on his editor's desk by morning. Emily and her grandparents were asleep in the two little rooms beyond the kitchen, and, in Meg's elegant bedroom, Miss Warburton, who had been induced to leave her lonely cottage for the night, brushed out her limp hair before the looking glass.

In the study, where it was warm and the air was blue with tobacco smoke, the coal fire ticked softly as the white ash fell and was audible in the silence which had fallen between the two men. Luke was at the desk. The Canon had insisted on his taking it because the little bits of paper on which he seemed to keep his notes worried him. Avril lost notes himself, often in the pulpit, and he had a very lively appreciation of the nuisance they could become. The Chief Inspector appreciated his motive, because he was setting himself out to understand every minute detail of the man.

As Campion had recognised when he first met him, Charlie Luke was destined to become one of the great policemen. He possessed the one paramount quality which appears in all the giants of his profession quite apart from any other merit which they may display. He had that utter persistence which only derives from an almost unnatural interest. The man was a living question mark and he hunted his quarry with the passionate patience of a devotee hunting salvation. After thirty-six sleepless hours, his red-rimmed eyes were bright as a bird's.

Sergeant Picot and his men had been working on the St. Petersgate Square angle all day and they had gleaned only a little. Luke had digested the scraps they had given him and now he was working on them. He had been talking to the Canon about Jack Havoc for a long time, expending the precious minutes deliberately, putting everything he had into the job, feeling his way, watching like a cat, letting his intuition stretch out beyond where the mind could take it.

Old Avril was listening. He sat in the worn chair, his uncunning fingers folded across his black vest. He looked both wise, and good, but there was no telling what was going on behind his quiet eyes. Luke found himself hoping he never had to play poker with him. He tried again.

"Usually, you see, sir, we know these lads like brothers." He stretched his left hand out and closed it as if it held another first. "We know their families, and if we don't exactly love them we are close to them. Havoc is an exception. We know nothing of his life before his first conviction in 1934. He was sixteen then, or so he says, and that seems to be all they ever got out of him. It's not his real name, of course."

"No?" The old man did not appear surprised, merely interested.

"It doesn't sound right to me. Does it to you?" Luke was appealing. "It's too suitable. I should say he invented that, as a boy might, trying to sound big. We seem to have accepted it. I suppose we had to. Anyhow, it was as Jack Havoc that he went to Borstal, and as Havoc, J., he's on the C.R.O. files. He said he came from nowhere, no one came forward to claim him, and from our point of view his life started then."

As Avril did not speak, he spread out his hands to him.

"All I know about him is what I've been able to get from the records. No one has had him on their short list for five years, because he's been safely in jail, and for some time before that he'd vanished, presumably into the Army. I've come to him fresh, and the outstanding thing about him from my point of view is that, according to listed information, he's been able to disappear twice before in his life just as he has now."

The Canon nodded his tousled grey head. "I see," he said, as if he was reluctantly convinced. "You feel that he must have friends among the people the police do not—walk hand in left hand with. I understand."

"It's so obvious, isn't it?" Weariness was uncovering the Chief Inspector's vital force and the words came pumping out of him, bright and alive, like blood from an artery. "Where did he get the suit he's wearing? Mr. Levett says it was made for him, and that's a thing he'd know. Where did Havoc get it so quickly? Who had it laid out for him? Who was waiting for him to make his getaway?" He waited himself, his head on one side. "It's significant," he went on at last, "because the only person known to have been in communication with him whilst he's been in prison is an old woman in Bethnel who keeps a lodginghouse he once stayed in. She's well known to us, and the instant we heard of his escape we got on to her, but he didn't show up there and she and her contacts have been watched ever since. It wasn't she. Who was it?"

He leant back in his chair and put his hands behind his head.

"Of course," he continued with disarming humility, "for all our talk the police are not so blessed thorough. This old girl has two daughters who both work in different West End stores. Although an eye has been kept on the mother, because she was known to be corresponding with a convict, no one has bothered about the daughters. Yet they live in the same house. Anyone at all could have kept in touch with him through one of them. They're hard-faced pieces, both of them. They've been through it today, but they're not talking. Why should they?"

Avril sighed. "Sixteen years old, and no one came forward

to claim him," he said slowly. "How very terrible that must have been."

His quiet tone had not altered, but pain was conveyed so poignantly that Luke was jerked off his course. He had made up his mind that he was going to hear the argument from the opposite point of view, and had been prepared to listen to the story of the sufferings of a respectable family when one of its sons betrays it. That was the aspect which most appealed to his own imagination, and he had prepared a case against it without much enthusiasm. Now he was doubly put out.

"Very likely, sir," he agreed bitterly, "but he doesn't sound to be my idea of a lovable kid. He and two other boys stole a laundry van, ran over a postman, maimed him for life, and pinched his bag, leaving him in the road. Then they smashed up the vehicle whilst fighting over the mail. One young brute was killed outright, the second was seriously hurt, and Havoc was arrested trying to run away. At the enquiry it was found that the injured youngster had met Havoc for the first time that afternoon, and the parents of the dead boy couldn't identify him either. All marks had been picked out of his clothes, mind you, so he knew what he was doing. That was in May '34, in Ilford."

He finished the recital with a certain amount of savage satisfaction and regarded the old man hopefully.

Avril said nothing. His chin had sunk on his chest, and his eyes stared unseeing at the polished wood of the desk pedestal. Luke felt sure that the story was news to him, but he could not tell what effect it had had. He went on very cautiously.

"Mrs. Cash," he said, "the woman who lends money. We had great hopes of her, you know."

"Ah. The sports coat. I thought you might. Where did that lead you?" Avril's direct intelligence was comforting.

"Not very far," Luke admitted. "Her story, when Picot got her alone, was that a dealer asked her to get it for him, and that was confirmed by the man. He says that Duds came into his shop in Crumb Street and asked him if he could get him an old coat or suit of Martin Elginbrodde's, and he mentioned this address. He explained that he was an actor and that he was due to give an impersonation of his old officer at a reunion dinner. The dealer saw no harm in it and he knew that Mrs. Cash, who did little bits of business of the kind, lived in this square, so he got in touch with her. He sticks to that. We can't shake him."

Old Avril nodded. "Ingenious," he said unexpectedly. "Mrs. Cash is not involved."

Charlie Luke eyed him curiously. "I understand you've known her for a long time, sir. She told Picot it was over twenty-five years."

"Twenty-six," the Canon agreed. "My wife persuaded me to let her live in that little cottage twenty-six years ago, the Michaelmas quarter."

"And she was a widow then with one child, a little boy. Is that right?"

Luke, who was not usually so self-conscious, hoped he was not sounding heavily significant.

"Perfectly. Did she tell you that?"

"No. That came from your Mrs. Talisman. We haven't worried Mrs. Cash since last night. She made a very full statement to Picot and let him see over the house, which she needn't have done. Since then we've merely kept an eye on the place, as we have the whole square. Not too easy, this weather. She hasn't been out today."

"So she told me. She seems to have a cold."

Luke sat up. "Was that when you called on her this afternoon?" He was annoyed. He had been saving that, and the old man had forestalled him. Avril seemed mildly surprised by his tone.

"Of course," he said. "That was the only time I saw her."

"Do you mind telling me why you called?"

"No. I asked her if she could possibly come and hunt for the minutes of the last meeting of the Diocesan Education Committee. She couldn't. She said she had a cold."

Luke sat looking at him blankly. He found that the only certain thing he knew about the man was that he would not lie. Of that one fact he had no doubt in the world.

"I see," he said at last. "I hadn't thought of that. I suppose that, like everybody else, your work has to go on, whatever happens around you."

The old man smiled at him. "It ought to," he agreed, "but

some of it is very trivial, you know. Perhaps paper should be
made a little more precious than it seems to be. These forms
we keep sending each other nowadays remind me of an old
parlour game we used to play called Consequences, except
that the results were very much more humorous, or so we
thought."

Luke grinned. He liked the man.

"So Mrs. Cash has a cold, has she?" he said. "I wonder if
it's in her feet. Did you notice if she looked ill?"

"I'm afraid I did not. It was dark in the doorway."

"I know. And you didn't stay a minute. I heard that." Luke
brushed the incident aside and returned to the heart of the
business. "This son of hers," he began without looking up,
but raising and lowering his hand as if he were estimating the
height of a child, "do you happen to remember, sir, exactly
when he died?"

Avril hesitated. "Not the year," he said at last, "but it was
just after Epiphany—that's early January. I was in bed with
influenza, and the Memorial Service was delayed."

"That's what they told me." Luke sounded dubious. "Mrs.
Talisman says it was in January '35. The boy was then four-
teen or fifteen, but well grown." Now that he was about to
test the one and only theory which had occurred to him as
being even faintly tenable, its flimsiness dismayed him, but
he went on resolutely. "My information is that the child died
down in the country, where he had been for some time, and
his body was brought to his mother's house for a night on its
way to the cemetery up at Wilsford. You were in bed, but
your wife, the late Mrs. Avril, went in to see the mother for
you. Now, sir, this is the only question I have to ask you. Mrs.
Talisman is certain that when Mrs. Avril returned she mentioned that she had seen the body. The child used to sing in
the choir at the church, so she knew him well and she said
she'd seen him when he was dead. Do you happen to remember that?"

Avril raised his fine head. "Yes," he said. "My poor Margaret." His face changed only for an instant. The grief upon
it appeared and passed like the shadow of a leaf in the wind,
but its intensity was so great that Luke, who was still a young
man, was dismayed to learn that it could exist.

The Chief Inspector was taken aback. The dark colour appeared on his cheekbones and he cursed himself for trying to make bricks without straw. He had no wish to torment his new friend, whose regret for his dead wife was clearly quite terrible. He shelved his "substitution of the child" theory completely. It had been a forlorn hope from the beginning. It had come to him when Picot had been telling him that Mrs. Cash was hard. He knew something of the hardness of certain women and it had occurred to him then that a self-centred widow who was making money in a shady way under cover of great respectability might have preferred to let her neighbours believe that her son was dead rather than to allow him to become a permanent danger to her, and this more especially if she was then free to do what she could for him secretly.

The actual manoeuvre of substitution would not have been easy, but not, he thought, impossible for a woman with so many impoverished folk beholden to her. It was a peculiar district. He had even known some very shady undertakers in it.

It had been the dates which had interested him most. In May a boy went to Borstal, and about the same time another boy had been "sent away to the country because he was difficult," and in January he had died. However, if Mrs. Avril had actually seen the dead child, then that was the end of it.

He took up the official photographs of the wanted man, which lay before him on the desk. They were not good. Mrs. Talisman had not picked them out of a bunch of others, and Picot had not blamed her. The face was wooden and lifeless.

Luke pushed the card across to Avril, who glanced at it and handed it gravely back.

"That's the bird we're after, sir."

"And when he is taken, what will they do with him?" For the first time rebelliousness had crept into the curl of the old man's mouth, and his tone possessed a hint of bitterness. "Argue over him, lock him up for three weeks, and finally hang him, I suppose, poor fellow."

The epithet stung the righteous sheep dog in Luke on the raw, and anger, naked and oddly naïve, shone out suddenly from his diamond eyes.

"That man," he exploded, "has killed a doctor who was trying to help him, a snivelling caretaker old enough to be his father, an invalid woman in her bed, and a boy I'd give my right hand to have here with me on the job. I nipped in to see his mother today, and I couldn't look the old girl in the face." He was so angry that he came within an ace of tears, but he kept control of his great rackety machine and managed to be impressive in his forcefulness. "That man is killing mad," he rattled on savagely. "He's knifing right and left as though human life had no value and any poor beast who gets in his way had no right to exist. And what's he thinking of? Nothing but a parcel of buried treasure out of a storybook, which may well turn out to be nothing more exciting than a bottle of gin. He's got no right to life. There's no place for him under the sun. Of course they'll hang him. Good heavens, sir, wouldn't you?"

"I?" The old Canon sat back in astonishment. He had been watching the other man's rage with the look of acute apprehension which is usually reserved for the contemplation of some very painful but familiar operation, the extraction of a tooth, perhaps. There was sympathy but no sharing of the sensation. "I?" he repeated. "Oh no, my boy, not I. I should never have made a judge. I've often thought that. What a very terrible job that must be. Consider it," he added as Luke sat staring at him. "However carefully a judge is protected by the experience and the logic of the law, there must be times—not many, I know, or we should have no judges—when the same frightful question must be answered. Not faced, you see, but answered. Every now and again he must have to say to himself, in effect, 'Everyone agrees that this colour is black, and my reason tells me it is so, but on my soul, do I *know?*'"

The eyes which met Luke's were frank with dismay at such a prospect.

"That must be a most dreadful moment," said Avril. "So much depends on it for *himself*. If he didn't consider his own position he'd be inhuman, and of course none of us are. I should have failed hopelessly, wouldn't you?"

Charlie Luke made no comment. It was not a subject he had ever expected to have to consider. It passed through his cheerful mind that the old fellow might as well start talking Greek to him.

"Well, guv'nor," he said, "what *would* you do?"

"I've been thinking of that all day." Avril spoke absently and sat watching the dead fire dropping quietly to dust. His placid face wore the authoritative but withdrawn expression which only appears in a man when he is actively engaged upon his own skilled work. Behind his untidy head the dark bookcase made a tapestry of subdued colour, and presently, as the silence lengthened, Luke felt that his inquisitorial desk had gradually become merely one in a classroom. Finally the old man stirred and his delightful smile broke the spell.

"Mine is a very technical job," he said apologetically. "I don't see that there's anything I can tell you that would be of any great use to you, except perhaps this, if you'll forgive a great impertinence. I should not dream of mentioning it in the ordinary way, but it comes within my province, and since you may have overlooked it, it might be helpful just now. Beware of anger. It is the most difficult to remove of all the hindrances. But it is the alcohol of the body, you know, and the devil of it is that it deadens the perceptions."

He spoke so earnestly and with such obvious good will that it was impossible to be offended, and Luke, who had expected almost anything else on earth, was startled out of his wits. The eyes which met his were as shrewd as the Assistant Commissioner's own.

Avril got up. "You ought to have something to eat before you go," he said. "This country seems to be determined to atone for its sins by instituting a perpetual Lent, but there must be something in the pantry. Let us go down and see."

Luke refused with genuine regret. It was not merely that he was hungry. He liked Avril and would have been delighted to go on being surprised by him. But there was a night's work waiting for him at Crumb Street. Presently he strode away through the fog, still not quite sure what warning had been intended in that last unlikely phrase.

He did not think that his perceptions were deadened and he could not imagine where he might have been misled, but he was always ready to admit that he might have overlooked something important. The fact that he had done so was not his fault. No one had thought to tell him that the Canon never used the word "poor" to describe men or women merely because they were no longer alive. That habit in one of his profession would have struck him as denoting either illogicality or gratuitous rudeness.

All his household knew this so well that it had not occurred to the old man to explain it to Luke. When Uncle Hubert spoke of a fellow human being as poor, he meant to convey that either by accident or intention they had done something wrong.

SIXTEEN
ASSIGNMENT

When Canon Avril had made sure that the front door was locked, somewhat to the amusement of Sergeant Picot, who was seated in front of it, he went to bed, or at least he would have done so had not Miss Warburton appeared in his path with a cup of steaming milk-food in her hand.

She was in her dressing gown and was so determined not to be in any way embarrassed by the fact that she achieved a skittishness not at all suitable in the circumstances.

"So there you are at last, you roistering old man!" she announced loudly. "Sitting up until I don't know when, chatting to policemen. Here, take this and do drink it down. I've put something in it to make you sleep, for if you don't have a good night you'll only be fagged out tomorrow, and goodness knows what that's going to bring forth if today is anything to go by."

Avril looked down at her kind plain face, soft now with a flush of belated youthfulness, and smiled at her with great fondness. Neither of his sisters had been in the least like her, but he wished they had been. Dear "Decimal Dot"! She was very good to him.

He thanked her gravely for the milk, which he had no intention of drinking, and took it carefully into his bedroom, which was on the ground floor just behind the sitting room, while she lingered against the doorpost, dying to gossip but quite incapable of taking a step inside.

"Hubert," she said briskly, "suppose this murderer comes

here looking for Martin's letter? Oh, I know he'll be caught at once. The house is infested with detectives. But—well, it won't be very nice, will it?"

"Who for?" He could not resist teasing her, she looked so worldly-wise.

"Oh, don't!" She might have been ten suddenly and he eleven. "I know I'm old-fashioned about these things, but there's been no word of St. Petersgate Square in the newspapers yet, and do you know, I'm very glad indeed. Besides," she added with the brightness of the truly unimaginative, "he might kill us all."

"The man will not come here." The Canon spoke with complete authority, but she was loath to let the subject drop.

"How do you know?"

Avril frowned. He was wondering what she would say if he explained that he knew Havoc would not come to the house because he, Avril, seemed to have arranged that he should not. He could imagine her face changing just as Mrs. Cash's face had changed when he had knocked at her door that afternoon and made the unprecedented request that she should come and hunt through his house for some papers he had mislaid.

He could still see the look, first of incredulity and then of fear, on that broad bold countenance, and his soul still writhed when he remembered the knowing smile which had followed and heard again the abominable words.

"No, Canon. I won't come out. I've got a cold. But you needn't worry. We'll take your word for it. There's nothing to read at the rectory."

The speed with which she had given a meaning to his request, and the quick diagnosis of the weakness to which she had ascribed his motive in making it, still shocked him.

It filled him with doubt too. Had he made the move because he guessed more than he admitted to himself and was afraid for his household? Or had he known, subconsciously, that a trap would be set at the rectory and he could not bear that even the wildest of animals should step into it? Or had he merely obeyed an impulse so strong that it could have been called a compulsion? Honestly, he did not know. There had been no plan in his mind, of that he was certain, for now he came to think of it, the letter *was* in the house at that time, although he had not known it. The idea of taking such an extraordinary step had come to him without ulterior motive as soon as he had heard the story from his nephew, and he had acted upon it there and then, telling Campion he had a call to make and must go out. It was only after Mrs. Cash had reacted that he had wondered at himself and her.

Miss Warburton bore with his silence but misunderstood his expression.

"Oh, you *are* worried, aren't you?" she said with concern. "That's why I want you to sleep. Drink that up. Otherwise I suppose you'll read—What were you thinking of reading tonight, Hubert?"

He nearly told her *The Adventures of Sherlock Holmes* but desisted because that would have been unkind. In common with so many worthy ladies of her age, she was fascinated by what she was pleased to call the "Theory of the Thing," and he knew she was itching to discover how he would approach the problem of Havoc from a professional point of view.

Theology and Christian Morals, thought old Avril grimly, all of them neatly locked up in great books to the making of which there was no end. If only it were true. If only anyone could tell anybody else anything. If only one could know by being told.

"Do tell me, Hubert," said Miss Warburton, and she was very sweet.

"My dear girl," he said seriously, "if you confronted a physician with a patient whom even you as an unpractised observer could see was certainly about to die, what would you think of the stupid fellow if he rushed off to his library and began to read?"

She missed the point completely. "Oh, so you mean you know what to do with him? Then why can't you tell me?"

"I mean I don't know," said old Avril, wagging a finger at her vehemently, "and if ever I do, it will not be because I have read it, but because when I read it or hear it or have it thrust inescapably under my nose it will then have pleased the Almighty to cram its reality into my thick and unworthy skull. Or, if you prefer it, life will then have so turned me about that the eye which is necessary for that particular piece of seeing will then be focused upon the fact. Now that really is all there is to it, my dear. You run along, or you'll catch cold. The 139th Psalm is the only one if you're frightened. Good night."

He began to remove his jacket and she hurried off at once, as he had known she would. Left to himself in the dark little bedroom which had been his wife's private parlour in the days when they had used the whole house as a single residence, he covered the cup of milk with a book lest he should forget and drink it inadvertently. He did not want to sleep. Now was no time to deaden the perceptions with any drug, anger or aspirin. He had just seen how the boy Luke had been hampered. Avril approved of Luke. A dear fellow, he reflected; untried as yet, of course, but sound and shrewd and very likeable. How amazingly close he had come to the truth—always supposing it was the truth.

Old Avril did not know. If he had, then perhaps it would have been his duty to tell. He was not too sure about this last point, but he felt reasonably certain that his heart would have directed him rightly had the occasion arisen. As it was, he did not know, and to have presumed knowledge would most certainly have made mischief.

He remembered his dear silly Margaret, with her wide eyes which were like Meg's eyes but not nearly so wise, sobbing out her confession on that third day of her last illness, when they had both known what was in store. What a silly wayward little tale it had been! The changes in money values during the first World War had taken her by surprise. Avril's masterful unmarried sister, who had managed his monetary affairs until she died, had not been sympathetic towards her extravagance and so she had borrowed. It had been such a trivial sum and the woman Cash had made her pay so much, not only in money but in agony. Avril's face grew stern as he remembered, and relaxed again as he also remembered that mercifully it was not for him to judge.

He had been angry at the time, though, and his anger had deadened his perceptions and he had paid for it. He was still paying for it. He could not remember, he could not recall, what it was exactly that she had said as she lay sobbing on his shoulder, with the fear of death upon her sweet stupid mind. Had she said she had actually seen another child in the open coffin, or had it been merely that she had been told to say that she had seen the boy when she had not, and had so suspected that it might not have been he? Avril could not tell. All he could remember was her pain.

He had thrust the widow Cash out of his universe from that moment on. It had not occurred to him to take any material revenge such as to dispossess her of her cottage. It was not so much that he was above it as that the idea never entered his head. His only notion of his ultimate personal rebuke of another human being was to cut him off, to shut him out of his heart, to eschew him, in fact, as evil. The move was not disciplinary, but self-protective. Mrs. Cash must have observed a coldness in him, but that was all. He made no attempt to avoid her, and when she knelt in church before him he included her in his blessing, for not to have done so would have been presumption, since in that house he was a servant.

But as he stood remembering, his shirt half over his head, he felt himself growing angry again. It terrified him and he prayed against it hastily lest he should lose his understanding. Avril had only one prayer which he used in private nowadays. He had reached that stage in his development when its few lines seemed to him to contain the absolute maximum which, from a purely personal point of view, he dared ask of his Creator. As he climbed out of his clothes, folding each garment carefully as he had been taught sixty years before, he repeated it, drawing the blessed sense out of every exact word.

"Our Father . . ."

When he came to the part which was most important of all to him that night, he paused and said it twice.

"Lead us not into temptation, but deliver us from Evil."

That was it. That was what he meant. Lead us not into temptation, for of that we have already enough within us and must resist it as best we can in our own way. But deliver us, take us away, hide us from Evil. From that contamination of death cover us up.

That was his prayer, and tonight it was not going to be answered. He noticed that when he found that he had put

on his thick bedroom slippers, the ones with the leather soles.
He was preparing to move about that night.

It occurred to him that the psychologists could explain that
phenomenon and could tell him how his subconscious mind
was planning to do something that his ordinary upper mind
shrank from. What fun all that sort of thing was! What a
delightful study! He pulled himself together. There he was,
as usual, sneaking off into the luxury of idle intellectualism,
lazing, arranging to be elsewhere when the new task, and he
felt it coming very close, was about to be put before him.

He got into his thick dressing gown to go up to the bathroom. It was quite a journey to the first floor, and Meg, who
loved that sort of conceit, had made him a robe from the
formula laid down in the archives of a thirteen-century mon-
astery. The directions had been easy to follow: "Of stout black
woollen cloth take four equal pieces, each as long as the
height of the Bro. from nape to heel, and as wide as will
stretch across his shoulders from elbow to elbow. Let the first
cover his left breast and the second his right, and the third
shall cover him behind. Then let the fourth piece be folded
into three, and of these the first shall be for his left arm, the
second for his right, and the third and last for his head. So
shall he be covered and two ells of common rope encompass
his middle."

Avril had objected to the rope as theatrical and used a
pyjama cord, but the simplicity and warmth of the garment
pleased him, and his household were used to meeting his
cowled figure striding down the draughty passages. The unfortunate Sergeant Picot, however, who had not been warned,
had the shock of his life when, on turning at a sound, he saw
"a black monk" behind him near the foot of the stairs. The
Canon was carrying the cup of milk. He was most anxious
not to hurt Dot's feelings by letting her find the draught un-
touched in the morning, and was preparing a little guiltily to
pour it away. Picot's violent start on catching sight of him,
however, struck Avril as clear evidence of overstrained nerves,
and he handed him the sedative with relief, delighted to find
a good use for it.

The sergeant was not a milk drinker, but he had not eaten
since a belated lunch and had a long cold night in front of

him. He took it as a very kind thought of the old gentleman's. He expected the stuff to taste unpleasant and was not surprised when it did. He drank it down to the dregs, unaware that Miss Warburton had added two of the barbituric sleeping tablets which her doctor had given her after her last attack of influenza. One had made her sleep like a log, but she put in two because she did want Hubert to have a good night. When Avril returned from his bath, Picot was nodding peacefully at his post.

Once back in his room, completely ignorant of what he had done, Avril still pottered about, waiting for something, he knew not what. He recognised his own mood. It was one which had come to him very seldom, perhaps only four or five times in his whole life, and always it had preceded some experience in which he had been called upon to play a principal but not particularly personal part. Its chief characteristic was its strange sense of absolute peace.

For a fleeting moment he perceived it quite clearly and recognised that he had no existence, no will, no responsibility save in obedience. He was aware most vividly of the great stream of the world's life on which he floated. He felt it above and below him, gathering speed, moving faster and faster towards unknown rapids. He could almost see the dark waters and hear their roar. But he himself was very quiet, very small, but alert and ready to fulfil his purpose, only fearful lest he should miss the opportunity when it came. Most oddly, he was not frightened. That alone he had learned from experience. With the danger would come the courage.

The moment of clarity passed and he became a worried old man again, preparing to go to bed. The small clock on his mantelshelf said ten minutes after one. The house was silent, and from outside the only noise which reached him was the far-off booming of the shunting trains at the terminus.

He stripped the paisley coverlet from his bed, noted the hump which the stone hot-water bottle made under the blankets, and then, switching off the light, he felt his way over to the window to draw the curtains. The window gave on to the stone staircase between the house and the church, and because it was on ground level it had been fitted, when the house was built, with slender iron bars on the outside. Avril always drew the curtains because he liked the sun to wake him, and always turned out the light before he did so. It was a habit of the war years and he had never corrected it.

The square of grey light, tiger-striped with bars, filled him with pleasure. He did believe the fog was lifting at last. He peered up to see if the familiar triangle of sky, just above the high wall and bounded by the spire, had stars in it. He could see none. But for the first time in days the triangle was clearly visible, a lighter grey than the rest. As he stood watching, the corner of his eye caught something else. It was faint and very brief, and when he looked properly it had gone, but he knew at once what it had been and he felt suddenly sick with apprehension.

He had caught a flicker of light, swift as the flash of a kingfisher's wing and just as brightly blue, high up in the grey walls above him. A light from inside the church, the beam of a torch perhaps, had passed across the east window, catching the azure robe of the saint in stained glass who prayed there unceasingly. Avril stood transfixed.

Now that he saw the rapids, now that the trend appeared, the whole workaday reality of the position rose up before him with complete certainty, and he knew as clearly as if someone had just informed him of them all those facts which, as the psychologists could have told him, his under-mind had known all along.

For instance, he knew that when Mrs. Cash had shown Sergeant Picot over her little house she must also have shown him the minute yard at the back with the door of the coal shed in it. It was not probable that even the thorough sergeant had opened that door, which, situated as it was in the wall of the very foundations of the sacred building, must have appeared to have very little depth. Even if he had, Avril thought it unlikely that he would have stared beyond her small stock of fuel to the heavy door behind it.

Twenty-six years before he had given Mrs. Cash permission to make a coal shed out of the service entry to the crypt. This entrance had been made for the convenience of the original verger, who, in wealthier times, had lived in the cottage, and it was recessed deep in the thick wall. As landlord, Avril had paid for the alteration himself and had stipulated at the time that the old door at the back should be kept locked and the key given to Talisman.

Now for the first time it occurred to him that it had never been done. In the light of his present knowledge of all the people concerned, he was sure it had not. The old way must have remained open, and the crypt, now never used for lawful purposes, must have stayed open for Mrs. Cash to enter and use as she chose.

He went on to think of the missing men and their hiding place. It was so simple, so convenient. They must have approached it from the church itself, entering not from the closely guarded square but from the avenue behind. The building was kept locked when not in use, for there had been many cases of pilfering in that part of London in later years, but there was a loose stone in the lintel beside the small door of the vestry and under it the idle Talisman had kept the key since the end of the first World War at least.

The man who called himself Havoc would have known of that key, and once in the church it was simple for one who knew the way to go down to the crypt from inside.

Old Avril, standing alone in the dark, realised that Luke would never have believed it had he gone to him at that moment and told him that all these highly pertinent facts had never become assembled in his mind before. Yet it was true. Until now, not one of them had occurred to him to have any bearing on the other. He was not usually so obtuse.

Avril accepted his stupidity as a mystery which would be explained. In his strange peacefulness, his own unprecedented intellectual shortcomings appeared to be only a part of something much greater and more important. He waited, and presently he found himself perceiving the reason for his visit to Mrs. Cash that afternoon. Of course, by conveying to her, and through her to the man behind her, that Martin's letter was not in the rectory, he had also conveyed that he knew where it was, and in fact that he had hidden it somewhere else.

Avril knew where the boy would look for it. Doubtless he was there now, rummaging through the old black folder which the Canon kept under his lectern in his pulpit. He must have felt he was safe in the small hours, but his torch had betrayed him if only for a second, and in that second Avril had seen it.

Suddenly, his forward mind shrinking as it had been shrinking all the evening, Avril raised his head to see where the stream was carrying him, and he saw what he was about to do.

"No," he said aloud in the darkness, "no, that is madness." Yet in that moment he had recognised the demand and knew that he would submit to it. All his human weakness, his casuistry and his common sense, rose up to betray him and turn him from his work.

It resolved into an argument between the two Avrils conducted politely but vigorously, as though between two old brothers who had lived together amicably for a long time.

"My dear fellow," protested the wise prelate in him reasonably, "this is one of those cases when no single human being must interfere. If you go down and attempt to talk to that wretched boy alone tonight, he will kill you as he had killed four other people, and it will be suicide on your part and murder on his. You are not particularly afraid of dying, but if you do, who will suffer? Everybody you love best, Meg, Sam and his missus will have to find a new home, for no new incumbent is likely to put up with them. William and poor Mary Talisman and Emily, who will shelter them? Dot Dear Dot. It will destroy Dot's reason for living, and, my sad overconfident soul, what good would it do?"

"I do not know," replied the essential Avril, who was shrinking and mindless and without existence save in obedience. "I only know that events have so arranged themselves that I have no choice."

"Listen," said the practical man in him, "telephone the boy Luke. Do it now. He is the professional man whose job this is. Tell him all you know, commend your soul to the Almighty, and go to bed. If you want to talk to the other boy, you can do it when he is in jail. That way you will protect him as well as yourself. Who are you to lead him into such monstrous temptation?"

"Again I do not know," said the naked Avril. "I do not ask. But if that had been the way, I should have known what I know now tonight when I was talking to Luke."

At that point his sense of humour, which was always hindering him, began to laugh. "You are standing here, talking like Lancelot Gobbo to his fiend," it remarked. "Don't be a fool, Avril. Telephone Luke."

"I will call him when I return."

"You won't return," said his common sense. "Why on earth should he spare you, of all people? He hated and feared you in spite of everything you ever did for him, and that was when he was a child. Why on earth should he listen to you now? You are the last person to have any influence over him. Do you remember when you caught him alone in the church mocking the service, and how after you had watched and made certain it was not innocent naughtiness but intentional sacrilege you put him across your knee? That boy is of Evil. He was of Evil as a babe. Deliver yourself from it while you can. There is a telephone in this room, put there for your salvation. Use it. You don't have to remember a number, even. Ask for the police and go on asking until you get Luke."

And then, as he still stood irresolute, his reason became cunning.

"At least take a sensible precaution," it said. "Get hold of Luke and tell him to meet you in the church in half an hour. He may come sooner, but that will not be your fault. Leave the rest to Providence, but do telephone now."

Avril moved over to the telephone in the dark. It was an extension from the main instrument in the hall and had been put in during the war for A.R.P. purposes. He was greatly troubled and he took off the receiver unhappily.

The complete silence over the wire comforted him. He was, of course, the one person in the house whom Sam had forgotten to tell of his new arrangement, and he had no idea that downstairs the whole system was switched off.

He took the silence as confirmation. He dialled, but there was no answering buzz and he sighed and hung up.

"There, you see," he said to himself, "I was quite right. I thought so."

He went quietly out of the room and down the corridor.

Picot's snores were loud in the hall and the Canon let himself out quietly so that he should not wake the weary man. The fog was clearing rapidly and he could just discern the tulip tree in the square. No one was about. The detective on duty outside had only that moment entered the kitchen to call his opposite number, and for the first time that night the coast was clear.

Avril was unaware of this. He walked like a child amid the pitfalls, climbed the stairs to the avenue, and passed round under the high wall to the church gate, crossed the paved yard without stumbling in absolute darkness, and made his way to the vestry door.

It was unlocked and it opened with the quietness of recently oiled hinges and let him into the blackness inside. He was physically frozen and his heart thumped in his breast, but deep within him he was still very quiet, very happy, very much at peace.

His long robe brushed against the woodwork of the vestry wall and he pushed open the inner door and stepped into the misty darkness of the great building, sweet with the dry scent of paper and flowers, and paused and looked round into the dusk.

"Johnny Cash," he said in exactly the same voice which he had used so many years before, "come out."

SEVENTEEN
ON THE STAIRCASE

The beam of Havoc's torch cut through the darkness like a blade and found Avril where he was standing in the side aisle. For an instant it trembled there, transfixed, and, recollecting his dressing gown for once in his life, the old man pushed back his hood and let the light play on his face.

"Come down, my boy," he said in the slightly schoolmasterish tone he always used when he wanted something done quickly. "There's nothing there for you at all."

The acoustics of St. Peter's of the Gate had always been a problem, and tonight, with the building empty, the echoes seized upon the voice and threw the sound ricocheting up to the roof and down again. "At all . . ." they sang hollowly, "at all . . . at all . . . at all . . ."

As soon as he spoke and his voice was recognised, the beam shot away from him and sped to explore the entrances one after the other. It was a series of startled glances seeking out a trap, but the blank doors, baize-lined with red, stood steady and the silence was absolute.

Meanwhile, during one of the flashes, Avril had noticed a pew beside him and now he felt for it and seated himself, folding his hands in his lap. His body was afraid and its trembling embarrassed him a little, but his mind was peaceful, relieved, and extraordinarily content. He felt at home in the church, as he always did, and presently he cleared his throat with a loud pre-Litany "Hur-ump!"

"Shut up!" The whisper was the most violent sound the old

building had ever heard within its walls. The torch beam died like a falling tape and in the darkness there was a scuffling, light footsteps on polished wood, and then silence again.

After it had lasted a fraction too long, the shaft of light reappeared to dart round the entrances again. It leapt from one to the other suspiciously, waiting, going out and reappearing in the same place, finding nothing. The building remained silent and deserted.

The soft laugh when it came at last had so much relief in it that it was almost gay. It astonished Avril because it was so close to him, but although there was sweat on his forehead he did not feel alarmed.

"You're alone." The whisper had incredulity in it as well as amusement.

"Of course I am," said Avril testily, and reaped the habitual truthteller's only reward.

"You've telephone, though. You've put out a warning." The man had ceased to whisper, although he spoke very softly. The voice was more mature than Avril remembered it, but it still aroused the uneasiness in him which it had always done. It was a false voice, every true thing in it hidden rather cheaply.

"No," he said, thanking his stars that he had been protected from making that mistake and so could answer. "No. No one knows that you and I are here."

"You —— old fool." The monstrous adjective was so uncleanly that it passed over Avril's head. Either his ears actually rejected it or he did not believe them. He made room beside him in the dark.

"Come and sit down," he said.

There was no immediate reply, only light movement so soft that it could have been no more than the scurry of a rat over the tiles, and when the voice spoke again it was behind him.

"This'll do me best." And then, in the artificial wide-boy idiom which the Canon found so unpleasing, "What's the big idea, Padre? Not Prodigal Son stuff, surely?"

All the worst in Avril rose up at the approach and he might have failed at that first hazard, but he kept his temper and his perceptions and he smelt creeping to him, through the scent of the paper and the flowers, the one odour which every animal, human or otherwise, recognises the first time it assails him. Avril smelt fear.

With it came a portrait of the boy as he remembered him at fifteen, and as he had half fancied he had just discerned him under the hard shadows and unrevealing highlights of the police photograph. He saw again the same disfiguring stamp of tragedy on the young face, with the short upper lip and the flat eyes, blue as gentians but with nothing behind them.

On the run. The horror of the reality shut out every other thought in his mind.

"You must be so tired," he said.

The mutter in the blackness was too soft for him to catch. He became aware of astonishment and mistrust and rising anger, not in himself but behind him. The man was very close.

"What exactly are you playing at?"

The question only just reached him, it was so quiet, but its menace was unmistakable. "Ma said you *knew* this afternoon when you came round to her, and she swore you'd never let on. We didn't risk it. We made her get us another place. But I came back because I remembered you used to hide things in here. . . ."

"Not hide," protested Avril. "Keep."

"Quiet. Where do you think we are, in the middle of a wood? What are you up to, coming in here to find me alone?"

Avril made no answer because he had none. All the worldly intelligence he possessed—and it had never been very much—was asking him the same question. The loneliness and the danger were apparent to him, but he pushed them away and ceased to tremble. He was glad of that because he felt a hand brush over his shoulders, feeling for him, finding out exactly where he was.

"Are you my father?"

The enquiry came out abruptly in the night. The enormity of all it implied was not lost on Avril, but it did not shock him. Human sin in any form, real or imagined, never did. It was his greatest strength. His entire attention was taken up with trying not to hurt.

"No," he said, and he sounded matter-of-fact, regretful

even, "not your parent. I am, or ought to be, your spiritual father, I suppose. I'm your parish priest. I don't seem to have been very successful in that. The man who begot you died, poor fellow, fighting in a public house. Your mother was left a widow and after some little while my wife found her present cottage to get her out of the district where the tragedy occurred."

"And she was paid for it later, I suppose?" The sneer was very bitter. The boy was disappointed not only because he was convinced, Avril knew, but because he had been searching for a reason for the Canon's charity towards him and it was not the shameful one he had chosen.

"I suppose she was," Avril said sadly. "In those days respectability seemed to matter very much."

"Don't I know it! Ma came within an ace of burying an empty coffin for the sake of respectability. She got one of her clients to fix it. Think of it, a whole funeral procession costing pounds, and all it did was to give me a hold on her. She didn't think of that."

"I wonder. She held you, if only in that way."

"Cut it out. Look, time's short. This is an unhealthy place for me and you're wasting my time."

A hand was biting into Avril's shoulder now and the stink of terror was enveloping him.

"Why are you here? You're not trying to save my soul, by any chance?"

"Oh no." Avril gave the little grunting laugh which showed that he was genuinely amused. "My dear boy, I couldn't do that. The soul is one's own affair from the beginning to the end. No one else can interfere with that." The idea interested him and in spite of himself he went off on a little intellectual digression, knowing quite well how absurd it was. "What is the soul?" he enquired. "When I was a child I thought it was a little ghostly bean, kidney-shaped. I don't know why. Now I think of it as the man I am with when I am alone. I don't think either definition would satisfy the theologians."

"Then for God's sake," said the agonised voice behind him, "why the hell did you come?"

"I don't know," said Avril, and struggled on, making the truth as clear as he could. "All I can tell you is that, greatly against my will, I had to. All today every small thing has conspired to bring me here. I have known something like it to happen before, and I believe that if I have not been misled by some stupidity or weakness of my own I shall see why eventually."

To his amazement, the explanation, which to himself sounded utterly inadequate and unsatisfactory, appeared to be understood. Behind him he heard the man catch his breath.

"That's it," said Havoc, and his voice was natural. "That's it. The same thing happened to me. Do you know what that is, you poor old bletherer? That's the Science of Luck. It works every time."

Now it was Avril's turn to understand and he was frightened out of his wits.

"The Science of Luck," he said cautiously. "You watch, do you? That takes a lot of self-discipline."

"Of course it does, but it's worth it. I watch everything, all the time. I'm one of the lucky ones. I've got the gift. I knew it when I was a kid, but I didn't grasp it." The murmur had intensified. "This last time, when I was alone so long, I got it right. I watch for every opportunity and I never do the soft thing. That's why I succeed."

Avril was silent for a long time. "It is the fashion," he said at last. "You've been reading the Frenchmen, I suppose? Or no, no, perhaps you haven't. How absurd of me."

"Don't blether." The voice, stripped of all its disguises, was harsh and naïve. "You always blethered. You never said anything straight. What do you know about the Science of Luck? Go on, tell me. You're the only one who's understood at all. Have you ever heard of it before?"

"Not under that name."

"I don't suppose you have. That's my name for it. What's its real name?"

"The Pursuit of Death."

There was a pause. Curiosity, fear, impatience bristled behind Avril. He could feel them.

"It's a known thing, then?"

"You did not discover it, my son."

"No, I suppose not." He was hesitating, a torn and wasted

tiger, but still inquisitive. "You've got it right, have you? You have to watch for your chances and then you must never go soft, not once, not for a minute. You mustn't even think soft. Once you're soft, you muck everything, lose your place, and everything goes against you. I've proved it. Keep realistic and you get places fast, everything falls right for you, everything's easy. Is that it?"

"That is it," said Avril humbly. "It is easier to fall downstairs than to climb up. *Facilis descensus Averni*. That was said a long time ago."

"What are you talking about?"

"The Science of Luck." Avril bent his head. "The staircase has turns, the vine climbs a twisted path, the river runs a winding course. If a man watches he can see the trend and he can go either way."

"Then you know it? Why are you soft?"

"Because I do not want to die. A man who pitches himself down a spiral staircase on which all his fellows are climbing up may injure some of them, but, my dear fellow, it's nothing to the damage he does to himself, is it?"

"You're crazy! You're on to a big thing, you can see what I see, and you won't profit by it."

Avril turned round in the dark. "Evil, be thou my Good— that is what you have discovered. It is the only sin which cannot be forgiven because when it has finished with you, you are not there to forgive. On your journey you certainly 'get places.' Naturally; you have no opposition. But in the process you die. The man who is with you when you are alone is dying. Fewer things delight him every day. If you attain the world, you cannot give him anything that will please him. In the end there will be no one with you."

"I don't believe you."

"I can hear that you do," said Avril. "Suppose you had got to Ste. Odile——"

"Where?" The sudden eagerness did not warn the Canon and he went on steadily, throwing away what he felt was worthless information in his anxiety to make clear the important truth.

"Ste. Odile-sur-Mer. In English, Saint Odile on Sea. A little village to the west of St. Malo. Supposing you had got there and uncovered treasure worth a king's ransom. Do you think that you would then become somebody else? Do you believe that this weary unsatisfied child who is with you when you are alone would not go with you then? What could you buy for him to make him happy?"

Havoc was not listening. "Is that the name of the house or the village?"

"Both. But you must put that out of your mind. Geoffrey Levett has gone there tonight."

"Has he? By sea?"

"Yes. But the fog is lifting. He will be there by tomorrow, or the day after." Avril was impatient. "You must forget that. That is over. The ports are watched and you are hunted, my boy. Now is your last chance to think of yourself."

Havoc laughed aloud. "Got it!" he said. "The Science of Luck, it's done it again. See how it's worked? That's why I came back, see? See what we're doing, you and me?"

"Passing on the stairs," said Avril, "rather near the bottom." And he sighed.

"You cut that out." The hand was on his shoulder again. "I won't hear it. You're wrong. You've told me the only thing I want to know, and I came to hear it. You don't even know why you came."

"But I do." Avril was quietly obstinate. "I came to tell you something which is perhaps more obvious to me than to anyone else whom you may meet."

"You came to tell me to go soft. I should say so. You silly old fool. You go home to bed and——"

His voice died abruptly. In the silence the chill grew so intense that it was painful. Far above them the ghostly figures on the windows had begun to take shape as the morning light began to strengthen.

The long fingers closed round the bones of Avril's shoulders and the trembling force of the man shook his whole body.

"Look. Swear. Swear it on anything, anything you like. Swear you'll keep quiet."

Avril saw the temptation into which he was led. "Oh," he said wearily, "you know as well as I do that for us who watch there can be no half turns. I can swear and you can let me go, but as soon as I am gone what will you think? If you do, and you come to grief as soon as you must, you will blame that one act and will go down believing it. That is not good, John. The time has come when you must make a full turn or go on your way."

"You fool, you fool, what are you doing? Do you want it? Are you asking for it?" The boy was weeping in his weary rage and the tears fell on Avril. The old man felt the agony of them and was helpless.

"I want very much to stay alive," he said. "Enormously. Much more than I could have believed."

"But you've done it, you've done it, you've put the doubt in my mind. I daren't. You know it, I daren't go soft."

Avril bent forward to put his head in his hands. His resignation was complete.

"I cannot help you," he said. "Our gods are within us. We choose our own compulsions. Our souls are our own."

He had reached the end of his secret prayer when the torch blazed and the knife struck him.

The fact that he felt it at all was significant. For the first time Havoc's hand was doubting and because of that it had lost some of its cunning.

EIGHTEEN
THE WHEEL TURNS

Thirty-five hours later, in the morning, when the sun was shining through the newly cleaned windows of his office as blandly as if no such thing as a London fog had ever existed, Charlie Luke sat at his desk in Crumb Street and considered the situation with the complete detachment which arrives with exhaustion.

Thirty-five hours. Two nights and a day. Thirty-five hours of rushed and unrelenting work, growing public hysteria, confused sympathy and censure from an excited press, anxiety in high places which from being stern was becoming querulous, and nothing, not one pointer, not one useful clue.

Havoc, Tiddy Doll, the brothers, and Bill had vanished again as utterly as if the sewers had swallowed them.

This morning Stanislaus Oates, the Assistant Commissioner, was with the Home Secretary. Chief Superintendent Yeo was at the Great Western Hospital, hoping to get an interview with Canon Avril. The old man had been out of danger since midnight and it was hoped he would be able to say a word or two as soon as he awoke.

Dear, *silly* old fool. Luke thought he could just understand him and hoped to be able one day to forgive him. Sam Drummock had saved his old friend's life. He had come creeping down in the very early morning, intending to take his boxing article to Fleet Street, and had found Picot asleep, the front door unlatched, and Avril's bed unslept in. It had taken the frightened household twenty minutes to find the old man where he lay on the vestry floor, which was as far as he had got before the loss of blood had doubled his legs under him. The actual nature of the wound was one of those miracles which Luke decided he would never understand. Why a man of Havoc's skill should suddenly miss his mark by inches, so that the collarbone took most of the blow, or why, having surely known he had missed, he had not struck again, completely defeated him. Pneumonia had not followed either. That was just God looking after His own, he supposed. "Surprisingly little loss of bodily heat," the surgeon had said, "as if the system had suffered very little shock."

Luke dragged his tired mind away from the subject and, although he was for the moment quite alone, made a gesture as if to throw a crumpled ball of paper over his shoulder into the wastepaper basket.

He was open to bet that Yeo would get nothing from Avril voluntarily and he knew his *Archbold* far too well to expect that there would be any attempt to drag much from him. Page 483 . . . *"while in strict law the privilege does not exist, the minister should not be required etc. . . ."* It did not fit the case, of course, because no one supposed that there had been any question of confession, but it was near enough if the old fellow didn't want to talk, and he wouldn't, Luke was sure of that. Besides, what news could he tell? Havoc had been his attacker. His prints were all over the blessed church. As to the rest, Luke could hardly suppose that the chap would have had a chat with the old man before he did his handiwork, much less mention where he was going.

Luke had been working. As he sat, his dark head resting on his hands, he reflected that they could put that on his tombstone: "Thickheaded but Thorough. R.I.P." He had taken the church apart and the crypt, with its clear evidences of recent occupation, had been gone over with a toothcomb. The miserable Sergeant Picot, still weaving slightly from the drug (and what a fantastic crazy piece of bad luck *that* had been!), had found the way out through the coal cellar of the cottage.

As Luke sat staring red-eyed at the notes before him he checked every point, his own slightly racy language colouring the dark list.

Ma Cash was in a detention cell downstairs, held on an accessory charge. She had refused to speak all yesterday and he was giving her until zero hour, just before the midday meal, before he tried her again. What a flinty old besom she was! As he considered her, his diamond-shaped eyes widened and there was a gleam of unwilling admiration in their depths. "I don't know, I can't help you. Find out." That was all she had said to every question, just like the gangsters in the movies. Not a bad line either, he conceded, except that there were no smarty lawyers around to bung in a writ of habeas corpus, so the old lady could sit there while the police asked for her case to be remanded for a week or two.

Luke did not think she would crack yet a while, if she did at all. There was something very strong in that bright flat face with the knowing eyes. He was not at all sure even now that there had not been something in his "substitution of the child" theory, after all. Mrs. Avril could have been mistaken. Something certainly was giving the wicked old girl in the cell a remarkable amount of courage.

He sighed. All this was getting him nowhere. Routine, that was the only thing. Well, that was going on steadily and relentlessly, despite the help from the public which was no help at all. Two men for whom he could have found better employment were needed to control the traffic in St. Petersgate Square this morning. Mercifully, old Sam Drummock was good with reporters, and Miss Warburton too; when she could be prised away from the hospital, she showed a lot of common sense. He thanked his stars that the other four were out of the way, and allowed his mind to wander to them briefly on their treasure hunt.

He expected to hear from them at any minute now. There had been some delay in the crossing. That was all he had gathered so far. And it was curious, in a way, because he had wired, and yet Meg Elginbrodde had not telephoned about her father.

He returned to his list. "The cottage." There the routine had all but taken the paper off the walls. Havoc's prison clothes, or what was left of them when they had been shovelled out of back of the boiler, had gone down to the Forensic Science Laboratories at Hendon. They would provide sufficient evidence to take care of the old lady for a while, or he was a Dutchman. Then there were the cash memoranda books. They were the only hope. Thirty-four in all, little fat black books hidden under a loose board in the bedroom. Picot had brought them to the station in a borrowed suitcase, and four experienced men had spent the better part of yesterday on them.

By six in the evening they had brought him their little list, three hundred and twelve names and addresses of men and women who still had outstanding reasons for hesitating to refuse to do Mrs. Cash a favour.

The Chief Inspector's brows had risen several times on his dark forehead as he had read. Little things which had puzzled him about some of the most respected residents of his district suddenly became plain. An attempted suicide which he had never understood emerged as almost reasonable. One of his own men, now on leave, became due to make some explanations.

The lodginghouse keeper who had visited Havoc in prison appeared prominently on the list, but the favour she had done Mrs. Cash had been investigated already, so that her name could be eliminated.

That left three hundred and eleven and, just after seven o'clock, five picked officers, which was more than could be spared, had set out from Crumb Street to visit and question each one. They were still at work and so far none of their reports, which had come in at three-hourly intervals all through the night, had contained anything helpful. It was slow work but it had to be done. In the end the result would be worth the delay.

Delay. The word hung in Luke's mind. That was the keynote of the whole enquiry. From the start there had been a perverseness in the whole business. Little snags had developed at every weary step, and although on the face of it the thing was inevitable, it was taking its own time and nothing and nobody, it seemed, could hurry it. As his own old grandmother would have said, it was as though the devil had got into it. He grunted. A fat lot of good that was. The Assistant Commissioner didn't believe in the devil.

Meanwhile, there was plenty to do. His desk was stacked

high with dockets. There were the Flying Squad's confidential memos, containing news and gossip from informers. The whole of the fraternity were leaving Havoc strictly alone, by all accounts. The underworld had never liked him and now considered him dynamite.

There were copies of all the more hopeful telegrams from police headquarters all over the country, reporting suspicious characters observed or detained. There were details of every car theft reported in the Metropolis in the past three days. There were seven bona fide "confessions" from people who were now being held for medical reports on the state of their minds. And there was one highly ingenious theory that the killer was a well-known politician masquerading as Havoc (who had been his first victim), offered in all seriousness by an expert just too eminent to be directly snubbed.

The maze of tinted paper towered in front of Luke's hot eyes, looking like the Blue Ridge Mountains. He surveyed it thoughtfully and reached for another barley-sugar lump.

Andy Galloway, his clerk, an earnest youth who had served in the R.A.F., had been feeding him with this for days in the belief that it would keep him from dropping in his tracks. Luke reckoned he must have eaten four pounds of the stuff and wondered idly whose ration he was robbing.

His mind was off the main problem only for a second, but in that little pause the wheel turned and suddenly the long march of events began to race.

As he put out his hand the pile of paper on the right side of the desk toppled over and slid slowly to the floor. He dived after it, but one flying sheet eluded him and he had to lean over under a chair for it. As he fished it out to place it with the rest he glanced at it, and one paragraph caught his attention. It was a reply to a query of his own which he had put to Sergeant Branch while that officer had been reporting on Havoc's companions.

Why, Luke had asked, did two fishermen spend the war in the Army when all such men had been directly instructed to join one of the two sea services? It was a minor point and he had forgotten making it, but good old Branch had been busy. After enormous difficulty he had identified the two as Roland and Thomas Gripper of Weft, near Aldenburgh, Suffolk, and the photograph in his report which had caught Luke's eye said simply:

On leaving school the two brothers joined their father, Albert Edward Gripper, who owned a fishing smack, and worked for him until 1937 (December), when he was charged and convicted of various offences connected with the shipping of uncustomed goods. He received a sentence of twelve months imprisonment and was severely fined. The boat appears to have been sold to meet these demands, and the brothers then left the district. Evidence points to the fact that they were simple ignorant men, most of whose lives had been spent on the water, and it looks possible that they felt it safest to disclaim any knowledge of their former calling, hence their appearance in the Army soon after the outbreak of war. The father died in 1940, but a mother and sister still live at Weft.

As the Chief Inspector finished reading the private telephone on his desk tinkled and Chief Superintendent Yeo's deep voice came through to him.

"Charlie? . . . Good. Listen. Canon Avril spoke to Havoc and told him (a) that the name of the place where the stuff was hidden was Ste. Odile near St. Malo, and (b) that Geoffrey Levett had gone after it. That's all. Nothing else so far. The old gentleman is very weak, but they say he'll live. I shall be here for the next half hour but I wanted you to have that information at once. Anything new with you? . . . No? . . . Very well, keep at it. Good-bye."

Luke's hand was still on the receiver, and the expression of incredulity was still on his face when Picot appeared, looking as excited as anyone had ever seen him.

"Chief," he burst out as he slammed the docket on the desk, "here's a small van found abandoned at Tollesbury in Essex. First reported 10 P.M. yesterday and just been traced to a family called Brown who run a little bakery in the Barrow Road here. They're all at home and they're lost without the van for the business, and yet they haven't reported it. Old

Mrs. Brown, who owns the shop, is on Mrs. Cash's books. She owes her three hundred pounds."

Luke sat looking at him. "Tollesbury? Where's the nearest town to that?"

Picot's solid face flushed with disappointment. "You must know Tollesbury, Chief. Everybody knows Tollesbury."

"Never heard of it." Luke uttered the blasphemy in all innocence.

"But it's so near Town," protested Picot earnestly. "A wonderful place. You *must* know Tollesbury! Yachts, oysters, fishing boats——"

Luke's sagging body jerked to attention.

"Is it on the sea?"

"The estuary. Right out on the marsh, yet only forty-odd miles from London. It's littered with little seagoing boats, all of them out in the river well away from the village, and the dinghies lie around on the mud with no one to mind them. If anybody should want to pinch a seagoing craft it would be the one place on earth to get away with it. Chief, *suppose those lads tried to stage the raid again.*"

Charlie Luke, the Londoner, to whom all water-borne traffic was a holy mystery, stared at him in stupefaction, and Picot hesitated, trying to find some way of conveying the desolation of that grey-green expanse of marsh and sky and sea, where, in November, the black geese and great saddleback gulls seem to live alone.

"The locals don't worry," he went on, "because the place is the devil's own job to get away from if a man doesn't know the mudbanks. But any East Coast fisherman would know the lanes like his own back yard."

Luke rubbed his eyes, one of his more ingenuous and endearing gestures.

"Wait a minute," he said. "There were just three hours early yesterday morning when no cars were stopped on the Southend By-pass. There was the pa and ma of a smash between two milk lorries and an all-night coach, and all available men had to go down there. Havoc couldn't have had luck like that."

"He's had all the cards so far." Picot was thinking of the milk-food.

The D.D.C.I. seemed still bewildered. "Anyone down there lost a—a seagoing boat?"

"Nothing's come through yet, sir, but it's early. People have to sleep, people other than us, I mean. I don't suppose a man would notice for twelve hours or so that his craft had gone, and then he'd think she had broken away."

Luke stretched out a long arm. As in most other professions, the one certain way of cutting through red tape in police matters is to have a private word on the telephone with a very old friend in another department.

Once again the luck held. Superintendent Burnby of the Essex C.C. had walked a beat with Luke in the far-off happy days when they were both prepared to put the world right if given only half a chance and another sergeant, and within a few minutes, although it was such an awkward hour of the morning, the well-remembered voice was drawling over the wire.

"Wotcher, Charlie boy, how are you? See you've kind of mislaid someone up there in the fog. It's funny where they get to, ain't it? Never mind, it's a nice drying day today. . . . What? . . . Boat from Tollesbury? That's a very strange thing, so there is now. Got it on my desk this minute. Just come in. What are you trying to do, confess?"

Luke spent a few precious moments in lucid explanation and the other voice lost its banter at once.

"It could be," he said briskly, "it well could be. You may be on to something. This is a smack of eighteen tons, the *Marlene Doreen*. Here it is: Lister Diesel engine fuelled up for one week, stores on board, hatch possibly left unlocked (if it wasn't it wouldn't signify. Two little old girls could lift it off bodily), owner Mr. Elias Pye. He saw her last lying out in the Fleet just before 11 P.M. the day before yesterday. His son missed her yesterday afternoon about three. Until dawn this morning they thought she must have fouled her anchor. They spent a bit of time thinking about that, and notified the Tollesbury Police an hour ago. Customs have been informed. Anything else you want? We can't always do it like this, so make the most of it."

Luke mentioned the van. "Wouldn't five strangers be noticed on this marsh of yours?" he added.

"Not on a November morning if they knew where they were going and drove straight to Woodruff and the yacht stores. Owners and their agents are always popping up and down that road." Burnby's voice had not quickened, but some of Luke's own rising excitement was echoed in its drawl. "Charlie, I've seen that van. I've been down there this morning on some other business. That's why I'm here so late. Lucky you rang me. It was a baker's van and quite empty except for one thing our chap happened to find on the floor. He showed it to me, but we didn't think there was much to it. It was a lens out of a pair of dark glasses. It meant nothing then, but now you start me thinking. I thought it had dropped out of a pair of those sun shields, but our fellow showed me it was a real lens all right. I've seen your circular, of course. Wasn't one of the five wearing dark glasses?"

Charlie Luke's spirits rose so violently that they took his breath away. The luck had come. He knew it as surely as the dairy hand knows that the cream in the churn has turned. For all the delays which had dogged him so far he had received ample compensation in the last quarter of an hour, when every minute thing which had emerged had dovetailed together and built up rapidly in his hands.

Burnby was still speaking. "I'll have the van tested for prints and rush 'em to you, to be on the safe side. Meanwhile, I'll get the water people out. The *Marlene Doreen* will be sitting on a mudbank by this time, as sure as Christmas, unless your blokes are fisherfolk born."

"Two of them are. Suffolk folk from Weft."

A thin whistle came over the wire. "That's torn it. She only carries a crew of two. Where will they make for? Do you know?"

"Ste. Odile, near St. Malo."

"Ha, I know. They'll be there by now, then."

"What?"

The violence of the exclamation set up a resistance in the countryman. "Well, it's just after one, isn't it? And they must have taken her out on the tide yesterday morning. High water was ten after 10 A.M. Everything went right for them, by gee. That gives them, let me see, twenty-four, twenty-five, twenty-six hours approx. Yes, that's about right. If their luck held and they didn't go aground they should be there just about now, or they soon will be."

"Are you sure of this, Len? It matters."

"I think so, Charlie. I do a bit of sailing when I can, you know. It's the sport round here. St. Malo from Tollesbury Fleet, yes, twenty-six hours with luck *if* they know the way, and if they're fishermen they will. She's small, you see. She wouldn't have to go out round the Golmers Gat, but could slip through the Spitwee and Burrows Swatch, through the Sands to Margate. And then outside the Goodwins. It's been ideal weather since the fog cleared, and she carries sail as well as the Diesel, so she could make speed. Depend upon it, they're due by now."

He paused and, as the silence lengthened, laughed apologetically.

"Well, I see you've got plenty on your plate, boy, so I won't detain you. All the best. Let me know if there's anything you want. I'll chivvy the Customs and see to the prints. Goodbye."

Luke hung up. It was not often that he found events outstripping his mental speed, but now he found himself staggering rather than rising to the occasion.

"The French police," he said to the startled Picot. "Radio the French police. Here are the details. While I write them out, get me Chief Superintendent Yeo at the Great Western Hospital and ring that bell for Andy."

He cocked an eye at the window, which showed a square of limpid sky, and his dark face began to glow again as the fires of his energy reddened once more.

"If it's a good drying day, Len, you old so-and-so," he murmured, "it's good enough for flying, isn't it?"

NINETEEN
MYSTERY OF ST. ODILE-SUR-MER

"If one was not anxious to avoid the profane," said the lady in the Citroën, who was really so anxious to display her English, "one would remark that the devil was in it, would one not?"

From the front seat of the Talbot, Meg Elginbrodde smiled polite agreement and for the third time the two ladies relapsed into silence and watched the little waves receding so slowly from the road.

The November afternoon was as mild as early autumn and in the sunlit stillness the neat countryside lay like a scarf of purple and green and soft gold under a sky of pearl.

Geoffrey, who had been dozing at the wheel at the head of the growing line of traffic which waited for the tide to fall so that it might pass, lit yet another cigarette.

"I feel," he observed over his shoulder to Campion and Amanda in the back, "as if I had been playing a game of snakes-and-ladders."

Amanda laughed and nodded towards the dark wedge-shaped hill before them just across the falling water.

"We can see it, anyway," she said. "I never thought we should. I've travelled unhopefully. Wake up, Albert."

"Why?" enquired Mr. Campion not unreasonably. "Every vehicle—is a channel steamer a vehicle?—in which I have set foot in the past two days and nights has stopped dead for an hour or two when just within sight of its goal, and I've developed an ability to drop off, as they say, in self-defence.

The thing that amazes me, if you'll forgive me, Meg, is why you, as well as the travel authorities, thought to tell us everything about this doubtlessly delightful village except that it was an island. I understood that it was Ste. Odile-*sur*-Mer, not *sous*-Mer. I am not grumbling because I am not that kind of clot, but, purely as a matter of academic interest, what induced you to forget it?"

Meg did not turn her head, which was all but lost in the collar of her travelling coat.

"When I was here it wasn't an island," she said. "This only happens at high tide."

"Which is twice a day," murmured Geoffrey, his hand tightening over hers where it rested beside them. "Feeling happier, beautiful?"

"Much." She smiled at him, her eyes as vivid as her little blue cap, gay against the fur lining of her tweed coat. "I've been happy since last night. Suddenly, just about midnight, everything seemed all right. I'm sorry I made such a fuss. It was that boat being so late after all the delay at the beginning, I suppose. I wanted to get on."

"You didn't, you know," said Amanda. "You wanted to go back. I think Geoff was wise not to wait at St. Malo. Of course the tyre trouble at Les Oiseaux was utterly unforeseeable."

"And for some hours irremediable," muttered Campion. "Let us come and live in Les Oiseaux, Amanda. No papers, no policemen, no garages, no drains, no lights, no post office. Probably no wars. Nice food, happy smiles, and always a nice long day tomorrow. London, Paris, even New York may have blown themselves sky-high by now. We shouldn't know. How lovely if it was always like that."

"That's age," said his wife, "or more probably that second omelette. What on earth induced you to eat two?"

"Hogliness," said Campion simply, and the lady in the Citroën, who had been following the conversation with increasing difficulty, gave up in despair and emitted a little cry as her husband let in his clutch.

Geoffrey stirred himself. "He thinks he can make it now, does he?" he murmured. "Where France leads, shall England hesitate?"

Campion opened one eye. "On our present form we should

get halfway across before we float out to sea," he observed. "Where are we going? To the village first, or straight up to the house?"

"Oh, the house." Meg turned round to him. "Please. It's so late, nearly two. It'll be dark if we don't. The road divides when we get across here and the village is down there to the west. If we take the east road up the hill we'll be there in ten minutes."

Mr. Campion's reply, which concerned the unwisdom of prophecy where their luck was concerned, was drowned in a hysterical outcry of hooting behind them, and a black car shot through the traffic in their wake, grazed their offside wing, and took to the shallow water like a duck throwing out a wake on either side. Geoffrey glanced after it with interest.

"See that?" he said. "The gallant gendarmes. Quantities of them. The police, the police, can we never get away from them? They're across, by Jove! Yes, there they go, away down the west road. We go east, do we, darling? Right, well, now for it. We'll take it steadily." He let his engine race and then the heavy car moved smoothly into the tide.

As they came up on the other side the road forked and they edged up the narrow way, leaving the rest of the traffic to take the main track to the village.

The hill rose steeply between high hedges, golden in the sun, and the air was clear and peaceful save for the buzzing of a little silver scout plane which sailed low across the sky, swooped, and turned back again.

"What's *he* doing?" murmured Campion, but no one was listening and the journey was so pleasant that he closed his eyes again. Meg was sitting forward, her eyes eager.

"It's somewhere here, Geoff. A white gate. You turn in and drive for a long way up to the actual house, nearly a mile, I should think. Yes, here we are."

They turned out of the road into a lane which ran up across a broad bank of meadow, bare and desolate. The sparse grass grew in tufts on the poor soil and was grey rather than green. There was no cover anywhere, no tree to break the arc of earth against the sky. The house appeared suddenly and with it the dark green sea and the ragged broken line of coast, lace-edged with surf, stretching out to the horizon on either side.

It was a little stone house, squat and solid as a castle, with a single turret and a wall round it which would have withstood a siege. Until they were almost upon it, it looked as neat and circumspect as ever it had done, but as they passed under the arch leading to the forecourt they saw it was deserted and in bad repair. There was no glass in the windows, and grass had grown through the crack which split the stone before the nail-studded door.

They climbed out in silence. The lighthearted mood of a moment before wavered before this sudden picture of desolation. The house was dead, a casualty, and since death has no dignity save that which the living can give it, its uncared-for carcase was ugly and pathetic.

"I hate this bit of it," said Meg, who looked young and forlorn despite the sophisticated swagger of her mink-lined cheviot, which was a wedding present. "Come through here."

Slender silk-clad legs, seeming too fragile for her boxy shoes, carried her across the small courtyard to a door in the wall. She put her weight against it and it creaked open, dragging a fringe of sere grass and weeds with it, and they followed her through into the wreckage of what once had been a formal garden sloping to the edge of the cliff and bounded there by a wall in which there were now many breaches. Despite its position, it seemed strangely airless, and the rents in the masonry through which the sea gleamed so dangerously far below were welcome.

Amanda sniffed. "Rosemary," she said, "and box, and what is it? Oh yes, wormwood. Here it is. That silver stuff. Smell it? Oh, Albert, this garden must have been so sweet."

Mr. Campion slid an arm round her fur-clad shoulders and his lips were near her ear.

"Now it's like a horrid old tooth, a big black back one, don't you think?"

"That is dirty and disgusting," she said. "Oh, look, they've found the icehouse. Is that it really?"

Meg and Geoffrey, who had gone on ahead, had paused before a small stone building which crouched in the angle of the main wall. It was not large and was constructed in a pit,

so that little more than half its walls and its conical roof was
visible among the rank grass surrounding it. The two stepped
inside as Amanda spoke and they followed them.

The inside was a surprise, for it was light. The whole of
one corner had fallen away with part of the outer wall, so
that now there was a ragged window at breast level looking
out over the cliff to the sea. The effect was unexpectedly
enchanting. Sky and sea merged on the horizon, and the afternoon sun, streaming out over the green water, slashed it
boldly with gold, while violet shadows and plumes of surf
made marblings between.

A little boat lying at anchor, her red sails furled, bobbed
in the foreground, a focal point in the seascape. At that distance she was no larger than a matchbox, and the name, a
two-letter word painted boldly in white on her dark side, was
unreadable.

"How very lovely!" Just for an instant the brilliant vision,
so unexpected and so beautiful, took all their minds and Meg
spoke with delight. "There's smoke, too. A little bit of smoke
on the horizon. Can you see it? Otherwise she's absolutely
alone."

Geoffrey laughed. "First sign of life since we turned east,"
he said. "Nice to see it. I thought we'd come to the end of
the world. Now, Campion, the great moment."

They looked at each other and for the first time since the
journey began admitted to themselves the sadness and absurdity of the quest. All save Meg were past first youth, and
the pathos of the little legacy hidden in this crumbling tomb
touched three of them at least. Meg alone was radiant.

"You say it's fire irons, and you say it's something you've
forgotten. And you, Amanda, say it's a set of priceless glass,"
she said, glancing at them each in turn. "But I say that whatever it is, it's mine, and I shall love it very much. Now then,
Geoff, no more secrecy, we're all alone. What have we got to
do? Get the floor up?"

"No." Levett had crossed the stone to the edge of the gully
where water once had run, and was looking at the uncompromisingly Victorian cement garden figure which kept a mil-
dewed guard there. It was a clumsy, cumbrous affair which
had never been beautiful or even pleasing. It was an insipid

shepherdess, much too large for life, seated on a formalised tree stump and holding a very small vase in an ill-proportioned hand. Her wide skirts were large as a barrel and about as graceful, and since she was now crumbling badly, and had flaked with an effect frankly piebald, she was, as Lugg himself might have pointed out, "no ornament."

"It's in here, whatever it is," Geoffrey said. "The postscript simply said 'The Treasure is hidden in the statue.' I think our best way is to put it down, Campion, so that we can see the base. Shall we try?"

Together the two men, solid-looking in their greatcoats, took the figure by waist and shoulder and tipped it slowly back. It was heavy, but it stood on a plinth a little too small for it, and the wall of the gully steadied it as they lowered it at the first try very gently to the moss-grown flags. It lay there, misshapen and ridiculous, the flat base of the log and barrel skirt together making a ragged O, like an oyster shell.

That they had found the hiding place was obvious immediately. The original cast had been hollow, for the cement outline of the inner wall was clearly marked, but the inside had been plastered over inexpertly and there was a fold of some sort of material, blanket possibly, just visible in the white mass. Campion tried it with his nail and marked it slightly.

"It's soft, but not quite soft enough," he said. "I think we need expert help with this, you know, as the thing is so fragile. It's not three yet. Suppose we go down to the village and get the local mason. We can't possibly get at it without tools."

"Isn't there something in the car?" It was Meg, her cheeks bright and her eyes dancing as Elginbrodde must have seen her when scarcely out of her teens.

"No." Geoffrey linked his arm through hers possessively, and his virility and happiness were aggressive in the little space. "No, Albert's right. It's delicate, you see. My letter stressed that. You be patient, sweetheart. No good coming all this way and smashing the thing. We'll go down to the village. You and Amanda can get us rooms at the pub while we hunt out the workmen. I think it might be easier to move the whole thing—— What's up, Amanda?"

"Nothing." The older girl drew her red head into the building again. "I thought I heard something, but it was only the door swinging back. Go down to the village, shall we?"

"You three go back. Amanda can see to the hotel, Geoff can get hold of the authorities, and Albert can hunt up a mason. Let me stay." Meg spoke earnestly and disengaged her arm.

"I shouldn't," said Amanda promptly. "You'll only get cold, if you don't fall over the cliff."

"But I'd like to stay with my Treasure. Do you mind, Geoff? It matters to me rather. Do you mind?"

Mr. Campion did not interfere. In these matters he was a very old bird. His pale eyes rested on Geoffrey's face, where a fleeting flame of jealousy had flared and died of shame.

"Do anything you like, my dear," Levett said awkwardly at last. "Stay if you want to. It'll make us hurry back."

"That's what I thought." She was as delighted as a child. "I'll just sit here and look at it and wonder what the Ste. Odile mystery can be. Hurry, or I shall die of curiosity."

The Sacred Mystery of Ste. Odile. A private Hollerith in Mr. Campion's mind went smoothly into action. He was a boy of ten again, standing behind his redoubtable Mama in the Eglise de la Collegiate at Villeneuve over the bridge from Avignon, struggling to translate the rolling phrases booming from the official guide.

"This work of art miraculous without something-or-other alone in the world except for a sister (that must be wrong) in the custody adoring of the family private of one of the most big gentlemen in France. They call it the Mystery, the Mystery Sacred of Ste. Odile-sur-Mer."

"My hat!" he said in sudden excitement. "This is going to be interesting. Let us do as Geoff suggests. We'll just go and get a truck and cart the whole thing down to the hotel. We'll leave you there to fix things up with them, Amanda. You stay here, Meg, since you want to, and we'll do it in under the half hour."

He swept Amanda out with him, and Geoffrey, hesitating, turned and kissed the girl. He was not often demonstrative and she was taken by surprise.

"Darling, how very nice."

"Are you going to be all right?"

"Don't be silly. Hurry back and we'll see what it is."

"Right. Twenty minutes. Don't go too near that hole in the wall."

"I won't."

Meg sat down on the deserted plinth and put her fur-lined sleeve on the base of the statue. It was exquisitely quiet. She heard the car start quite distinctly and listened to the sound of the engine dying gently away until it was lost in the deeper and more caressing growl that was the sea. The sun was still shining and the tinsel streaks on the water so far below had become a deeper gold. The little boat was still there, but a sail had altered slightly. She watched it with eyes narrowed hopefully. Perhaps it was going to open out like a red butterfly.

There was another boat, too, far away as yet and beetle-sized. It was dark, with a long white tail of foam which showed its speed.

The roar of a plane passing very low over the garden spoiled the peace and she resented it mildly.

She ran an exploring finger round the plaster filling of the cast and thought of Martin with great tenderness but no sorrow. The process of her mourning was complete. He had been gay, he had been kind, he had been brave, and he had been absorbed into the fabric of her life, which was the richer for him.

She was very anxious to see her new responsibility, and as she rubbed the plaster idly a shallow disc of it flaked away, exposing a deep rift in the packing. She was so interested in its possibilities that she did not hear the soft rustle of the box bushes outside in the garden, and by the time she had opened her bag and unearthed a long nail file nothing could have disturbed her.

Her fragile steel wand probed the weak spot cautiously, and unexpectedly a whole chunk of the dry, powdery composition came away, disclosing a dusty bulge covered with something which must at one time have been a blanket. Feeling very guilty, but incapable of resisting the temptation, she worked on and very soon had a cavity nearly a foot deep and wide enough to take her hand.

She was so excited that the step on the stone behind her

was purely welcome and she turned her head briefly to catch
a glimpse of a blue jersey and beret dark against the bright
doorway.

"*Bonjour*," she said politely and, returning to the work,
went on without looking at him. "*Qu'il fait beau. Est-ce-
que——?*"

"Speak English."

"English?" she said. "What luck. I wish you'd appeared
before."

Another piece of plaster had broken away and she was absorbed in edging it gently out. His voice had sounded husky,
but it had made no deep impression on her. No dominant
force had been revealed in it.

"Do you work here? Or no, I suppose you're fishing. Is that
your boat?"

Another lump of plaster came away as she spoke. She set
it down carefully beside her and put in her hand for more,
still chatting with the easy friendliness of her age.

"Doesn't it all look wonderful from here?"

Havoc did not move. He had slept for an hour on the boat
but no more, and now he could feel the earth heaving under
his feet like the sides of some vast animal, alive and uncertain.
He was nearly done, nearly exhausted. The final effort up the
cliff had drained the barrel of his resources, but he had made
it.

He put one hand on the doorpost, spoke, and was frightened by the lifelessness of his own voice.

"What are you doing?" The question was ridiculous. He
could see what she did, and none of its significance was lost
on him. He did not expect her to answer. Her appearance
there was as unreal to him as every other fortuitous happening had been to him ever since he had gone back to the
church at night and the old man had told him without even
the asking the one thing he wanted to know.

From that moment the Science of Luck had ceased to be
a cult which he followed painfully, a mere series of opportunities which he could seize or miss. From then on it had
revealed itself as a force which had swept him on without
even his connivance. It had been a whirlwind nightmare in
which everything went right without once losing the essential

nightmare quality which is fear. The sequence of events had been dreamlike, and in his exhaustion had seemed one. He remembered the old woman at the bakery, hiding them in the shed where the van stood. He remembered Roly knowing the way, the deserted roads where no one stepped out to halt them, the dinghy already afloat at the lapping water's edge. It all passed through his mind like the slow-motion details of a fall, or a car smash, smooth, irrevocable, and a finality.

The moment of lunacy had occurred when Tom had greeted the *Marlene Doreen* with a cry of recognition, a crazy belief in which he had persisted despite all his brother's angry arguments. She was the same sort of boat as their old man's, that was all, but Tom thought he knew her and the brothers could handle her, and on her smooth planks they stood taller and became different men.

They were on her now, still sitting there expecting him to return, the blamed fools: blissfully trusting him, even though Bill, who was lying sick as a dog in the bows, was swearing pitiably at them for their idiocy.

They would still be sitting there when the police launch came up. By all he had heard, the French coppers carried rifles on a job like this. However, one way and another they would all be busy for quite a reasonable time. The old Science was certainly holding. The Luck was more than just with him: he couldn't go wrong.

There was only Doll even to be considered. Havoc had seen him drop into the water while he himself was still lying panting on the cliff after the climb which had become so much more grueling since he had achieved it last. Doll had seen the red light and come after him. The old brute was shrewd and he was game, and the Treasure had got him. But he'd never make the cliff. He must be somewhere on the face now, just under that second overhang perhaps, clinging there, looking like a white slug with a black head. Tiddy Doll with one eye working and patent dancing pumps.

Meg's reply to his question took him utterly by surprise. As an obstacle she was so negligible he had forgotten her existence. Sex had long ceased to interest him, and her fragile beauty, graceful in the flowing fur and wool, made no impression upon him. She might have been a grasshopper sitting there at the mouth of his treasure cave.

But her voice when he heard it reminded him of itself when she was a child, clear and kiddish and with an irritatingly better accent than his own. He remembered that absorption in her, too, which had hurt his pride then and struck him as fantastically ridiculous now when at least she should have seen her danger.

"I'm trying to get something very fragile out of here without breaking it," she was saying. "It's something which has been left to me and I don't know quite what it is. I've got to get all this packing out, you see. It's still held quite fast, or it may be just very heavy. You wouldn't care to have a go at it, would you? Be very careful."

He lurched forward, stumbling as he let go the post. He was much weaker than he had thought. But what did that matter? It was all being done for him, wasn't it?

He saw her horrified look as the light from the breach in the wall fell upon him and his first thought was that she had recognised him from their childhood. But her exclamation dispelled that flattering illusion.

"Good heavens, are you all right?"

Her concern reminded him infuriatingly of Avril.

"You look most terribly ill. Please don't bother about this. The others will be back in a minute, anyhow. This doesn't matter in the least. I'm awfully sorry. I didn't realise. Can I do anything for you?"

"Get out of the way." There was no power in him. He noticed it and thrust the thought aside just as he thrust aside the hand she put out to steady him.

As for Meg, he looked so ghastly, his skin so pallid under the three-day beard, his bones sticking up through the shoulders of his jersey, and his eyes so dull within their caked rims, that she saw no tiger there.

She rose from the plinth and he dropped on to it and thrust his hand into the cavity she had made. He worked feverishly, his powerful fingers breaking away the plaster and clawing it out into the gully. The stimulus of touching the long-sought hiding place fanned the ashes of his energy, and she watched him, fascinated, misled by the show of strength.

The hard core of the discovery, a bundle wrapped in several thicknesses of cement-soaked blanket, began gradually to take shape. It appeared to be roughly cylindrical, about five feet long and the base not quite two in diameter. Twice before he had cleared the inner end of it he made attempts to drag it out bodily, but it resisted him and he went back feverishly to his scraping and shovelling. The white dust covered him, turning his hair and the blue jersey he had found in the *Marlene Doreen*'s locker to matted grey.

Meg eyed him dubiously. She was not afraid of him, but for him, and she was relieved to hear the vague buzz of activity which was becoming slowly more and more noticeable both from inland and the sea. She was inexperienced in illness, but he looked very bad, she thought.

A plume of spray streaking across her living seascape caught the corner of her eye and she turned just too late to see the craft whose wake it had been. The little boat with the red sails was no longer visible either. Its wings must have opened after all.

"Your boat has moved," she said. "Did you know? Perhaps I can see it if I come round here."

"It's not mine. Pull the side of this thing."

The command had come back into his voice and it surprised her into immediate obedience. She stepped down into the gully and took hold where he indicated.

As she moved, there sounded very faint and far away from the sea below a splatter of sharp little noises, followed by a long bodyless cry like a sea bird's. It was only just audible and barely a tone higher than the ceaseless soporific soughing of the waves. Havoc heard, but his busy hands did not falter. Rifles. He thought so. Doll's pallid torso must have made a wonderful target.

The whole incident had passed clean over the girl's head, he noticed. The Science was not faltering, the Luck was holding. He could feel it sweeping him on.

At last the bundle moved. "Pull," he commanded, "now." And again, "Pull."

She had as much strength as he had, he realised, and it bothered him fleetingly. It was queer to find it in a girl. The flaking mass slid forward on the slippery powder.

"Pull," he repeated, unaware that he whispered. "Pull."

"No. Look, it's caught. There. See?"

She touched the side of the original opening.

"This stuff on the base is harder than the rest. It's this jagged bit here, that's what's stopping us. Wait a minute."

She tried to dislodge it with her ridiculous file.

"What we need," she said, splitting the words as she made her futile efforts, "what we really need is a good—strong—knife."

She was not looking at him, and anyway, even under his mask of plaster, his face did not change. He felt under his jersey. His fingers found the familiar sheath, and he sighed as the knife handle slid comfortably into his palm.

Meg laughed aloud as she saw the blade on the cement.

"I *said* you were lucky." Her voice sounded joyful, like a child's.

"I am lucky," he said, and struck.

The fang of plaster and the bright steel blade split together and together fell to join the other débris.

"Oh!" She was concerned at his loss. "I'm so sorry."

He did not hear her. He was listening to the rhythm of petrol engines, still too far away to be anything but an undercurrent to the breeze blowing up from the valley. He flicked the useless shaft over his shoulder and caught the bundle with both hands.

"Take care, oh, please take care! It's very, very delicate."

She bent forward to help him and he permitted it, because he knew the thing must surely be too heavy for him to lift alone. Together they set it down softly on the moss-padded stones.

The roar of an aeroplane engine, heavier than the one belonging to the little silver scout of earlier in the afternoon, swooped down through all the other noises which were converging on the icehouse. Its proud clamour as it began to circle over the smooth pasture on the cliff top drowned the revving engines in the valley and the shouting from the sea. Neither of the two in the house in the garden heard it at all. The stiffened blankets round the bundle had rotted and they fell away easily from the main structure, which lay solid and uncompromising before them.

It was a wooden chest hollowed from a section of a single elm bole, white and seared with age and worm but hooped like a barrel with iron. For a moment its impregnability was too much for the man, and his hands flickered over the gnarled surface with awful helplessness.

"It opens here. Look, there's a hinge and a catch." Her voice reached him without any personality, as if it were the voice of the Science itself, and in the same unreal way he saw her stoop across the box and heard the gentle whine of the dry hinges.

The rounded lid fell back, disclosing a lining of fine embroidery and stump work on silk so old and fragile that a breath must rend and destroy it.

Inside there was a mound, covered prosaically with modern cotton wool, pounds of it rising up absurdly like whipped cream on a cake.

Suddenly he was so frightened that his outstretched hand paused in mid-air and Meg was before him.

Very cautiously she drew back the covering and the Ste. Odile Treasure lay regarding them with the same sweet innocent solemnity with which it had regarded all the cruelties, the bawdinesses, and the unconquerable hope of six hundred years.

It was a Virgin and Child in ivory, fourteenth-century work, and carved out of a single curving tusk so that the main figure bent slightly as if the better to support its gentle load.

It was not quite the twin of its more famous sister at Villeneuve-les-Avignon. That exquisite work of art has been damaged and there is a strange sense of pain, as well as a trace of oriental oversubtlety, in some of its detail. But this, the unknown master's other surviving work, was perfect and without blemish. It was a later product by a man who, though still a prisoner in a strange land, had known the mercy of his inspiration. The work's serenity flowed up naturally from the breath-taking drapery at knee and hem to the medieval face, not yet a saint's nor yet a child's.

For a full minute the two stared at it in a silence which nothing could penetrate. Meg sank down on her heels in the dust and her eyes grew slowly wider and wider until the tears formed in them. It was the time-honoured reaction, the Sa-

cred Mystery which had given the treasure its name. Honest
women wept when they saw it first. It was a phenomenon
which had been noticed during eighteen generations.

As the drop fell on her hand she started, coloured, and
turned apologetically to the man who had helped her.

"I didn't expect it," she said huskily. "I didn't expect anything like it. It must be the most beautiful thing in the world."

He did not move and she was spared the sight of his face.

It was typical of him that in that moment of disaster Havoc
remained realistic, as it was his pride to be. He was a modern.
He kept his feet on the ground. He had inherited at least
that much grace from civilisation's hard-won store. He made
no attempt to humanize his Science of Luck and so to credit
it with cruelty, or deliberated deception. The self-discipline
which had rendred him capable of discerning the reality at
all had made that mental escape impossible.

He saw the position immediately and with perfect clarity.
The mistake was his own. The Science of Luck was an impersonal force, vast as the slip stream of the planets, relentless
as a river winding down a hill. He had realised that from the
beginning. That was why Avril had frightened him so when
he had appeared to say the same thing. He was sorry to have
had to put the old chap out before he could part up with a
bit more information. He had no comforting illusions. The
only human, and therefore blamable, element in this whole
catastrophic mistake was himself.

As he crouched by the open box his body seemed to con-
tract and grow smaller as a corpse does when the life leaves
it.

There was no other mystery about the Treasure save the
little miracle which it had already performed when Meg had
wept. The figure filled each crevice of the ancient case, which
had been hewn to fit it. There was no space left for a secret
cache of jewels or other lesser trove. All there was lay before
him, open to his hand.

Overhead, the pilot of the police plane shut off his engine
and prepared to land. Where the road forked eastward, a car
full of men in uniform hooted violently at the Talbot which
had passed it on the corner.

Havoc scrambled to his feet and swayed over the girl.

"What will it fetch?" He was clutching at a straw, as he knew better than anybody. Even supposing the wretched thing could be moved without busting, then what was it? A few shillings' worth of junk.

Her reply only just reached him.

"Who could possibly buy it?"

That was the answer. He could hear any of the dealers giving him that one. He let a fantasy which he knew was moonshine creep into his mind. Didn't they hide things in images in the old days? Perhaps there was something worth having buried inside it.

"I'll smash it," he said aloud.

He saw her swift upward glance in which there was no fear, only a deepening of the concern which had so infuriated him earlier. Then, very smoothly and with much more certainty than he possessed himself over his movements, she closed the lid of the chest and quite calmly sat down upon it.

"You're ill," she said, and the authority in her voice was frightening because she sounded so strong, like a nurse or someone long ago. "You listen to me. You may not know it, but you're out on your feet. You've helped me and I'm very grateful to you and I'm going to pay you back. I feel guilty because now I look at you I don't think I ought to have let you exhaust yourself."

He found he could only just see her. She looked tall and quiet and the power in her was greater than his power because he was so tired.

"You've broken your knife, too," she was saying, not realizing how it sounded. "Anyway, let me square up with you for that."

He still stood before her, unaware that he was not terrible. He could see her bag and guessed that it contained at most a few thousand francs. There was her coat, of course, which looked all right if he only had somewhere handy to flog it. Her hands were so covered with the plaster that he could not see if her ring—and she only wore one—was any good or imitation.

He shook his head and motioned to her to move. He did not want to have to touch her, because he needed all the strength he possessed and time was short. All the same, he thought he would smash the doll. There might be something in it and it would be a satisfaction anyhow. The girl was still sitting there like a fool, and he let her have it.

"Get up!"

She seemed to be much further from him than he had thought, for the blow missed her entirely and all but over-balanced him. Her sudden laughter was the most terrible sound he had ever heard, for he knew what she was going to say a fraction of a second before he heard the words.

"You look like the little boy next door, Johnny Cash, who took my toy theatre and tore it up to get the glitter out of it, and got nothing, poor darling, but old bits of paper and an awful row. Do lie down. Then you'll feel better."

Old bits of paper, yellow and red and thick tinny gold, lying on the coal-shed floor. A cardboard horse on which the colours were running. His best shirt covered with dye. And outside, the locked door, Nemesis thundering on the boards. It was not even a new mistake. He had made it before.

He turned from her blindly, shambled across the floor, and staggered out into the airless garden, yellow and overgrown and reeking with its strange bitter smell.

Now the whole hillside was alive with noise and from down on the rocks hoarse exclamations floated up as men, whose very tongue sounds excited to Anglo-Saxon ears, fished for a pallid body in the shallow water.

The man who fled lurched against the door into the court-yard. It did not give because it opened the other way, and that was lucky for him. He heard a footstep on the stones within and had just time to drop down behind a dark bush beside the post before the door swung inwards and Luke, followed by his opposite number from the Sûreté, came charging through on his way to the icehouse.

At the same moment the Talbot and a police car raced each other into the yard.

Havoc edged a step backwards, missed his footing, and rolled over into a ditch which had been completely hidden by the long grasses. His luck was persisting. It had never failed him since he found its key. Where he directed, so it led him safely.

It was soft and cool in the ditch and he could have slept

where he lay, but he resisted the temptation and crawled on a foot or so to find that an old conduit pipe, quite large enough to take his emaciated body, passed under the wall and out on to the open hilltop.

As he emerged, lifting his head wearily amid the weeds, he discovered that the cover continued. He was in a disused waterway, a deep narrow fold in the open plain, with the house to his left. He could stand in it, even, without his head showing above the dry grass on its edges.

Behind him the noise and commotion, the shouting and the signals from cliff to beach were all receding, and as he stumbled painfully on they grew fainter.

He could not tell where he was going, and the curve in the hollow was so gradual that he was never aware of it. He moved blindly and emptily, asking no questions, going nowhere save away.

The ditch wound round towards the cliff edge, where the coast was deeply indented, as if the sea had one day taken a single bite out of the rocky wall. The tiny bay thus made was now almost three parts of a circle, and long before falling water draining off the land had worn deep sides to a pool two hundred feet below.

Havoc paused. The great beam which had been let into the bank on either side to save any unfortunate animal swept away by the rains supported him at breast height, and he hung there for some minutes looking down.

Beyond the bay the sea was restless, scarred by long shadows and pitted with bright flecks where the last of the winter sun had caught it. But the pool was quiet and very still.

It looked dark. A man could creep in there and sleep soft and long.

It seemed to him that he had no decision to make and, now that he knew himself to be fallible, no one to question. Presently he let his feet slide gently forward. The body was never found.

ABOUT THE AUTHOR

MARGERY ALLINGHAM, who was born in London in 1904, came from a long line of writers. "I was brought up from babyhood in an atmosphere of ink and paper," she claimed. One ancestor wrote early nineteenth century melodramas, another wrote popular boys' school stories, and her grandfather was the proprietor of a religious newspaper. But it was her father, the author of serials for the popular weeklies, who gave her her earliest training as a writer. She began studying the craft at the age of seven and had published her first novel by the age of sixteen while still at boarding school. In 1927 she married Philip Youngman Carter, and the following year she produced the first of her Albert Campion detective stories, *The Crime at Black Dudley*. She and her husband lived a life "typical of the English countryside" she reported, with "horses, dogs, our garden and village activities" taking up leisure time. One wonders how much leisure time Margery Allingham, the author of more than thirty-three mystery novels in addition to short stories, serials and book reviews, managed to have.